PRAISE FOR THE LAST CHANCE LAWYER AND WILLIAM BERNHARDT

"*The Last Chance Lawyer* is the kind of book you want to read in one sitting and then read again to savor the deeper meaning. I look forward to watching this series develop...."

— RICK LUDWIG, AUTHOR OF *MIRRORED*

"A brisk tale with a ~~deeply~~ ~~sympathetic~~ protagonist who ~~is~~ ~~the~~ ~~best~~ ~~way~~ ~~to~~ ~~savor~~ winning series."

— *KIRKUS REVIEWS*

"Once started, it is hard let [*The Last Chance Lawyer*] go, since the characters are inviting, engaging and complicated. I recommend that you find and read this book. You will enjoy it."

— CHICAGO *DAILY LAW BULLETIN*

"William Bernhardt is a born stylist, and his writing through the years has aged like a fine wine...."

— STEVE BERRY, BESTSELLING AUTHOR

"Bernhardt is the undisputed master of the courtroom drama."

— *LIBRARY JOURNAL*

THE LAST CHANCE LAWYER

THE LAST CHANCE LAWYER

A Daniel Pike Novel

WILLIAM BERNHARDT

Ebook ISBN: 978-1-948263-35-1

Print edition ISBN: 978-1-948263-36-8

For everyone yearning to breathe free

Give justice to the weak and the fatherless; maintain the right of the afflicted and the destitute. Rescue the weak and the needy; deliver them from the hand of the wicked.

— PSALM 82: 3-4 (ESV)

THE HAND OF THE WICKED

CHAPTER ONE

"What's my name?"

"I do not know."

"I don't believe you."

"I never know. Never."

"You're lying. I'm going to put you back in the box."

"Please!"

"I'll turn up the music. Bring back the needle."

"Por favor! No!"

"I want to hear my name. Tell me my name!"

"I do not know!"

Luciana raced across the four-lane highway, oblivious to the oncoming traffic. Even this late at night, cars buzzed over the hill at eye-blurring speed, unrelenting.

Her eyes were wet and unfocused. She could barely see anything. The roads felt slick and her feet were bare. Her gown was torn and filthy.

Didn't matter. She had to keep moving. They were coming for her. *¡Correr!*

A car slammed on its brakes, skidding to a stop only a few feet from her. It spun sideways, screeching and infusing the air with burnt rubber. She froze.

She could barely make out the headlights of another oncoming car. She stumbled backward just in time to avoid a tailspin, falling to her knees, skinning the palms of her hands.

She rose again and rushed forward, only to see another pair of headlights careening toward her. She increased her speed, rolling forward, diving. She tripped and fell, scraping her knees, but the car skidded past, missing her by inches.

Her knees bled badly, but she scrambled back to her feet and ran. She hit the lawn and kept moving. Something sharp dug into one of her feet. She ignored it. She had to keep moving. She wasn't going back. She would never return to him, to that life, what they had forced her to do. How long had she been a slave? How long had she been powerless? Her mind raced, trying to put it all in order, trying to make sense of what was happening, what she was doing. The needle made it harder. Everything did.

Don't give in, she told herself, but the fog would not subside.

She had to escape, had to find her way south. The only thing worse than what had happened to her was the knowledge that it would soon happen to somebody else.

She glanced over her shoulder, still running as fast as she could. She was miles from the box now, or so it seemed to her muddled brain. Was someone back there? She thought she heard something, but she couldn't be sure. What did it matter? She knew they would come for her. Soon.

Her only hope was to find her sister, but she wasn't sure where to look. Somewhere. Near here. She raced down the sidewalk, passing the coast and brilliant neon signs. Where was she? She tried to remember, but it was so hard. Everything was so hard. Her mind was disintegrating and she knew it. If she didn't escape this time, she never would.

The bright lights blinded her. Her mind was flooded with a series of disconnected images. It was almost as if her whole life passed before her eyes. But she wasn't dying—was she? She remembered her mother, so long ago, back in the old country, cradling her. Her mother told her to be strong. Her mother told her to fight. But she hadn't fought. She had conceded. And she was destroyed.

She was alone now. And no one should be alone. No one. Never.

She saw a bright fountain in front of a big hotel with water dancing above it. She was suddenly overcome with thirst. But the grass was wet and her bare feet slipped. She tumbled forward, falling on the stone ring encircling the fountain. Her head made a sickening cracking sound.

Lights ignited behind her eyes. Blood dripped down the side of her face. She lay on the grass, stunned, barely able to think. *¿Qué he hecho?*

She didn't know how much time passed before the people arrived. The one who had tormented her so long, and the new one, the friend. She feared him most of all.

"See what happens?" one shadowed figure said. "You're only making this worse on yourself."

"Kill me," she whimpered. "Please. Show mercy."

"Wish it were that simple. But it's not. You're on the books. Too many people watching."

"Just make sure she doesn't talk," the other figure said, in a slow flat voice.

"In time." The needle appeared. "Don't move." She tapped all the strength she could muster, squirming from side to side. Her head was still swimming, like she had severed a vital connection in her brain.

"You move, it's only going to hurt more." A hand clamped down on her mouth. "Do you need to be unconscious? Because I can arrange that."

She stopped squirming. The needle entered her arm. She felt a hot liquid coursing through her veins, radiating throughout her entire body. It hurt.

"You have become far too dangerous. I hope you weren't stupid enough to talk to anyone. Not that anyone would believe you if you did."

She felt darkness creeping across her like a spider. Was this the end? Finally? Her mind was bruised, ruined. She should just bash her brains against the wall and end this torture. She raised her head—

And a strong pair of hands grabbed her, immobilizing her.

"Back to the box for you."

"WHAT'S MY NAME?"

"I don't know."

"I don't believe you."

"Please stop this. I cannot bear it. I want to die."

"If you die, you know what will happen to the girl."

"No!"

"What's my name?"

"No sé!"

CHAPTER TWO

DAN SCRUTINIZED THE MAN IN THE WITNESS STAND, MICHAEL Herrin. Herrin's testimony could convict his client and send him to prison for eight years—depending upon what happened in the next five minutes.

His favorite law school professor told him that if you observed a person carefully, you could learn everything you needed to know. So that's what he did, every time he met someone new. He took photos with his eyes and filed them away, then used them later to make connections. Connections that led to greater conclusions.

He scanned Herrin top to bottom. Comb-over. Crow's feet. Crooked tie, didn't match. Leaning forward.

As it turned out, Professor Tepker was right.

"Mr. Herrin, do I understand that you were seated at your desk, staring out the window, around eleven p.m. on the night of October twenty-third?"

"That was my testimony." The man straightened slightly. He was obviously apprehensive. Which meant nothing. Everyone was apprehensive on the witness stand, and especially during cross-examination.

"Awfully late to be working, wasn't it?"

"That's why I'm the second associate vice-president," Herrin said, with more than a hint of pride.

"But despite how late it was, you could still see outside clearly?"

"The streetlamp illuminated the sidewalk."

Herrin had testified that he'd seen a drug deal go down across the street, and that the dealer in question, the man later arrested with over ten thousand in cash in his pockets, was his client, Emilio Lòpez. The prosecution's case hinged on this ID. All the other evidence was circumstantial at best. In fact, the prosecutor, Jazlyn Prentice, a generally savvy lawyer, would not have bothered bringing charges but for this one eyewitness. Destroy the eyewitness, destroy the case.

He pulled a document out of his backpack. He preferred backpack to briefcase—easier to carry, didn't slow you down when you needed to move fast. "Mr. Herrin, would you please look at defense exhibit number fourteen?"

Herrin thumbed through the heavy evidence notebook till he reached tab fourteen. "This is the statement I gave the police just after I contacted them." He raised his chin slightly. "That's my signature at the bottom."

"You're sure that's your signature?"

"Of course I am. I can see it plainly with my own eyes."

He smiled. "Yes, that's the crux of this whole case. What you saw, or could see, with your own eyes."

He felt a stir in the courtroom, some of it from the prosecutor's table, some of it from the bench. His reputation preceded him, it seemed. They all knew something was about to happen. They just didn't know what it was.

"I notice, sir, that you have more pronounced crow's feet, and a deeper line between your brows, than I would expect from a man in his thirties."

The witness appeared thrown. "Is that a question?"

"Each time you focus on a document, you raise your chin slightly, but look downward. You did it just now, and I noticed it before when you examined the prosecution's exhibits."

More silence. He could tell the prosecutor—Jazlyn to him, outside of court—wanted to object, but wasn't even sure what he was saying, much less what she should say in response.

Jazlyn slowly pushed herself to her feet. "I'm sorry, your honor. Is Mr. Herrin's chin... relevant for some reason?"

Judge Zimmerman arched an eyebrow. "Is that an objection?"

"Sure. That's an objection. On grounds of relevance."

"I will admit to sharing the distinguished prosecutor's mystification, Mr. Pike."

He nodded. "I can make it all clear in about three questions. May I?"

"I'll hold the objection in abeyance. For a little while."

"Thank you." He pivoted away from the defense table, then sprang forward. He loved his Air Jordans. They matched his tie and pocket square, didn't violate the court rules, and always put a bounce in his step. "Mr. Herrin, are you wearing contact lenses?"

The question startled him. "Yes, as a matter of fact, I am."

"Are those, by any chance, bifocal contacts?"

"Ye-es..."

"If I understand correctly, the top half of the lens enhances far vision, while the lower half is for near vision. So when you're looking far away, you look upward. And when you're looking at things that are nearby, like the document you're holding, you look through the bottom part of the lens. And here's a human quirk—we tend to raise our chin before we look downward."

He almost felt sorry for the witness. Herrin still wasn't getting it. But a glance at Jazlyn told him that she did. She was three steps ahead of the witness. But he was about ten steps ahead of them both.

"Mr. Herrin, when you spotted someone allegedly making a drug deal outside your window, how far away was he from you?"

"I'm not sure. I'd guess somewhere around thirty feet."

"Would you be surprised to hear that it is in fact exactly forty-six feet from your desk to the place where the incident allegedly took place? I measured it myself."

"Okay. Forty-six feet."

"Would it be safe to say, given your extreme nearsightedness, that you wouldn't be able to see forty-six feet away clearly unless you used optical aids?"

"If you mean these contacts, forget it. I just got these a week ago. I wasn't wearing them last October. I had normal glasses then. To correct my nearsightedness. So I could see from a distance."

"Were you wearing those glasses when you gazed out the window that night?"

"Yes, of course. I mean, I assume.... I mean..." His voice trailed.

He could spend the next ten minutes establishing Herrin's complete lack of certainty, but Herrin had already done that adequately himself. "Sir, I'd like to show you a still photograph taken from the surveillance camera operating inside your bank. Unfortunately, the camera wasn't focused on the street outside, so it doesn't help us identify who was involved in the alleged sale. But it gives us a great photo of you. Your honor, may I approach?"

The judge nodded.

He handed the photo to the bailiff, who passed it to the witness. "That's you, isn't it?"

Herrin didn't want to answer. He'd already seen his mistake. "Yes, that's me."

"But you're not wearing your so-called normal glasses, are you?"

"I... am wearing glasses...."

"You're wearing reading glasses, right? Cheaters. Granny glasses, the kids call them. Which makes sense, since you're sitting at your desk, reading documents." He stopped, just to make sure the jury was with him. "But those reading glasses wouldn't help you a bit when you needed to see something forty-six feet away, would they?"

Jazlyn rose to her feet. "Your honor, I must object."

Well, you must try, anyway.

"The witness has already given his statement," she continued. "He identified the defendant. He picked the man out of a lineup."

"Which only suggests that my client looked more like what Mr. Herrin thought he saw that night than the other four people in the lineup. It is not proof that my client is the man Mr. Herrin saw on the street. In fact, my client was the only person in that lineup who even came close to the description Mr. Herrin had already given the police. My client was the only possible selection—even if his original view was extremely fuzzy."

The judge understood. He probably didn't like where this was going, but he knew what he had to do. "The objection is overruled."

He could've quit there. He had already impeached the witness' testimony. But why not remove all doubt? "Mr. Herrin, do you by chance have your reading glasses with you?"

"Yes. In my coat pocket."

"I'm going to ask you to participate in a little demonstration."

Again, Jazlyn rose to her feet. "Now I seriously object, your honor. In-court demonstrations are supposed to be approved in advance. We all know how much potential there is for manipulation and stagecraft. This case should be decided based upon the evidence, not theatrics."

"Your honor," he replied, "since the witness misled us regarding his visual acuity and I only now discovered it, how could I have given the prosecutor advance notice?"

The judge's dour expression did not change. "Given the seriousness of the charges, and the importance of this witness' testimony to the prosecution case, I will allow this…demonstration."

He pounced. "Thank you. Mr. Herrin, I will ask you to remove your contact lenses and put on your reading glasses."

Herrin hesitated. "I… don't have a contact case to put them in."

"As it happens, I have one here." He winked. "May I approach, your honor?

The judge nodded.

A minute later, Herrin was wearing his reading glasses and ready to proceed.

"Mr. Herrin, I placed five men in various locations on the next to last row of the gallery of this courtroom. As it happens, the distance between where you're sitting and where they are now sitting is almost exactly forty-six feet." He paused like a good game show host, allowing suspense to build. "I will now ask the men to raise their hands." They did so. "Mr. Herrin, you are now confronted with a new lineup, a lineup in which the five choices, instead of looking completely different from one another, look somewhat similar to one another, though far from identical. One of them is my client, but he has changed out of the jacket and tie he wore this morning. The other four are not my client. Can you tell the jury which of these five men is the one you saw on the street that night?"

Herrin hesitated. He leaned forward, straining. He tried looking through the glasses, then over the glasses. It was clear that either way, he was not getting the clarity he needed.

"Mr. Herrin? We're waiting."

Herrin hesitated. "I… I think maybe…"

"Don't guess, Mr. Herrin. This is of the utmost importance. It determines whether my client leaves this courtroom a free man or leaves in chains. Can you tell the jury with certainty which of the five men in the rear of the courtroom is the one you saw on the street?"

Herrin gave it a few more minutes, then conceded. "I'm sorry. I cannot."

"I appreciate your honesty, sir." A slow smile spread across his face. "Your honor, I move to dismiss the charges."

CHAPTER THREE

IN THE HALLWAY OUTSIDE THE COURTROOM, DAN SHOOK HIS client's hand.

"Dude, I cannot thank you enough." Emilio pumped his hand with vigor. Arm guns. Pink muscle shirt. Dreadlocks. Scar from left temple to cheekbone. Probably could be fixed—if he wanted it fixed. But perhaps it helped convince everyone of his "gangsta" status. "You are like a miracle worker, man. A courtroom miracle worker. Santo Daniel, that is what I call you."

"Just doing my job."

"My bros said it couldn't be helped, that I was doin' time, but you pulled my fat outta the fire, just like you did before."

"I'm glad it worked out well."

"Needless to say, you will be paid, my man. Every penny. Just need to make a stop at the warehouse."

"That's fine."

"I will have one of my boys deliver to your office tomorrow." He grinned. "What is it gonna be this time? Another Porsche? A Maserati?"

"Oh, those are so last year. I'm feeling Britishy today. Maybe a Bentley."

"You are some kind of cool." His cell phone beeped. He

glanced at the screen. "Sorry, business calls. Remember, you are on retainer. You're my main man. I got you, dog."

"Understood." His client departed.

He felt jubilant, and relieved, and the two made for a heady mix. How to celebrate? He hadn't seen Liz in a while, and steak and lobster by the bay seemed like a good way to—

A middle-aged woman approached him. Hair escaping from ponytail. Bruise on arm. Cross dangling from neck. Exercise suit. "Are you Daniel Pike?"

"I am."

"Are you the one they call 'the miracle worker?'"

"Modesty forbids me from acknowledging this. But yes."

"Are you taking new clients?"

"I don't know. Do you have any money?"

"My sister needs a miracle worker. She's trapped in a poisonous marriage—"

He held up his hands. "I don't do divorce. No Family Court for me, thank you very much. Too messy. Not profitable."

"She won't even leave him, much less divorce him. But that man is beating her up almost every night. Her eye is swollen shut. He broke her arm. It's only a matter of time till he kills her."

"You should report—"

"I've been to the police, but they won't do anything unless she presses charges, and she says she can't do that to the kids. I was thinking maybe a protective order."

"Will he contest it?"

"Of course he will."

"Do you have any idea how long that will take? You'll need witnesses, evidence, a judge in the right mood..."

"You're saying it's impossible?"

"I'm saying it will take time. And in my line of work, time is money."

"I have just over $300 in my Christmas savings account."

"That will almost cover the cost of this conversation."

"Maybe you have an intern you work with?"

"No. I'm in a firm, but I work alone. And I won't take your money unless I can deliver. I would recommend that you contact Family Legal Aid. They have an office—"

"I already called them but they said it was hopeless."

"Until she's ready to press charges, it probably is." He checked his Van Cleef watch. "If you'll excuse me. I have a three o'clock." He turned, making his way as quickly as possible to his imaginary appointment. Unfortunately, he walked so quickly he nearly collided with the prosecutor he had just trounced in court.He knew Jazlyn was pissed, but she was way too cool to let it show. Brown dress. Great hair. Visible bra strap. Stern expression. Ring on the left hand, but no diamond.

Jazlyn pursed her lips. "You must be feeling good about getting that model citizen off the hook."

"Depends on what you mean. I think Emilio is a walking waste product. But I won't let the government railroad my clients. And your witness was a liar."

"Perhaps. But you do realize that even though you won, even though I had to fold, it doesn't prove your man wasn't guilty."

"What it proves, Jazlyn, is that you had no case. It all hinged on one eyewitness, and frankly, even if you didn't know about his eyesight issues, I think you sensed how shaky his testimony was. You shouldn't have gone to trial."

"A little presumptuous, aren't you?"

"You initiated this conversation. I'm tired of prosecutors acting as if they represent all that's holy and defense attorneys are demon spawn. We exist for a reason. To keep you and the cops in check."

She placed a finger square on his chest. "This isn't law school, it isn't sociology class, and I don't need your theory of the universe. Your pestilential client is one of the worst drug dealers on the Southside of St. Pete. He's destroyed more lives in a year than most people encounter in a lifetime. At least thirteen gang-related murders have been associated with him."

"Then why haven't you brought those charges?"

"If I had the evidence, I would. People like your client have a nasty habit of not leaving traces. Or finding fall guys to take the rap."

"So I should stand aside and let you convict people even when you don't have evidence, because you think they're bad people. Basically, change the standard from 'beyond a reasonable doubt' to 'prosecutor has a strong suspicion.'"

"We saw an opportunity to try to get Emilio off the streets, so we took it. And you prevented it. You are a destructive force in our community. You think winning is everything."

"Winning *is* everything." He started to sing. "Weeee are the champions, my friiiiiend..."

"Stay cool, Freddie Mercury. There's a war on out there."

"That's exactly right." He was tempted to poke a return finger into her chest, but of course if he did to her what she had already done to him, he'd be charged with sexual harassment. "The government is waging a war on private citizens. Civil rights are being eroded. Privacy is disappearing. We continue to perpetrate the myth that people are 'presumed innocent,' but as soon as you bring charges, most people assume the accused is guilty. You get plea bargains from people you could never convict because they're afraid to run the risk. And the only thing that stops this screwed-up system from persecuting the innocent is people like me."

"Messiah complex much?"

"Defense attorneys are the thin blue line separating a free society from a fascist *1984*."

"Are you calling me a fascist?"

"True or false. You convict three times as many black and Hispanic people as you do white people."

"You know it's true."

"Why do you think that is?"

"Presumably it's because they commit more crime."

"Bull. It's because, first, many dirty cops are also bigots, and second, it's easier to convict minorities. They're less likely to be able to afford a defense and more likely to be convicted by a jury of white retirees. The Innocence Project says there are more than a thousand wrongful convictions in the US every year. That means about four percent of the people in prison didn't commit the crime."

"Is that your excuse for the way you practice?"

"You don't think I'm a good lawyer?"

"Oh, you're a terrific lawyer. And I admire you." She paused. "But I don't respect you."

"Ouch. That stings." He knew he shouldn't be so obnoxious. He actually liked Jazlyn and admired her dedication. But this was a subject he felt passionately about. "Whether you respect my work or you don't, defense lawyers play an essential role in making the system work."

"Do you recite this speech to yourself at night? Like when you're trying to sleep? Which, given the state of your conscience, I would think you find very difficult."

"Would you like to help with that?"

She blinked. "Seriously? You're propositioning me?"

"Only in a consent-based, respectful way. How about dinner? We both have to eat. Why not do it together?"

"There is no way in hell—"

"Dinner at eight, just the two of us, Chez Guitano."

Her lips parted. "I've never been there."

"Best meal in St. Pete."

"And the most expensive."

He shrugged.

"This is completely inappropriate—"

"Am I pressuring you in any way?"

"No...I suppose not."

"And we are not currently working on a case, you are not my boss or underling, I have no authority over you, and you are free to walk away at any time."

"Which I think I will."

"As you wish. But the lobster thermidor at Chez Guitano..." He kissed his fingertips. "*Magnifique*. Are you in or out?"

"I can't believe you're asking me to dinner. Can you not see how angry you're making me?"

"I like it. Turns me on."

"And you think if you buy me an expensive meal I'll go to bed with you?"

"Nah. I never have sex on the first date."

She arched an eyebrow. "Is that a fact."

"If I wanted to impress you, I'd cook. But that would be overkill on the first date."

"You can cook?"

"And circle gets the square. Yes, I've completed two gourmet courses. Got the certificates and everything. But I digress. Are you joining me for dinner?"

"I must admit, you have a unique seduction technique. Trounce a girl in court, insult her in the hallway, then invite her to dinner."

"You probably go for the bad boys. So?"

Jazlyn stared at him, hands on hips, breathing through her nostrils like a dragon. Finally, she spoke. "Can we make it eight-thirty? I want to go home first and change."

"Perfection."

She poked him again in the chest. "And you may not talk about this afterward. I'll deny everything."

He nodded. "I never eat and tell."

She turned on her heel and walked away.

"Red is your best color," he said, just loud enough for her to hear. "Ditch the earth tones."

CHAPTER FOUR

HE SAT BEHIND THE DESK STARING AT THE TWO PEOPLE HE HAD invited to this private meeting in a darkened room. Dark by choice. He preferred it that way. He couldn't afford to have any witnesses. And he didn't particularly want to see their faces.

"I think you know why I selected you," he said. "You are both highly placed operatives within your organizations. You, Luis are trusted by Emilio, and as I'm sure you already know, he is once again a free man. You, Diego, are trusted by your brother. Both of your bosses are in St. Petersburg at the moment. And they both hate each other."

He drew in his breath slowly, then continued. "The question is, how do we get these two... businessmen, let's call them...to meet."

"Emilio will never meet that bastard," Luis said.

"Why? Doesn't he want to expand his business?"

"Maybe."

"How's he going to get a foothold?"

"By killing every whore-dog who gets in his way." The hostility in Luis' voice was plain, but whether that was a sign of aggression or nervousness was unclear.

"And what about you, Diego?"

"The same. My brother doesn't want people to know he's in the country. He won't consider any kind of meeting."

"He would if he had a good reason. We just need to figure out what that reason is."

"He has nothing to gain."

"I disagree. They both have something the other wants. That's the key." He rose, towering over the desk. "Sanchez wants to expand his business into the states. Emilio wants to cut into Sanchez' business. Sanchez probably wouldn't object to taking over Emilio's business. At the end of the day, they are both self-centered, petty little gang lords willing to risk everyone and everything to gain a little turf. They would put any life on the line, including yours, if they thought it would help their bottom line. All we have to do is convince them that the meeting will be to their benefit."

Luis spoke up. "And that ain't never gonna happen. Meet out on the street? That's gonna get people killed. They will both assume it is some kinda setup. A hit."

"But what if they thought differently? What if we chose a more upscale location? What if each of them believed they were going to get the drop on the other?"

Luis was slow to respond. "That could never happen."

"You could make it happen."

"What are you saying?"

He spread his hands across the desk. "Simple. You don't tell Emilio you're arranging a meeting. You say you're arranging an assassination. Same for you, Diego. You let each of them believe the other doesn't know they'll be there. That somehow you've gotten inside information about their enemy's movements, which presents an opportunity to eliminate the opposition and seize their business. They'll love that."

Luis shook his head. "Man, do you know what you are saying? People are going to get hurt. Maybe dead."

"Some of them should be dead."

"That's sick. I have spent years tryin' to turn this business into something legit."

"And that has cost you, hasn't it? Now you need money badly, money I can provide. And most of all—you need Emilio gone. Back behind bars, or perhaps something even more permanent." He turned his attention to the other shadow in the room. "Same offer for you, Diego. Isn't it about time you stopped being your big brother's play toy?"

He reached down, grabbed two briefcases, and slid them across the desk. "Inside you will find everything you need. More than enough money to grease the wheels. Make this happen. And remember—I'll be watching you."

CHAPTER FIVE

DAN SMILED AT JAZLYN ACROSS THE DINNER TABLE. "I CAN'T believe one of your no-doubt-numerous suitors hasn't taken you to Chez Guitano before."

"I work too much to have no-doubt-numerous suitors."

The restaurant was crowded, but they kept the tables adequately separated to maintain some illusion of privacy. Waiters in white coats attended to their every need, and they had a great view of the ocean. Of course, he saw the ocean every day from his boat. But somehow, a good view improved every dining experience.

"That explains nothing. You look terrific, by the way. Especially in that red dress. Very fetch."

"I suppose I must convey my thanks."

"What's going on with you?"

"You know perfectly well what I do."

"But outside the office. Do you have...a life?"

"You don't get to the head of the office by having a life."

"From what I hear, you got there by being the DA's apex predator."

"I plead *nolo contendre*."

"Regrets?"

She shrugged. "I am well past thirty and my bio clock is ticking. I think I would've liked being a mother..." She sighed. "But it's not going to happen."

That was a problem he didn't want to help with. "Focus on all you've got. You look great. You're smart. You're a terrific prosecutor. Rumor is you'll run for the top spot in a couple of years. Do you need a marriage?"

"Enough about me." She nibbled a bite of her lobster. "Why aren't you with someone?"

He pondered a moment. "I suppose the most honest answer is—because I don't want to be."

"I get that. Seems like even when you're with someone, you're not really with someone. Kind of a lone wolf, aren't you?"

"Just because I'm single?"

"I never see you with anyone from your firm. You're always in court alone."

"Goodness. This is getting personal." He tugged at his collar. "Friedman & Collins does not have an extensive criminal law department. I'm their token dip into brackish waters."

"Then why be there?"

"Because I want to practice law, not fill out forms and handle administrative crap."

"So you use them. Just like you probably use women. But you're not really *with* them."

"Hold on, Nessie. I may be single, I may not want to burden myself with constant discontent, but I do not use women. Ever. I respect and love women. I want everyone to be happy."

"Is that why you asked me out? To make me happy?"

He popped an oyster into his mouth. "I was hoping the happiness would be mutual."

"Is this the part where you try to lure me back to your apartment?"

"Boat."

"Excuse me?"

"I live on a boat. Big sailboat. *The Defender*."

"You live on it?"

"Keeps down the rent. Don't have to worry about mowing the lawn. Completely guarantees you don't become a hoarder. Wanna see it?"

She tossed her head to the side. "I have to admit, I'm curious."

He smiled and raised a hand. "Check, please."

CHAPTER SIX

DAN'S EYES OPENED. HE WAS IN BED, ON THE SAILBOAT.

Quick bed check. Nope, he was alone. He tried to retrace the previous night through his pre-caffeinated haze. She had come back with him after dinner, mostly out of curiosity, but she left quickly and he didn't try to stop her. Third date, maybe. First date, he'd be a gentleman.

He checked his phone. He spotted a text from John Stoddard, managing partner at the firm. Wanted to see him in Conference Room Three. The big one. Ten a.m. sharp.

He closed his eyes. Stoddard must've heard about the big win in court, or more importantly, how much money he'd brought into the firm's coffers. Probably had some kind of party or reception planned. Hail the conquering hero.

His life was everything he'd ever dreamt it would be. He wished his father had lived to see this. Despite a few missteps here and there, he'd made a success of himself.

His life was perfection. Right?

DAN LOVED EVERYTHING ABOUT KITEBOARDING. THE WIND

whipped his face and the sun chapped his skin and the saltwater spray made his eyes water. Paradise.

He liked to push himself, which he supposed was what drove him to extreme activities. Nothing excited him as much as trying something new. In the last six months, he'd surfed at least once a week, zip-lined over the canopy of the Costa Rican rainforest, caved on Kauai, scuba-dived at Turtle Bay, jumped out of an airplane at ten thousand feet, and kissed a dolphin (long story).

But kiteboarding was his new favorite. Basically, he harnessed the power of the wind with a large controllable kite that propelled him across the water on a board, similar to a surfboard, but smaller. He preferred to go freestyle—no foot straps or bindings. He loved to get "big air," jumps so high he could try tricks while airborne. He had managed a 360 flip. Next time he wanted to do it and land on the board.

This morning, he used a smaller twintip board and a first-rate kite to get good boost and hangtime. His goal was to set a new St. Pete speed record. So far as he knew, no one around here had cracked fifty knots yet. Why shouldn't he be the first?

As far as he was concerned, that's what life was about. Being the first. Being the best. Staying unchained and untethered, as free as the kite in the sky.

Boundless. Right?

———

AFTER HE PUT HIS GEAR AWAY, HE DROVE TO WORK. HE TOOK I-175 almost all the way in his convertible 911 Turbo S Cabriolet Porsche with the top down, enjoying the perpetually perfect St. Pete weather, feeling the breeze and inhaling the smell of the ocean. Perfection. That's what he kept telling himself. He had built a life of boundless perfection.

He entered the lobby of his firm, Friedman & Collins, striding like Caesar returning to Rome after crossing the Rubicon. I came, I saw, I devastated.

He was not impressed by the response. He stopped at the receptionist's station. The receptionist was a British woman named Gemma, cute in a bad-teeth sort of way, and he usually bantered and flirted a little on his way in. This time, as he approached, she quickly grabbed the phone receiver and acted as if she were talking to someone, though when he glanced at the phone bank, he noticed that none of the extension buttons were lit.

He rounded the corner and approached his assistant's station, now a bit more guarded. Before he had even spoken, he could tell Kathy was uncomfortable.

He decided to take the full-frontal, oblivious-to-the-world approach. "You heard about the case?"

She nodded, her left eye twitching slightly. "I definitely heard about the case. Congratulations, Dan. Another notch on your belt."

"That's very kind of you." Something was definitely amiss. There was an elephant in the room and his assistant knew its name—but he didn't.

For that matter, as he glanced around the office, he got the distinct impression that everyone was looking the other way. He'd expected to be met with congratulations and accolades. Instead, he was getting more of a pariah vibe.

Kathy cleared her throat. "I think John wants you in Conference Room Three."

"I know. Should I wear a party hat?"

"Probably best if you just...get it over with."

He didn't like the sound of that at all. He left his backpack in his office, admired the beach view for a moment, grabbed a legal pad, and headed for Conference Room Three.

———————

IT WAS NOT A PARTY. HE WAS ONLY THREE MINUTES LATE, BUT all eight senior partners were seated around the table, not talking, not smiling, including the most senior of them all, Barry Friedman, who gave the firm its first name. Friedman didn't even come into the office most days—he was well into his seventies. But he was here today.

And he was not smiling. Hair dyed black. Reagan uniform—blue suit, red tie. Missed a spot shaving. Rolex watch.

John Stoddard, the managing partner, sat at the far end of the table. Immaculate suit, Brooks Brothers. Gold tie clip. Obvious perm. iPad on display, though he probably couldn't use it. Good with clients, though mentally negligible.

Stoddard had never liked him. Probably thought Dan was lower class, since Stoddard came from old money. Always seemed to have a deprecating expression when they talked. Smirky McSmirkface.

There was an empty chair at the opposite end of the table, obviously reserved for him.

"Please take a seat," Stoddard said.

Dan did as instructed. And then he noticed the most ominous clue of all—no granola bars. When he joined the firm, he'd objected to the Krispy Kremes laid out at every meeting. Fried dough, horrible for you. He suggested granola bars. Made some low-fat macarons for those needing a little sweetness.

Scanning the table, he saw no granola bars, much less macarons. The doughnuts were back.

A very bad sign indeed.

Stoddard cleared his throat. "Are you feeling okay, Dan?"

He beamed. "Moister than an oyster. What's up?"

"I'm afraid we have something...serious to discuss. Serious and rather...unpleasant."

Just get to the point already, you weasel. "You did hear that I won the case yesterday, right?"

"We all know that, yes."

"In fact, I destroyed the prosecution so thoroughly they didn't even submit the case to the jury. They just folded."

"We heard that as well."

"Our client was extremely pleased and—"

Stoddard interrupted him. "Yes. Your client."

He craned his neck. "He's so pleased he's going to have our fee hand-delivered today."

Stoddard nodded. "He's already done that. The money arrived first thing this morning. All in cash." He exchanged some side-eye with his fellow partners.

"So I assume everyone is jubilant," he continued, almost tongue-in-cheek, since it was obvious that no one at this table was jubilant. "We provided our client with a fantastic defense. And he paid his bill. Isn't that our business model? Isn't that how we define success?"

Friedman opened a manila folder resting on the table, his hands trembling slightly. "There's more to it than that, Dan."

"We won. And winning is everything."

Friedman stared at his hands. "No, winning is *not* everything."

Stoddard cut in. "Have you listened to the news this morning, Dan?"

"I'm afraid I haven't had time."

"Well, you should. There was a horrible shootout last night, in the tourist district, not far from the Trademark Hotel. Looks like some kind of gang confrontation got out of control. Six people were shot. One person is dead."

"I'm sorry to hear that. That's horrible."

"It's more than horrible. It's...disastrous."

His brow knitted. "I don't want to seem heartless, but this is Florida. We do have gangs, we do have drugs, and I don't think that's a newsflash to anyone."

Stoddard cleared his throat. "The police are still gathering information. The investigation is in its preliminary stages. But it appears that one of the major players in this blood-soaked drama"—he drew in his breath—"was your client. Emilio Lòpez."

Now he saw where this was going. He was normally ten steps ahead, but this morning, he was two steps behind.

Stoddard continued. "Looks like your client wanted to have some kind of...celebration. Mixed with business, of course. A rival gang was not so excited that their ace competition, your client, was back on the street. Shooting ensued."

"This is a terrible event, I agree. And my thoughts and prayers go out to the families of those who were hurt. But from a business standpoint...Emilio does have us on retainer. If he or any of his buddies are charged, they'll come to us for representation. And that could be worth—"

Friedman pounded his fist on the table, startling everyone. "No, he will damn well *not* be coming to my law firm for representation."

Stoddard laid his hand on Friedman's forearm, trying to calm him. Friedman looked as if he might stroke out at any moment. "Dan," Stoddard explained, "we will not be taking that case. We will not be taking any more business from this man."

"Are you kidding? Emilio is a gold mine. Don't you think you're overreacting?"

Stoddard looked as if he had an unpleasant taste in his mouth and couldn't get rid of it. "I just texted you a photograph, Dan. Take a look."

He pulled out his phone. His lips parted. His stomach roiled.

It was obviously a crime-scene photo. The victim was a young girl, maybe fifteen. Blood covered her entire body and pooled around her head. Her limbs were twisted at an unnatural angle.

He set the photograph down, trying to keep his hand steady. He'd seen crime-scene photos before, of course. But this was beyond dreadful. And the age of the victim didn't make it any better.

"This is one of the victims of the...incident?"

"She's in critical condition. She may survive, but the recovery will be long and she may have brain damage." He paused. "Her name is Mandy Donahue."

"As in—?"

"That's right. As in Alan Donahue. Donahue Petroleum, the largest offshore driller in the state—and our five-hundred-pound gorilla. Best client we have. Best client we ever had. What she was doing in the middle of this mess, no one knows yet. Maybe she was just out with friends and got caught in the crossfire. Or maybe she was being a teen rebel and hanging with some bad characters. But the point is, this tragedy would never have occurred except that a member of this firm got a vicious gangster released by employing a courtroom stunt."

So the managing partner was concerned about the bottom line. Completely on-brand. "That's my job, John."

"Every lawyer has to temper his duty to represent his client with common sense. And common decency."

"I had no way of knowing this would occur."

"You had no idea this...Emilio was involved with gangs?"

"Half the criminal defendants in this town are involved with gangs. That doesn't mean anything."

"And you had no idea he had been linked to previous crimes?"

He remembered what Jazlyn had told him the previous day. "I've heard some rumors..."

Friedman shook his head, as if lost in an uncomprehending daze. "We cannot have this," he mumbled quietly. "I built this firm from nothing, and I didn't do it so we could be known throughout the state as child murderers."

"No one is going to blame us for—"

"What the hell would you know about it? Some people already blame us. Some people always blame the lawyers. I won't have this. I never thought we should handle criminal law in the first place."

"You wanted a full-service firm. That's why you brought me onto the team."

"The team?" Stoddard said. "When did you ever care about the team? You never work with anyone else, much less consult anyone or toss any hours their way. You're a kingdom unto yourself who just happens to have an office here, probably so we can handle all the grunt work while you play courtroom superstar."

He decided to let that slide. "I think you're angry because this case is in the newspapers and that doesn't comport with your Old-School vision of the firm as some New-York-brownstone affair with white Harvard graduates sipping Earl Grey from china teacups."

Stoddard raised his hands. He appeared to be trying to keep the meeting professional, but the dam was breaking. "Dan, we've already taken a vote, and we've decided that it would be best if you were not a member of this firm."

"You're joking. You're firing me...for being really good at what I do? For being too profitable to the firm?"

"We aren't accepting any of the...cash ...your client delivered."

"That's insane. You're just throwing me to the dogs? No severance package? Not even an Edible Arrangements bouquet?"

"You keep Emilio's money. We don't want it. You'll also get a fair distribution package, something resembling the bonus you would've likely received at the end of the year. We don't want any hard feelings." He inhaled slowly. "We just don't want you to have anything to do with this firm. Ever again."

"You're making me the scapegoat to protect yourselves. Has the press release gone out yet?"

"We are simply doing what we think is best for the long-term reputation of the firm. We would appreciate it if you cleaned out your desk today. I don't know that you're doing any work for any of the cornerstone firm clients. You keep all your pending cases, keep all your existing clients...and just get the hell out of here. As soon as possible."

CHAPTER SEVEN

DAN POINTED A FINGER AT THE BARTENDER. ANOTHER MULE, his eyes said. Pronto.

He dominated his barstool at Beachcombers like it was his own private office. Maybe it should be his own private office, he thought, now that he didn't have an office. What couldn't he manage from here? He had a phone in his pocket. He could bring in a laptop. They had Internet connectivity and they must have a printer somewhere. Or he'd get one of those portable Canon jobs. What else did he need?

He certainly didn't need those stuck-up snobs downtown. He should've gone out on his own a long time ago. He should be thanking them for giving him the push he needed to jumpstart his solo practice. Yeah, that's the ticket. *Thanking* them.

Except he wasn't thanking them. He didn't want a solo practice. He wanted to be a lawyer, but he didn't want to be buried under paperwork and bookkeeping. He just wanted to do his job. And he didn't need the ignominy of being fired from the top firm in town, either.

The bartender brought his drink with a smile, but the smile had a pronounced edge. "Need me to call a taxi?"

"No. But thanks for asking."

"You don't want to get into trouble."

He understood the man's concern. He had been here since the sun went down and was still here as the clock approached midnight. For all he knew, he might still be here when the sun came up again. But he could walk back to the boat. Another thing he loved about Beachcombers—it was one of the few 24/7 bars in St. Pete. Made sense, since they were only a short walk from the pier. Boats came in at all hours of the night.

"Just keep them coming." He could be drinking down at Chez Guitano, but that watering hole was way too upscale. Everyone at the bar was either a con man, a hooker, or a pickup artist. Beachcombers had the real people.

Like the real person sitting to his left, belching and finding it just as amusing as a ten-year-old might. African-American. Jean jacket. Chain belt. Bow legs. Excessive tattooing. He looked to be about 270, maybe 280 pounds, but whatever was needed to intoxicate that body weight he had imbibed a long time ago.

"Rough day?"

The man responded with a mysterious combination of chuckle and sneer. "Damn straight. Lost my job."

"Me too, as it happens."

"For real?" He made the sound again. "Must be somethin' goin' around. Third job for me in three months."

"Is that a record?"

"Record for big hot mess."

"Why'd you lose the job?"

"Boss says I was drunk. But I wasn't."

"Hadn't been drinking?"

"Well, I didn't say that. Might've had a snort or two at lunch. But I certainly wasn't drunk. I mean, after what happened last night, who could blame a man for needing a drink? The boss was out to get me. He's been on my case since the day I started. Oughtta be something you can do about someone like that. Aren't there laws? Can't I sue him?"

"Anyone can sue. But you wouldn't win. Florida is an employment-at-will state. Bosses don't need a cause. They can fire anybody they want for any reason they want, or for no reason at all."

"That sucks."

"It's the law."

The large man signaled the bartender for another shot. "You sound pretty smart." His speech slurred, but not so badly as to be incomprehensible. "You some kind of lawyer or judge or something?"

"I'm a lawyer. Never a judge, heaven forbid. I would be a horrible judge."

"Why?"

"Because I've got a perpetual soft spot for the underdog. Because I fight for justice, which is not always what courts dispense. And because I'm always suspicious of the government."

"Yeah, the government sucks. Why can't they get out of our lives?"

"Basically the same argument I made in the courthouse yesterday."

"We should take this country back for the people!"

Maybe it was time to extract himself from this conversation. Soon his new friend would be talking about his underground survival cellar and the semi-automatic weapons he keeps in his pickup. "You got a ride home, my friend?"

"I can walk. Should've gone home hours ago. Just not sure I can face it."

"Haven't told the wife you lost your job?"

"Oh hell. She's used to that. We got far worse to worry about."

"Family problems?"

"Yeah. My brother-in-law got shot last night, in that shootout at the Trademark."

He felt a cold chill creep down his arms and legs. "I am... sorry to hear that."

"He wasn't doin' nothin'. Just mindin' his own business. Didn't know about drugs and gangs. And he gets shot. He's in the hospital now. Might lose his leg. Sister depended on him. We're getting together in the morning to figure out how to handle it."

He tried to play it cool. "If you've got a big meeting in the morning, you'd better get home. Give yourself time to sleep this off."

"I don't wanna sleep it off!" His fists tightened. "I wanna get the bastard who's responsible for what happened to Benny."

"Leave it to the police."

"Easy for you to say. Did you know any of the victims?"

He hesitated. "Not personally."

"They say one of the guys who started it got outta jail that afternoon. And was already killing again. Did you know that?"

He had the distinct feeling that it was time to go. "Look, I need to head back to my boat…"

He started to rise, but the large man clamped a hairy hand onto his shoulder. "Oh hell. You said you're a lawyer. You said you were at the courthouse yesterday. Are you the one who got that mofo off?" The man was practically spitting in his face with each syllable. "You put this bastard back on the streets."

He didn't know what to do. No one was flying to his rescue. "You don't know what you're saying, man. You just need to go home and—"

"You bastard! You filthy stinking bastard!" The man grabbed him by the lapels and slung him back against the bar. "I'm gonna pound your face into hamburger meat. I'm gonna do the same thing to you they did to our Benny."

The bartender tried to intervene, but the large man ignored him. Unless he had a shotgun behind the bar, there probably wasn't much he could do. "You put that murderer back on the street. What the hell did you think you were doing?"

"My job." He brought his hands up fast to break the man's

grip on his lapel, then pressed a hand against his chest. "Look, I don't want to get into a fight."

"Who says you got any choice about it?"

The man reared back his fist, but tottered and lost his balance. Someone behind grabbed him under the arms and kept him from hitting the floor. Two more men rushed between them.

"Come on," someone muttered to the fallen man. "Let's get you home. You need some rest." He noticed they both gave him serious stink-eye as they left. They wanted him to know they weren't doing him a favor. If they had their way, they'd probably deliver the beating the drunk man wasn't capable of mustering.

Once they were gone, he tried to relax back onto his barstool, but his heart was pounding, and he realized he was covered with sweat. He polished off his mule in a single swallow, then signaled for another one.

It didn't steady his nerves. That guy had seriously shaken him up. What bothered him most was knowing that hothead wasn't an outlier. The man was expressing what everybody in this town probably thought.

The man was expressing what the inner voice in his head had been saying to him all night long.

"Dangerous place to be drinking tonight?"

His head snapped to the right. An attractive woman with long thick black hair sat on the barstool beside him. Lustrous brown skin tone. Immaculately manicured nails. Real eyelashes, better than most fakes. Earrings matched her bracelet. She'd been there for a while, but she hadn't shown any interest in him. Mostly she stared at her phone, like so many people in bars these days.

"He may lose a family member. He's understandably upset."

"So he's taking it out on the defense lawyer?"

Apparently she'd overheard most of their conversation. Or did she already know? "That's what everybody does. The media fans the flames of the kneejerk redneck reaction. Everybody hates defense lawyers—until they need one. Just like everybody assumes anyone charged with a crime is guilty—until it happens to them. Then the system is flawed, rigged, unjust. And the defense lawyer they despised before can't do enough to help them."

"That's one way of looking at it."

"Could we talk about something else?" He sat up straighter and took in a few quick breaths. There was a rumor floating around that inhaling air quickly sobered you up. He doubted it was true, but it did at least make him feel more alert. "What brings a woman like you to a place like this in the dead of night?"

"Seriously? That's your best pickup line?"

"I was just trying to initiate a conversation. No ulterior motive. Would you rather I asked about your astrological sign?"

"Keep trying."

"Fun facts? Icebreakers? Bar tricks?"

She shook her head. "I've seen it all."

"Why don't we just have something that approximates a real conversation? I'm Dan."

"I'm Maria."

"Unwinding after a hard day's work?"

"In fact, I'm still on the clock."

"You work here?"

She laughed. "Perhaps I'm a lush. Or a complete loser."

He squinted slightly. "You're not a lush. You ordered a wine spritzer, and you haven't touched it. No alcohol on your breath. And you're also not a loser. I can tell from your voice and your vocabulary that you're well read, probably well educated. You're wearing Jimmy Choo shoes and a pair of Gucci Genius jeans that cost ten times what I paid for mine. To be fair, they make your ass look fantastic."

She fluttered her eyelashes.

"Just stating the obvious. No offense intended."

"None taken." She smiled. "I'm a legit snack. You'd be lying if you pretended you didn't notice. Now I see what Mr. K was talking about."

"What? Who?"

"You're quite the observant one."

"It's what I do. Connecting the dots. Uncovering the larger story. Our lives are all a tangled web of interconnecting stories. You just have to find the points of intersection."

"This is important to practicing law?"

"Vital. Here's what you have to understand—everyone lies. Even the innocent. You have to make some connections on your own."

"And that's why you were staring at my jeans?"

"Point being, you're not a loser, and I don't think you come to this bar frequently. I doubt you've ever been here before in your life. But you're here tonight, and even though half the stools at the bar are empty, you've chosen to sit beside me." He pivoted slowly. "Which either means you were drawn by my irresistible animal magnetism...or more likely, you came looking for me."

"Maybe I'm drawn to skinny drunk guys feeling sorry for themselves."

"More likely this has something to do with what happened last night at the Trademark. Are you packing? Is this a hit?"

"Aren't you the drama king."

"I doubt you came to thank me."

"True dat. I came to deliver an invitation."

"To your place? Sorry, Maria, not on the first date. I'm not cheap."

"More like a business meeting. And it isn't coming from me. Mr. K is issuing the invitation. He's my boss. He's had his eye on you for a while, apparently. But now he says you've become available."

"Mr. K? Who the hell is that?"

"Check your cell phone. He sent you a text two hours ago. If you looked at your phone more frequently, I wouldn't have had to come to this dive tonight."

He withdrew his phone. Sure enough, he had a text from an unidentified caller. MEETING AT 11 AM. MR. K. Judging from the address, it was probably one of those nice homes or condos on Snell Isle, one of the most desirable neighborhoods in the city, with its own harbor. Ideal for water enthusiasts, and just a short stroll from everything in the city that mattered. "The drive should be pleasant. But why on earth would I want to do this?"

"You seem to be unemployed at the moment. What have you got to lose?" She slid off the barstool. "Here's a guarantee I can make. This meeting will change your life."

CHAPTER EIGHT

DAN AWOKE ON HIS BOAT, THOUGH HE WASN'T ENTIRELY SURE how he'd gotten there. His head pounded. Apparently, there was a little man with a hammer and anvil inside his skull beating time. Had he remembered to drink lots of water before he went to sleep? Take a couple of aspirin? He couldn't remember. All things considered, he should probably count himself lucky he made it back to his bed. *The Defender* was his safe haven, and right now, he needed one. Maybe no kiteboarding this morning.

He reached for his phone. There was a message there from someone called Mr. K. Like Special K? Circle K?

And then it came back to him. The bar. That strange if gorgeous woman stalking him. Maria. Who wanted him to come to a meeting, but inexplicably didn't want to come back to his boat.

She already knew he'd been cut loose by the firm, so someone had a serious ear to the pavement. Although for all he knew, Barry Friedman had given a press conference to brag about the dismissal.

What did Mr. K want? What was the meeting about? He might be out of the firm, but he was hardly broke. Then again, his stash wouldn't last forever, and he didn't actually have anything else to do today.

He pushed himself out of bed and began the arduous task of putting his act together.

Nice of Mr. K to schedule the meeting for late morning. It was almost as if the guy knew he'd be hung over and was trying to cut him a break.

DAN HAD THOUGHT MORE THAN ONCE ABOUT GETTING A place on Snell Isle, not because he needed a house but for the enormous showoff factor. Having a home on Snell Isle was a sure sign you'd made it. He cruised past the palm trees and pelicans and perfectly mowed lawns, drinking it in.

He pulled his Porsche in front of the designated address and released a soft whistle. Nice place. At least 5000 square feet, possibly more. Hard to tell how many bedrooms the two-story terra-cotta mansion might have. But it was big and well-kept, landscaped, gorgeous. Apparently Mr. K had made the big time...somehow.

He approached the front door and knocked. Barely an instant later, a smiling man opened the door. Friendly. African-American. Fiftyish. Somewhat thick around the middle. Holding a half-finished crossword puzzle. Wearing a sweater vest.

"You must be Dan?" the man said, hand extended.

He nodded. There was something inherently creepy about a scenario in which everybody else knew who you were and you didn't have a clue who they were. Or why you were here.

"I'm Jimmy Armstrong. Glad you could make it. Come inside."

The living room was just as plush as the exterior. A big semi-circle sofa, two recliners, and a fireplace with a huge flat screen television hanging over it.

"And this is your...office?"

"This is the lobby. We have individual offices upstairs. Converted bedrooms. We use this room for conferences, team meetings, that sort of thing. And the weekly Gloomhaven game."

"Gloomhaven?"

"Yeah. It's like Dungeons & Dragons, only cooler."

"And you play this once a week?"

"It's a firm requirement." Jimmy gave him a friendly slug on the shoulder. "I'm playing with you. You don't have to do anything you don't wanna do. But it'll be your loss."

They approached a bar outside the kitchen and met another man, younger, probably late-thirties. Way too tall. Drawn face, serious expression. Long fingers. Whitest teeth he'd ever seen.

Jimmy introduced him. "This is Garrett Wainwright. He's a wizard."

"He's...what?"

"In the Gloomhaven game."

Garrett leaned in and shook hands. "And a lawyer in real life."

"He's been on the team the longest. FYI, he's your biggest advocate in the room."

"I didn't realize I needed an advocate in the room."

Garrett nodded. "You don't. Your record speaks for itself."

"My...record?"

"In the courtroom. Your winning streak. Your ingenuity."

"I'm not sure everyone admires my ingenuity. Especially right now."

Garrett shrugged. "You certainly don't lack for talent. Maybe just for...direction."

"You're part of this firm? Or whatever it is?"

"Have been for years. Love it."

"Not many lawyers talk about how much they love their work."

"I don't even think of it as lawyering. In my mind, I'm part of a search-and-rescue team."

"And you like that?"

"I do. Someone rescued me once. I'm glad to be able to pay it forward. We need more of that in this world. Less government, more entrepreneurs, more private charity. A nation of leaders, not leeches."

He was relieved, if that was the right word, to see a familiar face emerge from the back of the kitchen, even if the face was staring at her cell phone. "Maria, right?"

She looked up. "Maria Morales. Pleased you remember. I wasn't sure you would."

"Don't sell yourself short. You're very memorable."

"Yes, and you were very drunk. Glad you could make the meeting."

"Are you the reason I need an advocate?"

She glanced at Garrett and Jimmy. "I am...not going to lie to you. I wasn't in favor of bringing you in."

"Didn't want to sully yourself with a criminal defense lawyer?"

"Don't be a jerk. We're all criminal defense lawyers. I was only concerned about your...ethical issues. And to be blunt, I didn't think Brian could be replaced."

"Who's Brian?"

Garrett jumped between them. Clearly he was the peacemaker. "Maybe someone should give you the nickel tour. I'll volunteer."

"Sounds okay."

"Downstairs are the common areas. The living room. The kitchen. Two conference rooms. A small gym. A meditation room."

"A meditation room?"

"What do you think we are, barbarians?" Garrett continued. "Upstairs are all the private offices, where you can meet clients, or just chill, put in some me time. You'll take the one at the end of the corridor. You can decorate anyway you like. I favor prints from the Dali Museum. Maria likes Restoration Hardware and boy bands."

"And Jimmy? Let me guess—Gloomhaven."

"Mostly DC superheroes, actually."

"And you're okay with that?"

"All except Maria." He winked. "She's more of a Marvel fan. Big rivalry."

Maria nodded. "DC is lame."

Jimmy drew up his shoulders. "DC is the house of writers. Marvel is for movie zombies."

"Calm down, children." Garrett glanced at his phone. "I just got a text from Mr. K. He's ready to start the meeting."

"Is he here?"

"Oh no. He's never here, not in person. He's joining us by Skype."

"Just couldn't make the drive downtown?"

"Downtown from where?"

"He doesn't live around here?"

"I have no idea where he lives. None of us do."

"But he's the head of the firm?"

"And then some. Have a seat on the sofa, Dan. I'm going to Airplay the call up to the television."

Given the size of the screen, he thought, this was not going to be so much a conference call as an IMAX movie screening. He settled onto the sofa. He had no idea what he was getting into. But at least it didn't look like it was going to be boring.

The screen blipped a few times, refocused, and eventually resolved. To a blank screen. He expected to see a big face peering down at him. Instead, he saw absolutely nothing.

"Good morning, Dan. Thank you for joining us." A friendly, tenor voice radiated from a Bose sound bar. "I hope you're feeling okay this morning. Jimmy has a dynamite hangover remedy, if you want it. Never fails."

He checked the reactions of the other three people in the room. None of them seemed to think anything was strange or amiss. But the television was a solid blue field. Audio, no video.

"Your image isn't coming through," he said.

A chuckle emerged from the television set. "It never does. I like it that way. Want the Jimmy special?"

"I'm okay, thanks. Maybe next time." How was he going to scan someone he couldn't see?

"Let me get straight to the point, Dan. I'm the one they call Mr. K."

"Does the K stand for something?"

"That's not important. I'm just giving you a moniker. People seem more comfortable when they have a name to put with a voice. I expect you've already figured out why I've invited you here. I'd like you to join our little law firm."

He glanced around. "This is a law firm?"

Jimmy brushed imaginary dust off his shoulder. "Are you throwing shade at our office space? I'll have you know I spent six months on the interior decoration, matching colors, choosing carpets. Hell of a lot of work."

"I just meant—"

"That it isn't a real office unless the decor is bland?"

"It just seems...atypical. More like a rich man's pleasure palace than a workspace."

"And what's wrong with that?" Maria asked. "Most lawyers spend far more time in their offices than they do at home. And yet they spend thousands making their homes comfortable, while their offices look like a floor display from Office Depot. Insane."

Mr. K cut in. "I have gone to some trouble and expense to create a pleasant environment. I want my people to look forward to coming to work."

"It just doesn't look...lawyerly."

"Right," Maria said, "and you're probably traumatized that I'm not wearing one of those plug-ugly pantsuits female lawyers sport. Maybe with a silk shirt and a little bow at the neck. High heels, perhaps?" She made a snorting noise. "Forget it. Unless I'm going to court, I'll stick to my Guccis."

This was a bizarre change from the law firm norm. But he

had to admit it appealed to his maverick streak. "Maybe you should tell me more about your law firm, Mr. K."

"It's simple enough, and the three people in the room with you can confirm everything I'm about to say. Garrett has been with me the longest, but Maria and Jimmy have been around long enough to know the score. Here's the bottom line. You'll work for me. I'll assign your cases, and I expect you to get them done, with all the dedication and vigor you've always brought to your work."

"You'd be telling me what to do."

"I'll give you assignments. I will never tell you what to do. I don't need to. You clearly know your way around the courtroom. You have the best win-loss record in the county. I'll bring the cases. You do the magic. And the best part is, you don't have to worry about billing clients or any other annoying administrative duties. I'll take care of all that. With an assist from Jimmy."

"What's the workload like?"

"One case at a time."

His eyebrows rose. "You're joking."

"I'm not."

"Impossible. Lawyers have to juggle fifty cases at a time to make ends meet. Otherwise, they have no one to bill when one case isn't active."

"And that approach ends up diluting their energy and attention and compromises their work product. No, there may be instances when emergencies require divided attention, but in the main, you'll be given one case at a time."

"I already have pending cases."

"I know. You'll want to wrap them up. But you're not limited to cases I send you. If you have time and inclination, you're welcome to take pro bono work on the side."

Pro bono? Better cut to the bottom line. "You haven't said anything about money. I'm hoping there is some?"

Another chuckle from the television screen. "You will be

handsomely compensated. Better than you got at your former law firm."

"Better than Friedman & Collins?"

"Much better. You deserve it. You're enormously talented, and I'm not gonna make you sit on your underpaid butt for ten years till you make partner. As far as I'm concerned, you're a partner on day one and you'll be rewarded accordingly. By me. Not your clients. Me."

"How does that even work? How can you afford it?"

"You let me worry about that. You worry about winning the cases."

He checked the people sitting on the sofa around him. They all acted as if this was the most natural thing in the world. "I don't know. This sounds pretty strange."

He could hear the challenge in Mr. K's voice. "Are you afraid of strange?"

CHAPTER NINE

IN TRUTH, DAN HAD ALWAYS STRUGGLED WITH THE traditional concept of the modern law firm, which paid lip service to ethics and clients, but too often focused on billable hours and extending conflicts rather than resolving them. He was usually bored stiff by the dated look of most law offices and couldn't abide the cookie-cutter personality of many lawyers. So he was hearing a lot that he liked. But still something left him feeling uneasy. He was accustomed to going his own way, not taking assignments, and certainly not being forced to work with other people. "How can you even call people your clients if they aren't the ones paying you?"

"Surely you don't subscribe to the myth that someone becomes a client when they give you a dollar bill," Mr. K replied. "Read the Rules of Professional Conduct. Someone becomes your client as soon as they reasonably believe you agreed to represent them. It has nothing to do with money. You'll get a monthly salary check from me, just like you got from your previous law firm."

"I don't know..."

"Aren't you the one who complains that money corrupts the justice system?"

"Yes."

"Aren't you the one who complains that justice is only available for those who can afford it? That minorities are prosecuted disproportionately because they can't afford to purchase a decent defense?"

"So this is a big public defender's office?"

"No. You won't be overburdened with a caseload that compels you to settle cases. You won't be working for the government. You'll have appropriate distance, so you can deal with prosecutors in the manner you think best. I'm not casting shade on public defenders. Most do a fantastic job under tough circumstances and are ridiculously undercompensated. But they can't do everything."

"Okay. What do you call this outfit?"

"I call it the Last-Chance Law Firm."

"Oh, that's classy. Where do I sign?"

"Not meaning that you last-chance lawyers are on the bottom of the talent pool. Meaning you're the lawyers for people who have run out of options. You represent people in serious danger of being railroaded by a system driven by money and ambition. You're hope for the hopeless."

"I like to think we're what every lawyer would like to be," Maria added. "Weren't you full of idealism, back when you were in law school? Then you hit the real world and—pow. Everything changes. The system, the old-school paradigms, plus the need to pay the rent, end up pushing most of us in a different direction."

"Ok. Query for Mr. K. Why are you footing the bill for our perfect practice?"

"Take a look at the world around you, Dan. There's a serious need for justice. I think you already know this. That's why you spend so much time toiling in the fields of criminal law."

"Nah. I'm just after the bucks."

"We live in a world where the rule of law is threatened. People in positions of authority trash lawyers, courts, judges, anyone who might stand in the way of their personal agenda.

They create scapegoats instead of addressing problems. They play on people's fears, insecurities, and bigotries."

"What's that got to do with us?"

"There's a third branch of government for a reason. The judiciary serves an important function. A branch free from politics and populism. A place where the rule of law is applied as fairly and justly as humanly possible. But that only works if people defend the system and protect it. Justice is a choice. We decide it matters." He paused. "I've been fortunate. I've acquired the means to help lawyers do what lawyers are supposed to do. Prevent injustice. Protect the weak and powerless. Replace wrath with kindness. Improve people's lives rather than destroy them. Fight hate. Speak out when the emperor has no clothes."

He pursed his lips. "Where do you find these last-chance cases you're going to be assigning?"

"It isn't difficult. There are some organized enemies of justice out there, and I'm doing what I can to hold them at bay. But I will promise you this. You will always be fighting the good fight. You will always be on the side of the angels. Even if it occasionally seems otherwise."

"He's right about that," Maria said. "I was with a law firm before I came here too. Never liked it much. Mostly corporate clients, big entities squabbling over money, arguments I didn't believe made so someone could delay paying their bills. More like prostitution then lawyering. This is much better."

"And we always work together," Garrett added. "We're a team. No matter how deep the water gets, you'll always know there are three people who've got your back. Four, counting Mr. K."

"And there's the weekly Gloomhaven game," Jimmy added. "Don't forget the weekly Gloomhaven game."

Maria and Garrett smiled.

Mr. K cut in. "I bet you're feeling the energy in this room, Dan. Friends. Family. I think you need a family. So I'm going to give you one."

"But why would I—"

"We know how strong your courtroom skills are. Maria is also excellent in the courtroom, and a terrific trial strategist, though she prefers to let someone else take the lead during trials. Garrett is the best researcher you've ever seen. Does all that boring stuff you don't much care for. He can find the obscure precedent you never knew existed. And Jimmy is the best networker in the state of Florida. He knows everybody at the court clerk's office, in the DA's office, and pretty much everywhere in the state of Florida. He can grease the wheels, find the person you need. It's the ideal firm. No duplication. Everyone has an important role to fulfill." Mr. K fell silent for a moment. "Dan, I think Maria mentioned that I've had my eye on you for a long time. More than once I thought about recruiting you, but it didn't seem like the time was right. After what happened yesterday, that changed."

If Jimmy knew everybody, that might explain how they were so instantly aware that he was no longer with the Friedman firm. "Speaking of what happened yesterday, I think there might be some...aftermath. I expect my client to contact me about a possible murder charge."

"You don't need to worry about that," Jimmy said. "Your pal Emilio found a different firm to represent him. They've entered an appearance."

"Why would he do that? He loves me. I've never lost a case for him."

"But unfortunately, you've been mentioned in the newspaper articles about the 'Tragedy at the Trademark.' That's what the press is calling it. In fact, you've been unfairly implicated in some op-ed pieces. It wouldn't look right for Emilio to go into the courtroom with you. He was advised to find someone else."

By whom? he wondered.

"So you're free up," Mr. K said. "And as it turns out, I've got a case for you, for all of you, that needs immediate attention."

He hesitated. This was intriguing, to be sure. But also strange as hell. "May I ask why you're not here in person?"

"That's just the way I roll."

"Do I ever get to meet you?"

"Probably not."

"And I'm supposed to be okay with taking cases from a disembodied voice? Like some weird Charlie's Angels law firm?"

Mr. K laughed. "If you want to put it that way. Except I am absolutely nothing like Charlie."

"Are you even in St. Petersburg?"

"That's not relevant. And don't bother asking Garrett, because you can't tell anything from my Skype address. So—can I count you in?"

"Can I think about it for a little—"

"No. I've got a client who needs help. I want an answer from you right now."

"I can't think about it for twenty-four hours?"

Some static, followed by a much quieter voice then Mr. K had used before. "Dan, I think you just need to ask yourself one question. What would your father want you to do?"

His teeth clenched. Seems this son of a bitch knew everything about him. Or thought he did, anyway. "All right, I'm in. For now. But this is a probationary period. I'm trying you out. I reserve the right to withdraw if I don't like it."

"Nobody can force you to stay if you don't care to stay. Nor would I want you to. Jimmy, can you draw up the papers? Make this man a full partner in the firm."

Jimmy bounced off the sofa. "Coincidentally, I have already prepared them."

He arched an eyebrow. "You were that sure I would say yes?"

Maria leaned forward, eyes sparkling. "We were hoping."

CHAPTER TEN

DAN STARED AT THE FILE IN HIS HANDS. MR. K WASN'T LYING about having a client waiting in the wings. The client was a nine-year old orphan named Esperanza Coto. The file only contained the barest details, but she appeared to have some kind of immigration problem. She faced immediate deportation but didn't want to go. Despite the law and the current climate on immigration, he was supposed to find a way for her to remain in the United States.

They drove to a home on the Southside of St. Pete, past Lake Maggiore to a much sketchier neighborhood, so they could meet their client. Maria and Jimmy came with him, in a souped-up Jaguar F-Pace SVR they referred to as the "company car." Maria drove. Jimmy sat in the back with enough files and gizmos to qualify the car as a mobile office. Garrett stayed at the office to begin exploratory research.

He wondered if Maria was entirely comfortable with the drive. Given her Sundial St. Pete appearance and the Hermes bag she carried, she might be uncomfortable in this neighborhood. If she minded, though, she didn't let it show. And Jimmy seemed too busy to notice where they were. "You got enough to do back there?"

Jimmy didn't even look up. "The guy who handles the paperwork is always busy. You flashy courtroom types get all the praise and act like celebrities, but you'd be lost without people like me feeding you briefs."

"Actually, I've always written my own briefs."

"Well, that's about to end. Everything we do here is a team effort."

"I never agreed—"

"Take a chill pill, control freak," Maria said, not taking her eyes off the road. "Everybody gets a chance to give input on this team. But Jimmy is fantastic at what he does. The judges say he's the best legal writer they've ever seen."

"True enough," Jimmy agreed. "Even my spouse grudgingly acknowledges my writing skills."

"She's a tough audience?"

"He."

"Oh, sorry, how stupid, I—"

"No worries. You're more evolved than most people in this town. I'm aware that we live in a sadly heterosexual-normative world."

Maria filled in the blanks. "Jimmy and his husband have been married for twelve years."

"That's wonderful. I don't think I've had a dog for twelve years."

"Yeah," Jimmy said, "I won't tell Hank you compared him to a dog. He's sensitive that way." He shuffled more papers around. "Just so you know, Hank's white, thirteen years younger than I am, favors Hawaiian shirts...and is a physician. You can imagine how much he loves us lawyers."

"And this relationship works?"

"Strangely enough, it does."

He turned his attention back to Maria. "Tell me more about the mysterious Mr. K."

She shrugged. "Not much more to tell. Best job I've ever had."

"It doesn't bother you that you don't know who he is?"

"I know who he is. I just don't know his name. I know *what* he is. And I know that if there were more people like him in the justice system, there would be far more justice."

"You're not from around here, are you?"

"Are you doing that Sherlock Holmes thing again? Connecting the dots?"

"I can't help myself."

"I guess. True, I'm not from around here. I grew up in Chicago, but I like to tell myself I've lost all traces of the accent."

"You haven't."

"I grew up on the north side, so don't expect any 'dese' and 'dose.' I got tired of the big city. Tired of the cold winters. And tired of feeling like a cog in a moneymaking machine. Moving to St. Pete for this firm was the best thing I ever did."

"What do you do in your spare time? Hobbies? Sports? You're very fit. Tennis? Doubles or singles?"

"Doing a little fishing?"

"I just wondered."

She laughed. "You haven't had a chance to Google me yet. So I suppose a little fishing should be expected."

Jimmy piped in. "Don't even try to get her to talk about her personal life."

He tilted his head. "Is there something I should know...?"

She drew in a deep breath, then slowly released it. "I was just in a relationship." The timbre of her voice dropped. "It...ended." She checked the mirror and licked her lips. "Anyway, let's get our heads back on business. We've arrived."

_____

CLOSER TO A SHACK THAN A HOUSE, DAN THOUGHT, AND seriously in need of work. A strong wind might blow this place over. A Florida hurricane would end it. Typical of Southside St. Pete.

"I'll stay in the car and finish up," Jimmy said. "You two go meet the client."

"As you wish." He hopped out of the passenger seat, walked to the front door with Maria, and knocked.

After a few moments, a middle-aged Hispanic woman came to the door. Floral print dress. Rosary in pocket. Broken front tooth. Deep-etched forehead lines. "Yes?"

"Hi. I'm Daniel Pike. I think you're expecting us. I'm a lawyer."

"We don't need no more lawyers."

He looked at Maria out the corner of his eye. "Apparently... someone thinks you do. We were told—"

"We don't need no lawyers. Please leave."

Maria chipped in. "Do you know Esperanza Coto?"

The woman shook her head. "Please leave."

She started to close the door. He raised a hand to block it. "There must be some kind of mistake. May I see Esperanza? I think we're expected." He heard a voice from somewhere behind her, in the corridor.

The woman holding the door pushed harder. "Go away or I will call the police."

He put on his serious face. "I'm a lawyer, ma'am, and my client is somewhere behind you. If you prevent me from conferring with my client, I'll call the authorities. Who knows what they might find in this neighborhood?"

The woman looked at him with daggers in her eyes, but she weakened her hold on the door.

He pushed it wider. "Esperanza?"

A small girl approached the doorway. She was petite, thin, probably undernourished. Apparently nine, though she looked a little younger. Her eyes were dark and wide. "I am Esperanza. Are you my lawyers?"

He looked down at her and smiled. "We are."

DAN QUICKLY LEARNED THAT THE WOMAN AT THE FRONT DOOR was named Gabriella Valdéz. She had been some sort of unofficial guardian for Esperanza since the girl lost her parents in a horrible traffic accident. She took her protector role seriously.

How had Mr. K managed to contact the girl and offer representation without Gabriella knowing? He couldn't imagine, but this didn't seem like the right moment to ask.

With considerable reluctance, Gabriella showed them into her tiny living room—two folding chairs and a ratty sofa.

"Nothing personal," he said, "but I'd like to speak to Esperanza in private. Perhaps in the kitchen?"

Gabriella folded her arms across her chest. "No. She doesn't leave my sight."

"Ma'am, I'm sure you want to protect your charge, but you can't prevent a lawyer from speaking to his client. You could get in trouble just for attempting it."

"Then you will talk to her right here. I got my eyes on you, Mister Lawyer."

No doubt. "Attorney-client conversations are privileged. If there are third parties present, it violates the privilege. Could lead to a loss of confidentiality, which could seriously hurt Esperanza in court."

Gabriella did not budge. "I am not going anywhere. And neither is she."

"How about you stay here, and we sit in the kitchen? You'll still be able to see us, but if we whisper, maybe we can have some semblance of confidentiality." Though he was speaking to Gabriella, he watched Esperanza closely. Her face was mostly a mask. She had likely learned to keep her emotions in check. But he did get a strong impression that she wanted to speak to him.

"No," Gabriella said. "Here, or not at all."

He drew up his shoulders. "Ok, let me tell you how this is going to play out. First, I'm going to call the sheriff and tell him you're preventing a minor represented by counsel from speaking to her attorney. He'll send a deputy to make sure I get to speak to her. If necessary, he'll put you in cuffs. I will get to speak to her. The only question is whether you want to spend the rest of your day in handcuffs. Possibly in the back of a police car."

To his surprise, Gabriella stepped closer to him. "You do not scare me, Mister Lawyer."

He almost smiled. He liked this woman. Even if she was a pain in the butt.

Maria stepped between them. "Okay, let's all calm down. You're both tough. We've established that. Now let's figure out what's best for the girl."

"It is not best for her to be misled. To have false hopes raised."

"Is that what this is about?" he asked. "You've already assumed she'll lose?"

"She has one hope. And it is me."

"Look," Maria said, "here's a thought. How about you two grown-ups talk this out in the kitchen? I think you need to clear some air. I'll sit with Esperanza. We'll just talk about..." She glanced down at the girl. "Do you like Hello Kitty?"

Esperanza's eyes widened. "Yes! Very much!"

"Okay. You two go work this out. We'll stay here and talk Hello Kitty." She leaned in closer to him. "But don't take forever. Because I really don't know much about that fat cat."

"Works for me." He led the way into the kitchen. After a moment's consideration, Gabriella followed him.

"Look," he said, "I think this caught you off-guard. I can see you're distraught."

Gabriella waved a dismissive hand. "I'm tired. The past two days have been...difficult. Not much sleep."

"I get that you don't want to lead this little girl astray. Tell me more about her situation and I promise I will give you—and her —a fair appraisal of your chances. I won't pretend you have a case if you don't."

"We have talked to lawyers before. They said it was hopeless."

"Which I guess explains why you're down to the last-chance lawyers. Why is she about to be deported?"

"She is not a citizen."

"Were her parents illegal?"

"No, no. Protected."

"How so?"

"They emigrated many years ago from El Salvador. Her father supported the Contras—as did the US government secretly, during the Reagan years. Her mother fed rebels and helped them when injured. Buried a few. But you know how that conflict ended. Afterward, their lives were threatened. Bricks thrown at their home. Father's name was called out on a radio station. Death threats. Said his body would be found in the streets with his private parts stuffed in his mouth. That's when he decided to leave."

"American foreign intervention forced them to leave their country."

"Originally, they had Temporary Protected Status here. But you know what happened to that."

He knew that El Salvador and several other countries had been cut from the protected list by the current administration. More than 300,000 foreigners, some of whom had been here for more than two decades, suddenly faced deportation. Their choices were either to go underground as undocumented illegals, or to return home. "Has Esperanza ever been to El Salvador?"

"She was born there, while her parents made a brief visit. But she's been in the US ever since. This is all she knows."

As he suspected. The relevant legal touchstone, he knew, was US Code Section 1226, an infamous law that had received much attention of late. It provided the official definition of "alien status" and set forth what the federal government could do with aliens. Which too often was anything it wanted to do. As interpreted by the current administration, the Immigration and

Nationality Act allowed them to detain without hearing, without even a bond hearing, anyone subject to deportation. People who lost TPS could apply for permanent residency but it was typically denied, even for adults who had been here for years and had become productive members of society. An orphan with no parents and no means of support had no chance.

"You'd think they'd make an exception in this case."

"In this world?" Gabriella said. "In this zero-tolerance time? When families are separated at the border? Condemned because they want a better future for their children? This country used to be a beacon for the entire world. Now it is a closed door."

"Did Esperanza's parents work?"

"Her father did lawn work. Her mother cleaned houses. It wasn't much, but they made do."

"They were paid in cash?"

"Primarily."

And thus they avoided paying taxes. But the federal government had no record of them working. "Did either of her parents ever apply for public assistance?"

"Barely. Twice, and not for long."

Twice was twice too often. From the government's standpoint, they didn't work but freeloaded off the taxpayer. "She'll need to be formally placed with an adult. Maybe an adoption."

"Many would be willing to adopt her. But again, the government objects."

He wasn't surprised. The government actively thwarted anything that looked like a quickie adoption or marriage so someone could get a green card. They would only permit adoption by a relative or someone who had known the minor for a significant period of time. "Any viable adoption candidates?"

Gabriella gave him a long look. "Me."

Now it began to make sense. "You want to adopt her. You're a US citizen?"

"Of course."

"And a relative?"

"A distant cousin. But my home is poor and I make little money. I hold two jobs and did some...freelance work for a local businessman, but it's never enough. And I have a record."

"Does she have any other relatives?"

"I have a sister. But she is not well. Not healthy."

"Anyone else?"

Gabriella's eyes closed. "Yes. Her closest relatives are in El Salvador. That is where she will go if she is deported. And that is the last thing I want."

"Who are these relatives?"

"The leaders of a major cartel."

"They won't send a little girl to a gang lord."

"Of course they will. No one can prove anything. If anyone cared about her, they wouldn't be so determined to get rid of her."

"Either you adopt her or she's shipped out to a drug kingpin?"

Gabriella's eyes rose. "Drugs? I said nothing about drugs."

"I assumed..."

"I might be able to live with it if it were just drugs. A drug lord would have money. He would send her to a private school where she would be safe."

"But you mentioned a cartel..."

"Sex traffickers."

He took a step back. Literally staggered. "No."

"They say it is the biggest sex trafficker outside of Asia. Pimping every girl they can lay their filthy hands upon."

"And you think...you think if Esperanza were sent there...she might—"

"There is no might. It is a certainty. Young virgins are their most precious asset. A pretty girl like Esperanza could be worth half a million dollars. Maybe more."

He fell into a kitchen chair. "This is...that is..." He shook his head, eyes wide. "I'm sorry, I don't know what to say."

"There is nothing to say. You are only telling me what the other lawyers said. Why they sent us away."

He slowly pushed himself to his feet, eyes steely. "No, that's not what I'm telling you. I'm telling you we will win your adoption case. I don't know how, but we will." He looked her straight in the eyes. "I will protect this girl as if she were my own."

CHAPTER ELEVEN

DAN FOLLOWED GABRIELLA BACK TO THE LIVING ROOM.

Maria and Esperanza were in the midst of an animated conversation. But Maria did not appear disappointed to see him return.

"There you are," Maria said. "Got everything worked out?"

"I think so." He smiled at them both. "How have you two been getting along?"

"Like long-time BFFs. Did you know Hello Kitty has a last name? She's Kitty White."

"I did not."

"And did you know that the creator of Hello Kitty got the idea for her name from reading Lewis Carroll's *Alice in Wonderland*?"

"I'm embarrassed to say that I was completely ignorant of these facts. And here I thought I was well read."

"And did you know that Hello Kitty is the second most successful franchise in the entire world? Second only to Pokémon."

"I did not—but Esperanza did?"

Maria nodded. "This is one precocious young girl. With a head for business. And Hello Kitty."

He looked down and spoke to her. "Your friend Gabriella and I have come to an agreement. She wants to adopt you. I will be handling the case—if that's okay with you."

"Yes, absolutely." She beamed. "That is all right with me. I like you."

He blinked. "You do?"

"I can tell that you are smart. I think that's important for a lawyer."

"Some judges might disagree."

"And I like that you listen more than you talk. The other lawyers Gabriella took me to see, they talk talk talk all day long. You watch. And listen."

Smart girl, this observant little nine-year-old...

"And you don't get all excited like some people do. Even when Gabriella was yelling at you."

Maria laughed. "It's his legendary inner calm."

"And most of all," the girl continued, "I like that you are kind. Otherwise you would not be here."

"Don't let that get around, kid. You'll destroy my reputation." He squatted down so he could look straight into her eyes. "So this adoption is okay then?"

"Absolutely!" She hugged Gabriella's side.

"Good. We'll file the appropriate concurrent immigration papers as well."

"Have you succeeded with adoptions before?" Esperanza asked.

"Actually, I've never handled one before."

The girl was not disappointed. "That doesn't matter. You're smart. That's what's important." Esperanza threw her arms over her head and bounced up and down. "I will be able to stay in the United States! I can go to the movies and the mall. And I can buy all the Hello Kitty stuff there is."

He raised a cautionary hand. "One step at a time."

A small frown line appeared on the girl's forehead. "May I ask you a question, sir?"

"Yes. And none of this 'sir' stuff. Just call me Dan."

"Do you like children?"

That caught him by surprise. He pondered a moment, then decided to play it straight. "Not as a rule, no. Too noisy and needy."

"That is what I thought. But you like me, right?"

A grin spread across his face. "Totally correct."

"That is another thing I like about you. You tell the truth. People who tell the truth are the best people."

Although not always the most successful lawyers, he mused.

The little girl laid her hands on his shoulders. "You are going to win this case, Mr. Dan. I can tell you are. And then I can stay here forever." She suddenly lurched forward, wrapping her arms around him. "I knew you would be the one who saved me. I knew it the moment I saw you."

He felt his stomach tighten. "I'll do everything I can. You have my promise."

HALF AN HOUR LATER, THEY WERE BACK IN THE CAR, MARIA driving. Dan didn't mind. It gave him a chance to scribble some of his thoughts down on paper.

"I'm driving us straight to the courthouse," Maria said. "We need to get our petition filed as soon as possible, since Esperanza could be deported at any moment. A pending motion might justify a temporary restraining order."

"Or it might not," he replied. "Immigration and Customs don't have to wait around for adoption proceedings. But it's a shot."

"Jimmy? Have you got the adoption petition ready?"

He replied from the backseat. "Printing everything as we speak."

"How is that even possible? We just got back to the car."

Maria explained. "I texted him as soon as I realized where

this was going." She checked her watch. "Think we can file today, Jimmy?"

"It's going to be close."

She floored it. "I might have to break a few traffic laws. Fortunately, cops love lawyers."

He gave her a long look.

She stopped at a red light. While the car was stationary, she dialed a number on her Carplay touchscreen. A few moments later he heard Garrett's voice.

"Did you get my text?" Maria asked.

"Yes. Already running LEXIS-NEXIS searches. I've got the general idea, though the sooner you can forward the rest of your notes to my phone, the better. I've downloaded everything I found online about Esperanza's status with Immigration."

"How's the law look?"

"I've barely started. But you know the score. When it comes to deportation, the federal government holds all the cards. This Temporary Protected Status business began decades ago. No one expected anything to change, until of course the current administration abruptly changed everything. Now people who've been here for decades suddenly face expulsion. Over thirty thousand have already been deported. And our client, with no parents and no means of support, has about the weakest case you can imagine."

"But you'll think of something, right?"

"As I said, I'm still researching. I think her case is sympathetic. But at the end of the day, judges have to rule on the law, not pathos."

"You never know. Many of the district court judges are Democratic appointees and they've struck down recent executive orders. Let's hope for a sympathetic audience."

"You can do more than hope," Jimmy said. "If you know the right people."

He twisted his head around. "Are you seriously suggesting

you have some way of influencing judicial assignments? These days, it's all done randomly by computers."

"Nothing is random," Jimmy replied. "You just have to understand the algorithms."

"I have no idea what you're talking about."

"Which is why you need me on this team."

He sighed. "Just get me to the courthouse."

"Okay, Garrett," Maria said, "I'll check back with you later." She pushed a button on the touchscreen. "Dan, I think that girl softened up your tough-guy lone-wolf facade."

"I don't know what you're talking about." He thought a moment. "I never like it when the government implements policy without a thought to how it affects people's lives. Let's face it, whether you're liberal or conservative, the immigration policy in this country has been irrational and chaotic, totally changing from one administration to the next. It may be all slogans and posturing for politicians, but people like Esperanza get caught up in the cogs."

"There is something rather evil about trying to deport a nine-year-old orphan."

"And yet, I'm sure no one involved sees themselves as evil. They just have jobs to do. It's not wrong to have reasonable policies or secure borders. But it is wrong to let a little girl on her own in the world suffer."

"I think that's exactly why Mr. K thought she needed the last-chance lawyers."

He nodded. "I'm beginning to see that."

CHAPTER TWELVE

DAN JUMPED OUT OF THE CAR THE INSTANT MARIA SLOWED IN front of the courthouse. Jimmy followed close behind. They both raced, taking the stairs rather than the elevator, but they still didn't make it into the court clerk's office until 5:02.

Fortunately, the door was still unlocked. A woman stood behind the counter. Extra-large blouse. No makeup. Ink stains on her fingers. Slippers instead of shoes.

"Shawna, sweetie, so good to see you." Jimmy rushed up to her with open arms, one hand clutching a bundle of papers. "My favorite court clerk."

She gave him a dubious look. "Give it a rest, Jimmy. We're closed."

"Aw, come on, sweetie. I'm only a little late."

"Office closes at five. You know that. Come back tomorrow."

"Tomorrow may be too late for us. Got a sweet little girl who needs this filed today."

"What, you think the statute of limitations will run?"

"Worse. She's about to be deported."

That slowed Shawna a step. He could see she wasn't a heartless woman. But somebody else made the rules, and she was supposed to follow them.

"Come on, Shawna."

"All these documents get time-and-date stamped, Jimmy. You know that."

"And I know how easy it is for you to adjust that."

"Rules are rules."

"Who's gonna know?"

Shawna held up her hands. "Do you know what you're saying? You're basically asking me to falsify documents. I could lose my job. You could be disbarred."

Jimmy squinted one eye. "What if I threw in one of my special super-duper strawberry cream pies?"

"Seriously? You think you can bribe me with a pie?"

"It's a really good pie."

"I'm still offended by the suggestion."

"Haven't you heard the word on the street? My pie is better than anybody's pie."

She put her fists on her hips. "Are you flirting with me? Does your husband know you flirt with women at work?"

"Why would he care? It's not like I'm trying to get sex."

"No. For that, you'd need at least three pies."

"Come on, Shawna. Cut us some slack. Keeping this little girl from being railroaded by the government is more important than a two-minute filing discrepancy."

Shawna glanced over both shoulders. No one else was in the office. "Fine. Whatever. I'll stamp it as 4:59. You can't tell anyone about this. No bragging in court or anywhere else. If word sneaks out, I'm coming after your chubby butt. And I still expect the pies. And don't ever ask for a favor like this again."

"I won't. Except...any idea what judge will get this case?"

"You know that's randomly assigned."

Jimmy inhaled slowly. "I know that's how it looks on the outside..."

"Meaning what?"

"I've been around a long time."

"It shows."

"Consider me wounded. What I was saying was, I have detected certain patterns. Such as how Judge Buell never gets the nasty child custody cases."

"Buell hates child custody cases."

"But it's funny that he never gets one. Since everything is randomly assigned. And I've noticed that Justice Franklin never gets antitrust work."

"She says those cases make her head hurt."

"My point is, there seems to be something occasionally less than random taking place. Like maybe you have some way of inserting an anti-randomizing agent when you log in the cases."

"Completely untrue."

"Right. I didn't do it, nobody saw me do it, nobody can prove anything. But still, I'm thinking you have what we gamers call a cheat code."

"Which I deny."

"Which of course does not mean it doesn't happen."

"No, but it does mean you're never going to hear about it from me. There aren't enough strawberry cream pies in the entire world."

Jimmy raised a finger. "I think you just admitted these cheat codes exist."

"I did nothing of the kind."

"And we both heard it."

Her face reddened. "You're wrong. Now get out of here."

"You can't stop me from speculating. Maybe in random anonymous posts on social media. Judicial bulletin boards, that sort of thing." He paused. "You know how Maria loves to tweet around."

"Now this is becoming downright nasty."

"Look." Jimmy smiled. "I don't want to cause you any problems. But if this adoption case gets assigned to Conrad or Hindlemeyer, it's dead in the water."

"Probably true."

"I'm thinking Judge Hawkins would be a good choice. She's a

mother. And a grandmother. I'm relatively certain she has a heart."

"Softest touch on the bench," Shawna confirmed.

"It would really make me happy if this case was assigned to Judge Hawkins."

"And now, Jimmy, you are totally crossing the line." Shawna twisted her neck. "I do not appreciate you putting my job in jeopardy. You're putting all of us in jeopardy."

"And I'm willing to do that," Jimmy said softly, "if it saves this little girl. Take a look at those papers. See if you don't think this is a worthy case for clerical mercy."

Shawna grudgingly riffled through the papers. "This girl lost both parents the same day?"

"You got it. And her temporary protected status has been revoked and she could be deported at any moment. And sent to a sex-trafficking cousin."

Shawna twitched slightly.

Jimmy continued. "We can't stop the wheels of justice. But we might slow them a little. You've already helped a lot by getting this petition filed today. If it's assigned to the right judge, Dan here might be able to get a restraining order against any immigration activity pending a full hearing."

"Very likely. But still..."

"I'm not going to pressure you anymore. You do what you think is right." Jimmy tucked his papers into his satchel and headed toward the door. "It's all in your hands, Shawna."

She called after him. "And you're good with that?"

He nodded. "Judge Hawkins isn't the only person in this building who has a big heart."

CHAPTER THIRTEEN

OUTSIDE THE COURTHOUSE, WAITING FOR THEIR RIDE, DAN gave credit where due. "Kudos, Jimmy. That was quite impressive."

"Just doing what I do."

"Query. When you make your strawberry cream pies, do you use a flour crust or a graham cracker crust?"

Jimmy made a snorting sound. "I've never made a pie in my life."

His eyes bulged. "You promised that woman three pies!"

Jimmy smiled. "Didn't I hear you can cook?"

DAN WENT STRAIGHT TO THE COURTHOUSE FIRST THING NEXT morning. He met with Judge Hawkins and, without doing anything inappropriate, made sure she understood the urgency of the situation. She agreed to issue an order requesting that the government delay deportation proceedings pending the resolution of the adoption case. "Requesting," of course, being the nice word courts used when issuing orders to the government. He also managed to get the judge to set the adoption hearing down in her earliest setting, near the end of the month. Since he would represent Gabriella, the court appointed a guardian ad litem to represent Esperanza.

He felt good about it. But he wondered why Mr. K thought his crack team needed to get involved in an adoption. He had said something vague about "powerful forces," and to be sure, some people had strong feelings about immigration issues, but surely no one would take it out on this poor girl.

He expected to have a free day he could spend decorating his new office, or perhaps scuba diving, or thinking about what nonsense he would buy with his generous new salary.

He was not expecting to be greeted by a sea of dour, mournful faces the instant he entered the office.

Why was it every time he felt happy—no one else was?

"What's happened?" he asked, surpassing the niceties. All three of his new partners glanced up from the kitchen counter, but no one spoke. "What's gone south?"

"Our adoption," Maria said, stirring her pumpkin spice latte, or chai tea, or whatever it was.

"I just spoke to the judge," he replied. "We're set for the 29th, first up. It's gonna happen."

Garrett frowned. "He doesn't know."

The gloom must be contagious, because he felt it creeping across his body. "Know what? What happened to Esperanza?"

Garrett cleared his throat. "It's not her. It's Gabriella. She's currently residing in the city lockup. Since late last night."

"Why?"

"Murder One."

"No way. Who died? I didn't hear about anything."

"It's that big mess near the Trademark."

"They think she murdered the gang lord? I thought the cops were going after Emilio!"

"He's been arrested too," Jimmy explained. "Gossip down at the courthouse is that she was in deep with him. Worked with him. Part of his gang."

"That's absurd. Did you look at her house?"

"Could be a front. As the cops tell it, the whole confrontation at the Trademark was a trap. They knew the rival gang would come after Emilio when he got out, so they set up a counter-hit."

"And they think Gabriella was a conspirator?"

Jimmy took a deep breath. "Dude—they think she was the shooter."

"No way in hell."

"That's the charge. Emilio has been arrested on a conspiracy rap, but they think Gabriella pulled the trigger. I got a look at the evidence sheet. They've already logged in a gun that ballistics says was the murder weapon. And the CSIs say her prints are on it."

"But that—that—"

"They found it hidden at her house."

He felt as if the room had suddenly started spinning.

"So," Maria said, handing him a coffee, "it would appear that Mr. K had uncommon insight. As usual."

"What do you mean?"

"Seems we need our criminal law expert after all."

He remained completely flabbergasted. "This makes no sense. What possible motivation could Gabriella have to kill anyone? You met her. Did she seem like a killer?"

"Sometimes people fool you."

"They don't fool me. She's not the type. She's got a pending adoption, which this obviously screws over. She loves Esperanza. She has nothing to gain from murder."

Garrett pushed a file in his direction. "Except, perhaps, she did."

He grabbed the file and thumbed through. It barely took a second to grasp Garrett's point. "The victim who died was Jorge Sanchez. That's Esperanza's cousin. The sex trafficker."

"The one Gabriella feared might recruit Esperanza into his

virgin prostitution ring." Garrett arched an eyebrow. "See any motivation yet?"

He closed the file. "The police think she did it to protect the girl?"

Maria looked him right in the eyes. "Isn't that the exact same reason you took on this case?"

CHAPTER FOURTEEN

DAN DROVE TO THE JAILHOUSE WITH HIS NEW PARTNERS. Garrett split off for the court clerk's office to see what had been filed so far. Jimmy worked the front desk for the holding cells, greasing the wheels with an elderly man named Joe he had apparently known since the dawn of time. Joe decided who got to see the people being detained, and at this stage, it was a challenge even for lawyers to get in. They weren't attorneys of record yet and no one had asked for them. Until they spoke to Gabriella and she retained them, technically they didn't represent her. Unfortunately, unlike on television, you couldn't just declare yourself to be someone's lawyer and bully your way inside.

Jimmy got them in with a combination of bonhomie, chitchat about whether Superman was stronger than the Incredible Hulk, and tickets to a Rays game. Inside, they were escorted to a visitation room decked out with rows of small booths, each divided by a Plexiglas screen and augmented with an old-style telephone receiver. These always struck him as something out of a Turkish prison movie, not something you'd expect to see in the land of the free and the home of the brave. Who exactly was this set-up supposed to protect, and from what? Were they protecting the lawyers and loved ones? The inmates? Did they fear someone might make a break for it, in this tiny room with guards posted in six different places? It seemed unnecessarily oppressive, another reminder that the government held all the cards and everyone was expected to conform and obey.

A FEW MOMENTS LATER, A FEMALE GUARD BROUGHT GABRIELLA into the room. She looked horrible. Technically, she had only been behind bars a few hours, but she looked as if she'd been there for a week, maybe a year. Her hair was a rat's-nest mess. Her eyes seemed sunken and hollow. Even her skin seemed paler, though realistically, a few hours in jail shouldn't have made that much difference. Maybe it was the phosphorescent lighting.

Gabriella picked up the phone receiver. "What happened to Esperanza? Is she safe?"

He explained. "The marshals took her into custody when you were arrested. She's been taken to an ORR camp run by ICE. I'm sure she hates it, but she's safe. We'll visit her as soon as they permit it."

Maria leaned in. "We will take care of her, Gabriella. Anything she needs or wants, we'll provide."

He hoped that brought Gabriella some measure of comfort. "The state has brought charges of first-degree murder against you. Would you like us to serve as your lawyers?"

"Do I have a choice?" Her face somehow seemed both sad and expressionless. She had a zombie cast, almost as if she weren't really there. Perhaps she was trying to distance herself from this horrific situation. Some kind of psychological astral projection.

"Of course you have a choice. You can hire anyone you want. And if you don't, the state will appoint a public defender."

"I can't pay you anything."

"I'm not asking you to pay me anything. I'm asking whether you want me to represent you."

"Fine. It will not make any difference."

Maria leaned into the phone receiver. "Gabriella, can I bring you anything?"

"You can bring it, but they will not let me have it."

"Are you getting everything you need? I know how rough it can be for a woman to survive in a place like this." She paused. "Most of the guards are not tuned into the...particular needs of a woman."

"I need nothing. What does it matter? We all know where this will end."

He gazed at her, trying to figure her out. She acted as if she had already been convicted. Was this a manifestation of despair? Or guilt? "Let's start at the beginning. I want you to tell me everything. Please. Do not hold anything back, no matter how embarrassing or potentially incriminating. If you keep secrets from your lawyers, you're shooting yourself in the foot. It will come out at trial and we won't be prepared. Tell us—"

"I did not kill that man. I did not shoot anyone."

He would never have posed that question. Every defense lawyer knew it was best not to ask. If the client confessed, it put you in an impossible position, since you are ethically barred from assisting any client in lying to a court. "Okay. Good to know. But there is a lot of evidence stacked against you."

"It is a frame. They need a scapegoat and they want me out of the way."

"Slow down. I don't know who 'they' are. Get me up to speed. Start at the beginning. Sanchez is the sex trafficker from El Salvador, right?"

"True."

"When we talked at your house yesterday, you didn't mention that he'd been killed."

"It makes no difference. His operation will be taken over by his brother."

"The police say you worked for Emilio López."

Her eyelids fluttered shut. "Also true."

His heart sank.

"I had nothing to do with…his business. I just ran errands for him. Small tasks. I needed to survive. I worked two jobs, but it wasn't enough. After Esperanza's parents were killed, my needs were even greater. The girl needs clothing, food, school supplies—"

"You don't have to explain to me how expensive life is," Maria said.

"Easy for you to say, in your fancy clothes, carrying a handbag that cost more than I make in a month. Do you have children?"

"No."

"Then you have no idea what it is to care for a child. Or how expensive."

To her credit, Maria did not appear to take offense. "Nobody's gonna fault you for working, even if the job wasn't perfect. We've all held jobs we didn't love. We've all worked for bosses we couldn't stand."

"But just to be clear," he rejoined, "you're saying you didn't do anything illegal."

"I'm not deaf and dumb. I heard the talk. But I had no part in drugs or anything illegal. You've seen my neighborhood. Everyone is some kind of crook. And the other neighborhoods are not interested in someone like me. What are your choices? What jobs are available? None, unless you want to clean hotel rooms for the rest of your life."

"So you worked for Emilio. Fine. Why was there bad blood between Emilio and Sanchez? Why this big shootout? As far as I can tell, they ran different businesses. Sanchez was involved in sex trafficking. Emilio's world was drugs."

"They both wanted to expand," she explained. "Turf wars, that is a part of life in the gangs. Hard as it is to imagine, street drug sales are diminishing. Too much competition from opioids. Prescription drugs that are technically legal. Emilio's thugs can't compete."

"But sex never goes out of style," Maria said. "There's always some would-be pimp looking to ruin a girl's life."

"Why was Sanchez in the United States?" he asked. "You said he ran his operation from El Salvador."

"I do not know, but they knew he was here, and Emilio didn't like it. Some say Sanchez set that trap for Emilio, but people in our neighborhood think Emilio set the trap for Sanchez, to eliminate him so he could take over the sex trade."

"Did Emilio know about Esperanza?"

"Yes. And so did Sanchez. He...wanted her."

"For his business?"

"As I told you before, she could be very valuable to him."

He felt his stomach churning. It was disgusting, even to think about. Worse, it gave Gabriella a strong motivation to eliminate Sanchez.

"Sanchez knew I wanted to adopt her," she continued. "He could tell lies about me, try to ruin everything so he could have Esperanza for himself."

"You were present at the shootout, right? The police say they have video taken from a security camera and you're in it. True?"

She nodded her head slowly, almost robotically. "I was there."

"Why?"

"Because Emilio asked me to be there. To bring him a package."

"What was in the package?"

"I do not know."

"Guns?"

"I do not know. I did not kill Sanchez." Her teeth clenched. "But I would have, given a chance. I would have done so happily, if I thought it made Esperanza safe."

He was glad attorney-client privilege prevented the police from recording this particular phone conversation. "The police have found a gun they're calling the murder weapon. They say it belongs to you. Do you own a gun?"

"Of course I own a gun. You have seen my neighborhood. Only a fool would not own a gun."

"Did you take it with you to the Trademark meeting?"

"That would get me killed. It was hidden in my bedroom. Strictly for emergencies, if crazy gangbangers invade our home."

"The police say your prints are on it."

"Of course my prints are on it. It was my gun."

Good point. Somebody planning a murder would have the sense to wear gloves. "The police say they found the gun in your backyard. Hidden under a hedge."

"And you believe that?"

"I believe they might've found it there. I find it hard to believe you would've put it there. You're not stupid."

He spotted the slightest trace of a smile. "Thank you for giving me that much. If I had wanted to dispose of a weapon, I would've taken it farther than my backyard. The police searched my house the night of the shooting. They found nothing. Then magically two nights later they find a gun. It is a frame."

"Was anyone else present when the police searched the first time?"

"Yes, a friend. Ramon Alvarez."

"Why was he there?"

"I think he is...sweet on me. Trying to be protective. But I wasn't interested."

"Do you mind if I talk to him?"

"No, if you can find him. He seems to have disappeared."

"Could he have planted the gun?"

"I doubt it."

Maria jumped in. "We should bring a motion in limine. Get a hearing. Try to keep out the gun evidence."

"We can try." He turned back to Gabriella. "Is there anything else you can tell us? Anything that might help explain this confusing situation?"

"Is it confusing? This is what happens in our neighborhood, in our part of the world, all the time. People turn to gangs because there is no other way to survive. They can't get good jobs. They can't get into good schools. They can make more money faster with the gangs. The gangs compete for territory. People are killed. Lives are ruined." Her eyes seemed glassy. "I don't care about me. I care about Esperanza. You must protect her."

"We'll do everything we can," Maria said.

He knew she was trying to keep Gabriella from becoming despondent, but he couldn't help thinking he had to be honest with her. "I'm sure you realize that these charges are...not going to help the adoption."

"I assume these charges terminated the adoption."

"No. But they don't make our chances better." Now he was soft-pedaling the truth. There was no chance of adoption by a woman facing capital murder charges.

He took a deep breath. "We'll do everything for you we possibly can. We will leave no stone unturned."

"What happens next?"

"You've already been booked and had your first appearance. Next there will be an arraignment. It's purely a formality. They'll read the charges. You'll enter a plea. But given the gravity of the charges, they may call a grand jury."

"Why a grand jury?"

"Florida law requires it for murder charges if..." He swallowed. "If they pursue the death penalty."

She remained stone-faced. "Will they?"

"For a violent gang shooting? Almost certainly." He kept talking, moving forward as quickly as possible. "But the grand jury, too, is largely a formality."

"Will I have to testify?"

"I will not permit you to testify. There's no point. It's the prosecutor's playground. I'm not even allowed to go in. I don't know that you ever need to testify, but you're certainly not testifying in any arena in which I am not present."

"Then we won't win."

"Not with the grand jury, no. Grand juries almost always return an indictment. Why shouldn't they? It's not as if there's been a real trial, or they've heard both sides of the case. They're just deciding whether the prosecution has enough evidence to proceed, and since the prosecutors will be in there explaining the case to them, the prosecutors get what they want. After that, it's discovery and a long wait for trial." He took a breath. "I want you to identify everybody you know who was involved with Emilio. Or Sanchez. Anyone who knew Esperanza well. Anyone who might have an interest in the outcome of this case."

After some thought, she gave him a list of names, although she knew little about most of them. Garrett was supposed to be a crack researcher. Time for him to go to work.

"After the grand jury, I'll ask for a bond hearing. Try to get you out of here. But given the seriousness of the charges..." He let the sentence trail off.

"If Esperanza were free, that would be different. If she is going to be detained somewhere—it would not be right for me to be free."

Even though it appears to be killing her, he noted. "I'll try, just the same."

"I...have not led a blameless life," Gabriella said slowly, as if measuring each word. Her eyes welled. "I have made mistakes. But Esperanza is blameless. She is without sin. She has so much potential. All I wanted was what was best for her, to be able to care for her and give her the childhood she deserved." Gabriella leaned forward, pressing her hands against the Plexiglas divider. "Do not let these people destroy her future. Not the government, not the gangs, not those who would sell her skin for money. Protect that little girl." Tears spilled from her eyes. "She's counting on you."

He nodded. "I know she is."

CHAPTER FIFTEEN

DAN JOINED GABRIELLA FOR THE ARRAIGNMENT. IT ALL WENT according to rote, another constitutional formality that was basically a waste of time. The arraignment was originally designed to prevent the police from locking someone up for indefinite periods of time without charging them. Now it was just rigmarole.

The DA's office assigned the case to Jazlyn. She charged Gabriella with both first-degree murder and, in the alternative, felony murder or manslaughter. Death penalty possible.

Gabriella entered a plea of not guilty.

After the marshals hauled Gabriella back to lockup, he took a moment to chat with Jazlyn. "Good to see you again. Wish the circumstances were better."

She nodded brusquely. "Agreed." Her manner seemed considerably colder than when he'd seen her last. Granted, this was not a date and they were not on his sailboat, but he got the sense that something more was going on.

"Has someone given you grief about having dinner with me?"

She seemed startled. "No. Why? Have you said something to someone?"

"Of course not. I was just...wondering. You do realize Gabriella is completely innocent here, right?"

That seemed to ruffle her feathers. "No, I do not realize that at all. If she were completely innocent, I would not have charged her. I charged someone whose prints were on the murder weapon, who was at the scene of the crime, and who left the gun in her backyard."

"No one is stupid enough to hide the gun in their own backyard."

"This is where we differ. I see far stupider every day of the week. I don't want to shock you, Dan, but some defendants are not criminal masterminds."

He tilted his head. He had to grant her that point. He'd seen far stupider too.

"We've already got a grand jury in session. If you have no objection, I thought we'd hit them with this case."

He nodded. Normally he would drag his heels, trying to buy time, realizing that speed was rarely to the defendant's advantage. But this was a different situation. He had a pending adoption hearing for a little girl who had no chance if Gabriella went up the river. "Sounds good to me. Any chance you'll let me sit in?"

Jazlyn smiled. "You know I won't."

"You can't possibly consider this a fair hearing when the defendant isn't represented."

"I'm okay with the defendant testifying. I just don't want you around."

"If I can't go in the room, neither will she."

"As I expected."

She turned on her heel and walked away without another word.

———————————

BACK AT THE OFFICE, DAN GATHERED EVERYONE FOR A

planning session. He wasn't sure what the protocol was regarding designation of duties. He didn't want to come off as the would-be bigshot who acts as if he's running the firm ten minutes after he joins. But someone had to take the lead.

"I think we can assume the grand jury will indict. I want everyone to focus first on the bond hearing, and second on the motion in limine."

Jimmy shook his head. "Both losers."

"But you'll still help, right?"

"Of course. Superman never says no."

Whatever. "Garrett. I know you've already started investigating. I got a list of potential witnesses from Gabriella. I'm hoping that by tomorrow you can give me enough background information to know who I should talk to first."

Garrett nodded. "I will get on it immediately. Fortunately, I don't need sleep."

He squinted. "Everybody needs sleep."

"Not me."

"I don't want to work with a sleep-deprived zombie."

Garrett smiled. "I'm a wizard. Jimmy's the zombie."

His eyelids fluttered. It would be a while before he got a grip on this team. "We need some research, too. Is there any precedent for releasing a defendant accused of first-degree murder on bond in this jurisdiction?"

Jimmy was not optimistic. "Virtually none."

"We can raise the money. We can bring in character witnesses. Maria, any thoughts?"

She was staring at her cellphone. Most annoying thing in the world. "I'm going to focus on the trial," she replied, eventually looking up. "I know you have your motions planned and it would be malpractice not to pursue them. But this is going to trial. Which means I need to start using my superpower. Strategy."

He did not disagree. "Have you learned anything about Esperanza?"

"Yes. She's been placed in protective custody. The Office of

Refugee Resettlement places non-citizen kids in shelters till they can be released to a family member."

"Esperanza isn't a refugee. And her parents are dead."

Maria nodded. "Still falls under their jurisdiction. She'll be held at the ORR facility in Tampa until they can process the paperwork to deport her."

"You still think they will?"

"Some would argue it's the merciful thing to do. Deliver her to her nearest relatives. Which by the way, now that Jorge Sanchez is dead, is his little brother, Diego, believed to be taking over the reins of the cartel."

"We can't let that happen." He felt his throat tighten. "Can you get us in to see her?"

"It takes time. But I played the lawyer card. Said we needed to speak to her in connection with a murder case."

"Will that work?

"Eventually. There's an immigration agent assigned her case. Jack Crenshaw. Nice guy. Immigration and Customs Enforcement—ICE. He's helping. He doesn't like what's happening to Esperanza any more than we do. He just can't do anything to stop it."

"Judge Hawkins issued a stay pending the adoption."

Jimmy brought him up-to-date. "She withdrew it. At the request of ICE. Their argument is that the adoption hearing is hopeless now, so they might as well deport."

"Did the judge dismiss the adoption petition?"

"No, the petition is still pending, but..."

"Hopeless?"

Jimmy shrugged. "Certainly doesn't look good."

Wonderful. "The grand jury convenes at ten a.m. tomorrow morning. I want to be there when they're called, even if they won't let me inside. Just to keep an eye on things. Can we meet again tomorrow morning at eight to see where we all are?"

Maria blanched. "Must it be so early?"

He nodded. "I'll bring your avocado toast."

Garrett agreed. "I'll be awake."

"Because you never sleep. Right."

"Maria has more trouble with mornings than I do."

"Not anymore," she insisted. "I have a new phone app that monitors my sleep."

Of course she did.

He thought for a moment. He wasn't one for giving Gipper-esque pep talks, but he felt something was called for. He decided to keep it simple. "Let's keep one thing in mind. We are representing Gabriella. We care about her, and we won't let her be railroaded. But our original client was Esperanza. Everything we do is ultimately in her interest. We have an obligation to that little girl. Let's make sure we live up to it."

CHAPTER SIXTEEN

"HOW THE HELL DID SHE GET A LAWYER?"

Shawna didn't know what to say. She was beginning to think she'd made a huge mistake. It seemed such a small thing at first. She'd worked at the clerk's office for twenty years and never made much more than it took to survive. And then a possible upgrade magically presented itself. Take a little money, provide a little harmless information. She didn't see that it could hurt anyone. And she'd be padding that college fund so Morgan had some hope of fulfilling his med school dreams.

But now she was having serious second thoughts.

"Everyone is entitled to a lawyer." She ran her fingers through her white hair. "Supreme Court said so."

"Everyone is entitled to a defense—meaning some government flunkey. Some court-appointed desperado. Not the best damned lawyer in the city."

"Hey, don't kill the messenger."

"Don't tempt me."

Shawna didn't know what to do. She really wanted to go. She was scared, right down to her core. "Well, then, I'll be gettin' back to—"

"I want to know every move this man makes. He and his little friends."

"I can certainly pass along anything that happens in the clerk's office."

"That's not enough."

Shawna felt a tingling sensation trickling down her spine. There was too little space between them, but she didn't think this was the time for a lecture on personal space. "I don't know what goes on elsewhere. None of my business, really."

"Make it your business."

"But how—"

"You know anyone in the courtroom?"

She thought for a moment. "I know Ken pretty well. He's Judge Le's bailiff."

"Good. He can tell you what goes on. Even in chambers."

"He's supposed to keep all that confidential."

"You want that nephew of yours to know how you plumped up his college fund?"

"No..."

"Then you get your friend Ken to talk. What about the consultation room?"

She stuttered a moment. "T—There's a little closet near the courtroom where lawyers go to talk in private."

"Anyone stationed in there?"

"No. That's kinda the point."

"Could you plant a listening device?"

She looked stricken. "What?"

"Cheap and easy bug. You can run it from your phone."

"I couldn't get that past the metal detectors."

"I can. Just activate it whenever anyone enters the room."

"This is making me very nervous. Maybe we should just—"

The hands around her throat choked off the end of her sentence. "I need to know everything this lawyer does. You have no idea how much is at stake. How much money. How many lives."

Her trembling was so intense she couldn't speak.

"You will do this. Or little Morgan will be missing more than a college fund. He'll be missing an aunt. Have I made myself clear?"

She nodded. The hands released. She crumbled to the floor.

"I've put too much work into this. I'm not going to see it fall apart now. You keep me informed. So far, they aren't anywhere near the truth. That probably won't change. But if it does..." The sentence trailed off.

"If it does?" she whispered.

The laugh was chilling. "Well, who the hell is going to miss a few lawyers?"

CHAPTER SEVENTEEN

DAN WAS AT THE COURTHOUSE WHEN IT OPENED, JUST AFTER the team staff meeting, and well before the prospective grand jurors arrived. He knew they would indict, but he thought he might learn something by reading the jurors' faces, which he did when they entered and later during bathroom breaks. He was still there four hours later when they departed. As they left, the jurors were stiff and glassy-eyed, as if they'd just sat through a long binge-screening of a Netflix series they'd already seen eight times. But they also appeared somber, as if moved by the gravity of what they'd heard.

Not a good sign for the defense.

Jazlyn emerged in the hallway surrounded by four other people he recognized as members of her office, all men. He watched them huddle and chat for a few moments, then disperse.

He waved at her. She spotted him and approached. "You been here all day?"

"You know how I am. If you won't let me inside the room, I can at least stay out here and absorb the ambience."

"Whatever floats your boat. The grand jury returned an

indictment against your client. I'll send a copy to your new office."

"That's all right. I know what they look like."

"You don't seem shocked."

"The grand jury is your personal plaything and we both know it. You can say anything you want in there."

"Are you suggesting I would lie to the jury? Because that's a potential ethics violation."

"I'm sure you wouldn't do anything that improper." He paused. "You might exaggerate a bit. Make your case sound stronger than it is. But we all do that."

She almost smiled. "We do indeed. In any case, the jury chose to indict. And it didn't take them long to decide either."

"You have a dramatic case. I'm sure you milked it for all it's worth."

"Don't discount the mental acuity of the grand jury. I don't think we give juries enough credit."

"Yes, they looked like they were chosen based upon IQ scores."

"More like randomly selected driver's licenses. But I think they followed the chain of evidence."

"Really? Because when the door flashed open for a moment about halfway through, it looked to me like one of them had fallen asleep."

"Be that as it may, the indictment is in. See you in court."

She started to turn, but he stopped her. "I saw your entourage a moment ago. Are they all working on this case?"

"Yes. I'm the lead prosecutor, but the other four are helping."

"The DA assigned five prosecutors to this case?"

"Are you surprised? It's Murder One. The case has received a ton of publicity. We can't let this slip through our fingers. Or be stolen from us by tricky defense lawyer tricks."

"Oh, you wound me. I don't actually have any tricks. I just prevent prosecutors from digging into their bag of baloney."

"Please."

"I suppose I should take this as a compliment. The DA thinks you need five people to counter little ol' me."

"What can I say? Someone up top really wants a conviction."

"And by 'up top,' you mean, higher than the district attorney?"

"I can't comment on interoffice activities."

"Like maybe someone at the federal level?"

"Again, I can't comment."

He didn't expect she would. But it was a reasonable inference. He'd handled high-profile cases before, but he'd never seen one allocated this level of attention.

Jazlyn still seemed antsy, unsettled. A few days before, she'd been relaxed enough to go back to a sailboat with him. Now she acted more like she wanted a restraining order. "Have I done something to offend you? Other than, you know, my job."

"I told you before. I'm fine."

"It's about the other night, isn't it? If I did something inappropriate, I apologize."

"You were fine. I shouldn't have gone with you. That was a mistake."

"Was it so horrible?"

"I'm not saying that. I'm saying it was inappropriate. I'm a prosecutor, you're a defense attorney and frequent opponent. I think the alcohol was talking to me more than common sense."

He peered into her eyes. He heard what she was saying, and in a cliché way, it made sense. But he couldn't shake the feeling that something more was going on. "Maybe we could try again? You have to eat."

"Are you kidding?"

"No, I'm pretty sure you have to eat."

"First, I have no spare time now that I'm lead prosecutor on this murder. Second, we're on opposing sides of a hugely publicized case. If the press saw us out together, my head would be on a platter."

"Well then, when the case is over."

"I think it's best we forget that happened and don't make the mistake of repeating it."

He continued staring into her eyes. "This isn't because the evening went badly. This is because it went well, isn't it?"

"I don't know what you mean."

"This isn't because you're embarrassed that you went to the sailboat with me." He tilted his head, still peering into her eyes. "Are you feeling insecure because I didn't push for sex?"

"Don't be stupid. I need to get back to my office."

She started to turn away, but he reached out and touched her wrist. "Look, I just didn't want to rush things."

"Seriously? You?"

"It's not inconceivable." She started to leave again, but he held her in place. "I can assure you it wasn't because I'm not attracted to you. In fact, I think you're drop-dead gorgeous and sexy as all get out. I was just hoping to... you know... get to know you better. First."

"And I'm supposed to believe this? Even though it goes against...everything everyone knows about you?"

"Maybe everyone doesn't know me as well as they think they do."

"Whatever. Please release my wrist before I file sexual harassment charges."

"As you wish, Princess Buttercup." He held up his hands. "You know, pardon me for stating the obvious, but you mentioned that you weren't having luck with relationships. I'm beginning to see why."

"I don't know what you're talking about."

"You said your clock was ticking, yadda yadda yadda."

"I should never drink wine. Please don't make this any cringier than it already is."

"I think we have things to discuss."

"Yes. The murder case. The prosecution will produce any and all exculpatory evidence at the proper time, though at the moment, I don't know what that would be. All the evidence points toward your client. We have a rock-solid case, so don't expect a generous plea bargain."

"Gabriella says it's a frame. She wasn't involved in Emilio's illegal activities, and knows precious little about Sanchez' illegal activities. She was only at the scene because she was running an errand, she didn't kill Sanchez, and she didn't see who did."

"And you believe that? Let me tell you, Dan, if you go into the courtroom with that story, we're going to destroy you."

He wondered if that was true, or if she was trying to be intimidating. Either way, he had a deep and substantial feeling that there was too much about this case he didn't know. He needed to start talking to people.

Jazlyn hesitated. "But let me just offer this to you, Dan. A bit of advice. Or if you prefer, a warning."

"This is the part where you try to scare me off the case, right? I'm not going anywhere."

She drew in her breath, then spoke slowly and carefully. "Whether you want to accept it or not, I'm only saying this because I do actually... care... somewhat, about you. In a vague sort of way. Listen to me. You cannot win this one. I know you've pulled a lot of rabbits out of your hat in the past, but this case will not be one of them. And if you continue to cause problems, we're going to slam back at you, hard."

"You think your case is that good?"

"I do. But that's not what I'm saying. Look into my eyes, Dan."

He did as she instructed.

"You cannot win this case. The evidence against your client is conclusive, and there are powerful forces who want this wrapped up cleanly and decisively."

"You're talking about feds? Immigration? Higher?"

"I don't want to see you get hurt. You just took a severe career blow. One more and you won't have a career. There will be no one to save you next time." She leaned in even closer. "Your client is going down. I don't want you to go down with her."

CHAPTER EIGHTEEN

DAN WAS BACK AT THE JAILHOUSE, WAITING TO BE ESCORTED to the visiting room, ruminating on its pungent odor, oppressive lighting, and stylish Plexiglas divider. This time, he wasn't here to see Gabriella. He would like to see her later if possible, but he came to see Emilio Lòpez. Which was a tricky matter, since he wasn't currently representing the man, and people awaiting trial for murder weren't typically granted visitation by non-relatives who weren't on the list.

He had chosen not to involve Jimmy. Jimmy had good connections, good work relationships with the staff, and he didn't want to wreck that by getting him involved in any nefarious schemes that might compromise him later. Instead, he traveled alone.

He approached Joe, the man at the front desk. "I'm here to see Emilio. I'm an attorney." He spoke loudly and clearly. Nonetheless, he hoped Joe didn't notice the subtle distinction between the article adjective "an" and the possessive pronoun "his."

Joe admitted him to the visitation room.

He took a seat in the designated chair, a plastic clamshell number that looked like it probably dated back to the 1970s.

And waited. A few moments later, a guard escorted Emilio into the room. Dreads combed. Flush complexion. Tats on display. Bounce in his step. He was handling jail better than most. Of course, he had more experience with it than most.

He tried to play it cool and act as if being here were the most natural thing in the world. If Emilio became distraught, or objected, that would end the interview instantly.

Instead, Emilio grinned from one ear to the other. He showed such effusive geniality people might think they were two old friends meeting at Starbucks for a jaw session.

"Dan! My man! Come to see your old buddy. I am touched."

"Good to see you too, Emilio. Glad you're holding up under pressure." He skipped the usual song and dance about attorney-client privilege, since there was none. "Food good?"

"Passable. I assume you're not here just because it's Taco Tuesday."

"True enough."

"Word on the street is you got dumped by your firm."

"And joined a new one the next day."

"That is so dope. Smaller outfit, right? Strange. No one is sure what to make of it."

"All anyone needs to know is that I'm still working—and I'm making more money." He didn't want to sound defensive. But he also didn't want word going around that he was washed up.

"I was advised to find a different mouthpiece this time. I hope there are no hard feelings."

"None."

"I hear you are representing my long-time employee Gabriella."

"This is true."

Emilio spread wide his hands. "Should we even be talking?"

"That is entirely up to you." He pressed on quickly, before Emilio had much time to think about it. "I'm just trying to figure out what happened."

"When you find out," Emilio said, "please explain it to me."

"I assume you weren't out on the street late that night by accident."

"No, man, I was celebrating. You cut me loose. With that wonderful courtroom prank. Even I thought I was doing some time, but you got me out. Happy days, right? So I was partying with my boys."

"Not exactly the neighborhood where I would expect you to be celebrating."

"Got a text. Inviting me to a party."

"Who from?"

"No ID. Probably one of those unregistered phones you buy at the 7-11."

"Who knows your cell number?"

"Too many people." He grinned again. "Coulda been you."

"It wasn't. What did the message say?"

"Said someone wanted to meet me. Owed me money. Wanted to deliver it."

"Some people are saying you threw the party."

"Why would I?"

"To take out Sanchez."

"That's cray-cray, man."

"And yet, he did end up dead."

"You need to talk to your client about that mess. Sanchez was out to get me. He wanted my turf."

"Another good reason to kill him."

"I would never do that."

Meaning, he'd get someone else to do it? "Why was Gabriella there?"

"Gabriella is like, my right-hand man. Or woman, you know? I never like to go anywhere without her. She and Luis. My BFFs, right?"

He'd heard about Luis González before. The second-in-command who ran the operation while Emilio was behind bars. "Gabriella says she wasn't involved in any criminal activities."

Emilio's smile transformed into a smirk. "That what she says? She's protecting that kid she love so much."

"You're right. She is protecting Esperanza. But that doesn't mean she's lying. Are you telling me she's lying?"

"I'm not gonna finger nobody. Not without good reason. I think that—"

"What the hell is going on here?"

He heard the loud voice behind him, slightly down the corridor. He didn't have to pivot. He knew who that would be.

A few moments later, Greg Russell stood beside him. He knew Greg well. He was another criminal defense lawyer who worked the St. Pete area. A prominent lawyer, though of course, not as prominent as he was. Russell had a solo practice and, so far as he knew, didn't have his own sailboat.

"This is completely unacceptable!"

Emilio pivoted slightly. "Hey, Greg, what happening?"

"My client is having a non-confidential conversation with another lawyer, that's what happening."

Emilio shrugged. "We go way back."

"As if I didn't know. But you're not representing him now, Pike. I am."

He cleared his throat. "I know that. He knows that. There's no confusion about that."

"Then why are you here?"

"We're just talking—"

"Bull."

Emilio jumped in. "Mostly about food."

"Really? Just sittin' here talkin' tacos?"

He raised a finger. "Hey, Greg, are you being racist? Tacos, because he's Latinx? That's wrong, dude."

Russell looked infuriated. "Do you think I don't know you represent Gabriella Valdez?"

"There is no secret about that, either."

"Completely unacceptable." Russell shoved him out of the clamshell chair and grabbed the phone receiver. "What did I tell you, Emilio? No conversations with anyone but me. None. Zero."

"I saw no harm."

"You are the defendant. I am the lawyer."

Emilio's feathers were completely unruffled. "I didn't tell him anything. Promise."

"Still not acceptable. This could totally screw up the—" He put his hand over the phone receiver. "I know you have the skeeziest reputation in the St. Pete bar, Pike, but this is low even for you."

"I've done nothing wrong."

"You're having an unauthorized conversation with another man's client. How would you feel if I snuck in and started talking to Gabriella?"

She has too much sense to talk to you, he thought, but opted not to say it aloud. "I tried to clear this. I sent a message to your office. I didn't hear anything back, so I assumed it was okay."

"In what parallel universe does silence constitute consent? I wasn't in the office. I didn't see your message until five minutes ago. That's why I rushed over here."

"I'm sorry if there was a misunderstanding. I can assure you I meant no disrespect. I would never deliberately do anything inappropriate."

"Spare me." He removed his hand from the receiver and spoke to Emilio again. "Did you talk about what went down at the Trademark? You cannot say anything that might undercut the deal we're trying to make."

His eyebrows rose. "What kind of deal would that be?"

"That's between Emilio and his lawyer. Which, as a reminder, is not you."

"Are you thinking about turning state's evidence?"

"Again, none of your business."

"If anyone turns state's evidence, it should be Gabriella. Emilio is the gang lord. She's just a single parent trying to survive."

"That's your story."

"That's the only story."

Russell chuckled. "Now you sound like a rank amateur. There's never just one story. Unless there's only one person involved. Which is never."

"Are you suggesting Gabriella was the head of this drug-running enterprise?"

"At the moment, the DA doesn't care who was in charge of the drug operation. They just want to know who killed Sanchez."

"And your gang lord liar is going to pretend it was Gabriella?"

"I've already said too much."

"I think you've said too little. I want to know what's going down."

"And I want you to leave. You've already learned far more than you have any right to know. Any negotiations I make with the District Attorney's office are confidential."

"I'm speaking to the prosecutor in charge. Immediately."

"Good. Then you won't be here. Never speak to my client again. I've put your name on the list. The Do Not Admit list. No one will let you near Emilio again. Now get out."

He glanced at Emilio, feigning a forlorn expression. "Sorry, old chum. Looks like this is our last hurrah."

Emilio pointed his finger like a gun and pulled the trigger. "Never say never, my friend. Never say never."

CHAPTER NINETEEN

THE INSTANT DAN LEFT THE VISITATION ROOM, HE RETRIEVED his cell phone and dialed Jazlyn. She didn't pick up. It was the middle of the workday, so she was likely busy, in conference or otherwise unable to take his call. Or she could still be stinging because he didn't go after her like a wolf the night they had dinner. Or there could be some other reason she avoided his call. The last possibility was the one that concerned him most.

He left a message and crossed his fingers that she would call him back, even though he knew it was unlikely. He would have to pester her if he wanted any answers. If she was pursuing some kind of immunity arrangement with Emilio, she wouldn't talk about it until it was completed.

He called Maria. "Any luck?"

Maria sounded chipper. "Yes. It's all arranged. We can see Esperanza this afternoon."

"Fantastic. Pick me up outside the jailhouse."

DAN WAS SLOWLY ADJUSTING TO BEING DRIVEN RATHER THAN driving. He tried not to see it in terms of a masculinity-driven need to be in control. The more evolved attitude, he told himself, would be to view this as a promotion. He had a driver now. A chauffeur. A perk of the new job. Though he thought it best he didn't refer to Maria as his chauffeur when she could hear.

They drove to Tampa, where the Office of Refugee Resettlement had Esperanza in custody. If traffic didn't pile up, as it often did near Tampa, they should arrive in about an hour and a half.

It only took ten minutes before he realized that he and Maria had very different musical tastes. He preferred classical music, while she preferred whatever was on FM radio this week. He didn't think he was a snob, but he could only tolerate drum machines covered by high-pitched voices singing sophomoric sex lyrics for so long.

Maria suggested a switch to podcasts, but still their tastes differed. She preferred dramatizations reminiscent of old-school radio shows. He preferred documentaries. If they didn't find common ground soon, he worried, they might be forced to converse.

At the light, Maria touched the little blue bird on her CarPlay touchscreen. "We're trending."

"Excuse me?"

"On Twitter. This case. In the St. Pete area."

"We're trending?"

"Yeah. But the wrong way."

"Oh."

"Females age thirty-to-forty think you're cute. Men in that age group think you're what's wrong with America today."

"How do they know I'm cute?"

"Online news photos. There's a story every day about the Tragedy at the Trademark. Part of why it was so hard to set up this meeting. That, plus the current administration's need to punish so-called undesirable immigrants."

"I don't think everyone in ICE is evil," he replied. "But I

think many are confused. The problem is the absence of clear and consistent authority. All the relevant statutes tell the government what they can do, but not what they must do. Or should do. They have the ability to put Esperanza in this detention camp, or to deport her, but the rules governing when and how and why are nebulous and tend to be created on an ad hoc basis."

"Situational rulemaking?"

"Something like that. They try not to be inconsistent or to show favorites. But the work is complicated by incoherent, inconsistent, constantly changing policies, too often driven by politics. Short-term policies designed to obtain short-term votes. And some of them are insane. Separating children from their parents. Throwing infants into cages. Deporting children. Fifty percent of all kids who go up on immigration charges are not represented by counsel. Nine out of ten are deported." He knew the stats by heart. He'd looked them up right after he took Esperanza's case.

"This is a nation of immigrants. Except for the Native American population, we're all immigrants. You'd think we'd have a more coherent immigration policy by now."

"Are you taking this personally?"

"How can I not take this personally? My father emigrated from Mexico. Met my mother in the United States. Worked hard all his life. Never for one moment was he on public assistance. He could have been, but he refused. He just worked and worked, so hard weeks went by when we didn't see him. Sometimes he was on the road, chasing a crop. Even when he was at home he worked such long hours we only caught fleeting glimpses of him."

"Sounds like a man who cared about his family."

"Dad worked here twenty-two years before he got a job that allowed him to go indoors. A podunk job with the highway department. But he thought he'd made it."

"Sounds like a great guy."

"I thought so. He wanted the best for his children. He wanted the best for me."

"And look at you now. Law school. Fancy car. Gucci jeans."

"You're really hung up on my jeans, aren't you?"

"I notice details."

"That sounds classier than, I'm constantly staring at your ass."

"Perish the thought."

"My dad taught me that appearances are important. Superficial though it might seem, dress is a major factor in making first impressions. He wouldn't want me running around town in thrift-store threads. Like those hideous jeans you wore at the bar the night we met."

"What's wrong with my jeans?"

"Nothing, if you like torn-and-tattered JC Penney's."

"I'd been kite-surfing! I have plenty of nice clothes. But I don't normally wear them to a bar."

"You might score more often if you did."

She had a point, but he wasn't about to acknowledge it. "Your father must be proud of you."

She fell quiet for a moment. "He passed away a few years back. But he lived long enough to see me graduate from law school. Couldn't have been a prouder man in the entire world."

"That's wonderful."

"As far as I'm concerned, he's still with me every day, looking down and smiling. These jeans make him smile. So I'm going to continue to dress nicely, thank you very much."

They approached Tampa, and predictably, traffic slowed. Everybody was in a rush to get to the beach, he supposed. Fortunately, the detention camp wasn't actually in the city but on the outskirts. They didn't have too much farther to travel.

"What's this place going to be like? I have visions of World War II Japanese internment camps."

"I haven't been inside one before," Maria said. "But you may be right. There's a rumor going around that someone in the government dug up blueprints from those old camps when they designed these."

"That sounds ghastly."

"Let's hope it's just a rumor. A lot of time has passed since WWII, and we're not involved in a global war, and the press gives detainment more scrutiny than it once did. Still, I can guarantee it's no pleasure palace. Esperanza doesn't have any private space. No one does. Ten or twelve girls to a room."

"That's nuts."

"The camp hasn't been open that long, but it's already overcrowded. They have no medical staff. If an emergency arises, and anyone notices, they send people out for care, which is an administrative problem and sometimes doesn't happen when it should. There's been a lot of controversy about the meals they serve. Quality is not great, and neither is the nutrition level. They have a hard time getting and keeping staff."

He felt his teeth clench. "There must be some way we can get Esperanza out of there."

"If there is, I haven't found it yet, and believe me, I've looked. The only relevant rule says that children will be placed in the shelter until they can be released to a family member. Which isn't going to happen. We can't get her out, at least not until she's adopted. Technically, we have no standing to even ask."

THEY FINALLY ARRIVED. HE COULD SEE AT A GLANCE THAT this was low-income housing of the worst sort. Looked like they had converted an abandoned warehouse, or something of that sort.

The only door admitted them to a small reception area. They waited twenty minutes while an underworked receptionist filled out papers and communicated to co-workers by text. He understood that she was probably not paid much, but still.

They were escorted to an interior reception room. Six roundtables filled the available space. A few moments later, two female guards escorted Esperanza in. Unkempt hair. Wrinkled t-shirt. Sunken eyes. Smudge on the left cheek. He didn't need acute observation skills to see that she was miserable.

As soon as Esperanza spotted them, she raced forward. The two guards yelled at her to stop, but she ignored them. A second later, she flung herself into his arms.

She wrapped herself around him and hugged tightly. "I knew you would come. I knew you would get me out of here."

He cleared his throat. "We came as soon as we could. Maria arranged it."

Maria smiled at her.

"I knew you would be the one to save me. I knew it."

He took her by the shoulders and pulled her back slightly so she could see his face. "We're here to visit, Esperanza. We don't have permission to take you away."

"Please don't leave me here. It's horrible. Please!"

He felt a sharp stinging behind his eyes. "Believe me, if we could take you, we would."

"And we're trying," Maria added. "We haven't figured out quite how to do it yet, but we haven't given up, either. As soon as we discover a legal remedy, we'll pursue it as hard as we possibly can."

He could see Esperanza was brokenhearted, but she wasn't going to fuss. Despite all that had happened to her, she was a strong girl. Some adults would succumb to self-pity under circumstances like these. But she kept her chin up. "I know you will. I know I can count on you. How is Gabriella?"

He swallowed. He had considered the best possible way to tell her about it. But he still wasn't looking forward to it. "The police have taken her into custody."

"Can you get her out?"

"I'm going to ask the judge to consider releasing her on bond tomorrow."

She smiled. "You will win."

He held up his hand. "No, in all likelihood, I will lose. Bond is almost never granted in cases like this. The charges against Gabriella are too serious. And the judge won't like..." He struggled to find a way to explain it. "...the kind of people she has associated with."

"Gabriella is good. She has only done what she had to do to take care of me."

"I know that," he said quietly. "How are you?"

A frown crossed her face. "People here don't like me," she said, as if reciting a fact, not playing for pity. "I don't know why. They say Gabriella sells drugs. And they say she killed people."

"You know better than to believe that."

"But I can't stop them from saying it. All night long. I'm forced to stay in a room and sleep with people who taunt me. Night and day. Sometimes they hit me and—"

He felt his heart sink. This was so damn messed up.

He tried to think of a way to buoy her spirits. "They're probably jealous of you, Esperanza."

"Why would they be jealous of me? I have nothing."

"I don't know about that. For starters, I bet you're the cutest girl in there."

Maria gave him a look.

"Me? I'm hideous."

"Don't be silly. You're cute as a bug. Smart too. Who else in this place has grades like yours?"

"I do not think they care about grades."

"Well, everybody else does. And they know smart girls like you will be successes in the world. You're a winner."

"They say I will be shipped to El Salvador. A place I don't know at all."

Shipped to people she doesn't know and a fate worse than death, he thought silently. "We're doing our best to prevent that." He saw the matron tapping a wristwatch. "Do you need anything? Can we bring you anything?"

Esperanza shook her head.

Such courage. If he had been in this place overnight, he'd have a want-list as long as his arm.

"What about the adoption?" she asked.

"The adoption is still pending." He sighed. "But realistically, we have to eliminate these charges against Gabriella. Otherwise she will not be permitted to adopt you."

Esperanza leaned into him. "If she cannot adopt me, will you adopt me?"

He stuttered. "M-Me? I—I don't have...I—I have no experience—"

"You would be a wonderful father."

"I'm not... any kind of father. I have no children."

That you know of, Maria mouthed over the girl's shoulder.

"Then I will be the first!" Esperanza clapped her hands together. "I will be a good daughter. I promise. I will never give you trouble."

"I know you wouldn't," he said. "But the court is never going to allow a guy like me to adopt." He saw Maria tossing her head back and forth, as if she doubted the statement. "I mean," he added, "under different circumstances, maybe that would be remotely possible. But in this case, you're not a US citizen, and you no longer have protected status. They won't let a random stranger adopt you. It needs to be a relative."

Her chin dropped. "You do not want to adopt me. You do not like me."

"I never said that." He looked pleadingly at Maria, who offered no assistance. He stuttered a few more seconds, then said, "Esperanza, if any plan, option, or idea ever arises that will help you stay in this country, I will not hesitate to do it. And that's a promise."

CHAPTER TWENTY

DAN WENT STRAIGHT TO THE COURTHOUSE, SINCE THE hearing had a first-up setting. He met Maria outside the courtroom.

She gave him a quick once over. "Look at you. Fancy-schmancy."

"First appearance before the trial judge. Want to make a good impression. I put on my best suit." He smiled. "Following your father's advice."

"To the max. What is that, Burberry?" She peaked under his cuff. "Ohmigosh. Zenga! Italian luxury." She nodded in admiration. "I guess I'm having a little influence on you."

"You did not invent nice clothing. I've always been a stylish dresser."

"If you say so. Ready to go inside?"

He was. Jazlyn was already seated at the prosecution table, flanked by her squadron of associates. He dropped his backpack on the other table, then approached.

"Good to see you this morning," he said, trying to make it sound sincere.

"Good to see you too. Is that a new suit?"

"This old thing? Nah." He changed the subject. "I have it on good authority you're making deals. With other people."

Her lips pursed. "Who's been talking out of school?"

"Greg Russell. Seems to think Emilio's going to turn state's evidence and finger my client."

Her head bobbed for a moment. "If we make any kind of deal, you'll be notified immediately."

"What's Emilio offering?"

"You will be notified of that as well, at the appropriate time and place. I run a tight, honest shop. We will not withhold evidence."

"Give me a hint. What lie is he peddling?"

"I don't have any reason to believe he's lying. To the contrary, he's in the best position to know what happened that night outside the Trademark."

"And the only way he can get his sorry butt off the firing line is by incriminating someone else."

"I can assure you we will attempt to verify any testimony he proffers."

"I can assure you I will too, except it will take time and cost me a bundle, so the sooner I know what the lies are going to be, the better."

"Why do you assume he's lying? Looks to me like this was a staged showdown designed to take Emilio out."

"I agree with the showdown part. The rest I'm not so sure about." Much as he was enjoying this badinage, he had probably said too much already. There was nothing to be gained from revealing his hand to the prosecution in advance of trial.

A rustling behind the bench told him this dog-and-pony show was about to begin. "Let's continue this conversation later."

Jazlyn nodded. He returned to his table.

"Learn anything useful?" Maria asked.

"Just enough to get worried."

A moment later, two armed marshals brought Gabriella into

the courtroom in chains. She looked terrible, even worse than when he'd visited her at the jailhouse. She was tired. Her face was drawn and her eyes looked hollow. Once she reached the table, in the slow half-steps that were all she could manage, one of the marshals unlocked the chains connecting her legs. She was still wearing jailhouse coveralls, but since they would only be seeing the judge today, not jurors, there was theoretically no prejudice. In truth, he didn't see how anybody could not be affected by witnessing someone in this condition.

"How are you holding up?" he asked.

Gabriella parted her lips as if to speak, then choked. A rush of tears spilled out of her eyes.

He felt his heart sink. He leaned in and whispered. "I know how hard this must be. But I need you to pull yourself together before the judge arrives."

She choked, gasping for air. "Tell me about Esperanza."

"We've seen her. She's fine. She misses you, but she's a tough girl. She'll get through this and so will you." He held her by the shoulders. "You are not alone."

She nodded, and wiped the tears from her eyes.

A few moments later the bailiff stepped out from behind the back door. "All rise."

The Honorable Jessica Le passed briskly through the door and took her position on the bench. "This court is now in session. Please be seated."

Although he had given it considerable thought and spent much of the previous night researching Judge Le, he still wasn't sure how he felt about this judicial assignment. A judge of Asian heritage in a case involving immigration issues might be a lucky break. She might be sympathetic. Or she might be judgmental, which was after all the defining characteristic of judges. Le's family survived the rigors of immigration shortly after the Vietnam War ended and became successful and prosperous—without acquiring a criminal record. She might feel others should be able to do as well. It was virtually axiomatic in legal circles that women were harder on other women. If you had a female defendant, you wanted as few women on the jury as possible. He feared the same principle might hold true for a female judge.

Judge Le called the case and asked if the parties were ready to proceed. "Mr. Pike, have you received the indictment?"

He rose. "We acknowledge receipt, your honor. Waive the reading."

"I realize you've already been arraigned. But how do you plead to the specific charges raised by the indictment?"

He turned to Gabriella, urging her to her feet. Her voice was barely more than a whisper. "Not guilty."

The judge nodded. "All right then. I have some preliminary motions we can take up today, while we're all gathered together." She glanced up. "Mr. Pike, you're looking particularly snazzy today."

What was it with women and this suit? "Thank you, your honor."

"I'm flattered that you bought a new suit to appear in my court."

How did they know? Had he left the price tag on the back?

"But still wearing the sneakers, I see." The judge made a tsking sound, then turned to the prosecution table. "I don't mean to slight you, Ms. Prentice. You look fine too. But you always do."

Jazlyn smiled. The judge returned her gaze to the papers. "As I was saying. Preliminary motions. I have a request from the defendant to set bond. I've read your motion and brief, counsel. Do you have anything to add?"

In truth, he had said everything in the brief. But when the judge gives you an opportunity to speak, you speak. "Yes, your honor. I would like to point out that, despite the gravity of these charges, my client has no incentive, much less means, to travel anywhere. She has a home here. She has ties to the community.

As I believe your honor is aware, she is in the midst of an adoption proceeding."

The judge shook her head, as if amazed anybody thought she had a chance of adopting a child at this point.

He continued. "She is not a young woman and she has never been incarcerated for a long period of time. This is extremely hard on her. I'm asking the court to show mercy. There is no risk. Why force the state to incur this enormous expense for no reason?"

The judge nodded. "Anything from the prosecution?"

"I'll say." Jazlyn took a tiny step forward. "I don't care what the incarceration costs the state. This woman is dangerous. She's been indicted on a capital offense. She owned a gun, the gun that forensic evidence has identified as the murder weapon."

He started to interrupt, but Jazlyn raised her hand. "I'm not going to start arguing the facts. But we have a rock-solid case here. Rock-solid. It is a fact that Ms. Valdez owned a weapon. It is a fact that she worked with gangs and gang lords. She has been linked to the drug trade and has a criminal record. She's a flight risk. With respect, I believe it would be irresponsible, and a hazard to the community, to let her run free pending trial."

He knew the judge was seconds from ruling. He cut in. "Obviously I disagree, your honor, but I will point out that there's no need, to use the prosecutor's words, to let my client run free. Give her a collar. Put a tracking device on her. The state can monitor her every movement. Restrict her to home, or a five-mile radius of her home. You'll know immediately if she goes anywhere."

Jazlyn looked disgusted. "I can't believe counsel is even making this argument, given the charges. Let this woman roam freely? Hope we catch her before she kills again? If she decides to go on the lam, she'll remove the collar and we won't know where she is. Honestly. Shall we give her the gun back too?"

He rolled his eyes. "Despite the prosecutor's dramaturgy, we are not talking about a major gangland figure here. We're talking about a poor woman who does not have the ability, means, or desire to go anywhere."

The judge cut in. "If she doesn't have the means to leave town, how could she ever make bail?"

He tilted his head. "Set an amount, your honor. I will do my best to raise the funds."

"No. It's nothing personal against you or your client. But I never allow bond in capital cases. I believe we have a responsibility to protect the community. If there's sufficient cause for the grand jury to bring an indictment, then there's sufficient reason to keep her behind bars pending a full adjudication. Bond is denied. Is there anything else?"

He drew in his breath. "I filed a motion for change of venue, your honor. This case has already received an enormous amount of publicity, in newspapers, online, and on television. TV anchorpeople are chattering about it incessantly. I've watched the shows. They can barely speak my client's name without sneering, or looking as if they're about to vomit. There is no way any prospective juror could watch that and not be influenced. Online, the chatter is worse. Last night I logged over one-hundred-and-forty websites or online bulletin boards discussing this case. I've made a list. And every single one, without exception, assumes based upon absolutely no evidence that my client is guilty."

The judge shrugged. "No one should trust online bulletin boards to know anything about anyone."

"My point being, your honor, there is too much prejudicial chatter going on in St. Pete. My client cannot get a fair trial here."

The judge pivoted. "Ms. Prentice?"

Jazlyn responded. "I don't doubt there has been a lot of discussion about this case. It's a horrible incident, the kind that rivets the community. But people are talking about this case all over the state of Florida, and probably in other states as well. I don't see that moving to a different venue changes anything."

She paused. "And I know your honor can overcome any bias that might arise."

"The court thanks you for the vote of confidence. The truth is, we have procedures in place to root out pretrial bias. I will allow both sides liberal opportunity to question the prospective jurors when the trial begins. I will double your normal allotment of peremptory challenges. But like the prosecutor, I don't see that moving to another venue improves anything. So long as I sit behind this bench, there will be no prejudice or bias. I will make sure nothing inappropriate happens." She gazed at the defendant's table. "And that includes inappropriate behavior, shenanigans, or courtroom trickery. Everyone clear on what I'm saying?"

He didn't pretend that she might be speaking to anyone other than himself. He nodded.

"This is an emotional case with many opportunities for plays on sympathy, racism, sexism, pathos, and the basest instincts of the press or the prospective jurors. I will not have it." She tapped her finger on the bench as if to emphasize each word. "Do you understand me? I will not have it."

She allowed an uneasy silence of several seconds before she proceeded. "Motion for change of venue is denied. Is there anything else?"

He'd been thinking about this all morning, but the judge's failure to set bond, not to mention the little speech she just gave, strengthened his resolve—despite the inherent risks. "Your honor, I would ask the court to set this case down for trial immediately. First available spot."

The judge's eyebrows lifted.

Jazlyn rose to her feet. "Is this a joke?"

"No joke. My client has a right to a speedy trial."

"Your honor," Jazlyn said, "we had no notice that this motion was coming. I don't know what counsel is up to, but no one is going to benefit from a rush to trial."

"Excuse me," he cut in, "but we just heard the prosecutor say she had a rock-solid case. If she's already got a rock-solid case, then let's start the trial and hear it." He turned toward Jazlyn, just to rub it in a little harder. "Look at all the lawyers the district attorney has allocated to this case. There can't be any prejudice to this gigantic brain trust if they've already got a rock-solid case."

Jazlyn did not have a reply.

The judge glanced at some papers on the bench. "How soon would you be ready to go to trial, counsel?"

"We can be ready tomorrow. Heck, we're ready today."

"I think that might be pushing it. But later this month might be possible. Are you sure about this? Have you discussed it with your client?"

"I have. And she's all in favor of it. She's eager for a chance to prove her innocence. She's also eager to get out of the hellhole in which she is currently incarcerated. As I mentioned, there's a pending adoption, and we have not given up hope of success. But it is hopeless so long as my client has murder charges pending, so we need to get this business resolved. The young woman she hopes to adopt currently faces imminent deportation. If we wait the usual year before trial, she'll be in El Salvador living a life of hideous degradation."

Jazlyn shook her head. "I don't even know what he's talking about, your honor. We have not been briefed on this. He's bringing in matters that are not relevant because for some reason he's decided it benefits his defense strategy to rush to trial. Is there something you're afraid we'll find out?"

"What is there to learn? You have a rock-solid case."

The judge covered her mouth. "He's right about one thing, Ms. Prentice. You did say you have a rock-solid case. And I think it would be best for the community if we resolved this matter as quickly as possible. Do you oppose his request for an immediate trial date? For your rock-solid case?"

He had a strong feeling Jazlyn would regret saying "rock-solid" till the day she died. But now her prowess was challenged. "If he can be ready for trial quickly, we can too."

Le spoke to her clerk, seated below and to the right, beside the court reporter. "Check my calendar, Murray. Assume this trial will take at least a week, possibly longer. When's the first available opening?"

Murray riffled through papers for about half a minute before he spoke. "Actually, your honor, you'll recall that the grand larceny we thought was going to trial settled yesterday. We theoretically could hear this case in ten days. On the 24th."

The judge gazed into the gallery. "You heard it. Defense counsel has asked for an immediate trial date. I can set this down for ten days from now. Any objections?"

He looked at Jazlyn out the corner of his eyes. She bit down hard on her bottom lip. He could imagine how much she must hate this. But she wasn't saying anything.

"All right then," Judge Le said. "This case will begin on the 24th. Given this expedited start date, I want counsel on both sides to cooperate. No discovery disputes. Fast track the exchange of exculpatory evidence. If you have any more motions to file, I want to see them by the end of this week."

"Understood, your honor."

"Anything else?"

No one spoke.

"See you all in ten days." She pounded the gavel on the bench. Everyone rose until she left the room.

Maria muttered under her breath. "I can't believe you just did that."

"I'm not entirely sure I believe it myself. And I can't believe it worked."

"We have a good team. We can pull this together in time."

"Glad to hear you say that." He scooted closer to Gabriella. "Do you understand what just happened?"

She nodded. "Is this wise?"

"Do you want to stay locked up for a year?"

"No." About that she was certain.

"I didn't think so, and I know with absolute certainty that if we waited the usual time it would take a murder case to come to trial, Esperanza would be deported."

"But I can't help her if I'm convicted. If I'm...executed."

He and Maria exchanged a dire glance. "Then we have to make sure that doesn't happen."

CHAPTER TWENTY-ONE

DAN SCRUTINIZED THE OFFICE DIRECTORY ON THE FIRST FLOOR of the federal building on State Street, scanning for the office of Immigration and Customs Enforcement. It was on the fourth floor. Stairs or elevator? He supposed a little aerobic exercise wouldn't hurt.

Maria, of course, was all in favor. "I didn't have time to run this morning. My Fitbit is nagging me."

But of course.

They opened the creaky door and started upstairs. "You didn't have to come," he said. "You're not keeping tabs on me, are you?"

"You wouldn't want to do this without your trusty girl Friday."

"That's incredibly sexist."

"But possibly how you see me."

"Wrong."

"Then as your chauffeur?"

"Thought never crossed my mind. What I meant was, you're not following me around everywhere because you think I need to be watched, are you? Did Mr. K ask you to monitor my activities?"

"He has never asked me to do that to you or anyone else. He lets us make our own decisions about how to handle a case. His theory is, if you hire the right people, you don't have to micro-manage their activities." She peered at him. "You seem to have a...strong antiestablishment strain."

"I know from first-hand experience that being charged with a crime is no guarantee of guilt. So pardon me if I rebel. If I fight hard. If I make sure cases are tried on the merits, and nobody's civil rights get trampled along the way." He calmed himself. "But now that I've ranted a little bit, let's talk to this guy. He has a lot to do with whether Esperanza stays in the USA."

They exited the stairwell and made their way to the office of Jack Crenshaw, the ICE agent overseeing Esperanza's case.

He peered through the door. The man he assumed was Cren-shaw held a long cylindrical tube to his eye. When Crenshaw spotted them in the doorway, he dropped what he was doing and came out from behind his desk to meet them. Tall. Slender. Works out. Cowboy boots and matching hat on the credenza. No ring.

Crenshaw extended his hand. "Hi, I'm Jack. You must be Maria? And I'm guessing you're Dan."

"Guilty as charged." They all shook hands.

"Come on in. Have a seat." Once they were settled, he retook his seat behind the desk, but it didn't seem like a hierarchal power move. That was the only seat still available. "What can I do for you?"

"For starters, you can explain why you are so relentlessly harassing a little girl." He hoped that wasn't too blunt, but he saw no reason to mess around.

Crenshaw drew in his breath. "You're referring to Esperanza Coto."

"Damn straight."

Maria jumped in. "She's never hurt anyone. She's persevered despite the worst possible circumstances. She's sweet, good-natured, makes good grades, and stays out of trouble, even though she lives in a neighborhood filled with bad influences. What's the problem?"

Crenshaw shook his head. "I don't have a problem. But I do have a job. And I am required to enforce the law."

"The law requires you to harass a child? I don't even understand why your office is involved. Just leave her alone."

"I understand what you're saying," Crenshaw replied. "But I don't have the option of leaving her alone. I wish I did. I see no great harm in letting Esperanza remain in the United States. But she has no legal status, no legal guardians, and no means of supporting herself."

"That doesn't mean you have to deport her."

Crenshaw tilted his head. "Actually, it kind of does. As you must be aware, the administration revoked temporary protected status for Salvadorans. It didn't revoke TPS for all nations—just six. We have to assume those six were not chosen randomly. To the contrary, we have to assume they were chosen because the executive branch has decided that we no longer want to shelter people from those nations."

"So we helped the Salvadorans when we were feeling guilty about the Iran-Contra fiasco. But now that time has passed and racist sentiment seems widespread, we're going to pull the rug out from under them."

"I know it must look like that to you, but here's the reality. Immigration policies change. All the time. They are constantly in flux. It has been that way since the dawn of this nation. This has never been a place where all immigrants could enter the country anytime they wanted in whatever numbers possible. We have rules."

"And that's why you're going to let Esperanza fall between the cracks."

Crenshaw raised a finger. "Now that's where I have to take exception. This girl has far from fallen between the cracks. I know all about her case." He patted a stack of files on his desk. "We have extensive files which I have read thoroughly. I have tried to do everything possible to help her. I was the one who told Gabriella Valdez she should pursue adoption. Because I thought that was Esperanza's best hope of remaining in the country. Sadly, the girl lost her parents. Her closest relative was Jorge Sanchez, and now he's dead too."

"Just as well, from what we hear," Maria interjected.

"I have to agree with you there."

"But you'll deliver her to Sanchez' little brother, who may be just as bad."

"That's not accurate. We'll deliver her to the El Salvadoran immigration authorities."

"And they'll deliver her to the little brother."

"Maybe. Frankly, it's a little presumptuous to assume we know better than other nations how they should handle their orphans."

"Gabriella thinks the Sanchez cartel is involved in sex trafficking. Does a lot of that go on in El Salvador? Or here?"

Crenshaw drew in his breath. "The answer to both questions is yes. Sex trafficking has exploded to previously unseen proportions in the past decade. We like to think that sort of thing doesn't happen in the United States, but it does. I have to wonder if that's why Sanchez was here. Trying to expand his operation. We believe that he, or the people he's working with, have some sort of operation by which they trade green cards for sex. That is, they grease the wheels and get people into the country, possibly even get them legal or protected status, in exchange for their work in prostitution rings."

"That's despicable," Maria murmured. "Prostitution should be illegal everywhere."

"Ma'am, prostitution has existed since the dawn of time. Always has and always will. Bernard Shaw called it the oldest profession. Since we can't get rid of it, the smarter approach might be to legalize it. Govern it. Sex slavery and abuse wouldn't be possible if it were run above-board, like other businesses. We could require medical examinations to prevent the spread of

STDs. We could tax it, which would add billions to the economy."

"I think that's a horrible idea."

"It's a realistic idea. But"—he added quickly—"not the official policy of the US government. Just my random thoughts on the matter."

"Do you have any idea how Sanchez got into this country?"

"We do not. We were caught off guard, and that's pathetic. If we can't track a major criminal like him, who can we track? Someone with his kind of money, unfortunately, has enormous resources. That gives him a huge advantage. We have the support of the United States government. But we do not have enormous resources. Our budget is modest, to say the least."

"So you can't stop a major gang lord, but you can deport a little girl."

"Let me put my cards on the table. I'm an immigration agent, and the law says people who no longer have protected status must leave the country. That includes Esperanza. If she isn't adopted soon, she'll have to leave. I know Gabriella has been charged with murder, which makes her chances of adoption slender, even if she's acquitted, which seems rather unlikely. The prosecutors tell me you haven't got a chance, Dan."

"Yeah, they feel they have a rock-solid case."

"Those are exactly the words they used. I think Gabriella is not adopting anyone, but if there's any way I can help Esperanza short of breaking the law, I will. I've been at this job for a good while, and it's not for the big bucks." He chuckled. "Most months I can barely pay the mortgage. But it does put me in a position to help people every now and then."

"I appreciate that," he replied. "But it sounds like there's nothing you can do for Esperanza."

Crenshaw pushed two tall stacks of folders across his desk. "I photocopied everything I have in my files. Some of it relates to Gabriella as well as Esperanza. I don't know that there's anything in there that will help you, but who knows? Maybe you'll see something I didn't. I hear you're good at finding escape hatches for hopelessly guilty defendants."

He realized he hadn't exactly been complimented, but he chose to take it that way anyway. "You've heard of me?"

"Checked you out as soon as I heard you were on the case. They say you're a hard worker. Take these files and see if they help."

"I'll do that." He didn't know if it was mere curiosity, or his brain making weird connections, but he felt compelled to ask an irrelevant question. "Mind if I ask what's up with the cowboy duds?"

Crenshaw grinned. "Not at all. When I hit forty, I decided I was old enough to start dressing to please myself. I love Westerns. Cowboys are my heroes, and some people think today's immigration officers are kinda like the Wild West's Texas Rangers. Patrolling the borders and making the nation a safer place."

"I guess that's one way of looking at it."

"I love seeing the world from a fresh perspective."

"Is that why you were peering through a kaleidoscope?"

Crenshaw opened a drawer and pulled out two kaleidoscopes just like the one on his desk. "Here, have one. Both of you." He tossed them across his desk. "Something else I've loved since I was a kid. Peer through the glass and see a different world. A lovelier world."

He took one of the kaleidoscopes from Crenshaw, held the glass to his eye, and turned the wheel. The colors danced and sparkled. The bland government office became a Technicolor wonderland.

"And after you've appreciated all that beauty," Crenshaw said, "remind yourself that the kaleidoscope isn't creating those colors. It's just forcing you to appreciate the beauty that surrounds us, that we tend to overlook, every day of our lives."

CHAPTER TWENTY-TWO

DAN WAS SECRETLY PLEASED, THOUGH HE WOULD NEVER ADMIT it, when Maria was unable to make the trip to meet Luis González. Not because he disliked her company—but because he had a strong desire to drive the Jaguar.

Garrett accompanied him to the meeting. He was good company, and apparently didn't have a compelling need to sit in the driver's seat. This was the first time they'd been alone together. Maybe he'd get to know the man a little bit better.

"How long have you been with Mr. K?"

"A little longer than Maria," Garrett answered. He had a slow easy way of speaking. "Before that, I worked solo, taking it easy, never working too hard. Handful of cases at a time. Played keyboards three nights a week at a local club. Lots of trips to Hawaii."

"I love Hawaii. Have you been scuba diving at Turtle Bay?"

"I prefer to stay above the water. Went for the Hawai'i Bowl last year."

"You're a football fan."

"You could say that. Box seats at Raymond James Stadium."

"You like the Bucs."

"Doesn't everyone? How about you?"

"I'm more into doing stuff than watching other people do stuff." He quickly amended. "That wasn't meant as a criticism. I just never understood why it's fun to watch other people play sports. I'd rather be doing it myself."

Garrett laughed. "That wasn't an option for me. I tried to play ball in school. Most uncoordinated person who ever lived. Law school was a better choice."

"And then Mr. K's law firm?"

"I worked in government for a while. Worked for the Florida Department of Law Enforcement. Spent four years on a state senator's staff."

"Republican?"

"Is it that obvious?"

"Nah. I just notice subtle things. Like the radio in your office is always tuned to Fox News."

"I think things are getting out of control in this country. We need to get back to basics. Remember why we fought for independence. Can't let the federal government become the new monarchy." He hesitated. "I guess you think that makes me a total whack job."

He thought for a moment. "Do you have a 'Hitler Was Right' bumper sticker on the back of your pickup?"

"Hell no."

"Then you're not a *total* whack job." He smiled and changed the subject. "Tell me about this man we're getting ready to meet."

"He's a high-ranking member of Emilio's organization. He ran the gang whenever Emilio was in lock-up, and he's back in charge again now."

He pulled up outside a large warehouse, not far from the ocean. The sign read SOUTHSIDE IMPORTS. It looked like a busy operation. Twelve different loading docks, all of them occupied.

"Looks like this guy is a mover and shaker. How did you get us in to see him?"

"It was easier than you might imagine. The man runs his business...like a business."

"We are talking about a gang, right?"

"A gang in the millennial era. Which apparently has come a long way since *West Side Story*."

"González keeps office hours?"

"And he has a Rolodex and an appointments secretary and everything."

He found a parking space on the street. Ten minutes later they were in the lobby. They only waited at the receptionist's desk about five minutes. A well-dressed woman in a short skirt escorted them inside. And then outside.

They were shown through double doors into what appeared to be a greenhouse. An arboretum, she explained. An arboretum about the size of Mr. K's house, and filled with greenery. Exotic trees, colorful flowers. He was no expert, but he thought he spotted a few orchids, African violets, and all manner of ivy, herbs, and succulents. Whoever put this place together put a lot of money into it.

At the end of the walkway, he spotted a small man holding a pair of shears pruning some sort of shrubbery. Vest, no jacket. Man bun. Posed, as if he knew he was being watched. Birthmark on the left hand.

"Mr. González?"

The man looked up. He was five foot two, maybe five foot three at best. Not an imposing figure. "Call me Luis. Are you Mr. Pike?"

He extended a hand. "Good to meet you. I think I've heard Emilio mention you."

"No doubt. We've been together a long time. And you are Garrett?" Luis shook his hand as well. "It's a pleasure to finally meet the man who has defended and protected Emilio on so many occasions. You've been of great benefit to our enterprise, and we're grateful."

Our enterprise? Not stereotypical gangsta. "What is it we're in? An overgrown sunroom?"

Luis chuckled. "I hope you'll forgive my indulgence. This is my passion. I love the green. I love flowers, especially bright colorful ones. They bring me great joy. It is a welcome respite from the quotidian tasks that unfortunately fill most of my days."

This man had neither the demeanor nor the vocabulary he expected from a gang leader. "You've done a terrific job making this appealing. I've seen botanical gardens that were not so well kept."

"I come here every moment I can. Of course, I have others who help with the upkeep. I've invested a great deal of money here. But you can't take it with you, right?" He chuckled a little. "I hope one day to make it even larger and open it to the public. I have not been blessed with children, at least not yet. I would rather spend my money on life than on sports cars."

Luis gestured to the collection of flowers to his left. "I obtained many of the seeds from the Kanapaha Botanical Gardens. Just outside Gainesville. Beautiful facility. I've modeled mine after it, making a few improvements here and there as I saw fit. Notice the gorgeous birds of paradise. Hard to grow here."

He nodded, assuming that the birds of paradise Luis referred to were not actually birds. "Lovely."

"And there are azaleas and camellias. Passion flowers, jasmines, honeysuckles. Pickerelweed. All present their unique challenges. But it sooths my soul."

He almost felt guilty disturbing this tranquil environment with a discussion of the case. "What can you tell me about your...operation? It's not what I expected."

Luis smiled. "I hope you're not indulging in the common misapprehension that since my friends and I are Hispanic, and we live in Florida, our activities must be illegal."

He drew in his breath. "I'm not racist, if that's what you

mean. But please remember, I have represented Emilio on several occasions. And he has always been connected with drugs."

Luis sighed. "I respect Emilio, especially the way he dug himself out of crippling poverty and did the same for others. But he has not always made the best choices when it comes to business associates. He grew up in a poverty-stricken neighborhood and many of the old ties persisted for far too long. Nonetheless, the business I run is 100% legitimate."

It seemed unlikely, but he hoped it was true. It would make their task so much simpler. "What kind of business are you in?"

"International trade. Imports and exports. We move a lot of electronics, but only where it is legal. The European Union. And now, Cuba."

"What do you import?"

"Oil, when we can get a good deal. Rare woods. As you might guess, occasionally exotic flowers. And yes, not to sound trite, but we do actually bring in Havana cigars. Now that it is legal to do so."

Luis kept mentioning the legality of his business. Which could be a sign that he had indeed straightened this business out. Or could make one wonder, to paraphrase Shakespeare, if he protesteth too much. "This has been a prosperous business shift?"

"Look around you."

"A cynical soul might suspect that the arboretum, and the whole import line, is a front for your drug-running."

"It is not. We have been exceptionally prosperous. One of the best and most profitable new businesses in St. Pete. We now employ more than sixty men and women, all of Hispanic descent. I target people who grew up poor, as Emilio and I did. I want to break the cycle of poverty that sends so many of our people spiraling in the wrong direction. We want to lower the crime rate and improve the reputation of south-of-the-border immigrants, one case at a time."

"Admirable. But no drugs?" He hadn't actually denied it yet.

Luis took a step to the right and pruned an ivied lattice. "We are developing, slowly, a line of pharmaceuticals. There is money to be made bringing prescription drugs from other countries where they are vastly less expensive. But the paperwork, and the government regulations that must be dealt with, are incredible."

"Just to be clear—you don't peddle street drugs?"

"Never."

"What about sex trafficking?"

Luis shuddered. He tucked in his chin. "The very thought disgusts me."

"But you are aware that there is an active sex trafficking ring that seems to have some sort of ties to this area. I believe the man who died in the shootout, Sanchez, was connected to it."

Luis' jaw clenched. He seemed to struggle to regain control of himself before he answered. "I know Sanchez dealt in that sort of thing. We have not. We would never."

"Even if there was a profit to be made?"

"What profiteth a man to gain the world but lose his soul?"

A gang lord who quoted the Gospels. This *was* a new era. "How do you like running the organization?"

"It is a great deal of work, but I'm doing the best I can." Luis bent down and picked up a rake, then smoothed the peat chips.

"As long as Emilio is in jail."

"I am not sure what you're saying."

"You have a strong reason to not want Emilio back on the streets. Your life is better the longer he remains in jail."

"Emilio is our founder."

"Forgive me if I read between the lines, but I know Emilio was involved in illegal activities, and you probably hated that. I suspect you've been fighting him tooth and nail for a long time, taking the money he made from the drug trade and steering it in more honest directions. You've only gotten this far because Emilio has been behind bars so long. If he gets out again, you could lose everything."

Again, the small shudder. Almost imperceptible, but he saw it, just the same. "You don't know what you're talking about."

He pressed on. "Some people believe Emilio was set up at the Trademark. That someone lured him to a rendezvous that could easily have led to his death. He told me he received a text from someone. I bet you've got Emilio's private number, don't you?"

"I begin to find your remarks insulting. I'm a legitimate businessman. I'm a member of the Chamber of Commerce."

"Which requires filling out a form and paying a $200 fee."

"Emilio is my brother. I would never do anything to harm him."

"Did you know your brother is working on an immunity deal? If it happens, Emilio could be out tomorrow."

He could tell that tidbit caught Luis by surprise. But he rebounded quickly. "I have not heard that. And I have many friends. People of influence."

"Like who?"

"Like the mayor of this city, for starters."

"She may not have much pull with the district attorney. Who I hear would like to be the next mayor." He took a step closer. "Convince me you had nothing to do with this mess. Tell me what happened that night at the Trademark."

"I do not know. I was not there. If Emilio had told me he was going, I would've told him not to. It was a stupid idea and typical of his—" Luis cut himself short.

"Typical of the stupid things he was always doing? The illegal gangland things he was always doing? Which is why you wanted him out of the way?"

"I see I am never going to convince you. I will respectfully have to ask you to leave." Luis snapped his fingers, and the woman who had escorted them in appeared at the end of the walkway.

He continued to push. "Answer one question for me. Why was Gabriella at the Trademark that night?"

"I assume because Emilio wanted her there."

"Why?"

"Isn't it obvious?"

"No, it isn't obvious to me at all."

"Are you not aware of how skilled Gabriella is with handguns?"

"Noooo..."

"Have you seen her temper?"

He glanced at Garrett. Garrett shook his head. News to him too. "Are you suggesting Gabriella was there...as Emilio's security?"

"More like his assassin. That woman is bad news. For everyone. And that includes the little girl."

"You know about Esperanza."

"I know you are making a very bad mistake."

"Is that a threat?"

"I am a legitimate businessman. I don't make threats. I take action against those who might harm me or my business."

He tilted his head to one side, weighing Luis' words. He made a point of appearing defiant, though in reality, he was scared to the tips of his toes. The last thing he needed was to be on the wrong side of St. Pete gang lords. "What are you threatening me with, Mr. Legit Businessman? Trade sanctions?"

Again the guarded smile. "As you can see, I know how to care for a garden. How to nourish and protect it. Shield it from inclement weather. And pests." Luis gestured toward the assistant. "Janine will escort you out of the complex. Please do not resist." He gave them both one last look. "And please do not return. Ever."

CHAPTER TWENTY-THREE

DAN STEPPED INTO JIMMY'S PRIVATE OFFICE—AND GASPED.

This was like no other office—if that was the word—he'd ever seen. The walls were lined with toys, dolls, and action figures, some mounted on the wall, still wrapped in plastic. A tall shelf housed what looked to him like an endless supply of tabletop games. He had a Star Trek pinball machine and a Foosball table. His desk was cluttered with superhero figurines and a small jukebox. There was barely any room for what must be annoyingly intrusive legal stuff.

"Now I know where all the Toys R Us stock went after the chain folded."

Jimmy grimaced. "There's nothing wrong with having a fun office."

"Do you bring clients back here?"

"And they love it. Their kids love it, too."

"That part I believe. Do you actually play with this stuff?"

"Dan, these are collectibles. You don't play with them. You admire them. From a distance. Would you play with the Mona Lisa?"

He stared at a colorful figure hanging on the wall. "Hey, I remember these."

Jimmy beamed. "The original Mego DC superhero figures? Classic. You read comic books?"

"Nah. Kid stuff. But I always wanted one of these. For some reason, I thought Aquaman was the coolest. Probably because I loved water sports. Never got one, though. We didn't have money for that kind of stuff."

"No cash for toys? Heavens to Murgatroyd. That's the saddest thing I've ever heard."

He kept admiring it. "You like these...Mego dolls?"

"I think they're hideous. But extremely valuable. Back then, that's all there was for the serious superhero fan." He checked his watch. "I wasn't expecting you back for at least another hour."

"The interview with Emilio's right-hand man didn't take that long."

"Because he didn't know anything?"

"Because he threatened to have me killed. I thought it might be smart to exercise the better part of valor."

"Just as well," Jimmy said. "We don't need to lose another teammate. I was surprised when you texted that you wanted to see the mayor."

"Luis name-checked her. They have some kind of connection. Worth a visit."

"A hard visit to get. But of course, I've arranged it. Ready to go?"

"You already got us an appointment?"

"I did. But please don't get us thrown out or threatened, okay? Maintain your cool demeanor."

He walked to a nearby shelf and pointed to a huge game box. "Is this the Gloomhaven game you keep talking about?"

"It is indeed."

"This box looks bigger than my travel luggage."

Jimmy laughed. "There are lots of parts. But it ships with more than ninety quests. So you can see why it would."

He had only the vaguest of notions what that meant. "You've played all ninety?

"We're about halfway through. We normally play on Saturdays, if everyone's free."

"And you're the dungeon master?"

"Gloomhaven ships with prewritten scenarios, so you don't actually need a dungeon master. Maria always ends up in charge, telling the rest of us what to do."

He wasn't surprised. "So did you join this law firm because you needed a job or because you needed playmates?"

"Both. As you may have noticed, I've had some of these collectibles a long time. I used to play with this stuff with my dad. An affection for nonsense was about the only thing we shared."

"I'm sorry. He's gone?"

"No. Well, not the way you mean. He's still alive. Big, burly guy. Worked most of his life as a stevedore down by the pier. We didn't have much in common. Except this stuff."

"But...no more?"

Jimmy gazed at the wall. "My dad hasn't spoken to me since I came out. And that was many years ago." He smiled a little. "But I'm keeping the toys close at hand, just in case he changes his mind."

THIRTY MINUTES LATER, DAN AND JIMMY STOOD IN THE LOBBY of Mayor Camila Pérez's City Hall office. He had to admit he was impressed. If Jimmy could get them in to see her this quickly, he had some serious sway.

A young African-American woman sat in the outer lobby. After she verified that he and Jimmy were on the schedule, she punched a few buttons, confirmed that the mayor was ready, and let them inside.

Mayor Pérez met them in the corridor. "Hello, gentlemen.

Please come in." Dragonfly brooch. Slight tummy. Frozen hair. Lots of teeth. She was shorter in person than she looked on television. Barely five feet tall, and even then he wondered if she might be wearing lifts. She looked good, especially for someone who was just sitting around the office. She was clearly of Latinx descent, but spoke without an accent.

The mayor spoke first. "I understand you're an attorney working on the Trademark case. You represent the accused."

"That is correct."

"I must tell you that my friends at the District Attorney's Office tell me your client is guilty."

"Did they say they have a rock-solid case?"

"Those were their exact words."

"That's what I would expect them to say to the mayor."

She nodded. "I know from experience, having lived in St. Pete all my life, that the police do not always get it right. But since we are part of the same team, I have to assume that they are handling matters as best they can."

"That may be. But it doesn't prove my client is guilty."

"Understood. We will agree to disagree. As the city's highest official, I must take a firm stance against violence."

"I understand," Jimmy said, easing into the conversation. "Tragedies like this leave everyone feeling unsafe. They weren't even in a particularly bad part of town."

"Exactly," the mayor replied. "They were in the tourist district. And we cannot afford to chase away the tourist trade. The city would crumble. We must be perceived as taking a strong stand against violence." She paused. "Would you gentlemen care to join me for a stroll on the beach?"

That caught him by surprise. He knew they were close to the ocean, but he didn't expect to go beachcombing with the mayor.

"I try to walk a mile each day," she continued, "but I haven't done it yet. And the beach just outside is my favorite walk. Join me, please."

He couldn't complain. Even though he lived on a boat, he

didn't spend as much time on the beach as he should. St. Pete had the best beaches in the world, in his opinion, not as crowded as Waikiki and some of the other candidates.

Ten minutes later he was on the beach, inhaling the salty air and feeling sand crunch beneath his Air Jordans. The sun shone and the sea spray lifted his spirits and he could almost forget why he had come.

Maybe that was why the mayor brought them here.

"Thank you for indulging me," she said. "I spend far too much time locked up in offices." She turned slightly toward him, catching his eye. "And the problem with offices is that they are full of people. And people have ears. Now what was I saying?"

"Something about taking a stand against violence," he said. "I may have helped you appear to be taking strong and swift action. We're going to trial in about a week."

"So I understand. Do you think that is wise? Speedy justice is good, but if it's rendered too quickly, we open ourselves to charges of unfairness."

"I understand your concerns," he said. "This must be a difficult situation for you. Tricky. You can't play favorites, but you also have to be careful not to alienate anyone."

The mayor did not disagree.

"So you're performing a difficult tightrope act. Not alienating minorities, distancing yourself from violence, being perceived as proactive. Almost impossible."

The mayor smiled. "That would be a good description of my job, virtually every day of the week. Almost impossible."

He returned the smile. He couldn't help but like her. If nothing else, she was exceptionally honest. Refreshing in a politician. "I understand you're going forward with the expansion of The Meeting Place. Bulldozers go to work on Monday morning."

"You've been talking to members of my staff?"

"No. But on the drive up, I read your Facebook page. And your Twitter feed."

"What a world we live in. When social media is the best source of information about a politician's activities. Welcome to the twenty-first century."

"This park expansion is going to be expensive. You need all the support you can muster."

"That is true every day. But Albert Kazan gave us a masterpiece with The Meeting Place. The best thing to happen to St. Pete in decades. It would be a crime not to finish it."

"You've worked closely with Kazan, right?"

"Dr. Kazan both designed and helped raise the funds. He has vision." She stopped walking. "Do you like bright colors, Mr. Pike?"

"Well, I have a kaleidoscope in my backpack."

"Good for you. Bright colors make people happy. They increase joy. Studies have shown that people exposed to light and color are happier and more productive. That's why I made sure the new downtown government offices were painted with vivid, electric colors. Fuchsia and magenta. They make people happy."

"As I recall," he said, "you got a lot of grief for that in the press. People asked if you were building an office or a kindergarten."

"Happy people work harder and live longer."

"And vote the mayor in for a second term."

"That is not as important as spreading joy."

"I recommend toys," Jimmy said. "People surrounded by toys are happy."

The mayor laughed. "I can see that you think like me. When people lose their inner child, they become unhappy. They think growing up means giving up everything that makes them smile. The result is a joyless world. People who wake up in the morning but are not particularly happy to be there, who have nothing to look forward to. That's not the kind of city I want to run." She pointed. The Meeting Place was just visible from the beach, over the horizon. "People questioned this new park, but to me, creating a safe haven for children, bringing joy to people of all ages, is worth a billion dollars. In fact, it's worth a great deal more."

"Some of your opponents disagree."

"And they always will. That is why they are called opponents. But the people of the city elected me. And I intend to make them glad they did." She smiled. "As much as I enjoy talking about myself, I feel this is probably not why you came. You would like to get back to what happened at the Trademark."

Again the blunt honestly. Impressive. "I just finished speaking to a man named Luis González. He seems to be Emilio Lòpez's right-hand man, although I think in his mind he may be Emilio's replacement. He heads a business called Southside Imports."

"I know the man of whom you speak."

"He dropped your name during our chat. I was surprised he knew who you were, much less that he considered you a powerful ally."

The mayor gazed out at the ocean. The tide was coming in. "He has donated to my war chest. We are already preparing for my reelection campaign."

"And you're comfortable taking money from him?"

She spread her hands wide. "So far as we are able to tell, he is running legitimate businesses, profitable ones. That is exactly the kind of donor we try to attract."

"I'm surprised he would even be on your fundraising radar."

"Actually, it was Dr. Kazan who suggested him as a possible revenue source."

The architect suggested they secure funds from a gang lord? That seemed unusual, to say the least. He made a mental note to follow up on that later. "Whatever surface businesses he runs are probably for laundering money. The real dough is coming from the drug trade."

"I believe that may have been true when Emilio was running the organization. But we have reliable information indicating that Luis has cleaned up the operation. And I applaud that. I want to support it."

"And you want it to support you."

"Now you are being unkind. There is nothing wrong with taking money from a legitimate business person. Of course, if any links to organized crime or gang activities are proven, we will distance ourselves and refuse further donations. But for the time being, I see no problem. St. Pete needed this park and now it needs the expansion. Luis has been most generous."

Jimmy stepped in. "You've also engaged in some real estate deals with Luis' companies. I found the records in the court clerk's office. Some of them look a little..." His voice drifted off. "Shady?

The mayor smiled, but the smile did not strike him as being as genuine as the ones that came before. "I am trying to persuade Luis to invest in our downtown renovations. To bring more corporate activity to St. Pete. We have a serious unemployment problem. The more people offering jobs, the less reason anyone has to join a gang. Surely you can see how that benefits the city."

"And you," he added. "Especially at reelection time."

The mayor smiled. "Mr. Pike, I see that you are a, well, what is the nice way of putting it? A cynical son of a bitch. But I don't see how challenging me helps your client."

She might be right. But there was something going on here that he hadn't uncovered, something that might concern Gabriella. It was possible the mayor knew more about this than she let on. And people on the defensive sometimes said more than they planned. "I want to know everything I can about Emilio and Luis' activities. And what went down at the Trademark. If you know anything that could bear on that subject, please share."

She gave him a steady gaze. "I can assure you that I know nothing other than what the district attorney has told me."

"Then I thank you for your time." He kicked at a small sand

dune. "But I also warn you that I will continue to investigate. I will leave no stone unturned. I don't have time to be genteel or deferential. I will find the truth. Whatever the cost."

The mayor tilted her head slightly. "Oh now, Mr. Pike. I'm sure you don't mean to cause trouble."

He smiled. "Then you don't know me very well."

CHAPTER TWENTY-FOUR

DAN MADE IT TO THE COURTROOM TEN MINUTES BEFORE THE hearing was scheduled to begin. Nonetheless, when he arrived, Jazlyn and her cast of thousands were already set up at the prosecution table.

This was worrisome. It was only a motion in limine, after all. It didn't require the whole office. Sometimes, for minor hearings that didn't involve a jury, prosecutors would make a great show of running in at the last possible moment, papers flying from their hands, reminding the court how incredibly busy and overworked they are, begging them in advance to forgive any failings because they have such an impossible workload but their incredible efforts are all that stands between us and the collapse of civilization.

Drama queens. All prosecutors were drama queens.

Except Jazlyn did not appear to be playing that game. This was one more indication that the prosecution was taking this case extremely seriously.

He dropped his backpack on his table and approached her, smiling big. "Good morning, Jazlyn. You look tired. Worried?"

"No. Up too late. Fundraiser for St. Teresa's."

"Which is?"

"A girl's prep school. I'm on the board of directors. Like I have time for charity work."

"You make time for it."

"Right. And now back to reality." She didn't look as irritated as she acted.

"Any news on your immunity agreement with Emilio?"

"Haven't quite clinched the deal," she replied. "But we're getting there. You know who he's represented by?"

"I do."

"Well, he's an even bigger pain in the butt to work with than you, if such a thing is possible."

"I will take that as a compliment."

"Exactly how it was meant. Want to withdraw your motion and save us all some time?"

"Nah. I had my suit cleaned."

"I think the judge likes people who don't clog her docket with pointless motions practice."

"Probably right. But I'm poor at predicting judges. I prefer to give everything my best shot and then see what happens. I've pulled off underdog motions more than once in my life."

"Not planning any big surprises today, are you?"

"Nope. Just the usual scintillating legal argument."

"Marvelous. I love a good show."

He returned to his table and got his papers in order. Barely a minute later, the bailiff asked them to rise. Judge Le entered the courtroom and got straight to it.

"We have a motion in limine," she said, pushing on her reading glasses. "The defendant moves to restrict all evidence regarding the discovery of a gun. Is that correct?"

He rose to his feet. "It is, your honor. The gun was found—"

She raised a hand, cutting him off. "We'll get to that. I just want to understand what we're doing. Is there any question about the fact that the gun in question is the murder weapon?"

"No," he said, "but there's a big question about—"

Again, the raised hand. "Patience, counsel. Patience. This is the murder weapon, regardless of who might've fired it or who might've left it where it was found."

"That's just the point," Jazlyn said, clearing her throat. "Regardless of the facts surrounding its discovery, we all know the effect on a jury if the prosecution can't produce a murder weapon."

"That's not an element of any of the crimes with which my client has been charged."

"Yes," Jazlyn said, "we all know that. Motive isn't an element either, but if you don't give the jury one, they feel like they don't know what happened and they won't convict, even if there's overwhelming evidence of guilt. It's the same for a murder weapon. If you can't produce it, jurors feel like the story is incomplete."

"That's no excuse for admitting prejudicial or misleading evidence."

"But this is neither. This is the murder weapon. The police did have a warrant to search the yard. And it does have your client's prints on it."

"All right," the judge said, "let's start at the beginning. Mr. Pike, this is your motion. No more than five minutes, and please remember, I have already read your brief."

Which is what judges always said, regardless of whether it was true. Today though, the judge did seem to grasp the points of contention. But he still was going to say anything he thought would help. "Your honor, we're not disputing at this time whether this was the murder weapon, although we may take that up at a later date, because there are some questionable details in the ballistics report I have not had a chance to track down yet. But let's assume for the purpose of this motion that it is the murder weapon. That doesn't tell us who fired it."

The judge cut in. "The gun was purchased by and registered to your client, right?"

"That's correct. But she had not looked at it in months."

"And she was at the scene of the crime, right?"

He drew in his breath. "She was present. But she did not fire the gun."

"So she says."

"And there is no dispute about the fact that the gun was not found at the scene of the crime."

The judge peered at the brief in her hand. "The gun was found in some shrubbery in your client's backyard?"

"That is correct, your honor. At least, that's what the police officers are saying."

"It was found two days after the shooting?"

"True. The police searched her home immediately after the shooting. But the gun was found two days later, and only then because they claim they received an anonymous phone call telling them where it was."

"And the tip was correct. They found the gun."

"But the fact that they didn't find it the first time they searched strongly suggests that it wasn't there at that time. And the fact that an anonymous caller told them exactly where it was two days later suggests that the caller planted the gun."

"All of which I'm sure you will bring out in excruciating detail at the trial."

"Your honor," he continued, "I know that I can discuss all this at trial. But introducing a gun found in my client's backyard is unduly prejudicial. It proves nothing—except perhaps that someone is trying to frame her."

"Or," Jazlyn murmured, "that she's the killer."

"But they didn't find the gun the first time they searched."

"Apparently they weren't looking in the right place. Yet."

"You're telling me your police officers failed to search Gabriella's backyard? If that's true, you've got the worst plain-clothes officers on the face of the earth."

"Move to strike defense counsel's negative reflections on our police officers."

The judge nodded and waved toward the court reporter.

"Your honor," he continued, "the test at a hearing such as this is whether the proposed evidence is more prejudicial than probative. If the jury is slammed with evidence suggesting that my client's gun is the murder weapon, found in her backyard, it will create a false impression difficult to overcome, even though in fact it is no indication of her guilt and may well be indicative of a frame. This kind of deliberate misdirection is all too common, particularly in gangland operations."

"Are you suggesting some kind of conspiracy to frame your client? I warn you, I'm not even letting you say the word 'conspiracy' without an offer of proof."

"At this very moment, the prosecutors are working in concert with a career criminal, Emilio Lòpez, trying to get him to turn state's evidence. He may well be the person who organized the frame. If he becomes the prosecutor's best friend, they will be able to support any wild claim they want. In the name of fairness, I ask the court to exclude this evidence. The prosecution will still have all the evidence they had at the time of the arrest, and perhaps some they've discovered since. But this gun is tainted evidence. Don't let them railroad my client."

The judge nodded. "Thank you, Mr. Pike. Anything from the prosecution?"

Jazlyn's manner was unemotional and matter-of-fact. "I agree with Mr. Pike about one thing. The evidence of the gun is prejudicial, but that's because it is so keenly relevant and such a clear indicator of his client's guilt. It was her gun. Her prints were on the gun."

He rose. "I dispute—"

Jazlyn waved him back down. "We all know you dispute. It's what you do. But the fact is, the prints were found on her gun which was found in her backyard. She was at the scene of the crime, and contrary to what Mr. Pike just indicated, we have strong evidence that she fired the gun while there. She had a powerful motive for taking out Sanchez. Don't cripple our case, your honor. We need to get dangerous criminals off the street.

We need to stop the constant gangland warfare that threatens the city. We need to take a strong—"

The judge waved her hand, cutting Jazlyn off. "Yes, yes. I know how important your work is. And I'm sympathetic, but it's not relevant to this motion. As Mr. Pike said, this is a simple question of whether the potential prejudice outweighs the probative value. And I find that it does not. The motion is denied."

He rose to his feet. "Your honor, I'll ask you to reconsider based on—"

"Denied. You're welcome to take an appeal, if you think that will do you any good."

He lowered his chin. The judge knew as well as he did that an interlocutory appeal, even if possible, would not be heard before their scheduled trial date.

Judge Le continued. "I understand there are some questionable circumstances surrounding the discovery of the gun. But I know that you'll read the jury chapter and verse about that during the trial. You will likely cross-examine each and every police officer involved, suggesting that they did something wrong, or that the gun was planted, or that it came from a parallel universe, or whatever. Given that the defendant is so ably assisted by counsel, I can't see that the evidence prejudices your client. Is there anything else the court should take up at this time?"

He had already started packing his backpack when, to his surprise, Jazlyn rose to her feet. "Yes, your honor. We would like to raise a counter-motion in limine."

He frowned. "Can she do that?"

"Call it a motion in limine then. Whatever works."

The judge stared at her. "I don't see a motion for that."

"No, your honor. I apologize. We have not had time to brief it yet."

He cut in. "Then it should not be heard at this time."

The judge raised a hand. "Normally I would agree. But given

the short fuse we are on, with an imminent trial date, which was your idea, Mr. Pike, let's at least hear what she has to say. If we can dispose of something at this time, it's to everyone's advantage."

Jazlyn cleared her throat. "Your honor, I would move to restrict all mention of the young girl that the defendant filed a motion to adopt. Esperanza Coto."

He shot to his feet. "On what grounds?"

"On exactly the grounds you just expressed. It is not probative. It is not relevant to the murder, but it could be keenly prejudicial. I've seen indications that defense counsel intends to use this little girl strategically to create sympathy for the defendant."

"That's not true."

"Of course you would say that. Some people have even suggested that the whole point of filing the adoption petition, which seems so unlikely to succeed, was to make the defendant seem like a nicer person than she is."

He was outraged. "The adoption was filed before the charges were brought against my client. Before we even knew this was going to happen."

Jazlyn continued. "The adoption petition was filed before charges were brought against the defendant, true, but after the Trademark incident occurred. Given that there is such strong evidence indicating the defendant is the shooter, it would be easy to foresee that she would soon be charged. This whole adoption business creates a false impression."

"That is not true."

"We all know defense counsel has a history of using trickery in the courtroom, emotional appeals intended to prevent jurors from thinking logically."

"I object!"

"This is just argument," the judge said. "It's not testimony."

"What I'm saying," Jazlyn continued, "is that defense counsel is planning to manipulate the emotions of the future jurors. And that is in fact more prejudicial than probative. I will ask the court to restrict all mention of this irrelevant young girl and especially the pending adoption hearing."

"And I completely object to that," he said.

The judge pondered a moment. "Can you explain why this business about the girl is relevant to the murder charge?"

He took a moment. Offhand, he couldn't think of a reason. But there probably was one, and he didn't want to make important decisions off the cuff. "If nothing else, it goes to the motivation that the prosecutor just mentioned. And it's an indication of character. I would like an opportunity to brief this."

"Well, I don't feel this motion is frivolous. I don't want manipulative pathos to replace evidence and logic at this trial."

"I would never do that," he said. "Let me brief the motion."

The judge nodded. "The defendant should be allowed a fair chance to respond before I rule. Briefs in two days?"

As if he didn't already have enough on his plate. "I'll get it done, your honor."

"Thank you. Anything else?"

No one spoke.

"Good." She banged her gavel and left the courtroom.

He went straight to Jazlyn. "What was that about?"

"Prosecuting a criminal?"

"I'm talking about the ambush. Raising a motion without notifying me in advance."

"Truth to tell, I just thought of it while we were arguing your motion."

"I don't believe you."

She seemed genuinely hurt. "Believe what you want. You've got time to brief it, so nothing unfair is happening. I'm sure you'll think of some brilliant response." She packed her briefcase and left the courtroom, followed by her minions.

HE PULLED OUT HIS CELL AND DIALED MARIA. "GUESS WHAT?

More work to do. Can you ask Jimmy to start on a brief? We'll need Garrett to do some emergency research. I'll text the details."

"Sure. But they'll want to talk to you. Where will you be?"

"I've got a date at the park."

CHAPTER TWENTY-FIVE

DAN HAD NOT VISITED THE MEETING PLACE IN MANY MOONS, and he was startled by how much, and how well, it had grown. He had a hard time finding a parking spot, and how often was that true when you visited a public park?

Once inside, he lost his way repeatedly, not because he was geographically challenged, but because the park was immense. Even though it swarmed with children, it did not seem crowded, and no one had to wait long for their turn on the tower, or the slides, or the teeter-totters, or the footbridge. He could see that the builders had done everything possible to make it safe. He supposed you could never eliminate the possibility of children falling and hurting themselves, but these padded foam bases had to help. He could also see that it was decked out in bright colors —perhaps the mayor's touch. This was one of the best parks in this part of the world, which people compared favorably to Central Park in New York City.

And he was about to meet the architect behind the operation. Winding his way past the museum—yes, an actual museum inside the park—he found a small camouflaged office space. Necessary, he supposed, but it had been disguised so as not to detract from the landscape.

He cracked the door open and peered inside. A thin man with a lean face looked up at him. Long hair, balding in front. Stud earring in left ear. St. Pete hoodie. Birkenstock sandals.

"Dan Pike?"

He nodded. "You must be Dr. Albert Kazan?"

"I am." He looked as if he had never been happier in his entire life than he was now to see Dan Pike walk into his office. "Did you have any trouble finding me?"

"Only a little. And I enjoyed every minute of it."

Kazan beamed. "That's what I like to hear. This park is supposed to be as pleasing to grown-ups as it is for children."

"You succeeded on that score. I need to come here more often. It's hard not to feel your spirit rise when you're surrounded by so many people having fun."

"That is, literally, the best compliment a park designer can get. Do you have children?"

"No. Maybe one day."

"Don't rush. Do it when the time is right." He closed his notebook. "Mind if we go outside? I've been in this office too long."

"Not at all."

Kazan opened an exit door. "Let's enjoy the sunshine and the children and the green. Even if we don't have the most pleasant topic to discuss, we can make the best of it."

He followed Kazan outside. The office had a rear exposure facing the skating area. Rolling hills of concrete, perfect for enthusiasts. And there were many taking advantage of it, on skateboards, rollerblades, even scooters. "So you made this park?"

"I designed it. We have a construction crew that handled all the hammer-and-nail stuff."

"But you oversaw that."

"I see my reputation precedes me. I do have a hands-on approach to the fulfillment of my plans. But that's how you make sure the job gets done properly."

"It's much the same in the law. Delegation is always tempting, but that's not how you get the best results."

"I can't take all the credit for this, though. I may have drawn the plans, but I didn't finance it. That was a concerted effort. We spent three years hitting up everyone in Florida with an active bank account."

"Yes, the mayor mentioned that you were involved with that. What did it cost?"

"What with all the eminent domain actions, demolition, bulldozing, planting, and construction, it ultimately cost almost a billion bucks."

He whistled. "I read that you did your best to help people who lost their homes find new places to live."

"True. And despite some of the caterwauling you may have read in the papers, it was always to their benefit. Let's face it—this was all low income, dated, in most cases not even safe, housing. We took people out of the slums and gave them an upgrade. That's a win-win. Particularly for some of these predominantly Hispanic Southside neighborhoods. We tried to help those who need it most. We may have been financed by the 1%, but they're not the ones who benefited most. We gave a lot of people jobs. And created a safe place for people of all ages, a place that doesn't require drug dealing or popping cops. Like I said. Win-win."

"You should feel proud."

"I was raised Catholic, and technically, pride is one of the seven deadly sins." Kazan gave him a side glance as they strolled toward the skybridge. "But yeah, I feel pretty good about it. Now how can I help you? You didn't come out just for the guided tour."

"I assume you've read about what the papers are calling the Tragedy of the Trademark."

Kazan nodded. "So pointless. Gang warfare has become too common in the poorer neighborhoods. It takes a big death toll before the papers seem to notice."

"I left this information with your receptionist, but just to be clear, I'm representing Gabriella Valdéz."

"Another woman caught up in the gang lifestyle that seems so difficult for those people to escape."

Did he detect a note of sympathy? Or was there something else, something about the way he said "those people." "She's being framed by powerful and resourceful people determined to make sure she disappears for a long time. Perhaps permanently."

"I don't see how I can help you. I'm an architect."

"The mayor said it was your idea to get gang money to finance the project."

Kazan sighed. He reached down and pointed at a wildflower. "Indian paintbrush. Isn't it beautiful? Hard to grow in this part of the world, but I found some that would survive and had them shipped in. At my own expense." He sighed again. "I suppose this is about Luis González?"

"He was a donor?"

"Indeed. Contributed a significant amount to the park fund. And got another of his associates to do the same. His name is on a plaque somewhere around here. That may have to be taken down now."

"Why would he want to contribute to a park?"

"If you want me to peer inside someone's heart and reveal their personal motives, you're asking the wrong person. That's not my strong suit. Whatever went on in that man's head and heart, he kept it locked inside."

"Were you ever in his office?"

"Yes. He expressed interest in contributing but hadn't done it yet. The feeling was that he needed someone to give him a personal push, and a visit from the architect, the man with all the dreams bubbling in his head, might do the trick. I spent about an hour with him. Got to tour that gigantic arboretum. And the next day he wrote a huge check. That didn't bounce," he added, winking.

"But why would he do that?"

"He told me he grew up on the Southside, still lived there, and was doing his best to help people. I know you think he engages in illegal activities, and maybe he does. But that's not what he told me. The office I visited was completely legit."

"Certainly looks legit."

"He told me about his import and export activities. Even showed me ledgers and profit-and-loss statements. Honestly, I had no reason to think I was getting into business with a shady character."

"So he did this because he wanted to help people?"

"He said it was part of his ongoing work to improve his neighborhood. I believe he even called it 'the hood.' He saw how many jobs we could create. I recall him saying something like, every time you give one young man from the hood a decent job, you decrease gang membership by ten. And I suspect he's right."

Time to shift gears, a tactic he had learned from many years of taking depositions. Most attorneys followed a linear, chronological dateline when quizzing people. Much smarter to jump around, back and forth, future to present, one topic to the next. Throw the witness off. Give them less chance to prepare. "You've also built a lot of hotels, haven't you?"

"Of course. We do live in St. Petersburg, after all. Tourism is our stock in trade. The more tourism, the more everyone benefits."

"Some people have called you the Trump of the Tropics."

Kazan laughed. "Yes, newspapers and blogs have a fondness for alliteration, don't they? Regardless of how inaccurate it might be. Because we're not really in the tropics. And I am nothing like Donald Trump."

"It didn't bother you? Dealing with people like Luis? I assume you met Emilio López too?"

"May I tell you the truth, Dan? I've worked with worse. You don't always get to pick and choose your financiers. You have to go with the money, you know what I'm saying? If you want to engage in billion-dollar projects, like it or not, you're gonna make some strange bedfellows. I'm sure you can understand that. You're a criminal lawyer. You have to represent whatever walks through the door, assuming they can pay your fee. Am I right?"

He remained silent.

"And I would be willing to bet that more than once you've suspected your clients were guilty. But you still represented them."

"Everyone is entitled to a fair trial. Without a fair trial, we can't make an equitable determination of someone's guilt. And unless someone is represented by counsel, they haven't had a fair trial."

"I understand the rationales. And here's mine. Projects like this beautiful park benefit everyone. So I'm going to be less concerned about who finances it."

"The ends justify the means?"

"I wouldn't put it that way. I would say ignoring donors like Luis benefits no one and changes nothing. But taking advantage of their financial clout could help people all across the city."

"Did you know Jorge Sanchez? The victim?"

"Only what I've read. Sounds like a slimy character."

"You haven't had any contact with prostitution rings?"

Kazan seemed genuinely disturbed. "Why the hell would I? What do you think I am?"

He held up his hands. "I don't mean to offend. But I have to ask all the questions. That's my job."

"If I had a job like that, I'd be looking for a new line of work. No, I don't have anything to do with sex trafficking. That doesn't interest me at all."

"But if Sanchez had come to you with a big check, you would've taken it."

Kazan's face flushed. "Not someone as disgusting as that. I would never ever *ever* take his money."

"So drug dealers are okay, but you draw the line at sex traffickers."

He could see Kazan was getting angry. "I don't know why you're coming down on me. You're the one representing the assassin."

His eyebrows knitted. "I was originally engaged to represent Gabriella in an adoption."

"And that never struck you as a bit contrived?"

Was Kazan trying to get his goat? Revenge for the sex-trafficking remark? "I don't know what you mean."

"Tell me if I've got the facts straight. Two days after the shooting, she talks to you about adoption and gets you to file a petition for her."

"True."

"But when you talked with her, did she ever once mention that she'd been at the scene of a major shootout?"

"Well…"

"Did she mention her gun? Her expertise with that gun?"

"It didn't come up."

"Do you think that might be relevant to the adoption? And yet she purposefully withheld that information. Why do you think she did that, Mr. Self-Righteous Lawyer?"

He had no answer.

"Maybe before you run around making accusations, you should ask yourself what exactly you're representing in that courtroom."

CHAPTER TWENTY-SIX

THE MAN SITTING IN DARKNESS CRUMPLED THE REPORT IN HIS hands.

Who did that arrogant lawyer think he was?

He hadn't worried at first, when he learned that Gabriella would be represented. He had expected it to be a public defender, but whatever. This slick-ass lawyer wouldn't be any better. He'd milk it for fees, then run. No one could get her off the hook. This honey trap was too deep for anyone to claw their way out.

But Pike had proven particularly resilient. He seemed to have an unerring instinct for deciphering who he needed to talk to, what stones to overturn. He was more than a token lawyer. He was a serious threat.

Something had to be done about him.

He could have Pike killed easily enough, but that might make matters worse. The trial would be delayed, and he didn't want that. He just needed Pike to get a message. A strong one. He needed to calm down. Lose some of his crusading zeal.

The best way to motivate or persuade someone, of course, was to determine what they most wanted. What did Pike want? He knew Pike got into this mess by helping that girl who wanted to be adopted. Was he in it for the girl? Fine. If the girl was what motivated him, let's give him a reason to think hard about what's in her best interest. It would be easy enough to get to her.

No one was really watching that detention center.

He'd dealt with lawyers before. They were all canker sores, barnacles on the hull of life. Pike needed to understand they weren't playing games here. If he didn't care about himself, maybe he'd care about someone else. And if the girl wasn't enough, he could go after the partners, or the client, the boat, the car, or blow up the whole damn office. Find his parents, siblings, friends—whatever it took. He was accustomed to taking decisive action. It was his job, really. And he was very good at his job.

He smiled, his fingers drumming on the countertop.

So many choices these days. What was the best way to send a package?

CHAPTER TWENTY-SEVEN

DAN PEERED AT THE BOUND-AND-INDEXED FOLDER IN HIS hands, feeling nothing but admiration. "Maria, you have done a sensational job."

"You think so?"

"I know so. I've never seen such a detailed trial map."

"I tried to find one of your old trial maps to use as a model."

"Good luck with that. I hate paperwork."

She nodded. "And you didn't have anyone to do it for you. Because you always worked alone."

He flipped through the pages. "You've thought through every foreseeable contingency here."

"Oh, I guarantee there will be surprises at trial. There always are. But we can try to minimize them. I told you long-range planning, strategy, was my forte."

"And you were right."

All four Last-Chance Lawyers sat in the living room area, thinking through their plans on the eve of trial.

"Does that mean you're not gonna kick us to the curb?" Jimmy asked.

"Can he do that?" Garrett replied. "I don't think we can be pitched. I think he can only pitch himself."

"You wouldn't do that, would you?" Jimmy asked again. "You wouldn't leave just after we got hitched?"

"Well, don't register us at Pottery Barn yet."

"But seriously. We like having you around."

He shrugged. "You just want a fourth for your Gloomhaven game."

"True. But that doesn't mean you're not indispensable."

"Your knowledge of this community is indispensable. I'll admit, when Mr. K first told me that you knew everyone and had connections that would be of great assistance, I was dubious. But he was right. I would never have been able to get in to see the people you got me in to see—at least not without a subpoena, and once that issues, everybody's tongue gets tied real quick."

Jimmy feigned modesty. "I do what I can."

"And that business with the court clerk? Brilliant. Possibly illegal. But brilliant."

Jimmy held a vertical finger across his lips. "Hush."

"What's this?" Maria said. "What secrets have I not heard about yet?"

Jimmy smiled. "That's why they're called secrets. I delivered your pies, by the way. Shawna was quite grateful. Seemed a little nervous, but she wanted to know all about the case. Kept me talking for twenty minutes. I think we made a friend for life, Dan."

"You can never have enough of those. And while I'm at it, Garrett, I stayed up late last night reading your research folder. First-rate. I feel prepared to handle whatever legal arguments Jazlyn throws at me."

Garrett bowed his head. "Thank you."

Maria agreed. "Garrett is chill. Low-key. And super-useful. But I'm sure you could do some research if you had to, Dan."

"No. I'll be the first to admit that research is not my strong suit. I mean, I know how it's done, in a vague sort of way. But I don't enjoy it. Books and paper. Ick."

"I do enjoy it," Garrett replied. "I would much rather be in the library than the courtroom."

"This is the way a team is supposed to work," Maria said. "Complementing one another."

Dan gave her a stern look. "If you say, 'You complete me,' I'm going to become violent. Or violently ill."

She laughed. "I would never commit such a heinous offense."

"I do kinda think we've got a nice gestalt here," Jimmy added. "Just saying. We're like a brave group of wandering warriors. We're like, the fellowship of the ring."

"Or," Garrett suggested, "a first-rate NFL team."

"Or Team Hogwarts," Maria said.

He arched an eyebrow. "Hogwarts? Really?"

"Oh, loosen up. Didn't you love the Harry Potter books when you were younger and less boring?"

"Actually, no."

"Too juvenile for you?"

"Too long for me."

Maria laughed. "Well, it's applicable, even if you don't know it. You, Dan, are our Harry Potter."

"I'm a scrawny geek with weird glasses?"

"You're the focal point. The wheel around which the spokes pivot. A natural leader."

"I don't want to lead anyone."

"Neither did Harry."

"I suppose you're Hermione? The smarty-pants know-it-all?"

"Aha. You do know a little about the Harry Potter universe."

"I've seen some of the movies. And you're obviously smart. I knew that the first night I met you in that bar."

"I don't think I like where this is going," Jimmy cut in. "You're not going to say I'm Ron, are you?"

Maria laughed. "Oh, Jimmy. You are so Ron."

"I'm pretty sure you're not suggesting we're gonna hook up in the end. Are you saying I'm the comic relief?"

She smiled. "You're the heart of the team."

"I like that better." He raised a fist. "Go Team Hogwarts!"

"I'm feeling left out here," Garrett said. "Who's left for me? Hagrid?"

Everyone burst out laughing.

"Surely we can find a better parallel," Maria said. "Who does the research at Hogwarts? Dumbledore? Snape?"

"I am not going to be Snape," Garrett insisted.

"I guess that makes you Dumbledore. You have been here longer than the rest of us."

"Now wait a minute—"

The doorbell rang. Through the windows on either side of the door, he could see that a package had been delivered.

Maria looked toward the door. "You expecting anything, Dan?"

"I did send some exhibits out to be photocopied. I'll bring it in." He opened the door and lifted the box. It was much lighter than he expected. He set it on a coffee table and started to open it.

"Want a knife? Scissors?" Jimmy asked.

"Nah. I prefer the brute-force approach." He ripped the tape off the top of the box, then opened it.

And gasped.

At first, he didn't realize what it was. Then, as he slowly removed the pieces, he figured it out.

It was a doll, a stuffed cotton doll, perhaps two feet in length. It had dark hair and a Hispanic skin tone. Young. Probably beautiful—before it had been ripped to shreds.

And splattered with blood.

He scratched some of it with his fingernail, then touched it to his tongue.

Real blood.

Maria hovered over his shoulder, then drew in her breath. "Wh—what is it?"

He felt his throat dry up. "A doll. An effigy. Bloody, mutilated, and dismembered."

"But—why?"

"It's supposed to be Esperanza." He paused. "It's a threat."

"Why would anyone threaten that beautiful girl?"

He laid it gently back in the box. "Because it's the best way to get to us. To stop what we're doing. Someone is worried we're going to get Gabriella off. And they don't like it."

Garrett rose. "Surely they don't think we're going to back off because we got a doll in the mail."

Silence.

"Well, we're not going to. Right?" Garrett's eyes scanned the room. "Right, Dan?"

He found it increasingly difficult to speak.

A doll covered with blood. Real blood. Some of it still wet. The odor rising from the box was horrific, like something stale and dead. He knew there were many nasty people involved in this case, and at least one capable of murder...but someone who would do this was capable of anything.

Fighting his flight instinct, he reached into the box and found something more. At first he thought it was scraps of cardboard, a message maybe. Then he realized it was a photograph torn to shreds.

He poured all the pieces onto the table and assembled them like a jigsaw puzzle. It didn't take long to see what it was. Or rather, what it had originally been.

Jimmy whispered. "It's a photograph of us. All four of us."

"When was that taken?" Maria asked.

He licked his lips. "Looks like we're in front of the courthouse. Maybe when we went out for the arraignment."

"I don't remember anyone taking a selfie," Garrett said.

"Because we didn't. This was taken by someone else. Someone watching us."

Jimmy stuttered. "L-Like you said. A threat."

"And a damn good one. Because if someone can shoot a camera at us, they could shoot a gun at us. And disappear into the background, no one ever knowing who did it." A word echoed in his brain. "Like an assassin. No trace left behind. We'd just be gone."

Maria's voice was mostly steady, but he could see that her hands trembled. "Do you think... we need to give this a second thought?"

Jimmy was still whispering. "At any rate, we need to tell Mr. K."

"No," Garrett said. "K won't put us in danger. He'll take us off the case."

Maria's brow was deeply creased. "Dan? What do you think?"

He drew in his breath, trying to keep his voice level. "This psychopath probably realizes we might not back down, if it's just our own lives in danger. Hence, the doll. What we might not do for ourselves—we might do for Esperanza."

"She's in that detention center all by herself," Maria said. "How hard would it be for someone to get to her?"

"If people can have inmates executed in prison, a detention center should be a cinch. And that's what our correspondent wants us to understand. In our hearts, we took this case for Esperanza." He slowly lowered himself into a chair. "And if we continue with it, we may kill her."

THE WEAK AND THE NEEDY

CHAPTER TWENTY-EIGHT

DAN RARELY SLEPT THE NIGHT BEFORE A TRIAL BEGAN. AT least it felt that way. Some inner voice suggested that he must sleep a little and not realize it, or he wouldn't be able to put one foot in front of the other come morning. But all he remembered was tossing and turning, flipping and flopping, not being able to stop thinking long enough to rest.

That was standard practice for a trial lawyer, and especially a criminal lawyer, whose work had life-and-death ramifications. He was always queasy the night before trial—and that was probably good. If he ever became so accustomed to this that it didn't bother him anymore, it was time to quit. It was the nervousness and nausea that gave him an edge. And the edge guaranteed that he did his best work.

The looming specter of the death penalty did not help him sleep. Florida was one of the most active death penalty states in the nation. Several people had been executed in the past few years, though happily, none of them had been his client. Early in 2018, a death penalty execution turned horrific when the convict screamed and struggled as he died, apparently in excruciating pain. Some pundits said enthusiasm for the death penalty was fading, that court rulings and waning public support might soon make it obsolete. He hadn't seen any evidence of that yet, but he hoped it was true.

Today he had an even more immediate threat to worry about. He couldn't shake the feeling that he was about to put his foot in a steel-claw bear trap—and he wouldn't be able to chew his leg free. He'd called Crenshaw, the cowboy kaleidoscope ICE agent, to notify him of the suspected threat. Crenshaw said he would notify the staff at the detention center and tell them to be doubly alert. He also instructed them to isolate Esperanza and not permit her any unknown visitors.

But he knew that might not be enough. There was always a way to get someone.

He hired two security officers to stake out the detention center. But of course, they couldn't go inside. All they could do was park a car nearby and photograph who entered. They had facial-recognition software that might help them identify suspicious visitors. But what if the person who mailed that package got to someone on the inside?

He had also hired a security team to watch him and the other members of Gabriella's defense team, but that gave him no greater sense of satisfaction or security. The officers could enter the courthouse and even the courtroom, but they couldn't bring weapons. The metal detectors prevented that. Theoretically, the metal detectors should prevent assassins from bringing weapons into the courtroom as well. But there had been incidents when people managed to smuggle weapons, sometimes made of something other than metal, into courtrooms. If someone with sufficient intelligence and resources really wanted to take out a lawyer, they'd find a way.

He and Maria took their positions at the defense table with Gabriella. Jimmy and Garrett stayed in the gallery. He knew Jazlyn would be flanked by her enormous staff, and he liked the image that would give the jury. Normally, an extensive defense team might make the prosecution look outgunned. Here, it would be just the opposite, with so many briefcases sitting with the prosecutor, but only two with the defendant. And one of those was a backpack. They would look like the underdog. That fit best with the trial strategy Maria concocted.

He warned Gabriella that jury selection was a long and tedious process, and that it was best she not be in the courtroom while it took place. He preferred that the jurors get their first glimpse of her when the trial began, after Maria made sure Gabriella was well scrubbed and well dressed. Nothing from Neiman Marcus, nothing that suggested they were trying to turn her into someone she wasn't. But respectable. Not someone you would expect to be a member of a gang, much less pistol-popping rival gang members.

Judge Le had not ruled on the prosecution's motion to preclude all mention of Esperanza and the adoption petition at trial. He certainly wasn't going to remind her. He wondered if the motion had slipped Jazlyn's mind because she had so much to worry about, or whether making the motion had been a gesture, something designed to make a point, rather than something she actually planned to pursue.

Judge Le had the option of conducting the jury examination herself, based upon questions suggested by counsel, but happily, given the gravity of the charges, she let the attorneys handle it themselves, sacrificing speed but giving the defense one less potential error to gripe about on appeal.

He and Maria considered hiring a jury consultant to advise on the selection. That was trendy these days, particularly in high-stakes cases, and Mr. K said he would pay for it. But ultimately, they opted against it. He didn't think they could find a jury consultant who knew anything he didn't know already. That might sound egotistical, and maybe it was, but he still thought it was true. They could study their charts and statistics all night long, but it was no substitute for the knowledge he had gained representing desperate, low-income clients, fighting tooth and nail against the government, spending hours on his feet in the courtroom.

Besides, he knew what the jury consultant would say. The general wisdom was, on the defense, you want African-American females, as many as possible, so you can get a hung jury. Maybe in this case a Hispanic female would do as well. But he didn't want a hung jury. Given the high profile of this case, the prosecution would almost have to retry it. He wanted to win, and he wanted to win the first time around. Otherwise, Esperanza would not remain in this country.

More general jury consultant wisdom: white middle-class men convict ninety-seven percent of the time. That was actually supported by some statistical evidence. And you could probably increase that when the defendant was a minority group member. He didn't need a jury consultant to tell him that the more diversity on the jury, the better.

He would let the prosecution do the overt political questioning. He preferred more subtle approaches. Instead of asking the jurors, Who did you vote for in the last election?—which might offend them—he asked, What television shows do you like? If they watched Fox News, or cop shows like *Blue Bloods*, they likely tilted conservative. Other shows, like *Will and Grace*, or *Last Week Tonight with John Oliver*, tended to lean liberal. Anyone who admitted they didn't believe in the death penalty would be removed from the jury quickly. He was looking for people who might accept the death penalty in theory but balk at actually implementing it, or who might be suspicious of law enforcement, or who might be more likely to sympathize with minority defendants. He wanted jurors who might actually apply "beyond a reasonable doubt" as the stiff standard it was meant to be.

The first eighteen called to the box were all familiar with the so-called Tragedy at the Trademark. Only a handful were foolish enough to admit that they had already formed opinions about who did what—and they were immediately removed. It would be his job to root out anyone who kinda sorta thought they knew what happened but wouldn't admit it, plus anyone who might think that one Hispanic was much like another, or all Hispanics were members of gangs. He didn't think rooting out racial bigotry would be that difficult, but you can never be sure. No one was going to admit it.

The hardest moment was his frustrating conversation with prospective juror number thirteen, a man who appeared to be in his mid-sixties, retired, in a white dress shirt with rolled-up sleeves and a white undershirt beneath.

He asked the juror, "How much do you know about this incident?"

The man shrugged. "Bunch of thugs shot at each other and one of them died."

"And when you say thugs, you mean—what?"

"Them gangs."

"How do you know gangs were involved?"

"They're always shooting themselves down on the Southside, right?"

"But the Trademark isn't on the Southside. It's in a tourist district."

"But those people came from the Southside."

"Actually, the victim was from El Salvador." He had to dismantle stereotypes whenever possible. "Visiting the country for reasons that are unclear." Out the corner of his eye, he saw Jazlyn rocking a little, wondering if she should object.

"Doesn't matter what country they come from. Still Hispanics."

"I gather you don't like Hispanics."

"I don't like murderers."

"Please answer my question. Do you dislike Hispanics?"

"I don't like or dislike people. I just want them to stay out of the way and stop ruining everything for real Americans."

He did a slow pivot toward the judge. "Your honor, I move that this juror be removed for cause."

Jazlyn rose. "Objection. He said he wasn't prejudiced."

"He said a great deal more suggesting that he is. My client can't get a fair trial from people like this."

The judge thought for a moment before responding. "The prosecutor is correct. He denied having any prejudice. If you hadn't asked the question, Mr. Pike, we might have cause to speculate. But since you did ask the question, and his answer was in the negative, I cannot say that you've established the existence of any inappropriate prejudice."

"Seriously? You're going to let this man remain on the jury?"

The judge gave him a stern look. "We've got a long trial ahead, counsel, and I can make your life miserable for every day of it, so I would advise you to respect the dignity of this court. I'm not going to remove this juror for cause."

"Then I will use one of my peremptory challenges."

"That you may do." She made a mark on her roster. "Juror Thirteen, you are excused. Please follow the bailiff out of the courtroom. And the defense has only two peremptory challenges left. Don't squander them."

As it turned out, he didn't have another dramatic need for them. He used them, just the same, to remove two more white middle-class men. But they still dominated the jury. He had seven white males somewhere between twenty-five and sixty years of age, two white females, one African-American male, and two Hispanics, a man and a woman. The composition of the jury did not remotely reflect the composition of the community, but that was almost always the case.

He never felt he handled juror examinations well and constantly second-guessed himself. But he knew that in capital cases sometimes this went on for days, and he was finished by early afternoon, so he considered that a success.

He expected the judge to call it quits for the day and start the actual trial first thing in the morning, but to his surprise, she did not. Instead, she allowed them a thirty-minute recess to gather their thoughts. "Looks to me like we ought to be able to get in opening statements, which by the way will be limited to thirty minutes per side, and you're encouraged to speak less. We can do those and perhaps even cover a few preliminary witnesses today."

Unexpected, but fine with him. They were on a tight deadline.

————————

DAN SPENT MOST OF THE HALF HOUR IN A QUIET consultation room near the courtroom, gazing at the marble walls. Everyone left him alone, probably assuming he was deliberating, contemplating, planning his opening, meditating, whatever. Something productive. But it wasn't true. Mostly he was just worrying, trying not to feel overwhelmed. He felt this way every time he was immersed in a lengthy, complex trial. It was as if he had been ripped out of the real world, submerged, buried, isolated in some remote polar outpost, with wind and snow howling and separating him from the rest of humanity. All his normal activities, contacts, and habits dropped off the map. Nothing existed but him and the trial.

Saving Gabriella was paramount, but so was saving Esperanza, and they had to get this murder case resolved before she was deported. He didn't want a Pyrrhic victory. He had to save that girl. She was depending upon him.

What was happening here?

He caught his reflection in the window and gazed at the eyes he saw peering back at him. Something had changed, something inside. He had always cared about justice, about curtailing government bullying, preventing what happened to his father from happening to others. But this time there was more. Everything was different. Like this firm, these people who kept calling him part of a team. He never meant to be part of a team. He never *wanted* to be part of a team. He wanted to be Daniel Pike, the rebel, the lawyer in the Air Jordans with the backpack, doing things his own way but always getting the job done. And putting his surfboard in the water in time to catch the best wave. That was who he wanted to be. He didn't need anybody else to be happy.

Or so he always thought.

Maria was right about one thing. That little girl had gotten to him. He could see those big brown eyes even when he closed his.

"I knew you would be the one who saved me."

He wasn't sure he could trust Gabriella. Every new thing he learned about her made him worry more. Made their case seem increasingly impossible.

But he had to win this. He felt that in the core of his soul. He *needed* to win this.

What was happening here?

Could there possibly be more in that reflection than the lawyer who always pulled a rabbit out of his hat?

CHAPTER TWENTY-NINE

APPARENTLY WORD GOT OUT THAT THE TRIAL WAS BEGINNING this afternoon, because by the time he returned to Judge Le's courtroom, it was packed. He spotted his two rent-a-cops on opposite sides of the courtroom in the middle of the gallery. He was glad they had managed to maintain their seats. Sometimes, for high-profile trials like this one, seats were assigned by lottery or random luck.

Just after he stepped in, he noted Crenshaw near the back of the courtroom.

Crenshaw stood to greet him. "Ready to ride out, cowpoke?"

He smiled a little. "You're the cowboy. I'm just a worker bee."

"Looks like you got your work cut out for you today."

He did not disagree.

"Look, I came by because I wanted to tell you—I've got everyone at the detention center on high alert. We're not gonna let anyone but you and your staff visit Esperanza Coto. We'll make sure that girl stays safe."

"Thank you. That makes me feel much better. As hard as that probably is on her, I think it's safer to keep her isolated from the other internees."

"You're afraid she might get picked off by another little girl?"

"You never know. Some of the girls detained there aren't that little. Some of them are drug addicts. Some of them never had five dollars in their hands. They may be readily susceptible to influence and bribery."

"I suppose you have a point. We'll keep her to herself as much as possible."

"Thank you. I appreciate it."

"I appreciate you." Crenshaw stepped a little closer. "I understand what you're doing here."

"I'm defending a woman falsely accused of murder."

"I mean with this over-the-top speedy trial. Trying to get it done as soon as possible. Trying to prevent Esperanza from being deported."

He didn't comment.

"You're putting your neck on the chopping block for that girl."

"Because you're about to deport her."

"We both have roles to play in this drama." His voice dropped. "But that doesn't mean I or any member of my staff relishes the prospect of sending Esperanza to El Salvador. I just can't stop it." He paused. "But I think maybe you can."

"Cross your fingers."

The bailiff opened the back door and let the jurors into the gallery. They started with the twelve primary jurors, plus six alternates, so that regardless of what happened, they would never fall short of having twelve people who had seen the entire trial. If the alternates were not needed, they would be dismissed when the jury retired to deliberate.

He returned to the defense table and sat between Maria and Gabriella. He smiled at Gabriella, took her hand, and kissed it. He couldn't check, but he hoped the jury was watching. He felt certain that at least a few of them would notice. Of course, he genuinely cared about Gabriella. But the point of this exercise was to send a message to the jury, to tell them that he wasn't afraid of her, didn't dislike her, and didn't think she was guilty.

A few moments later, Judge Le entered the room and called the court to order. "Please be seated." She read the style of the case, gave some preliminary instructions to the jury, and then looked toward Jazlyn. "Let's have opening statements. Madame Prosecutor, are you ready to begin?"

Jazlyn nodded and positioned herself squarely in front of the jury.

Her opening was powerful, obviously rehearsed but still effective. She ticked through the facts of the case, previewing what "the evidence will show." These were supposed to be statements, not arguments, but in actual practice there was little difference.

He noticed that she kept it as simple as possible, which was probably smart. Complicated cases put viewers to sleep. If you want a favorable verdict, keep it simple, stupid.

"Forensic evidence puts the defendant at the scene of the crime. Eyewitness testimony puts her at the scene of the crime. Her prints are on the murder weapon, which by the way, is her gun, which was found at her home. Let them explain that." She pivoted. "As you will learn, she had a strong motive for killing Jorge Sanchez. And you will hear even more compelling evidence as the trial proceeds. This is a simple matter, really, and though I'm sure defense counsel will attempt to complicate it, the facts speak for themselves, clearly and without doubt. Gabriella Valdez should be convicted of murder in the first degree."

Judge Le nodded. "Mr. Pike? Would you like to give your opening now, or wait until you present the defense case?"

"I'll speak now, your honor." As she knew he would. Because only an insane person, or a complete amateur, would let the prosecution opening weigh unrebutted on the jurors' minds.

Jazlyn had remained motionless as she delivered her speech, so he made a point of moving. He didn't know if that was better or worse, but at least they would know he was capable of walking and talking at the same time.

"Ladies and gentlemen of the jury. I will not bore you by

previewing everything you're about to see and hear. I will not tell you what to think. You can draw your own conclusions. But I will tell you this. Nothing about this case is simple. That's not because I'm going to complicate it. That's because cases of this magnitude are rarely as simple as the prosecutor just indicated. Suggesting that there can be no questions, no doubts, is frankly, absurd."

He walked through the case as presented by Jazlyn, making it clear that he didn't find the forensic or eyewitness testimony nearly as compelling as the prosecutor did. He still didn't know if Emilio would be called to testify, but he had to assume that was a possibility, so he said a few words about the unreliable nature of snitch testimony, evidence from people who received rewards in exchange for talking. And he made sure they understood that the gun was not found in Gabriella's yard until two days after the incident, and then in a location where only an idiot would leave the murder weapon.

"Whatever else you may conclude about my client, I can tell you with certainty that she is not an idiot. I hope you will pay close attention to the testimony offered by the agents of the government, law enforcement, the St. Petersburg police." He recited almost word-for-word from Maria's strategy notebook. "And I hope you realize how little investigation was ever conducted in this case. They assumed from the start that Gabriella was guilty, based on the word of an anonymous tipper, and they have never seriously investigated anyone else, although there are many gangland characters with far greater criminal records involved. You need to ask yourself, Why? Doesn't that seem odd? Doesn't that create doubt in your mind?" The word "doubt" of course being the million-dollar noun.

"Can you ever conclude that you know what happened, that you understand what went down, when the matter has not been thoroughly investigated? The police and the prosecutors were under intense pressure to charge someone, and now they're under pressure to convict someone. They grabbed the first possible suspect and stopped looking. They'll say they stopped looking because they found the culprit. But the fact remains—they stopped looking. Other avenues were never explored."

He drew in his breath and strolled slowly to the other side of the jury box. "During the defense case, we will provide evidence pertaining to many of those other avenues. It will be for you to judge whether they should have been pursued. You will decide whether they create doubt in your mind."

He provided a few more sneak previews of the case to come, but he didn't want to bore them. Better to let them be pleasantly surprised later. All they needed to understand now was that this was not a slam dunk. They were going to have to pay attention and take this seriously. He knew people have short attention spans and the worst thing he could do was overstay his welcome. He wasn't even going to use his full thirty minutes.

"One last note. The prosecutor used the phrase, 'Let them explain that.' Well—news flash. We do not have to explain *anything*. We do not have the burden of proof. The prosecution does. Before you go back to the deliberation room, the judge will give you many instructions, but the most important one is this: the prosecution must prove its case beyond a reasonable doubt. We don't have to put on a single witness or present a single piece of evidence. We will, but even if we didn't, it would still be the prosecution that must meet this extraordinarily high burden. Bear that in mind as you listen to the evidence and always remember that if they have not met their burden, if they have not proven Gabriella's guilt beyond a reasonable doubt, you must acquit her. You are not being asked what you personally think probably happened. You're being asked whether the prosecution has proven her guilt beyond a reasonable doubt."

He paused, scanning the gallery, looking each of the jurors in the eyes. "I am confident that by the conclusion of this trial, you will find that they have not met this burden. And you will set my client free."

CHAPTER THIRTY

Dan spotted Luis González sitting on the third row of the gallery, not far from one of his security men. That was surprising. He wouldn't think such a busy businessman—and it's all completely legitimate, really!—would have time to play lookee-loo at a murder trial. Even if Luis did have time, he found it surprising the man would show up. In his experience, no one even tangentially related to a high-profile or high-stakes case appeared voluntarily at the trial. Either you subpoenaed them, or they weren't there. This was what he liked to call the Perry Mason effect. If they were in the gallery, they worried, they might be called unexpectedly to the witness stand and cross-examined until the lawyer pounded a confession out of them—a result that transpired in every episode of *Perry Mason*, and never once in real life.

Gabriella appeared to be holding it together. He knew she was scared to death. How could she not be? But she kept it locked inside. He had advised her to maintain a poker face in the courtroom. Don't look confident, don't look scared. Poker face. Don't react to what the witnesses on the stand say, even if they tell the most outrageous lies. Poker face. The jurors would be watching, and they tended to be put off by defendants making expressions of surprise or contempt, headshaking and similar dramatic reactions.

He wanted to ask her the questions raised by some of the people he interviewed. Why didn't she mention that she was trained with a gun? Why didn't she tell him she'd been at the shootout the first time they met? But he decided against it. He didn't want to force her to lie. And he especially didn't want her to tell him anything that would cripple his ability to defend her.

"How do you feel?" he asked.

"Like I have been stabbed in the heart. And someone is slowly twisting it." She choked. "Every second it gets worse. And it doesn't stop."

He suspected that was one of the most accurate descriptions he'd ever heard of what it was like to be on trial for murder. "Hang in there. There's not much time left today. The judge won't keep the jurors past dinnertime."

"Why do they hate me so much?"

"I don't think anyone hates you. But they have to convict someone, or soon everyone in town will hate them."

"I did not do this thing. I could never hurt someone like that."

"I know."

"I have tried to be a good parent for Esperanza. Putting myself at risk puts her at risk. I would never do that."

"Stay strong. Just a little longer. Then you can rest."

She nodded, smiling slightly.

As usual, the prosecution led with the most boring witnesses. There were many experts who had to be called to fulfill essential elements of the alleged crimes. To tick off the boxes. It didn't make them interesting. He had wondered briefly if, given the short amount of time before the close of day, the prosecution might advance someone on their list, to give the jurors something exciting to think about when they went home tonight. But that didn't happen. Jazlyn was too smart to revise her strategy on the fly.

The first three witnesses were called to establish proof of death. If you're going to bring a murder charge, you have to prove someone died, even if it isn't in dispute. The first witness established the death. The second witness, an ER doctor at the hospital, testified that six people had been wounded, and one of them, Mandy Donahue, remained in the hospital in critical condition. He was not sure why they needed the third witness, or why Jazlyn saved the coroner for last, given that he alone could probably have provided the testimony of all three. Perhaps Jazlyn thought it would liven up the boring stuff if it came from three different witnesses.

Turned out there was more to it than that.

The coroner, Dr. Zanzibar, established that Sanchez had been killed as a result of two gunshots, one to the head and one to the heart. But he didn't stop there. Jazlyn continued to question him.

"Were there any other signs of injury?"

Zanzibar nodded. "Extensive signs of cutting on the body, some pre-mortem, some postmortem. Because the cutting and the gunshots came relatively close in time, it is difficult to distinguish the two."

"I will ask you to describe this cutting for the jury. And I will warn everyone in the courtroom that this testimony might be... disturbing."

Great. She was trying to get the jurors agitated, outraged by the horrific nature of the crime.

Zanzibar continued. "Sanchez' throat was slashed, although as I said, it was not necessary to inflict death. That was already a certainty from the gunshot wounds. He was stabbed repeatedly. Gutted. Even stabbed in the face."

This wasn't just a murder, she wanted the jurors to know. This was a mutilation. This was a crime committed by someone with a serious hate-on against Sanchez. The other injuries might be collateral damage, but Sanchez was targeted.

He considered objecting, perhaps on grounds of relevance.

But why? It was all true. And none of it directly incriminated Gabriella. Although objections were somewhat exciting, jurors resented it when attorneys prevented them from hearing everything there was to know about the case. He decided to reserve his objections for a later time when they might be of greater importance.

Jazlyn continued. "How much strength would be required for this mutilation?"

Gabriella was a petite woman, so the prosecution wanted to make sure the jurors wouldn't question whether she was strong enough to disfigure the corpse.

"Not that much physical strength," the coroner replied. "Just a strong desire to inflict harm."

That last bit was outside the scope of the coroner's expertise, but he let it slide.

"Would it be time-consuming?"

"Not necessarily. A few seconds would be enough."

"Would it require anatomical knowledge?"

The coroner shook his head. "No. Anyone could do it. A child could do it." His voice dropped. "Though I hope to God no child would ever want to."

Jazlyn nodded. "Would you say this mutilation was evidence of... a strong desire to inflict pain?"

She was pushing it now. This was a coroner, not a psychiatrist. That was why she spoke so tentatively. But she had chosen her words carefully.

The coroner agreed. "This is not something I normally see in gangland shootings. This is more than you would associate with a territorial conflict or rubout. This was personal. Like someone wanted this man dead. For personal reasons."

"Like," Jazlyn suggested, "to protect someone they loved."

Before he could make an objection, she added, "I'm sorry, your honor. I'll withdraw that last bit."

The judge nodded. But he knew what she had deliberately planted in the jurors' minds. The idea that Gabriella wasn't acting for herself, but to protect or defend someone else. Meaning Esperanza.

Which explained why Jazlyn wasn't pursuing the motion to preclude mentioning Esperanza at trial.

"I have nothing more, your honor."

He passed on cross-examination. There was nothing to be gained. He couldn't deny the fact of death or the cruelty inflicted on Sanchez' corpse. Battering the witness over trivia would only draw more attention to his testimony. The sooner the coroner was off the witness stand, the better.

CHAPTER THIRTY-ONE

THE NEXT TWO PROSECUTION WITNESSES CAME FROM THE ballistics department. Unsurprisingly, the first testified that the bullet that killed Sanchez came from Prosecution Exhibit 1—the gun. The second testified that the same gun was registered to Gabriella. Another forensic witness added that DNA traces matching Gabriella's had been found on the gun.

On cross-examination, he suggested that wasn't particularly surprising, given that it was her gun. "You would expect to find DNA matching the owner on the gun, wouldn't you?"

"I can't say that it would be unusual."

"Could you please answer the question? You would expect to find the owner's DNA on their own gun, right?"

"I suppose."

"But that does not in any way prove that she fired the gun or killed the man in question, does it?"

"It's almost impossible to fire a gun without leaving minute traces of DNA. Skin flecks. Sweat."

"What if the shooter wore gloves?"

He tilted his head. "If the shooter were gloves, they would probably not leave DNA traces."

"So in that instance, the only DNA on the gun would be DNA that was there before the shooting occurred. Right?"

The witness drew in his breath. "In your hypothetical scenario, I suppose."

"Let's get back to my original question, and perhaps this time you could answer it. The fact that Gabriella's DNA was on the gun does not prove she fired it, does it?"

"It shows she held it in her hand."

"At some time. Let me try again. The fact that her DNA was found on the gun does not prove that she fired it, does it?"

"I suppose not." The expert held out as long as possible before acknowledging the truth. He almost admired the man's perseverance.

"Did you conduct a paraffin test?"

"A dermal nitrate test. Yes. We did not find traces of gunshot residue on the defendant. But she was not tested until two days after the incident. She had changed her clothes and washed repeatedly."

"What you're saying is, you found no evidence that she fired a gun."

"What I'm saying is, the test did not prove or exclude the possibility that she fired a gun."

With the time remaining, Jazlyn called a witness named Brian Hancock. He knew that Hancock was a night watchman at the Trademark's parking lot checkpoint about a hundred feet from the shooting. One of the security cameras caught footage of Gabriella—and many others—at the scene of the crime. She was carrying something. You couldn't tell what she carried, but you could definitely tell it was Gabriella, and you could see her walking toward Emilio. About thirty seconds later, they moved out of range.

He rose to his feet. "Bench conference?"

The judge waved them forward. She covered the microphone. "Yes?"

"Your honor, I object to the admission of the security-camera footage. It is not probative. But it may be prejudicial for the jurors to see it."

Jazlyn's eyebrows knitted together. "Do you deny that she was at the scene of the crime?"

"No. In fact, I'll stipulate to it, so this evidence adds nothing. But seeing this videotape will create a prejudicial effect in the minds of the jury that vastly outweighs the tape's probative value, which is zero."

The judge almost scoffed. "You don't think it's relevant that your client was at the scene of the crime?"

"We're not denying that she was at the scene of the crime. This video footage is irrelevant to any point in dispute."

"I disagree, your honor," Jazlyn rejoined. "A stipulation has little impact. Even witness testimony doesn't have the same impact as a videotape. This removes all doubt that she was present. Plus, on the videotape, she speaks to a known criminal and she is carrying some kind of satchel which we maintain contained the murder weapon."

"She has no proof that it contains a weapon. Again, prejudicial, but not probative."

The judge shook her head. "I'll let it in. Mr. Pike, you of course will be free to cross-examine the witness about what the videotape shows and does not show. Although I would like to think that will be obvious to the jury."

In other words, she didn't want him to waste their time with a lengthy cross-examination about what was already obvious.

He returned to the defense table and tried to comfort Gabriella. "It doesn't matter." And to some extent, it didn't. He'd known all along he was unlikely to succeed. He was tilting at windmills. But he had to try.

After Jazlyn took Hancock through the lugubrious process of establishing his credentials, describing the function of the security cameras, and establishing the chain of custody of the tape, they showed the video on a monitor. He didn't watch the screening. He watched the jurors' faces. If he had learned anything from his years as a trial lawyer, it was that watching those faces was the best indication he would ever get of how effective a case, or witness, or piece of evidence, was.

The tape was having its intended effect. The jurors realized she was there, carrying something.

He realized the burden of proof had shifted. The jurors believed, at the very least, that Gabriella might be guilty. If he was going to save her, he would have to prove that she was not.

As it turned out, his cross-examination of Hancock was brief.

"Did you ever see my client, Gabriella, with your own eyes?"

"No. I wasn't even looking that way. Not until I heard the shots."

"So you have no idea what she did there?"

"That's correct."

"You don't know why she was there."

"That's correct."

"You don't know who she spoke to."

"True, although in the footage she appears—"

He cut the witness off. "I'm not asking you to interpret the tape. I'm asking what you know. Witnesses can only testify about what they know."

"I don't know who she spoke to," he said, properly chastised.

"And you have no idea what was in that satchel?"

He could tell what the man wanted to say. But he held it in check. "I can't say for certain."

"Thank you. No more questions."

CHAPTER THIRTY-TWO

DAN KNEW THE SECOND DAY OF TRIAL WOULD BE ALL ABOUT the gun. The first witness would be the officer who found the gun. The second would be the fingerprint expert who claimed Gabriella's prints were on the gun.

Jazlyn called Officer Treadway to the stand. Medium height. Slightly overweight. Crooked smile. Very white. He was an earnest officer, serious but not presumptuous, matter-of-fact but not arrogant.

Jazlyn led him through his testimony without undue elaboration. She knew the facts were inherently suspect and didn't want to draw attention to that fact. Instead, she rushed to the finish line. They found the gun in Gabriella's backyard.

"Officer Treadway, after you found the gun, what did you do with it?"

"I followed our departmental procedures for handling potential evidence," he explained calmly. "I tagged it and bagged it. Meaning I affixed a label indicating the location and time where and when it was found using a slip-tie that would not alter the condition of the gun in any way. I then put it in an evidence bag." He turned slightly toward the jurors. "Similar to the Ziploc bags you probably keep in your kitchen, only somewhat more durable. I labeled the bag, then I put it in a lockbox in my patrol car. When I returned to headquarters, I immediately took the box to the officer in charge of the evidence locker who logged it in and stored it for safekeeping."

"Has anyone touched that gun since?"

"I understand that it was sent out to various forensics scientists for examination, then returned to the evidence locker. No police officers have been anywhere near it. I checked the register this morning. It was only logged out twice for evidentiary purposes."

She nodded. "Thank you, officer. No more questions."

Judge Le turned his way. "Mr. Pike?"

He rose. "Thank you, your honor." There was so much to say he barely knew where to begin. "Officer Treadway, how long have you been working in St. Petersburg?"

"Just over five years."

"How long have you been working the Southside?"

"Almost the entire time."

"How do you feel about that? Must be dangerous work."

"Being a police officer is dangerous work," he replied. "But I didn't take this job because I wanted to be safe. If you're going to be a police officer, I think you ought to go where people need help. And that's the Southside. As you undoubtedly know, it has the highest crime rates in our city."

"Wouldn't you rather be somewhere else?"

"No. I probably could have finagled a reassignment to some cushy tourist neighborhood where far less crime takes place. But I'd rather be where I feel I'm doing some good."

"You're saying you chose to work in the neighborhood with the highest crime rates...and the highest Hispanic population."

For the first time, Officer Treadway paused. Probably because he could see where this was headed. "I don't know for a fact that your statement about the population is true. It may be. I just don't know."

"Most of the people you interact with in that neighborhood are Hispanic, right?"

"That is true."

"And many of them may be illegal aliens."

"That could be true. I don't know the statistics. I'm not an immigration agent." He was playing it cool and close to the vest, not providing any opportunities to suggest that racial prejudice might motivate his actions.

"When was the first time you encountered my client?"

"After the shooting," he explained. "She was spotted there. I personally interviewed her, with my partner, Stacy Yancey."

"Did you find the gun at that time?"

"No. We mostly just talked."

"Did you suspect Gabriella at that time?"

"Only because she had been seen at the shooting. Of course, many people were there and they weren't all killers. If anything, she struck me as least likely to be involved at that time. She was calm, cooperative, and she was raising a young girl. She seemed to take her parental duties seriously."

That was nice, anyway. He doubted that Jazlyn had coached him to present Gabriella as mother of the year. "Did you search the house? The grounds?"

"We did a cursory scan, not a thorough or complete search. Making sure she and the child were safe."

"But you did search the house?"

"Yes."

"And you did search the grounds, including the backyard, right?"

"Yes." Treadway knew where this was going and tried to defend himself. "But remember, it was late at night. About three in the morning, by the time we were searching. We looked over the backyard with flashlights, never the best search conditions. It would be easy to miss something."

"Particularly if it wasn't there yet."

Jazlyn rose to her feet. "Objection."

The judge nodded. "I'll instruct the jury to disregard defense counsel's remark. Counsel, your job right now is to ask questions. Please limit yourself to that."

He nodded, then plowed ahead. He knew that jurors had a hard time following objections and their aftermath. As long as he didn't look as if he'd been beaten, they might not grasp that the judge had chastised him, or even that he had lost the objection. "What inspired you to return to Gabriella's home?"

"Two days later, we received an anonymous phone tip suggesting that the murder weapon could be found in the defendant's backyard."

"Do you know who made the phone call?"

"As I said, it was anonymous."

"I get that they didn't identify themselves, but that doesn't necessarily mean you have no idea who it was."

Treadway paused again. "We don't know. We couldn't get a fix on the call. But it seemed credible, so we obtained a warrant and searched the yard."

"The caller accurately described where the gun was located, correct?"

"Yes."

"So the caller either saw the gun put there, talked to someone who saw the gun put there...or put the gun there himself."

"Or herself," Treadway added.

"If the gun had been there the night of the shooting, you would've spotted it, wouldn't you?"

"As I said, it was dark."

"Do you typically do sloppy work?"

Treadway twisted his neck slightly. "No."

"Does your partner do sloppy work?"

"No."

"You were using flashlights. Wouldn't a metal gun glint if you shone a light upon it?"

"Not necessarily. It was covered with mud."

"Officer Treadway, you do not strike me as incompetent. And let's face it, searching the backyard but missing a murder weapon that was simply lying on the ground would be gross incompetence." He could tell Jazlyn was deliberating whether to object, so he plowed quickly ahead. "In all likelihood, the gun was not there when you searched the first time, correct?"

"I can't answer that question. As I've said, it's possible we missed it."

Jazlyn rose to her feet. "Objection, your honor. The witness is not qualified to argue about the probability of overlooking a small object covered with mud hidden beneath a hedge in the dark of a moonless night."

The judge nodded. "Counsel, can you rephrase your question? And please limit your questions to the witness' actual knowledge or expertise."

He pondered a moment before proceeding. "Officer Treadway, you said you've worked this neighborhood for five years. To your knowledge, have you ever overlooked a murder weapon you were staring directly at?"

Again the twisting of the neck. "Not to my knowledge."

"What would be your opinion of a police officer who overlooked a murder weapon he was staring straight at?"

His lips thinned. "I would try to be understanding. It was a dark night."

"That's generous of you. What would be your reaction to an officer under your supervision who overlooked a murder weapon?"

Treadway didn't answer. He was searching for the right response.

"Would you give that sloppy officer a commendation?"

Jazlyn rose again. "Objection. Calls for speculation. There are no officers working under Officer Treadway."

The judge nodded. "Sustained."

He wasn't quite through with this yet. "Officer Treadway, the judge has asked me to limit my questions to your knowledge, so now I'm going to ask a question that directly pertains to it. Based upon your experience as a police officer for many years, at least five of them in that Southside neighborhood, do you think you overlooked the murder weapon the first time you searched Gabriella's yard?"

Treadway's jaw clenched. Eventually he spoke. "I don't know. It's possible."

"I did not ask you what was possible. I asked what you think, based upon your years of experience. Do you think you over-looked the gun the first time you searched those hedges?"

The officer's eyes darted toward Jazlyn, maybe looking for help, maybe wondering what the ramifications would be if he gave an honest answer. "No, I don't think I missed it the first time."

"And that means someone planted the gun later."

"Yes."

"And you don't know who planted the gun."

"The most likely candidate—"

"I didn't ask you to guess. I asked if you know."

"I know whose prints were on it."

He ignored that. "If Gabriella were going to hide the gun somewhere, putting it in her own backyard would be about the stupidest move possible, wouldn't it?"

Treadway tilted his head to the side. "Sometimes criminals do stupid things."

"No one is that stupid."

"She might've been concerned she'd be followed if she left her home."

"Do you think Gabriella would call in an anonymous tip telling the police to go find the gun in her backyard? Is she that stupid?"

"Probably not."

"And whoever made that phone call had to know that the gun had been placed under the hedge. So the person who called in the tip is most likely the one who planted the gun, right?"

"I don't know that. Maybe someone saw your client hide the gun."

"The truth is, you do not know who put that gun under the hedge. Right?"

"Correct."

"Thank you, sir. I have no more questions."

CHAPTER THIRTY-THREE

SCANNING THE GALLERY, DAN SAW THAT THE COMPOSITION OF the spectators had not changed much. Happily, his two security officers were still in position, closely monitoring anyone who came in or out of the courtroom. He still had no idea who sent that mutilated doll, and sadly, that wasn't because he couldn't imagine anyone doing it. It was because there were too many people he could imagine doing it.

He did notice that Albert Kazan, the park architect, was seated in the rear of the courtroom. What was his interest?

He pulled close to Maria and whispered. "How do you think that cross-ex went?"

"I thought you were terrific."

"I didn't get that much."

"There wasn't much to get. But you prevented the jury from thinking the discovery of the gun in Gabriella's backyard was proof positive of her guilt. You suggested some kind of skullduggery. Always good for the defense."

"I'm just implementing your trial strategy. We should put forward as many alternative suspects as possible. That includes people who might've planted the gun or made the anonymous phone call."

"Any leading suspects?"

"It doesn't matter. Just so they aren't Gabriella. Every new suspect makes it a little less likely she'll be convicted."

The judge returned to the courtroom and called the court back to order. Jazlyn called Dr. Brenda Palmer, their top expert on dactylograms—what the rest of the world called fingerprints.

Dr. Palmer walked to the witness stand. Serious expression. No jewelry. Pant suit, earth tones. Small scar beneath her left ear. About a size six.

Jazlyn spent twenty minutes establishing Dr. Palmer's credentials as a forensic scientist, which were indeed impressive. After extensive schooling, she'd spent twelve years in the CSI units in various Florida jurisdictions. She was consistently serious and scientific. Mr. Spock on the witness stand.

Jazlyn walked her through everything she did with respect to the murder weapon. Palmer identified two prints with the greatest clarity. A thumbprint was detected on the rear of the gun handle. And an index fingerprint was detected on the trigger. "That is consistent with how most people hold handguns."

After more scientific rigmarole, Jazlyn got to the key question. "Did you have access to the defendant's fingerprints?"

"Yes. I have the complete set taken when she was booked."

"Do they match the prints on the gun?"

"They are one-hundred-percent consistent with the prints of the defendant."

"Thank you." Jazlyn turned and smiled. "Your witness."

He positioned himself in front of the witness stand but off to the side, so he wouldn't block the jury's view of the witness' face. "You testified that the two prints you found on the murder weapon matched Gabriella's. In fact, you said it was a one-hundred-percent match. Is that correct?"

Palmer nodded, appearing pleased that the stupid defense attorney understood her testimony so well.

"But in fact, you did not have one-hundred-percent prints, did you?"

"I... don't know what you mean."

"On the gun. Did you have complete prints? Or partials?"

Palmer nodded. "Oh, partials, of course. You almost never find complete prints in the field."

"You didn't mention that before."

"The only time you're going to get a complete print is in a laboratory setting, or when someone is booked, when someone is deliberately trying to record fingerprints. In real life, when people pick up or touch an object, they don't lean in and roll their fingers around to make sure a complete print is left behind."

"How complete were these partials?"

"I'm not sure what you mean."

He pulled a document out of a folder in his backpack. "I've looked at your reports. I've seen reproductions of the prints you lifted from the gun. Not only do they not appear complete, it doesn't appear that you even had fifty percent of the print."

"That's probably true."

"So looking at less than half a fingerprint, you decided that it must belong to my client."

She cocked her head to one side. "Fingerprint evidence doesn't lie. As I'm sure you've heard, no two people have identical fingerprints."

"Yes, I've heard that, but I've never seen any proof of it. Has it ever been scientifically demonstrated?"

For the first time, the witness hesitated. "It is taken as... axiomatic in my field."

"But what I asked is whether there's any scientific proof that no two people have the same fingerprints. And the truth is, there isn't, right? It's one of those things people say, but it's never been proven."

"I...don't think I can agree with you."

"Can you direct me to a scientific study or analysis that has proven no two people have the same fingerprints?"

"Everyone knows it's true. Just as no two snowflakes are alike."

He smiled. "I was hoping you would bring that up, because that's another example of something people say without any proof. But in fact, a few years ago, a scientist did find two snowflakes that were just alike, and he did it without spending too much time collecting snowflakes. Are you familiar with the study I'm referring to?"

"I...did read something about that, yes."

"It appears that although there are many different snowflakes, it is not impossible for two to be identical. I can't help but wonder if the same is true for fingerprints. Particularly when you're not even dealing with complete fingerprints. The prints would only have to be fifty percent identical."

The expert squared her shoulders. "I examined these fingerprints personally. There is no question in my mind, based upon years of experience and expertise, that these fingerprints match the defendant's."

"Have you ever been wrong?"

After a beat, Jazlyn rose to her feet. "Objection, relevance. We're here to talk about this case, not others."

"The suggestion that an expert witness' track record is of no relevance is ludicrous. The prosecutor went to a great deal of trouble to establish Dr. Palmer's expertise. She's opened the door to evidence challenging that expertise, like for instance, evidence that the expert has made grievous errors in the past that have led to wrongful convictions."

The judge raised her hand. "The objection is overruled. You may proceed, Mr. Pike."

"Thank you." He returned his attention to the witness. "Have you ever made an incorrect fingerprint match?" He opened a file. "Like, for instance, in the case involving Miles Cortez?"

The witness' eyes hooded. This was clearly not her favorite

subject. "In that case, the prints in question were far less pronounced than what we have in this case. Barely even twenty-percent prints."

"So the quality of the prints affects the reliability of your testimony?"

"It affects the certainty of the results."

"In the Cortez case, given the poor quality of the fingerprint, I would understand if you had declined to reach a conclusion. But you didn't decline, did you? You declared that the fingerprints matched the defendant. Correct?"

The witness' jaw tightened. "What I said was that the partial fingerprints available appeared consonant to those of the defendant."

"And when you say consonant, you're using a fancy word to mask the fact that you said the fingerprints matched. Right?"

Out the corner of his eye, he could see Jazlyn bobbing, desperate for an excuse to interrupt the cross-examination. But she couldn't think of one. Because there wasn't one.

"I did, ultimately, use the word 'match.'"

"But the fingerprints didn't match. Subsequent DNA evidence proved that Cortez did not commit the crime. And he was released, though only after three-and-a-half years of incarceration. Is that accurate?"

"That is sadly correct."

"Your testimony put an innocent man behind bars."

"He didn't commit that crime. That doesn't make him innocent."

"Are you saying it's okay to put someone away based on false testimony, because they probably committed some other crime?"

"No."

"It sure sounded like that's what you were saying. Do you think we should lock people up regardless of the evidence? Especially if they're Hispanic?"

Jazlyn shot her feet. "Objection. The witness has said nothing to suggest any racial prejudice."

"It's not her words, it's her actions," he muttered.

The judge looked at him sternly. "This objection will be sustained. And I will not have any mindless mudslinging in my courtroom, Mr. Pike. Do you understand me? I will *not* have it. If you have no basis for making a claim of this nature, don't make it. We will not have reputations tarnished just to score a few points during cross-examination."

He drew in his breath. "Understood, your honor. I'll change the subject." Having already planted the suggestion in the jurors' minds. "You would be willing to acknowledge that you've made erroneous matches in the past, correct?"

The witness was not going down without a fight. "As I said, in the Cortez case, the fingerprint evidence was far less compelling than what we have in the present case."

"Are you aware that the Innocence Project says misleading fingerprint evidence leads to hundreds of wrongful convictions every year? Why is that?"

"I have no idea why they say that."

"But you have heard that before?"

"I have heard it."

"Do you disagree with it?"

"I have no way of knowing."

"But you would be willing to admit that fingerprint evidence has led to wrongful convictions. At least one that you know of personally."

Her eyelids fluttered. "Fine. Yes."

"Let's talk about your scientific procedure for a moment. When you talk about getting a match, jurors get visions of what they've seen on television, on CSI shows. High-tech labs and scientists running prints through computerized databases. But that's not your procedure, is it?"

"We do run prints through the FBI's IAFIS, when it's available."

"And since that only covers people who have attracted federal interest, like terrorists, how often in your experience has that led to a match?"

"Never."

"So after IAFIS strikes out, do you run the prints through some other computer database?"

"Unfortunately, we do not have equipment or records at that level of sophistication here. Few cities do."

"Then what did you do to determine whether the prints matched?"

"I brought my scientific expertise to bear."

"Meaning you eyeballed it, right? You held the two prints up, looked back and forth, and decided they were similar enough to call a match."

"That is essentially correct. And there's nothing wrong with that."

"Except—I wonder if you have perhaps misled the jury. You keep talking about your scientific expertise. But anybody could look at two pictures and reach a conclusion about whether they match, couldn't they? Children do that when they're working puzzles in *Highlights* magazine. 'Can you spot the differences?'"

"I think fingerprint analysis is more sophisticated than *Highlights* magazine."

"But at the end of the day, you looked at two pictures and decided whether they matched."

"And they did."

"Did they match perfectly? One hundred percent?"

"As I've already said, we did not have one-hundred-percent prints."

"But with respect to the partials, was it a perfect match?"

"It's never perfect. Fingerprints taken in the field are not perfect. They're dirty, smudged. Sometimes tainted with blood or body oils. You have to account for the realities of life."

"All of which is a fancy way of saying, no, ladies and gentlemen of the jury, the prints did not match perfectly."

"But they matched enough that I felt comfortable saying that the prints came from the defendant."

"Apparently you felt comfortable saying there was a one-hundred-percent match, although as it turns out, you didn't have one-hundred-percent prints, and what you had didn't match one-hundred percent either."

Jazlyn rose to her feet. "Objection, your honor. Mr. Pike has made his point, such that it is. Could we move on?"

The judge seemed sympathetic. "I do think you've made your point, counsel. Is there anything else?"

"Yes, your honor. I'm afraid so." He turned back to the witness. "How many people's prints did you compare to the prints on the gun?"

She squinted. "How many?"

"Exactly. Did you compare your partials with the prints of anyone other than my client?"

"No."

"How did you know to look at Gabriella's prints?"

"I was directed to do so by the prosecutors."

"Who had already decided Gabriella was guilty."

"As I understand it, they found the murder weapon in her backyard. That would make her the logical person to check prints on."

"I've already talked at length about the sketchy business of finding the gun in her backyard, the one place no one with half a brain would ever hide the murder weapon."

"Objection," Jazlyn said. "Move to strike."

"Sustained."

He continued unabated. "What I'm getting at is that the police asked you to look at one set of prints, and what a surprise, you found sufficient commonality to declare a one-hundred-percent match. Did you at any time look at any other prints, to see if you might find commonality there as well?"

"As I said, no."

"Did you look at Emilio Lòpez's prints? The gang leader at the scene of the murder? He's a suspect. Unless they turn him into a witness."

Jazlyn shot up. "Your honor! Objection. This is grossly prejudicial."

Judge Le pointed a gavel. "Mr. Pike, you are truly trying my patience."

He held up his hands. "I'm making a point, your honor. It's just frustrating having to wade through so much muck to get there. My point, Dr. Palmer, is that you didn't look at Emilio's prints, right?"

"True."

"Did you check the prints of Emilio's lieutenant, Luis González? Or the victim's brother, Diego Sanchez?"

"I've already said, I looked at no other prints."

"So you looked where the police asked you to look. And nowhere else. End of investigation. Tell the police what they want to hear, then quit."

"Your honor," Jazlyn said, "asked and answered."

"Agreed," Judge Le said. "Aren't you about done now, Mr. Pike?"

"There's one more thing."

The judge rolled her eyes.

"Dr. Palmer, with respect to the prints on the gun—is there any way for you to determine *when* those prints were made?"

"Not really. Sometimes, when prints are very old, they degrade."

"Did you see that here?"

"No."

"So those prints could have been left prior to the night of the shooting?"

"It's possible."

"What if the prints were placed two months before? When Gabriella bought the gun."

"I think I would know."

"Can you rule out the possibility? One-hundred percent?"

She sighed. "I suppose not."

"Thank you." He smiled at the judge. "And now I'm finished."

He thought he heard the judge whisper under her breath, *Thank goodness*.

CHAPTER THIRTY-FOUR

DAN HOPED JUDGE LE WOULD CALL IT QUITS FOR THE DAY. But there was still an hour and a half on the clock, and to his dismay, Jazlyn said the prosecution had a witness they could get on and off in that amount of time. Usually, when a prosecutor made offers like that, what they actually meant was that there was sufficient time for them to put on the direct examination. They didn't care whether there was time for cross. In fact, they probably hoped there wasn't. Everybody wanted to end the day on a strong note, so the jurors would go home mulling the as-yet unrebutted evidence. A cross-examination quickly covered the next day, early in the morning, when jurors were sleepy and wishing they had more coffee, might have less impact.

The next prosecution witness was a woman named Betty Fuller, a tourist, not a local. Print dress. Sandals. Friendship bracelet, probably from a child. Red nose. Bruise at the base of her neck.

Fuller happened to be walking down the sidewalk in the wee hours of the morning because she was having an allergy attack and hoped to find an all-night drugstore. Instead, she found something much worse. When she saw shadowy figures yelling at each other, she ducked behind a retaining wall on the outskirts of the hotel. After the firing started, she was too scared to move.

Eventually, Jazlyn brought her to the main point. "Did you recognize any of the people you saw in this confrontation?"

"I didn't recognize them at the time."

"But you recognize them now?"

Fuller pointed toward Gabriella. "She was there."

"Let the record reflect that the witness indicated the defendant was at the scene of the shooting."

Jazlyn turned back to the witness. "Please tell the jury what you saw."

"I saw her talking to a man about her height, also Hispanic. I couldn't hear what they said. He seemed extremely agitated. My impression was that she was trying to calm him down. Unsuccessfully."

"Were either of them holding anything?"

"The defendant was holding some kind of bag."

"Anything else?"

"After they talked briefly, she removed something from the bag and held it in her hand. A few moments later she extended her hand straight out from her shoulder. Like this." Fuller demonstrated what was clearly someone pointing a weapon.

"Could you see what she held?"

"I thought it was a gun. And a few seconds later, I heard a gun fire, several times. Her arm appeared to recoil in connection with the sounds. Then she disappeared."

"Could you see the body?"

"No."

"So she might have left to...tamper with the corpse?"

He sprang to his feet. "Objection. Leading."

Jazlyn nodded. "I'll withdraw that. Thank you, Ms. Fuller. I appreciate you coming today to offer your testimony. Your witness, Mr. Pike."

Before he stood, he glanced at the legal pad Maria passed over. She'd hastily scrawled a note.

She's just trying to help.

He understood, and appreciated the reminder. Fuller was not evil, nor was she part of any prosecution or police conspiracy, so there was no reason for an attack-dog approach. Which did not mean he couldn't expose the flaws in her testimony. He just needed to do so with a bit more finesse.

"Ms. Fuller, let me begin by echoing what the prosecutor has already said. I appreciate you being here today. I know you had to travel a long way and probably had better things to do. But we appreciate it."

Fuller nodded.

He cut to the chase. The videotape had already shown that Gabriella was at the scene of the crime, so there was no point in arguing about that. The only question was what came out of that bag, and whether Gabriella fired a weapon. "I noticed when you described what came out of the bag, you didn't exactly say it was a gun. Your words were, 'I thought it was a gun.'"

"That's correct."

"So will you acknowledge that you may have been mistaken?"

Fuller hesitated. "I was a long way off, but it looked like a gun to me. And her subsequent behavior reinforced my feeling that it was a gun."

"We'll get to the behavior in a minute. First I want to focus on what you saw. The murder weapon is a handgun, relatively small. I would think even in the daylight, from a distance, it would be difficult to know for certain what she held. But when you saw her it was nighttime, right?"

"That's correct."

"And there was no moon that night?"

"That's also correct."

"Some ambient light from the hotel signs. But basically, you were in the dark."

"That's true."

"Why do you think she held a gun?"

"I saw glints of light. It looked metallic."

"So what you're actually saying is that whatever she held, light reflected from it."

She shrugged. "I suppose."

"It might've been... a wrench?"

She tilted her head to one side.

"Or cellophane. Cellophane gives off light."

Fuller's eyebrows knitted. "Who would be carrying cellophane at two in the morning?"

"Do you know what gangs typically wrap drugs in?"

"No. I most certainly do not."

"If they planned a payoff, what would the money be wrapped in?"

"I'm sure I don't know."

"All in all, wouldn't it be more accurate to say you don't know what you saw in her hand?"

"I saw her extend her arm and point it outward, toward the other people." Again, she pantomimed holding a gun.

"A person might extend their arm for many reasons, don't you think? Like, for instance, if they're offering someone something, holding it out so they will take it, or at least see that it is being offered."

Fuller hesitated. "I don't think that's what I saw."

"In the darkness."

"I also heard gunshots. There's no question about the fact that gunshots occurred. And I saw her arm recoil. In coordination with the shots."

"Could you really tell, from your distance?" He reminded himself to be gentle. "Given your distance, and your undoubtedly terrified state, can you be sure?"

"It's... what I thought..."

"Gabriella heard the gunshots too. That might be a reason for pulling back her arm, don't you think? Maybe she was getting ready to retreat. You said, a few seconds later, she ran away."

"So did everybody who wasn't lying on the ground."

"Ms. Fuller, I'm sure you can understand why it's absolutely crucial that we be clear on what you did and did not see. The jury has heard too much evidence that under scrutiny turned out to be less than it was suggested to be. Are you certain you saw a gun?"

Fuller hedged. "I suppose I can't say I'm absolutely...certain."

"Could you tell me what kind of gun it was? Or even what color?"

"No."

"Can you say with certainty that you saw Gabriella fire a gun?"

"It's what—" She stopped. "No, I can't say it with absolute certainty."

"And you surely can't say that Gabriella fired the bullet that resulted in Sanchez' death, can you?"

"No."

"I appreciate your honesty. It's citizens like you that make the system work. No more questions."

CHAPTER THIRTY-FIVE

THAT EVENING, DAN RETURNED TO THE OFFICE, WHICH HE still couldn't bring himself to call an office, because it was so un-office-like.

"I thought the trial went spectacularly well today," Jimmy said, bubbling with enthusiasm. "You're like Superman in there, crusading for truth, justice, and the American way."

Maria smiled. "He was rather impressive, wasn't he? Mr. K was right about you."

"Mr. K is always right," Garrett added.

"I'll be honest," Jimmy said. "I thought this case was hopeless before we started. But now we're two days in, and I don't think Jazlyn scored a point. What has she proven? Gabriella was there and she bought the murder weapon a couple of months before. Honestly, that's about it."

"And I don't think that will be enough," Maria said. "Especially once Dan starts hammering the jury about reasonable doubt."

Garrett leaned back into the sofa. "Is anyone worried about the possibility that we might not be... serving justice? Does that concern you, Dan?"

"I'm not sure what you mean. If we keep the government from railroading someone, we're serving justice."

Garrett's head lowered. "I just don't want to be a part of a...miscarriage."

Jimmy peered at him. "Are you saying you think Gabriella is guilty?"

Garrett shrugged uncomfortably. "I don't know. I don't think any of us know. But I do think something has to be done about what's happening in this town. These gangland wars are getting out of control. Sometimes I feel like law and order is disappearing."

"The cure for that," Maria said, "is better education and more job opportunities. Not putting the entire Hispanic community behind bars."

"I agree with you," Garrett said. "But we have to support the people trying to protect us. And the prosecutors."

He knew Garrett tended to be conservative, but he sensed something more going on. "You think I'm attacking the police? And the prosecutors?"

"Well...aren't you?"

"No. I'm just doing my job. But there's more going on here than we know. And I don't believe Gabriella is the criminal puppet master behind it all."

Maria went to the door and returned with more pizza than they could eat in a week. He noted it was delivered by Delmonico's. One of the nicest restaurants in town, one he knew for a fact had the best pizza. He didn't know they delivered. He suspected that was just for special customers.

He took a bite of the specialty white pizza—five kinds of cheese and alfredo rather than tomato sauce—and his eyes rolled into his head. "That is absolutely delicious."

Maria smiled. "The secret ingredient is artichoke."

He raised a finger. "That's what I was tasting. I've got to try making this. It's fabulous." He glanced at Jimmy. "Have you tried a slice?"

Jimmy shook his head. "Thanks. I'm still a meat eater." He reached for a slice of pepperoni.

Maria winced. "He even eats sausage. Ick."

"The body needs the occasional animal-based protein."

"It so doesn't," Maria said firmly. "But that's all right. We love you even if you are a barbarian."

Jimmy took another bite. "Vegetarians are so self-righteous."

"We'll win you over in time." She took another slice. "What do you think Jazlyn will do next, Dan? How will she start the third day?"

"I've been wondering about that myself. She knows that even jurors who come into the courtroom assuming everyone accused is guilty are likely to be underwhelmed by the case she's put on so far."

"So what will she do?"

He shrugged. "The most likely ploy is Emilio."

Jimmy cut in. "I stopped by the DA's office on my way out today. A friend told me that they still hadn't made a deal with him. And I don't think he'd lie to me."

"Jazlyn would notify me if she'd clinched a deal. But I suspect she's working on it as we speak. She needs something to energize her case. He must be holding out. Probably asking for total immunity, for more than this incident. Possibly an expunged record. Possibly even witness protection. I'll bet Jazlyn's willing to give him more tonight than she was before. She needs him."

"This sort of testimony should be forbidden," Maria said. "It's basically witness tampering. If we paid someone to testify we'd be disbarred, but prosecutors do it all the time, offering people immunity or early parole. It's a complete double standard."

"Agreed. But we have to live with it. Has anyone talked to Esperanza lately?"

"I called the detention center today. I was allowed to talk to her briefly. She did not sound good."

He tried not to let anything show on his face. "How do you mean?"

"That normally upbeat, calm girl was distraught, excitable, edgy. Even screamed at one point. Not like herself at all."

"Worse than when we visited her?"

"Much worse. She's desperate to get out of there."

"Have they isolated her? Crenshaw promised."

"Yes. And that might be part of the problem. She feels cut off from everyone, even more so than before. I wasn't going to tell you about this, but...I don't think she can take this much longer. Without suffering some kind of...permanent damage."

CHAPTER THIRTY-SIX

DAN WAS NOT REMOTELY SURPRISED WHEN HE ENTERED THE courtroom the next day and Jazlyn told him she was calling Emilio as her next witness. What did surprise him was seeing the mayor, Camila Perez, sitting in the back corner of the gallery. Was that because she heard Emilio was testifying? She was tucked away in the farthest corner, but there was no way she could get here, or sit there, without being noticed.

Jazlyn gave him a copy of the immunity agreement, which had been signed late the previous night. While he and his crew were scarfing pizza, Jazlyn and Emilio were apparently locked in mortal combat. Each had something the other wanted, and each made it as difficult as possible to get. Emilio was granted full immunity, not only for all crimes relating to the shooting at the Trademark but for any and all crimes, discovered or undiscovered, occurring prior to that date. He had not asked for witness protection, but given this clean slate, perhaps he didn't need it. When he walked out of this courtroom, regardless of what he said on the stand, he had a squeaky-clean record.

"I do not want that man to testify," Gabriella said, whispering into his ear as the jury filed back into the courtroom. "I do not trust him."

"You're right not to trust him," he whispered back. "The only person Emilio cares about is Emilio. But there's nothing I can do about this."

"He will lie. He is the devil incarnate."

"Again, not disagreeing. I'll do my best to punch holes in any lies during cross-examination."

"It will not help. He is too smooth, too clever. Too experienced at the lying game. And he hates me. Even as I worked for him, he hated me, because he knew he could not control me. He could not have me."

He decided not to inquire into the details of what that might mean. He laid his hand over hers. He could see that some of the jurors were watching them. No telling what they might read into her current expression. "Poker face, Gabriella. Poker face."

Jazlyn called Emilio to the witness stand. They spent the first fifteen minutes establishing him as a legitimate businessman. But she followed with a series of surprises that not only caught him off guard, but reminded him why Jazlyn had risen as far and as fast in the prosecutor's department as she had. She was smart.

After establishing that Emilio had lawful enterprises, she introduced the topic of drug running. She knew that he would do it on cross if she didn't, and she knew it was possible to call any number of witnesses, including law enforcement officers, who would testify that there was at the very least a strong suspicion that Emilio was involved in drug pushing on the Southside. As Emilio told the story, though, drugs were something he had done in his early days, when he was young, before he knew better. Which was easy to admit, since he now had immunity for all past crimes. He explained that when he was fifteen, he was groomed by a man named Hector—the Emilio of the day. Hector gave Emilio his training, both as a businessman and a gangster. After Hector was rubbed out, Emilio took over. But he claimed he transitioned out of drug running as quickly as possible.

"I saw what drugs did to my neighborhood," he said, with an

almost palpable earnestness. "How it destroyed my friends, my family." He lowered his eyes. "My mother's still a hopeless drug addict, despite all I tried to do for her. I have seen how drugs wreck people's lives. I didn't want that to be my legacy."

Emilio was not only coming across as earnest, but as impressively intelligent. Most of the street jive had somehow been bled out of his speech. "I took office space down by the pier where I could afford it and tried to learn from the businessmen who surrounded me. I started by getting a piece of the fishing business, so lucrative here, and then moved into import and export. I specialized in south-of-the-border electronics—cheap stuff that large corporations sometimes overlook because the profit margins aren't large enough. If you do enough business, though, even small profit margins add up." He smiled. "I couldn't afford to get into a luxury market. So I got into a volume market."

"And you were successful, weren't you?"

"Success came slowly, and after much hard work. But yes. After about five years, we were doing more than a million dollars of business annually. A few years after that, we had a million dollars of profit."

"What did you do with all that money?"

"I created jobs. That was my goal, first and foremost. I wanted to create alternatives for the people on the Southside. I don't believe those neighborhoods are infested by drugs and gangs because my people are inherently bad. It's all economics. There are no good jobs. Sometimes there are no jobs at all. They can't afford to go to the University of Miami and get four-year business degrees. They take the path of least resistance, the jobs that are available. And in our neighborhood, too often that means gangs. I wanted to create an alternative."

"Some people believe you're a gang leader," Jazlyn said.

"I suppose that depends on how you define 'gang leader.' I had employees. I had people who worked for me. And we frequently operated in those poorer neighborhoods. But we were creating good jobs and promoting honest business operations. We were not involved in illegal activities. And we were certainly not involved in turf wars or shootings. That's what I was trying to get away from."

He heard Gabriella mutter under her breath. *Bullshit.*

He shot her a look. *Poker face.*

"Did you know the defendant? Gabriella Valdez?"

"I did. She worked for me, not full-time, but occasionally, when I had something for her. She was basically a gofer. She didn't have the training or experience to work in a more professional capacity. I have training programs, but she didn't want to do that. Her options were limited. I used her when I could. She was raising an orphan girl named Esperanza. Sweet little thing. I knew that created a financial strain."

"Tell us about the victim. Jorge Sanchez."

An unpleasant expression crossed Emilio's face. "A disgusting human being. I didn't wish him dead. But then again..." He glanced at the jurors. "No one will miss him."

He couldn't help but be impressed by what a fine job Emilio was doing on the witness stand. He didn't believe any of it. Emilio's constant arrests made it hard to believe he had left the drug business behind. But the man on the witness stand was not the smirking arrogant thug he had represented so often. He didn't know if this was the result of personal growth or coaching by Jazlyn, but he came off as a transformed man.

"Was Sanchez also a businessman?"

"If you want to use that word. Of course, he did have some cover businesses. He had a tequila line, if I'm not mistaken. Reasonably successful, good enough to launder money through. But that was not where the majority of his wealth came from. He bought and sold people."

"Are you talking about sex trafficking?"

"Prostitution, both genders, but mostly women. Sometimes adults, sometimes children. Transsexuals, bondage freaks, virgins —he catered to a wide variety of tastes. Word on the street was that he came to Florida to expand his business and to recruit more...employees."

"Did you have anything to do with his death?"

"Absolutely not. As I said, I didn't wish him dead, but I won't pretend we aren't better off without him. He was a blight on humanity. He gave my people a bad name and contributed to the stereotypical bigotry we fight to this day. And he was targeting my neighborhood."

"Did you put out a hit on him?"

"No. Never. I don't do that."

"Some have suggested that the shooting at the Trademark was a trap you laid for him."

"More like a trap he laid for me. Do you think I normally would be out on the street at that time of night? My assistant got word of an offer from Sanchez' camp. I was told that in exchange for a sum of money, Sanchez would release twenty women, women I knew to be sex slaves."

He watched Emilio carefully. This was not the same story he told back at the jailhouse.

"Did you believe it?" Jazlyn asked.

"Of course I did," Emilio replied. "Sanchez has sold women before, usually when he needed money fast. I didn't even know Sanchez was in the United States till I got the message. Apparently he'd been here for some time, keeping a low profile. But keeping a low profile is expensive. I know Sanchez has bank accounts all around the world, but he might not have been able to access them without revealing his location."

"And were you prepared to deliver the cash?"

"I was happy to do so, if it would set sex slaves free."

"Did you consider contacting the police?"

"That would not have been smart. At best, they might've arrested him. But they never would've found the women. By keeping the pipeline open, I increased the possibility that not only these women, but others, might be released."

"Did you know any of the women in question?"

"I knew at least one of them." He nodded toward the defendant's table. "Gabriella's younger sister. Her name is Luciana."

He heard a small gasp escape from Gabriella's mouth. She lowered her head.

He felt a chill race down his spine. *What was this?*

And what else had she not told him?

He exchanged a cold glance with Maria. She understood the significance as well as he did. Emilio wasn't just exonerating himself. He was giving Gabriella an additional motive for murdering Sanchez.

Emilio continued. "Gabriella very much wanted Luciana set free. Apparently her sister had fallen apart mentally. It happens a lot to women trapped in that barbaric, humiliating lifestyle."

"So Gabriella urged you to pave Luciana's path to freedom."

"Yes. And I tried to do it."

"Did you ask the defendant to be present on the night of the shooting?"

"She insisted upon it. I didn't want anyone there who didn't need to be there. But she came anyway. Said she wanted to make sure her sister was set free. Gabriella also feared that immigration would turn Esperanza over to Sanchez and that he would turn the girl into one of his prostitutes."

"We've all seen the video taken at the Trademark. Gabriella appears to be talking to you."

"Yes."

"What did you talk about?"

"I urged her to go home. Although I hoped this business transaction could be executed peaceably, I knew an outbreak of violence was possible. I brought security people of my own."

"The video also shows that she was carrying a satchel or bag of some sort. What was in the satchel?"

"She brought a gun."

There was an audible gasp in the courtroom. He wanted to turn around and see who it was, but he knew if he did, the jury would follow his lead.

"She brought a gun to this... business transaction?"

"I did not want her to. I thought it was an extremely bad idea. If anyone saw the gun, it could trigger violence. And sadly, that's exactly what happened."

"Please tell the jury what occurred, as you remember it."

He pressed his lips together, as if gathering his thoughts. "Gabriella removed a small silver handgun from the bag. It was a powerful weapon, small but efficient. I immediately told her to put it away, but she didn't. Sanchez' men saw it. They of course drew their weapons. Gabriella demanded the release of her sister, pointing the gun at Sanchez. She fired twice. And then we had a shootout."

"Did any of your men have guns?"

"Of course."

"Did they shoot anyone?"

"No, though they did fire. But the only one who killed anyone...was Gabriella."

More audible reaction from the courtroom, except this time, he was certain at least part of it came from the jury box.

"You're certain of that?"

"I saw it with my own eyes. I screamed at her to stop, but she didn't listen. She shot him twice. Killed him."

"She must be a very good shot."

"She's a crack shot. Trained."

"Was the exchange ever completed?"

"How could it be? Sanchez was dead. The operation was blown."

"Were the women freed?"

"Some of them. Including Gabriella's sister. I believe immigration authorities found them tied up in a storage locker the next day. Thank God. With Sanchez gone, they might've rotted there forever."

Jazlyn paused for a moment, giving the jurors time to absorb what they had heard. "Just to be clear, Emilio, let me ask the question straight up. Did Gabriella shoot Sanchez?"

"Yes."

"Are you certain of that?"

"I am. She hated that man. She blamed him for her sister's breakdown. And she believed he would force Esperanza into his sex slavery ring. She wanted to stop him. So she killed him."

CHAPTER THIRTY-SEVEN

"WHY DIDN'T YOU TELL ME ABOUT YOUR SISTER?"

Gabriella's head hung low. She did not respond.

"Do you remember when I told you to give me everything? *Everything?* When I told you that keeping secrets would make it impossible for me to do my job?"

"Yes, but—"

"Do you realize you just stuck your head into a noose?"

Maria cut in. "Ok, let's all calm down. Take a breath."

They were in the consultation space near the courtroom, waiting for the trial to continue. "You realize this revelation undermines our entire trial strategy. Everything you planned."

Maria remained calm. "Trial plans are made to be modified. We'll cope."

"I don't see how." He turned back to his client. "The worst of it is, you've not only killed your own chances of survival, you've virtually guaranteed that Esperanza will be deported." His voice rose. "And sent straight into that sex-trafficking ring!"

"Dan!"

Gabriella covered her face, tears streaming between her fingers. "I wanted to protect her. That's why I did everything. I thought if people knew about my sister, they would assume I was guilty. And then where would Esperanza be?"

"Better off than she is now."

"And I was afraid no one would help Luciana if they thought she was connected to a murderer. To drug pushers. She needs help. Her mind...it is completely shattered."

"We have to talk to her."

"I did not even know she was in the country until Emilio told me, the night of the killing. And she could not assist you. She's...gone."

"We could have found help for her. We have resources. But now we can't do a damn thing for anyone."

Maria laid her hand on his shoulder and whispered. "Dan, court will resume in a few minutes. You need to get a grip."

He wanted to say—What's the point? But he kept it in check. Maria was right. The jury had just heard devastating eyewitness testimony backed by a credible motive. If he didn't come up with something fast, it was all over for Esperanza.

"Did anyone else know about your sister?"

"I don't know. Maybe Ramon Alvarez. I told you he was at my house the night of the shooting."

"Great. Another potential loose cannon."

What he needed was someone else who witnessed the shooting. If Emilio was the only eyewitness, the jury would give his testimony disproportionate weight.

He hated dealing with so-called eyewitness testimony. Inevitably, jurors treated eyewitnesses as if they were the most dependable, most unchallengeable form of testimony. In reality, forensic evidence was far more reliable. Unfortunately, forensic evidence tended to be dull. It was easy to confuse jurors with scientific matters. But an eyewitness, someone who claimed they saw what happened with their own eyes? That was hard to beat.

In truth, eyewitness testimony was inherently unreliable. People believe that their memories are inviolate, that a memory is like a book shelved in the library. You take the book down later and read it just as it was originally written. Recent scientific studies proved that is completely untrue. Memories are more like computer files, changed every time they're accessed. Unconsciously, people tend to improve stories, to solidify or rewrite what they heard or saw.

Memories are even more unreliable if the witness is influenced by other factors, like what they read in the newspaper or saw on TV, or saw in a lineup, or heard from police officers. Prosecution witnesses are subjected to a daily diet of people reminding them what they saw or should have seen. It was virtually impossible to not be influenced by that. Studies showed that memories can be planted, even completely created, in less than a week's time. The so-called eyewitness can come to completely believe something that never happened.

They returned to the courtroom. He had no idea how to handle this cross-examination, and Maria wasn't passing along any brilliant suggestions. Gabriella insisted that Emilio's testimony was a pack of lies, but they certainly sounded plausible. Emilio's story made sense, and in his experience, that's what persuaded juries most. A coherent story that simply made sense.

Jimmy suggested making some kind of self-defense plea, but he knew that wouldn't fly. Gabriella was the one who brought the gun, and at least according to Emilio, she was the one who started the gunfight. Not the best scenario for a self-defense claim.

Another possibility would be to claim that she acted in defense of another. Sanchez did present a tangible threat to Esperanza. But to make that claim work, they would have to show an immediate threat. If Sanchez had pointed a gun to Esperanza's head, she might be able to get away with executing him. But absent that immediacy, no way. Her option was to go to the police, or perhaps the immigration authorities.

He decided to start the cross by discussing the immunity agreement itself. Surely the jurors would be somewhat skeptical of testimony that so clearly had been bought and paid for.

"Hello, Emilio. Good to see you again."

Emilio nodded.

"Last night you executed an immunity agreement with the prosecutors." He held it up so the jury could see it. "Would you please explain what that means?"

Emilio shrugged. "I agreed to testify. They agreed to drop all charges against me."

"And not just charges relating to this incident. All charges arising at any time prior to the shootout."

"That's the deal."

"Why would a legit businessman like you be worried about charges?"

"Just being careful."

"Why would they go after the savior of the Southside?"

"Prosecutors target Hispanics. You know it's true. You've represented enough people in my community. When the cops need a patsy, they drive south."

Harder to argue with something you suspect is accurate. "Do you have any evidence of that?"

"No one in my hood has any doubt about it. There are also many police officers who resent my financial success. They don't like it when, to quote a phrase I've heard many times, the homie gets uppity."

"So you agreed to testify for the prosecution, and in exchange, they gave you a get-out-of-jail-free card. They wouldn't do that unless you offered them something valuable, right?"

"I suppose."

"Basically, you agreed to finger Gabriella."

"I agreed to tell them what happened."

"Gabriella is from your neighborhood, isn't she?"

"True."

"We just heard about how loyal you are to people back in the hood, and the people who work for you, but today you're throwing one to the dogs. To save yourself."

"Objection." Jazlyn rose to her feet. "Argumentative."

He never understood why people made that objection. Being argumentative was the whole point of cross-examination.

"Sustained."

Didn't matter. The jury knew what he was saying. "If you told the prosecutor you had no idea who shot Sanchez, would they still offer you immunity?"

Again Jazlyn objected. "Calls for speculation."

"Sustained."

"Your honor, I'm trying to show that the witness could only get what he wanted if he offered them something good."

"And you have made that point, Mr. Pike. Move on."

"Emilio, you talked at length about your successful business ventures. But the truth is, you've been unable to oversee the day-to-day business for some time, right?"

"Sadly true. The police persecution I mentioned has kept me out of the office."

"In fact, Luis González has been running the business for several months now, correct?"

"Yes."

"And how long has he been with you?"

"Almost from the beginning."

"Isn't it true that he's the one who actually steered your operation toward more legitimate enterprises?"

"He has been a great employee, that's for sure. In the early days, he was one of the few people I had who knew anything about finance. He's got a degree in it now."

"Isn't it true that you and he have disagreed more than once about the direction of the company?"

"Yes."

"And isn't that because he wanted to eliminate the illegal activities like drugs, while you were reluctant to give up such a lucrative operation?"

"That is absolutely not true."

"In fact, you're been hoping to get into sex trafficking, haven't you?"

"No. That's a repulsive suggestion."

"That might be the reason you wanted Sanchez taken out. So you could take over his business."

Anger flashed across Emilio's face. "That is a lie."

"That's what Luis told me."

"I don't believe you."

"He said getting you out of the way was the best thing that ever happened to his business."

"You lying sack—"

Jazlyn rose. "Objection."

He turned toward her. "Any grounds? Or just trying to interrupt the flow?"

"This is provocative and non-probative."

The judge shook her head. "Overruled. And please don't interrupt again unless you have a real objection."

Jazlyn sat down, not chastised. She did what she needed to do, curbed Emilio before he blew all credibility. He wasn't sure he could get Emilio worked up again. But he had to try. "What if I called Luis to the witness stand? Do you think he'd tell the truth?"

Emilio's eyes narrowed. "I have known Luis many years. I do not believe he would lie."

"What if someone offered him an immunity agreement? People will say anything if they're offered immunity."

"Objection!" Jazlyn almost shouted. "This is outrageous."

Nah. This was pretty standard cross-examination. But she wanted the jurors to see her outrage. "Your honor, I'm entitled to question the validity of the witness' testimony."

The judge nodded. "Agreed. Overruled. But counsel, I would like to hear questions that have more probative value and less showboating."

In other words, stop asking questions that are only designed to make the witness angry. But he had no intention of shifting gears. "You've mentioned that the police don't believe you've stopped drug running. Is that because the police department is out to get you?"

"They are out to get everyone in my neighborhood. But yeah, they especially target someone who escaped the hood and draws down a whole lot more bacon than they'll ever make in their bigoted lives."

"You really hate police officers, don't you?"

"No. You know what Tupac says. The hate you give, man. I try not to hate. Just perpetuates the cycle."

"I bet that's hard sometimes. What do you think of Officer Treadway, the man who found the gun?"

"We know him. He's been around the hood for a long time."

"Would you say he was friendly to your community?"

"I wouldn't say any of them are friendly to my community."

"Do you believe he found a gun in Gabriella's backyard two days after the shooting?"

"Objection," Jazlyn said. "Outside the scope."

"That one I will sustain." The judge gave him a stern look. "Please limit cross-examination to the scope of direct."

"Of course. Emilio, isn't it true that the police arrested you shortly after the shootout?"

"Yes."

"Why was that?"

He shrugged. "Round up the usual suspects."

"Oh, there was more to it than that, wasn't there? You were at the scene of the crime and you had a bad-on against Sanchez."

"I didn't like what he was doing. Sex trafficking is vile."

"Worse than drug running?"

"Much. And I'm not saying drug pushing is good. But turning women into prostitutes. That's beyond the pale. That's rot-in-hell-for-eternity stuff."

"So you wanted Sanchez dead."

"I don't want anyone dead, man. I just want us to all get along. Be good to one another."

"What a philosophical soul you are these days. Practically Gandhi."

Jazlyn rose. "Objection."

"Grounds?" the judge asked.

"Infantile sarcasm."

"Sustained. And this is the last time I'm putting up with it, Mr. Pike. One more remark like that and I hope your colleague is ready to take over for the remainder of the trial."

Okay, maybe it was time to chill. But he still hoped to get a rise out of Emilio. "So you were arrested and the only way you were getting off the hook was if you convinced the police someone else committed the crime."

"I don't know what you're talking about, man."

"And you didn't want to lose anybody important to your operation, so you threw Gabriella to the pigs."

"I told them what happened. That's it."

"You realize, if you help them put Gabriella behind bars, you've doomed Esperanza. Sanchez might be dead, but his brother continues the operation. And he's now her closest relative."

"I'm just telling what I saw." Emilio rose slightly, bouncing on his toes. "I don't like the truth. But it is what it is."

"And you don't care if Esperanza is deported."

"I think she might be better off away from Gabriella. That woman is dangerous."

"You say you're an enemy of sex trafficking. But you just doomed a little girl to a lifetime of it."

"All I did was tell the truth."

"I get that you had to lie to save yourself. But dooming an innocent child to a life of slavery and prostitution to save your own sorry skin—that's rot-in-hell-for-eternity stuff."

"I ain't lying!" Emilio shouted. "I just told what happened."

"You told what saved your butt. But will it save your soul?"

"*What you expect me to do?* They were gonna put me away till the end of time! And they—" Emilio caught himself and fell silent.

He held off on questions for several beats, letting the jurors' imaginations finish Emilio's sentence. "Yes, that's what I thought happened. No more questions."

CHAPTER THIRTY-EIGHT

DAN MET WITH HIS COHORTS DURING THE LUNCH BREAK, BUT it was a despondent affair. Even the pizza seemed tasteless.

"Well," Jimmy said, wiping his chin with a napkin, "that was a thing that happened."

"Total switcheroo," Maria murmured.

He knew what she meant. Last night, they'd been patting themselves on the back, talking about how ineffective Jazlyn's prosecution had been so far. But she turned it around in a heartbeat. He did the best he could on cross-ex, but he doubted it was enough. Whether he wanted to admit it or not, all the evidence supported Emilio's story. All the evidence suggested Gabriella was guilty.

"Do we know anything about this sister? Luciana?" Maria asked.

"Not yet," Garrett replied. "But I've already started making calls."

"Have something by the close of business." He didn't want to seem like he was giving orders. But he was panicked. This couldn't wait.

Garrett nodded. "On it."

BY ONE O'CLOCK, THEY WERE BACK TO WORK. THEY FIRST MET in chambers and dealt with some procedural matters, pending motions, judicial docket issues, and a concern about juror number 11, who appeared to be dozing during the last witness' testimony. And if a juror could fall asleep during Emilio's testimony, he was apparently not gigantically engaged. By the unanimous consent of all parties, the juror was removed, sent home, and replaced by a more attentive alternate.

Back in the courtroom, Jazlyn called two more police officers who were not completely repetitive or redundant, but largely reinforced what had already been established. Gabriella was at the scene of the crime. She was found at her home afterwards. And her gun was found in the backyard two days later. One of the police officers thought he saw Gabriella running down a street not far from the Trademark, but that was the least of the cop's worries at the time and he didn't attempt to stop her. After the gunfire exchange, people scattered like rats from a sinking ship, and who could blame them?

He didn't even bother cross-examining these witnesses. He didn't think they contributed much, and harassing them over trivia would only make their slight testimony seem more important.

To his happy surprise, come four o'clock, Jazlyn said the prosecution only had one remaining witness, and they couldn't possibly finish in an hour or two. Judge Le reluctantly adjourned court for the day, hoping to finish the prosecution case the following morning.

Even happier news. Garrett tracked down Gabriella's sister, Luciana. She wasn't in a detention center.

She was in a psychiatric ward.

"How did this happen?" he asked. They left as soon as court adjourned, hoping to get in before the hospital closed for the day. Maria drove, of course. Garrett sat in the back seat, guiding them. Jimmy returned to the office to do the usual post-trial postmortem and to get their ducks in a row for the next day. There were several possible witnesses Jazlyn might call for her clincher. Jimmy wanted to figure out who it was. He was hoping to call some friends, learn if anybody had been spotted coming in or out of the DA's office.

"Apparently Luciana had a total mental breakdown," Garrett said. "She's illegal, though not here of her own volition. Found in that storage locker with the others and they couldn't handle her in the detention center."

She was in San Angelo Medical, a government facility. Not the place he would have chosen, but it was better for someone with mental health issues to be in any kind of facility than out on the streets like the homeless—most of whom also suffered from mental illness.

"Is anyone caring for her?"

"I'm sure they are," Garrett answered. "But there's only so much they can do. They're basically just biding time until Immigration deems her safe to deport. And then it will be back over the border for her."

"Is there anything we can do? If she's a critical witness, I don't want her disappearing suddenly."

Garrett shook his head. "I don't think she's going to be of any use to you. I don't think this interview is going to be of any use to you. The attendant I spoke to indicated that Luciana was barely coherent."

"I'll take my chances. They'll let us see her?"

Garrett tilted his head. "I may have... exaggerated the urgency of the situation somewhat. But yes, under direct supervision by the floor administrator, they will allow us to speak to her. For whatever it's worth."

"It's always worth a try. Especially now."

Garrett continued. "She's been sexually abused by Sanchez and his customers for a long time. Probably since childhood. Which sadly, was not that long ago."

"Prostitution?"

"Of the worst sort. Bought and sold. Farmed out to people with...depraved tastes. In some cases, to people with a predilection for sadism. And I don't mean the fun Fifty-Shades-of-Gray kind. I mean the real deal. Violence. Torture."

Maria closed her eyes. "Why am I starting to feel not sorry that Sanchez no longer inhabits this planet?"

His lips pursed. "And that feeling, of course, is exactly what Jazlyn and Emilio are trying to suggest motivated Gabriella. Revulsion about what happened to her sister, what might happen to Esperanza. Let's face it, it's a credible motive. You're feeling it now. If Sanchez were still alive and I put a gun in your hand..."

"I wouldn't kill anyone!" Maria said.

"You might be tempted."

"Yes." Her eyes darkened. "I might well be tempted."

SAN ANGELO WAS PROBABLY A NICE FACILITY FIFTY YEARS AGO, Dan mused, but now it needed a serious infusion of funding. Or demolition.

Inside, they met the supervisor on duty, a woman named Catherine Broglie. She seemed distant, but cooperative. Heavyset. No nonsense. White dress a size too small. Blunt-cut red hair.

"I've had lawyers in before," she explained. "It's going to be a complete waste of time, but I don't have the budget to deal with subpoenas."

"I appreciate your cooperation," he said. If that was the right word.

"Do not rile her," Broglie said, pointing a finger. "She'll get upset sufficiently on her own. Don't fan the flames. Her deportation papers have already been filed. We're just trying to keep her alive and calm enough to travel. Understood?"

"Understood." He quickly read the file. It didn't have much information. "You know anything more about her?"

Broglie gave him an impatient look. "How could I? She can't tell me anything. Babbles incoherently. The people who transferred her didn't know anything. She's been abused and tortured. Exposed to mind-altering drugs. Took a severe blow to the head. We don't know what happened to her before she was found in that locker. She's never been visited by friends or family."

Ten minutes later, Broglie led them into a much smaller room. No decorations. A metal table in the center and chairs on either side.

A moment later, they brought in Luciana. Tiny. Emaciated. Red eyes, like she'd been crying for weeks. Discoloration across one side of her head. Chewed nails. Tear in the sleeve of her gown. He assumed she was being fed, but you couldn't tell to look at her. Her eyes seemed sunken and hollow. Her hair, what was left of it, was a mess. She was in a wheelchair.

He didn't need his acute powers of observation to realize that this woman was in a bad way. And wouldn't live much longer unless something changed.

He had suggested that Maria take the lead. The woman might respond better to a female questioner. But Maria declined. "I don't want to wimp out," she said, "but I don't think I can hold it together. You're going to have to take this one."

He introduced himself. "May I call you Luciana?"

She stared at him, head tilted at a slight angle, as if he were an interesting bug she'd spotted on the wall.

"I'm representing Gabriella, your older sister. She's been charged with a horrible crime, but I'm convinced she didn't do it. That's why we want to talk to you. We're hoping you can give us information that will help her."

Still no response.

He leaned forward slightly. "You know Gabriella, right? Your sister? Your friend?"

"*Amigos?*" Her head twitched. "No amigos. No...friends. Friends, friends, friends. Do you have friends?"

The trembling was slight, but it was there, just the same. If he hadn't known better, he might wonder if she had Parkinson's. "I do."

"No friends. No friends. No friends."

"Do you know someone named Gabriella?"

The woman stared back at him.

He had to snap her out of it somehow. "What about Sanchez? Do you know a man named Sanchez?"

Her eyes widened and watered. The trembling intensified. "*¿Dónde? ¿Dónde?* Keep away!"

He reached across the table. "He's gone. Dead. Sanchez can't hurt you anymore."

She pushed up as if to leave. He noticed she was strapped to the chair. "Don't let them near me!"

Them. Not him. Them.

Out the corner of his eye, he saw Broglie was not happy.

"It's okay," he said. "Sanchez is not here. Sanchez is dead. Very dead."

"His brother?"

At last. A sensible question. "Diego Sanchez is nowhere near here. You have people protecting you. No one can get in. No one can hurt you."

She calmed slightly.

"Regardless of what has been done to you in the past, you're safe now."

"*Seguro?* No. Not safe. Never safe. No one is safe."

"These people are taking care of you, aren't they?"

"They? They? Don't let them near me!"

"Your sister is in danger."

Her breathing slowed. The twitching stopped.

"You remember your sister Gabriella?"

"Gabriella wants to help me. But all women—powerless."

Maria leaned in. "That's changing, ma'am. Slowly."

"Nothing changes. Nothing changes." Her eyes seemed wild and unfocused. "Nothing changes Sanchez."

"Except death. He can't hurt you. He can't hurt Gabriella."

Luciana nodded her head as if to the beat of a private song. "Gabriella is strong. She stood up to him. She knew what...happened."

"What...did happen...to you?"

"So young. So innocent. An orphan. The nuns could not take care of me. No money, no food. The men said they would care for me. I would have the best of everything."

"So you went with them?"

"I did as I was told. Men. Filthy men. Whips. Knives. Pricks." All at once, she jerked her gown off her left shoulder, exposing herself. "See this?" The scar ran down from her shoulder almost to the tip of her breast, red and prominent. He had to look away. "No one cared what the men did. Anything was permitted, if they had money. Do this. Do that. Come to America. I came."

"Why were you brought to America?" he asked.

"Sanchez wanted me."

He was puzzled. But to be fair, they weren't certain why Sanchez was here, either.

Luciana suddenly lurched forward, as far as her restraints would permit. "You must protect Gabriella. *Por favor!*"

"I'm trying. But Sanchez is dead and she's been accused of his murder."

For the first time, a smile played on Luciana's lips. "I hope it is true."

He felt a shiver race down his spine.

This conversation was not going the direction he had hoped. Probably unrealistic, expecting something of value to come from a conversation with someone so clearly suffering from mental illness. "Did you see anyone else? After you came to the United States? Did Sanchez have any other visitors?"

"Many. They talk. Talk, talk, talk. Franchise."

The sudden insertion of business jargon startled him. "Someone wanted to take over Sanchez' business? Or start another business like it?

"They need women. More women."

"Who were these men? The ones talking. Did you know any names?"

"They never told me names."

"Can you describe them?"

"Ghosts. Demons. *Diablos*."

Damn. "What else did they talk about?"

"Sanchez liked to give his visitors a gift." Her eyes were sunken and cold. "I was the gift. I ran. I escaped." She started rocking again. "But they caught me. They always caught me."

He tried to keep his churning stomach from spewing. "Can you describe these men?"

It was as if he was watching a flashback in someone else's brain. Her rocking accelerated, back and forth in the chair. "Don't let them near me. Don't let them take me again. Let me die!"

He knew this conversation would not continue much longer. "Please, Luciana, think. Can you describe the men? Or tell me their names?"

"The eyes," she said, her whole body trembling. "The eyes. It's the eyes. He wants me."

"The eyes? What eyes? Whose eyes?"

"The eyes, man!" she screamed. "The eyes, man!"

Maria cut in. "Can you tell us anything more?"

"I ran and ran and ran. They put us in a box. They used the needle." She was hysterical, ranting, screaming, rocking with enough force to stretch her bonds to the limit. "Then the police put me in a cell. Now here. Don't let them hurt me! Don't let them!"

Broglie cut in. "Okay. This conversation is over." She reached down and tried to comfort Luciana.

"Let me die!" Luciana screamed, spittle flying from her lips. "Let me die!"

Even as they wheeled her away, she continued to scream. "The eyes man. Please make him stop. *Por favor! Please!*"

CHAPTER THIRTY-NINE

ONE SECOND AFTER DAN TOOK A SEAT AT THE DEFENSE TABLE, one of Jazlyn's many flunkies brought him a note. The fact that Jazlyn was using a flunky, and that the flunky disappeared a second after he delivered the message, suggested he wasn't going to like what he read.

He was right about that.

One quick scan and he crumpled it in his hand, rose, and stalked the halls for Jazlyn. He found her just outside the DA's office, leading the usual entourage to court. "A minute?"

She tried to play it cool. "May I ask why?"

"I think you already know."

She frowned, then turned to her nearest associate. "Go ahead. Get set up. I'll be there soon." She turned back to him. "One minute."

"What the hell is going on?"

"I assume this is a reference to our next witness?"

"Yeah, the one who wasn't on your witness list."

"And I apologize for that. The name did not come to our attention until late last night. I sent someone to the courtroom to inform you as soon as possible."

"Actually, you could have sent me a text last night."

"My office does not allow confidential information to be transmitted electronically."

"So you waited till I was in the courtroom. When there was no chance I could prepare. You know I'm going to object."

"I do. But I think the judge will allow it, once I explain the circumstances. I'm not kidding you, Dan. We didn't know about this guy until late last night."

"And how did this witness magically drop into your lap at the last possible moment?"

"We received an anonymous tip."

"*Again*? And that doesn't make you at all suspicious?"

"I know there are many players in this drama who would not want their identities revealed—but still have a conscience."

"You said yesterday you had one more witness."

"And I was right. I just didn't know who the witness would be yet. Look, given what this witness has to say, it would be complete malpractice not put him on the stand."

"This is trial by ambush."

"Oh, stop spouting clichés. The defense doesn't even have to give us a witness list. Now that's trial by ambush. Every single time."

She had a point.

"You're the one who wanted a speedy trial, and anytime we go to trial this quickly, some of the procedural niceties will get left behind."

"Just remember that you opened this door. If you're gonna pull eleventh-hour witnesses out of your hat, you can expect the same from me."

"Everyone always expects all manner of courtroom trickery from you, Dan. It's like your one-line biography."

He tried to restrain a snarl. "See you in court."

HE DIDN'T KNOW WHAT BOTHERED HIM MORE—THAT JAZLYN

was producing a new witness at the last minute, or that she had managed to find somebody that Garrett hadn't tracked down. This was Ramon Alvarez, the man Gabriella had mentioned before, the one who was at her home the night of the shooting but had disappeared. How did Jazlyn even know to look for him?

Then he remembered. Gabriella mentioned Alvarez yesterday in the consultation room.

"Jimmy," he asked after he returned to the courtroom, "do you think it's possible someone could be eavesdropping when we're in the consultation room?"

"That would defeat the whole purpose of providing attorneys a place to speak confidentially with their clients."

"Agreed. But do you think it's possible?"

"I don't think anyone here would agree to it."

"But it's not impossible."

"For this case? Nothing is impossible."

He made a mental note. From now on, during all confidential conversations, all cell phones would be turned off and all laptops would be closed. And they wouldn't use that consult room.

Jazlyn called Ramon Alvarez to the witness stand. T-shirt. Stubble. Beer belly. Tattoo on his left hand, the all-seeing eye symbol from one-dollar bills. Black Payless sneakers. Too eager.

Jazlyn quickly established Alvarez' identity. He lived on the Southside and he knew both Emilio and Gabriella. He frequently went to Gabriella's house. He had worked for Emilio in the past, though he had recently obtained a better job at a convenience store and was trying to have as little to do with Emilio as possible. After the shooting, he went to Gabriella's home.

"Who was there when you arrived?" Jazlyn asked.

"Only the girl, at first. Esperanza."

"Not the defendant?"

"Not yet. She got there about five minutes after I did."

"Why did you go there?"

"I was concerned about them. I heard Gabriella was at the

shootout. I was worried she might be hurt. And I didn't want Esperanza to be alone."

"Did you know these two well?"

"As well as Gabriella would permit. I wanted to be...closer. But she held me at arm's length. I thought we might make a good set of foster parents, but Gabriella always pushed me away."

He glanced at Gabriella. Good poker face.

"How was Esperanza when you arrived?"

"Worried. She was shut up in her room. The word about the shooting was out, and the noise level was high. She knew something had happened. And she knew Gabriella had not come home yet."

"What did you do?"

"I tried to comfort the girl."

"And she allowed this?"

"Yeah. We had a good relationship and before the defense tries to suggest differently, there was nothing weird or wrong about it. I just wanted to be her friend. I think I helped her hold it together until Gabriella got home."

"Please describe for the jury what happened when she arrived."

He took a breath, licked his lips. "It was...frightening."

"How so?"

"For starters, she was covered with blood. She wore a white blouse, but there was almost as much red on it as white. She was dirty and covered with sweat. Obviously agitated. Breathing hard." He inhaled deeply. "And she was holding a gun."

Jazlyn showed him the murder weapon, still marked and in its plastic bag. "Is this the weapon she held?"

"It looks like it."

"How would you describe her mental state?"

He started to object, but Jazlyn jumped in first. "I'm not asking for a psychological evaluation. I'm just asking you to describe what you saw."

"She didn't seem particularly scared, if that's what you mean. I wasn't nearly as close to the shooting as she was, and I was terrified. If anything, I'd say she was...buzzed."

"Can you explain what you mean by that?"

"She was pleased." He hesitated a moment, then continued. "She checked on Esperanza, made sure the girl was okay, then went upstairs. I heard her running water, cleaning up a bit. She changed her top. When she came out a couple of minutes later, she was clean and she no longer had the gun."

"Did this surprise you?"

"Not particularly. It didn't take a genius to realize the cops would be swarming all over the neighborhood soon. She had to try to eliminate all traces of...what had happened."

"Did you talk about what happened?"

"A little. She sat down with Esperanza on the sofa, cradling the girl in her arms. I was only a few feet away."

"What did she say?"

"She told us everything was all right. Not to be scared. She told Esperanza, 'You don't need to be scared any more. You don't need to be scared ever again.'"

Jazlyn let those words sink in. "What did that mean?"

"She didn't explain. I thought she meant—"

He rose. "Objection. We want to hear what the witness saw and heard, not his subjective interpretations."

The judge nodded. "Sustained."

Jazlyn proceeded. "Did she say anything else?"

"Yeah. She leaned closer to Esperanza and whispered, but I was still able to hear."

Because you were creeping like a creeper, he thought.

"What did she say to the girl?"

"She whispered, 'I took care of everything.'"

"Thank you," Jazlyn said. "No more questions."

DAN DIDN'T LET A SECOND PASS, NOR DID HE WAIT TO BE invited to speak. He strode straight to the witness box, standing directly in front of Alvarez.

"Let's be clear on this. Did you ever hear Gabriella say, 'I killed him?'"

"What she said was, 'I took care of everything.'"

"Which could mean a lot of different things, couldn't it?"

"I thought it meant one particular thing."

"Because that's what you wanted to think?"

"Because she came home with a gun, covered in blood. Because Sanchez was dead and she was pleased." He chuckled a little. "Gotta hand it to her, she said she took care of everything. And she did."

"You were close to Gabriella and Esperanza, right?"

"Yeah."

"You said you cared about Gabriella and implied that you wanted to marry her."

"Also true."

"But she turned you down, right?"

He hesitated. "She didn't think I could take care of them."

"That must've made you angry."

"I was disappointed."

"So you wanted to get back at her."

"Nah."

"So you told lies about her in court."

"No way, man. I'm not perfect, but I'm no liar."

"In fact, you proposed to Gabriella more than once, correct?"

He shrugged. "Sometimes persistence pays off."

"This is the testimony of a jilted suitor who wants to teach Gabriella a lesson."

Jazlyn rose to her feet. "Objection."

The judge nodded. "I'll sustain that. The jurors can draw their own conclusions."

He continued. "The police investigated you after the shooting, correct?"

"They investigated everyone in the neighborhood. Everyone who had any connection to Emilio."

"Were any charges brought against you?"

"Nope."

"Did the prosecutors agree to not bring charges in exchange for your testimony?"

"No. There was no deal, man. I'm just tellin' what happened."

"You were at Gabriella's house frequently, right?"

"I was trying to help them. I could've done more, but Gabriella didn't want that. She shut me out." He frowned. "And look what happened."

"Let's be clear on this. You didn't see who shot Sanchez, did you?"

"I didn't *see* it, no. But I heard her voice. I saw the way she looked at Esperanza. There was no doubt in my mind what she was saying. She was telling that little girl that she killed Sanchez to keep her safe."

He was getting nowhere with this witness and feared he was making it worse, reminding the jury what he had said. So he sat down.

Jazlyn spoke. "No redirect. The prosecution rests, your honor."

The judge pounded her gavel. "Mr. Pike, are you prepared to start the defense case this afternoon?"

"Of course," he said, even though he had no idea who he would call first or what he would do to salvage the case.

This last witness changed everything. The outlook seemed bleak last night, but now it looked like an epic fail. Now the jury had eyewitness testimony about Gabriella all but confessing to the murder. How could he possibly refute that?

Unless he put Gabriella on the witness stand. He didn't want to. It was bad trial strategy and would probably cause more problems than it solved. Gabriella was too easily flustered, confused, and even if she hadn't committed murder, she had a lot of dubious activities in her past Jazlyn would bring out.

But if he didn't put her on the stand, how could he refute this new testimony?

Jazlyn had hammered the final nail into the coffin, not just proving murder, but premeditated, intentional, even gleeful murder. The sort of thing that got criminal defendants the death penalty.

If he didn't come up with something fast, Gabriella would be convicted of first-degree murder—and sent to death row.

THE MEANING OF JUSTICE

CHAPTER FORTY

DAN SLUMPED ON THE SOFA IN THEIR FRONT OFFICE, STARING at the big screen TV, which was completely blank. Didn't matter. He had his own show playing in his mind, and it wasn't a comedy. More like a tragedy of Shakespearean proportions.

He'd blown it. Sure, he started this case with bad facts, but he should've seen Alvarez' testimony coming. He should've tried harder to find the man. Alvarez made Gabriella look guilty. And he did not see the slightest indication that Alvarez was prevaricating. The despondent suitor was simply reporting what he'd heard.

He didn't protect his client. And now Gabriella was on a beeline to a lethal injection.

He shifted his head and saw the faintest traces of his face reflected in the television screen. How had he gotten himself into this mess? His life had been fine before, perfect. He did what he wanted, took the cases he liked, pursued his passion for justice. He did the best he could and didn't worry about it if a case went sour. He wasn't burdened with family, colleagues, or concerns. He wasn't dependent upon anyone.

Now he was in this weirder-than-weird law firm, surrounded by so-called teammates, burdened with an impossible case—

And a little girl who mistakenly thought he would be the one who saved her.

He cared about her so much it made his stomach hurt.

What was happening to him?

Maria emerged from the back room and sat beside him, not too close, but closer than he might've expected. "I know what you're thinking."

"I don't see how that's possible."

"It's written all over your face. You're blaming yourself."

"I should've prevented this."

"You're a lawyer, not a magician. Gabriella has a tall deck of cards stacked against her. We knew that when we started. There's a reason Mr. K calls us the last-chance lawyers, and it's not because our cases are easy."

"Thanks for the attempted pep talk, but it isn't working. I blew it."

Maria shook her head. "Brian used to get the same way."

"Brian?"

"The guy you replaced. In a manner of speaking." The suggestion seemed to make her uncomfortable. "He got this way at the same time—right after the prosecution finished presenting their evidence, when everything seems grimmest. Your outlook will improve once you start putting on your case."

"Except we don't really have a case. Or evidence."

"You have Gabriella."

"Putting her on the stand would be a huge tactical error."

"It's problematic, true. Less than ideal, certainly. But not a mistake. I don't think you have a choice. The only way the jury is going to change its mind is if she explains what she meant by, 'I took care of everything.'"

"We could put Esperanza on the stand."

Maria smiled. "But I know perfectly well you're not going to do that."

He was starting to get a bit annoyed with the Nostradamus act. "How can you know?"

"Because Brian wouldn't. He was much the same. Very idealistic."

"I'm not remotely idealistic."

"And sweet on children."

"I hate children."

"And a crusader."

"I'm just in it for the money."

She laughed, tilting her head so far back her hair flipped across the right side of her face, highlighting her eyes. "Yes, that's what he would've said. And yet, he always seemed to be on the side of the underdog, taking impossible cases, fighting tooth and nail, never giving an inch. He took each case personally, fought for each client as if they were his own children." She paused. "Just like you."

"You're trying to make me into something I'm not."

"I don't think so. And neither did Mr. K. He saw something in both of you, something he really liked. Perhaps even something that reminded him of himself."

"What happened to Brian, anyway?"

She sighed. Her eyes turned downward.

"Oh no. You said before you were in a relationship that recently ended. You and Brian were a couple, weren't you? And it went sour, so he quit."

She craned her neck. "There was more to it than that."

"The relationship ended and you got custody of the law firm."

"He had a bad result. An extremely bad result. Client went away for a long stretch. Tore him apart. Made him...well, impossible to live with. I think he cared too much. He couldn't handle the stress, the turmoil, the feeling of failure." She brought her eyes back around. "And now I'm afraid you'll become just like Brian."

"Impossible. I never date people at work. And you're not my type."

"That's not what I meant."

He didn't think of himself as a quitter. But he did feel like Gabriella's case was hopeless. "The judge is expecting me to call our first witness in about an hour. And I have no idea who to call."

"You did read my trial plan, right?"

He nodded. "Create doubt."

"And the best way to do that is to suggest other suspects. Other murderers."

"I can't build a case nearly as compelling as what Jazlyn created against Gabriella."

"You don't have to. All you need is a reasonable doubt. Not an equal and opposite doubt."

He pressed his fingers against his temples. "I suppose I can try."

She laid her hand gently on his shoulder. "You'll do more than try. You'll do a terrific job."

"That doesn't mean it will work."

"No. But it will mean Gabriella got the best possible defense. That's all we can promise. Not every case can be won."

He heard the words reverberating in his mind. He knew it was meant to be encouraging, but it rattled in his brain like a curse. *Not every case can be won.*

"So buck up, buckaroo. You're doing great. So far as I can tell, you've only made one major mistake."

His forehead furrowed. "And that was...?"

"When you said I'm not your type. I'm the girl you've been fantasizing about your entire life. But sadly, I don't date people from work anymore."

CHAPTER FORTY-ONE

DAN WAS SURPRISED WHEN JAZLYN STOPPED HIM ON HIS WAY back to the courtroom. Wasn't he usually the one making the interception play?

She got straight to the point. "Against my better judgment, my office has instructed me to offer your client a deal."

He raised an eyebrow, not at the suggestion of a deal, but at the suggestion that she took instruction from someone. "What have you got?"

"Your client pleads guilty to criminal manslaughter. We take intent off the table. I think she did intend it, I think it was deliberate and cold-blooded, but she wasn't thinking clearly. She was trying to protect that girl, or her sister, or both. So we'll give her manslaughter. She could be out in less than ten years."

"Do you know what ten years in prison would do to Gabriella?"

"I think it's better than a life sentence. Or a death sentence. Which is very much possible here. This was a gangland slaying."

"And she's a nonwhite defendant."

"I didn't say that."

"You didn't have to. But she wouldn't survive prison. And Esperanza would be deported."

"Look, I'm not a miracle worker, but I'm trying to do you a favor. And it's not because I think we're going to lose. I'm trying to bring this to a just conclusion. Take the deal. It's better for everyone."

"I don't think Gabriella will agree."

"But you will take the offer to her, since that's your ethical duty as her lawyer, right?"

"Right."

A new voice broke in. "You should listen to the lady and take the deal, pardner."

He turned and to his surprise saw Crenshaw, the ICE agent, lurking about in his cowboy duds. How did he know what the prosecutor was offering his client?

"This is none of my business," he said. "But look, your adoption is sunk. No judge on earth would put a child in the custody of a woman who just stood trial for murder, even if she got off."

"Then you'll deport Esperanza."

"No choice there. But this is still the best deal for your client. Don't turn it down because you've got some pie-in-the-sky hope of keeping that girl stateside."

He frowned. He didn't want to acknowledge it, but what the man said made sense. "I have to confer with my client. I'll get back to you."

HE WAS NOT SURPRISED THAT GABRIELLA DID NOT CARE FOR the idea. He was surprised when she burst out in tears.

He placed his hand gently on her shoulder. "This is totally up to you. It's just an offer. You can accept it or reject it. It's your choice."

"Do you—do you—" She couldn't finish the sentence.

He signaled the bailiff and held up five fingers. The bailiff understood. He was asking for five more minutes before court went back in session. He didn't want the judge or jury to see Gabriella like this.

"Do you think I should take it?" she finally managed to say.

"All I can do is tell you what the options are. If you're convicted of first-degree murder, you could get the death penalty. At best, you'll get a life sentence. That's not necessarily your entire life, but it's at least twenty years behind bars."

"I cannot do that."

"I know. If you accept this plea you'll do maybe ten years, depending upon the actual sentence and time off for good behavior."

"I did not kill Sanchez."

"But the prosecution has made an excellent case. I'm gonna fight like hell, but I can't make any guarantees. Jurors are ultimately unpredictable."

"So many white people are on that jury."

"Yes." He'd like to pretend that wasn't a factor, but he wouldn't lie to her.

"Do you want me to accept this?"

He clenched his jaw. This offer smacked too much of the feds and prosecutors working together to come up with a tidy solution that allowed them to claim they cleaned up a mess. But what if he advised her to reject the offer and then she was convicted? He would never be able to live with himself. "It doesn't matter what I want. It's what you want."

"Why is that woman offering this? Does she think she's going to lose?"

"Not necessarily. It's possible she's afraid she's going to win. She's not a heartless person, even though she might seem that way in the courtroom. Prosecutors have to be tough."

"She wants to make a name for herself."

Maybe. But he thought he spotted genuine sincerity in Jazlyn's eyes. He remembered when they'd talked the night they went out to dinner, which seemed like a million years ago. She'd mentioned the emptiness of her personal life, her regret about being unmarried and childless. She was honest then and he thought she was honest now. "I can't read minds, but I think she's making what she feels is a generous offer. She's trying to help."

Gabriella shook her head, at first slowly, then so rapidly he was afraid she might hurt herself. "I cannot do it. I cannot do it."

"Then don't."

"I cannot say I did something I did not. That I killed someone. How could I look at Esperanza again after I did that?"

"Are you sure? Final answer?"

"I will not plead guilty. Because I am not guilty."

He nodded, giving her shoulder a squeeze. "I'll tell the prosecutor."

CHAPTER FORTY-TWO

DAN WONDERED IF HE HAD EVER GONE INTO A CASE BLINDER then he was at present. He'd done his preparation, as much as the short fuse permitted. But he had no clear idea what he was going to do or how he was going to accomplish it. Thank goodness for Maria. In addition to conceiving the overarching strategy, she'd prepared witness outlines for everyone they might conceivably call. That didn't guarantee a great cross-ex, but at least it gave him something to work with.

He leaned in close to Maria. "If I haven't thanked you yet for everything you've been doing—thanks."

"You don't have to thank me. Helping is what teams do."

He noted, not for the first time, that she had one of those broad irresistible smiles that made everything seem better, even if it was completely irrational to feel better.

Judge Le called court back into session. Since he had already given his opening statement, they launched straight into the witnesses.

"The defense calls Mayor Camila Perez."

Thanks to Jimmy's subpoenas, the mayor was waiting in the gallery, flanked by an entourage of security people. Jimmy had hand-delivered the subpoenas himself, trying to circumvent any hostility that might arise from being served by a cold, anonymous process server. He knew she didn't want to testify. Why would she? But at the same time, they preferred that she not be completely hostile. And she couldn't claim this was too inconvenient, since she'd been visiting the courtroom on her own earlier.

He quickly led the mayor through the preliminaries, establishing who she was and what she did, as if anyone in the jury didn't already know. They had to be curious why the mayor was visiting, and he hoped that curiosity would pique their interest and keep them listening—even if they thought they already knew how they were going to vote.

Mayor Perez seemed calm and composed, energetic. A firecracker in a small but vivacious package. She was obviously accustomed to speaking in public but had the sense to tone it down here. She wasn't giving a press conference, and typically, jurors distrusted witnesses who seem to be putting on a performance. They preferred to feel they were flies on the wall, observing private conversations from a distance, getting the real scoop, not just what witnesses wanted them to hear.

"Mayor Perez, would it be fair to say you've made renovation and reconstruction a priority for your administration?"

"Indeed." She smiled. "I'm all about the infrastructure. I want those old houses, tattered neighborhoods, torn down. Everyone has a fundamental right to decent housing. And everyone has a right to a calm, happy living environment. Bright colors. Safe neighborhoods. And—"

He cut her off. She was edging into campaign-speech territory. "Have you been able to fund all these renovations with taxpayer dollars?"

"Of course not. Any time you initiate projects of this magnitude, you must fundraise. Private donors. Like-minded individuals who care about the future of St. Petersburg."

"One of your partners on the Meeting Place project has been Albert Kazan, right?"

"I love Dr. Kazan. The man is a genius at design, construction, and business. He's that rare dreamer who also has the ability to make his dreams a reality."

"You helped him make that park a reality."

"I helped him through the political hoops. Used eminent domain to seize land where necessary. Helped him circumvent the bureaucratic snafus."

"And in exchange, he's assisted you with your renovation projects."

"I doubt I would've gotten nearly so far without his help. Did you know he donated almost a million dollars just for paint? Bright vivid happy-making paint. We're splashing it all over the city."

All right. He'd given her enough rope. Now it was time to see if she'd hang herself. "You've also used Emilio Lòpez as a partner, correct? We heard from him earlier in this trial, so the jury is familiar with him and his...business activities."

"I have used many partners. Hundreds of them."

"But Emilio was a substantial donor, correct?"

"You need many donors to make a project of this magnitude work." If she was thrown, or irritated, she wasn't letting it show. "It was important to me that we have contributors from all walks of life, all neighborhoods, all demographics. Including the Hispanic community."

"In fact, you and Emilio originally hail from the same neighborhood, correct?"

"Many moons ago. I was a Southside baby. I would like to think that in some small way I have shown people there is always a way out. A way to better yourself. And a way to give back, to help others."

He could see why she had been elected. She was almost impossible to dislike. Even for him, the lawyer who wanted to make her look like a murder suspect. "You're aware that Emilio has been associated with Southside gangs, aren't you?"

"I've heard rumors. Nothing has ever been proven."

"You know he's been arrested repeatedly."

"And that saddens me." She paused. "But I also know arrests are a way of life in those Southside neighborhoods."

"Come on now. Conviction or not, everyone knows Emilio was a gang leader."

"I don't know that."

"Mayor, you took his money because you needed it. But you've also done your best to distance yourself from him, haven't you?"

"I don't know what you mean."

He held up a bright yellow brochure. "This is a piece of promotional material issued by your office. Do you recognize it?" He handed it to the bailiff, who then passed it to the witness.

She only needed to glance at it. "Yes. This came from us. We used it after the first stage of construction on the park was completed to attract new donors."

"And Emilio was involved in the first stage, wasn't he?"

"Yes, I believe so."

"But I noticed his name does not appear on the roster of donors in this brochure."

He was relieved to see she wasn't going to feign a lack of knowledge. "That is...true."

"You deliberately left his name off the list because you didn't want to be associated with a known gangland figure, right?"

She drew in her breath, then slowly released it. "What's true is that I knew there were rumors afloat. And sadly, in the world of politics, rumors can be deadly. So after considerable discussion and with much regret, we left his name off the list."

"Did you inform him that he would not be included in the brochure?"

"I called him personally. To his credit, he was most magnanimous about it. He completely understood."

"And you've continued to distance yourself from him, right? Someone wrote an editorial in the *Herald*?" He returned to his table and Maria handed him an exhibit. "You took a lot of heat because of your ties to Emilio."

"I remember the editorial. I didn't worry much about it."

"A politician who doesn't care what the papers say about her?"

"The *Herald* has never been my friend. I assume most of my constituency ignores that kind of editorializing."

"You stopped taking his calls."

"I am very busy."

"You turned down his offer of cash for the expansion project."

"It seemed prudent, all things considered."

"It must have occurred to you that your life would be better if Emilio...disappeared."

Her eyes narrowed. "What are you implying?"

"Many people believe that the so-called Tragedy at the Trademark was actually a trap set to execute Emilio, not Sanchez. Or perhaps both of them."

She leaned forward. "Are you suggesting that I put out a hit on Emilio? That I tried to arrange his execution?"

"You did have a motive. Your political career was on the line. And you'll be up for reelection soon."

She folded her arms across her chest. "I find this whole line of questioning offensive." She looked up, as if she expected the judge to get her out of it, which of course didn't happen.

"For that matter, you probably weren't crazy about having Sanchez in your town, were you?"

"I did not even know who this man was until I read that he was dead."

"A hands-on mayor like you? I find that difficult to believe."

Jazlyn rose. "Objection. Ask that the jury be instructed to disregard."

Judge Le nodded. "Sustained. The remark will be stricken from the record. Mr. Pike, please restrict yourself to asking questions. Relevant questions. No commentary."

"Yes, your honor."

"Anything more?" the judge asked. "I sense that you have

reached the end of the line."

He smiled a little. That was about as close as she could get to pushing him out the door. "I'm almost there, your honor. One last matter." He returned his attention to the mayor. "Were you aware that the prosecutor was planning to offer Emilio an immunity deal?"

She frowned slightly. "I did hear about that, yes."

"In fact, you tried to stop it, didn't you?"

Out the corner of his eye, he saw Jazlyn stiffen. How did he know, she wondered? And the answer was—he didn't. But he suspected Jazlyn wouldn't do the deal without contacting the mayor's office, and he didn't think the mayor would like it.

"I never favor these immunity deals. I believe people who have committed crimes should be punished to the full extent of the law."

"Even your old friend and business colleague Emilio?"

"Justice should be blind. Everyone should pay the price for their crimes. If they are guilty."

"Truth is, you were hoping he would go away for a long time, weren't you?"

"I had no hopes."

"If you couldn't kill him, then a long sentence at the penitentiary was the next best thing, wasn't it?

Jazlyn shot up like a rocket. "Objection!"

The judge didn't wait for an explanation. "Sustained."

"That's all I have." He'd made his point. A little high drama would help cement it in the jurors' minds. "Nothing more."

As it turned out, Jazlyn chose not to cross-examine. He could understand that. She had ambitions and she didn't want to anger the mayor—more than she already was.

He thought he had done a decent job of giving the mayor a motive to get Emilio out of the way, but there was no telling whether the jury bought it, even as a remote possibility. Some of it was a stretch. But of course, he didn't need to convince the jurors of anything. All he needed to do was raise doubt.

CHAPTER FORTY-THREE

AFTER A BREAK, DAN CALLED HIS NEXT WITNESS—THE architect, Dr. Albert Kazan.

Kazan was dressed casually, but nothing like the aging hippie outfit he had worn when they met before. Today it was sports jacket and slacks, with a pink open-collared shirt. Kazan leaned back in the chair and crossed his legs, presenting a relaxed appearance.

He quickly established Kazan's credentials as an architect and builder, primarily focused on the St. Petersburg area. They talked about the hotels, the resorts, the office buildings, and of course, The Meeting Place. He noticed smiles on the jurors' faces as they talked about the magnificent park. Regardless of how much it cost, who didn't love a park?

He glanced back at Maria and saw that she was pointing at her wrist, at an invisible wristwatch. In other words—the jury's getting antsy. Move it along.

"Dr. Kazan, we just heard the mayor admit to an extensive financial and business relationship with Emilio Lòpez. He contributed to her campaign and contributed extensively to her various infrastructure projects. You worked with him as well, didn't you?"

His lips pursed slightly. He was far less sanguine about the relationship than the mayor had been. "Yes, I was."

"You told me you took money from him, right?"

"He was one of many investors in The Meeting Place."

"You knew he was involved in drug pushing, didn't you? Some say he was the biggest gang leader on the West Coast of Florida."

"I didn't hear that at the start."

"But you did learn, at some point, that some of your funds had come indirectly from the sale of illegal drugs, right?"

He drew in his breath. "I heard about the possibility. Nothing was confirmed. It's my understanding that Emilio has never been convicted of anything. And never will be, thanks to the immunity agreement."

"And you told me you personally visited Emilio's assistant."

"That's true."

"So you had no problem with taking this money."

"I don't believe people should be convicted or ostracized based on accusations. There's too much of that going on in the world right now. The press writes an ugly article about someone and they end up resigning. A woman makes an accusation about a man in power, and suddenly no one will work with him. I think it's important that people not be destroyed until they've had a fair hearing."

"And you felt Emilio had not had a fair hearing? He's been arrested several times."

"And each time he was either acquitted or the charges were dropped. Look, everybody who's ever accumulated a fortune had to do something to earn it. If you dig deep enough, hard enough, long enough, you'll find something to disapprove of. That's the way the world works. If we get all holier than thou about fundraising, we'll never get any money from anyone." He turned to look at the jury. "And then there would never be a Meeting Place. No parks, no hotels, no tourist trade. St. Petersburg would fade away as so many other seaside towns have done. I didn't want that to happen."

"You also worked with the man who was murdered, didn't you? Sanchez."

"I never worked with him. I never took a penny from him."

"But you knew who he was."

"Not until shortly before he was killed."

"Who brought him to your attention? Emilio?"

"No, I learned about Sanchez when Jack Crenshaw brought him to my attention. He's an agent for Immigration and Customs Enforcement."

He tried to control his reaction. He'd never heard about this.

"He came to my office, investigating Emilio. Told me about Sanchez. Said Sanchez and Emilio were working together, or trying to kill each other, he wasn't sure which. For some reason, he thought I might know something about it."

"Have you had any involvement with Sanchez'...industry?"

"With prostitution? Of course not. I told you that when we spoke before. No, but Crenshaw had suspicions about some of the people who had contributed to the park."

"Based upon what?"

"How would I know?" He was becoming agitated. "Some of those rich contributors may be using escort services or Latin American whores. How would I know? Why would I care? This is America. Rich people can do pretty much anything they want." He shrugged. "Sleep with a porn actress. Pay her to keep quiet. No one cares."

"But Crenshaw thought you might know something about this?"

"So he said. He was a complete—" He stopped short. "He was damned unfriendly about it. Pushy. I suppose that's what he does, browbeating people, playing the bad cop, seeing what he can pound out of you. But I resented it. I've never done anything to deserve that kind of treatment."

"How did the conversation end?"

"Can you believe it? He threatened to stop the expansion. A billion-dollar project that we've been planning for years."

"How could an immigration agent stop it?"

"By freezing our bank accounts. Impounding the money. Claiming that it came from illegal operations. He threatened to shut me down if I didn't give him information about Sanchez." He leaned forward and spread wide his hands. "But I had no information to give."

"And yet, Crenshaw was convinced that you did."

"Or maybe he was just fishing." He shifted his weight. "Or maybe it was some bizarre plot."

He arched an eyebrow. "A plot? A conspiracy? People out to get you?"

"Is that surprising? You can't do anything significant these days without attracting detractors. Anybody in the public eye will be rewarded with critical trolls who don't know anything about them. Front-page editorials passing as articles in right-wing broadsheets suggesting that you're evil. Government flunkies trying to turn you into a criminal. It's outrageous and it needs to be stopped."

He seemed increasingly paranoid. "You felt ICE was out to get you? To shut down your park?"

"Isn't it obvious? Why else would Crenshaw be hassling me? Does anyone seriously think I was involved with sex trafficking?"

He decided to take a shot. "I did notice several beautiful women in your office when I visited."

Kazan rolled his eyes. "Newsflash. I'm gay. I'm not remotely interested in beautiful women."

He retrenched. "I'm sure Sanchez has gay prostitutes, too."

Jazlyn rose to her feet. "Objection, your honor. Even by Mr. Pike's rather low standards, this is completely inappropriate. And it's not relevant."

The judge pondered for a moment. "I agree that any discussion of personal sexuality is not relevant, and I would prefer that we stay clear of that." What she was not saying, of course, was that she didn't want it eliciting any juror bias. "But I can't say the discussion of ties to organized crime is irrelevant."

He nodded. "Thank you, your honor." He decided to lunge in for the kill. "Immigration believed you were involved with Emilio or Sanchez or both. You had a good reason to want to see those two men dead."

Kazan disagreed. "I don't have a violent bone in my body."

"You have a ton of money. You could hire someone."

"I'm a businessman, not the Godfather."

"But you're in bed with the Godfather. And you didn't wake up with a horse's head. You woke up with a billion-dollar park."

"You want to live in the real world?" he said, his voice rising. "Then you have to get your hands dirty. You have to break a few eggs."

"Meaning you have to deal with drug pushers and killers."

"If that's what it takes to get the job done, yes!"

"And then, when they start to threaten the whole project, you have to get rid of them."

"*Yes!*"

The courtroom fell silent.

Kazan didn't wait for another question. "I'm not saying I killed anybody. Or got them killed. I would never do that. I'm just saying I have to take care of business. Every professional does. If you need to distance yourself from someone later, fine. You gotta watch your back. Every white male in America's got a target on his back right now."

Out the corner of his eye, he saw Maria drawing a horizontal line across her neck, a signal telling him to cut it off.

He agreed. It was never going to get any better. "No more questions."

CHAPTER FORTY-FOUR

AFTER THE TRIAL ADJOURNED FOR THE DAY, DAN WAS exhausted. He knew they would rehash the case for hours, then plan for the next day. The last thing on earth he needed was a field trip. But Jimmy had somehow pulled more strings and gotten them in to see Esperanza again. She might be expecting them, and she might be desperate for visitors. He didn't want to disappoint.

Maria drove while he reviewed his notes. They waited in the holding room for almost ten minutes before Esperanza appeared. The matron in charge pulled him to one side.

"Do you still have people watching this place?"

"Two security officers outside. Night and day."

She nodded. "You may want to...increase that."

His jaw clenched. "Tell me what happened."

"Maybe it's nothing. But we found a place in our chain link fence that was partly cut. Like someone tried to get in. I think they got scared off before they finished the job. But still..."

"I'll double the security. Round the clock."

He felt a gnawing in his stomach that would not subside. First the bloody doll. Now this. "You keep Esperanza away from everyone but us."

She nodded. "Is this going to go on...much longer? We're all more than a little terrified."

He didn't blame them. He was scared too. "The trial will be over soon. One way or the other."

"This detention will be over soon too. We've received the first wave of Esperanza's deportation papers. The process takes about two weeks but...it's begun."

As if everything wasn't bad enough already. "You keep her safe. I'll work on the rest."

She nodded and went back to find Esperanza. A few minutes later, they returned.

He gasped when the matron brought Esperanza in. She was almost unrecognizable.

What happened to this little girl? Her hair was not brushed —in fact, it looked as if it had not been brushed for days. Her eyes were dark. She seemed dirty.

But the most remarkable change was in her face. The inner strength that seemed so powerful before had disappeared.

She ran straight up to him and pounded on his chest. "Liar! You said you would get me out of here. You said you were going to help me!"

He was stunned. His lips parted, but he could not form words.

Maria cut in. "Esperanza, honey, calm down. We're doing everything we can."

"Then why am I here? Where's Gabriella?"

"She's still in jail, honey. We're doing our best—"

"Liar! You're all liars!"

He still couldn't find the words. What had happened? He'd read about children removed from their parents by immigration officials following the new administration guidelines. The combination of fear, isolation, and separation from loved ones often had devastating psychological effects that lasted for years, if not forever.

Maria placed her hand on Esperanza's shoulder, but the girl

shrugged it off. She pounded again on his chest. "You said you would help me!"

"I—I am helping you."

"Then why am I here? I hate it here. I hate you!" She pulled away, threw herself down on the table, and pounded.

He saw the matron move toward them, but he raised his hand. "Give us a moment." He crouched down so Esperanza could see him. If she wanted to. He reached into a paper bag. "I brought you something."

The pounding continued, but perhaps slowed a bit and diminished in intensity. She was listening.

He reached into the bag and pulled out a pair of Hello Kitty sneakers, just her size. They'd stopped at Journeys on the way over. "I thought maybe it was time for some new shoes. And I thought you might like having Kitty White keep you company."

He could see that she looked at the sneakers, but ultimately turned away and resumed pounding. "I don't want shoes! I want out of here! I want Gabriella!"

He could hardly bear it. She had seemed so strong before. But she was too young for this. Too young to be held in detention so long. And putting her in isolation, even though it was for her own protection, had made matters worse.

His heart ached, physically ached. He didn't want to cut out on her. But he didn't feel they were doing her any good.

He looked at Maria and shrugged. Should we stay? Should we go?

Maria leaned across the table. "Esperanza, I know you're upset, honey. I don't blame you. I can't imagine what it's like, locked up in here all by yourself. But it's not forever. It will end eventually."

"And then they'll send me away! To another country, to people I don't know!"

His eyelids fluttered closed. The full horror of her situation had finally hit home.

He could see Maria hesitating. Even she wasn't sure what to

say. "We're doing everything we can to prevent that, Esperanza. Everything possible."

He managed to contribute a creaky one-word affirmation. "Everything."

"Liar!"

"The trial will soon be over."

"And then Gabriella will be free? I can go home with her?"

He slid in beside Maria. He so wanted to say what he knew she wanted to hear. But that would only make it more devastating if it proved incorrect. "No matter what happens in this trial, we will be here for you. I will be here for you. And we will do everything we can to keep you in this country. Safe."

"You won't let them send me away?"

"I will do everything imaginable to stop it." He gritted his teeth. "If I have to throw myself under the immigration truck, that's what I'll do."

She thought for a moment. Finally, a glimmer of the old light returned to her eyes. "Please don't do that. That would be stupid."

He tilted his head to one side. "It was more like a... metaphor." He swallowed. "Only a few more days and the trial will be over. One way or another, this will end."

"Will you visit me again?"

"Of course we will. You know we will."

She paused a long time, wiping tears from her eyes, then finally pushed herself off the table.

"You know," she said slowly, "there's a Hello Kitty backpack that matches these shoes."

A grin spread across his face. "Consider it yours."

CHAPTER FORTY-FIVE

DAN HAD ALMOST REACHED HIS PORSCHE WHEN THE newspaper stand caught his eye. He normally didn't even look at newspapers. He thought most of the so-called news was more repetitive than new and rarely of lasting importance. But this was different. How often did the word Sanchez appear in a headline?

ACCUSED THREATENED TO MURDER SANCHEZ

He wasn't carrying any change and it took him five minutes to access the paper on his phone. Why didn't newsstands take credit cards like everyone else in the world? Eventually he was able to read the article.

Quoting an anonymous source, *The Herald* reported that Gabriella, who it noted was a distant relative of Sanchez, had a sister who had worked for him as a prostitute. The article said she worried that the girl they called her ward, Esperanza, would be Sanchez' next sex worker. The witness, whose identity was withheld but was said to be under the protection of immigration officials, allegedly overheard Gabriella promising to murder Sanchez the day before he was killed. The article went on to implicitly suggest that Gabriella arranged the meeting between

Emilio and Sanchez and brought a gun for the purpose of assassinating Sanchez under the cover of a gangland shootout.

Damn. What now? He knew better than to go after the paper. They would hide behind anonymous sources and freedom of the press. But if he'd seen this article, some of the jurors had seen it as well. And even if they tried to forget what they read, realistically, how could they?

———————

THIRTY MINUTES LATER HE WAS IN JUDGE LE'S CHAMBERS WITH Jazlyn. Normally, he would move for a mistrial based upon a tainted jury. But in this case, he couldn't. If the court granted a mistrial, they would have to start from scratch. The earliest new trial date would be months down the road. Esperanza would be out of the country before they could start. He had to find another way to protect his client.

"I want to question each and every juror," he said. "I need to know if they've seen this article."

Jazlyn shook her head. "The judge instructed them to avoid all media coverage before the trial began."

"That doesn't mean they obeyed. And this isn't normal media coverage. This story didn't come out of the courtroom. This is the paper generating its own truth with some anonymous source who's probably a complete liar."

"Even so—"

"Hell, this headline was so large the jurors could've absorbed it before they knew what they were reading."

"And if that's the case," Jazlyn argued, "who's going to admit it? It's like asking a child to admit they took the last cookie. Who would?"

Judge Le leaned back in her black padded chair. "I have to agree with the prosecutor on this one. I think it's a waste of time. No one's going to admit to engaging in juror misconduct."

"They might," he said. "At least let me try."

"And even if some do admit it," Jazlyn said, "what does that get you?"

"I'll move to replace them with alternates."

"What if the alternates saw the paper? They're as likely to have a newspaper subscription as anyone else. We could end up replacing more than six jurors, in which case we don't have enough, in which case it's a mistrial." The judge looked at him directly. "Is that what you want?"

She knew perfectly well he didn't.

"Look," Judge Le said, "I'm not saying your point is frivolous. But this is exactly why I give jurors instructions about avoiding *all* media coverage—not just about this case. I ordered a complete blackout. Because if you're listening to the news or reading a blog or newspaper you could be reading about this case before you realize it."

"In today's world?" he said. "Completely avoiding the media is not possible. The latest news could show up in a phone alert. And good luck instructing jurors not to look at their phones. There is no judicial instruction in the world strong enough to wean some people away from their smartphones."

"I don't think we should assume that a mere headline is enough to taint the case," Judge Le said. "In my experience, most jurors try to do the right thing."

"I agree with you. But prejudice is insidious. It can influence people without their knowledge."

"Anything can influence people unconsciously," Jazlyn said. "That's why we have twelve jurors instead of one."

He felt supremely frustrated. Even if he got what he asked for, it wouldn't be enough.

"Look," Judge Le said, "I'll question the jurors. Even if they didn't see this in the *Herald*, they might've picked it up elsewhere. But I'll do the questioning. One juror at a time, in chambers. And I assure you, if I see anything that hints toward bias, I will remove the juror. Quickly and efficiently. And then we'll get on with this trial."

He nodded. It wasn't perfect, but under the circumstances, it was probably the best he could hope for.

THREE HOURS LATER, TWO OF THE JURORS HAD BEEN REPLACED by alternates. The judge didn't discuss it with him, but he assumed someone had been honest enough to admit they'd been exposed to the news and might have trouble putting it out of their mind. Still not perfect, but the best he could hope for under the circumstances.

He tried to reassure Gabriella. "This is good for us. Really. The more we can fine-tune this jury, the better."

"They do not like me," she said. Her eyes seemed troubled.

"Why would you think that?"

"I can tell. I can tell by looking at them."

"Don't jump to any conclusions. The jurors are just taking it seriously."

She shook her head. "They assume I am guilty. They have assumed it from the first day."

He tried to think of something that might help. "The judicial system is not perfect," he said. "But I'm going to beat them over the head with reasonable doubt."

"It will not be enough."

"Well," he said, squeezing her hand, "we're not going down without a fight."

CHAPTER FORTY-SIX

JUDGE LE RAPPED HER GAVEL. "MR. PIKE. PLEASE CALL YOUR
next witness."

"The defense calls Luis González." They'd had no small
degree of trouble serving Luis, and even then, he wasn't certain
Luis would show. For someone who claimed to be such an
honest, respectable, legitimate businessman, he could be seriously elusive and unavailable when a process server wanted to
drop a subpoena on him. Jimmy finally managed it, but only
because a friend revealed where Luis liked to get chicken and
waffles. Even then, given Luis' income and access to lawyers, he
could've found a way to make himself unavailable, knowing full
well they couldn't afford to delay the trial while hunting him
down.

But his concerns were for naught. Luis took the stand and
was sworn in.

His first few questions were designed to establish what Luis
did for a living. Unsurprisingly, he talked about imports and
exports and presented himself as a perfectly honest business
executive. Most of what he said dovetailed with the story Emilio
had given the jury. He thought he detected some skepticism
crossing the jurors' faces when Luis refused to acknowledge any

involvement with illegal drugs. Possibly Emilio had not made as good an impression on the witness stand as he thought.

"Were you surprised when the charges against Emilio were dropped?"

After a brief pause, Luis answered. "Everyone said the case against him was bullet-proof."

"You thought he would be convicted?"

"I thought it was possible."

"Which means you thought he committed the murder."

"I'm not saying that. I don't know what happened. But I know that if the cops want to put someone away, they can usually do it."

"You must've been disappointed."

His brow creased. "I don't follow you, man."

"Didn't you like being the head of the organization?" Rather than calling it a business, he called it an organization, which he suspected many jurors would translate to "gang."

"I won't lie about it. There's nothing like being the captain of the ship."

"And you changed the direction of the company under your administration, right?" He could see the wheels turning behind Luis' eyes, as the man debated how much he could admit. "Change" suggested Emilio was doing something different before.

"I'm only interested in legal business activities. I want to create a business that can employ people from my neighborhood for a good long time. I want people to respect us. That's why we made all those donations to the park. I want people to see that we're not a blotch on society. We can be good citizens, good role models. I wanted to improve the reputation of the Hispanic community."

"Were you concerned that Emilio might...revert the company if he regained control?"

A long pause followed. "I can't predict the future. No telling what someone else might do."

"What I'm hearing in that response is, yes, you were afraid Emilio would want to get back into drug pushing."

Jazlyn rose to her feet. "Objection. The witness never said anything about distributing drugs."

The judge's head pivoted a bit. "Sustained." Then under her breath, "I guess."

"Would it be fair to say you were concerned about the direction the company might take if Emilio regained the reins?"

Another long pause, but he finally answered. "Yes."

"You liked being, what was your word, the captain? And you didn't want to relinquish command."

"I felt like I was doin' good work."

"Did you tell Emilio that?"

"No point. Most of the men were still loyal to him. If I tried a hostile takeover, they'd boot me out on my—" He stopped. "I'd be ousted."

Nice save.

"It was not a publicly held company," Luis continued. "Still isn't. It's not like I own stock. I couldn't prevent Emilio from doing whatever he wanted."

He was reminded that Luis did have a degree in finance. "So if free, Emilio would've seized control of the company again, right?"

"He'd already started. Second he got out a prison."

"And that would've continued, but for the murder at the Trademark."

"I guess that's true."

"You know that's true. The shootout was the best thing that ever happened to you."

"Don't pin that on me. I didn't want anybody to get hurt."

"But you did want Emilio out of the picture. Which basically meant he either had to be behind bars, or he had to be dead. And that shootout could have accomplished either one."

"I'm telling you, I had nothing to do with that."

"And yet someone set up the meeting. Someone who had access to both Emilio and Sanchez."

"It wasn't me."

"But you're the one who benefits. What is it they say? Follow the money?"

"I got no money out of this. I barely pay myself a decent salary. I'm trying to build a business."

"And Emilio could have taken that away in a heartbeat." He returned to his table. Maria handed him a photograph, pre-marked as a defense exhibit. "You've probably heard about the Trademark security camera. We have some footage taken before the shootout."

"And I'm not in it. Because I wasn't there."

"Could you identify the figure in the upper right-hand corner of this still taken from the video?" He passed it to the bailiff, who brought it to the witness.

Luis moved the photograph back and forth, as if he were having trouble focusing. "This is a pretty sketch photo."

"Do your best. Take your time."

"I'm just not sure..."

"Come on, Luis. That's Everett Jefferson, isn't it?"

Luis slowly nodded. "It might be."

"He's your personal assistant, isn't he? I saw him when I visited your office."

Luis frowned. "Maybe."

"Was Everett at the shootout?"

"You'd have to ask him, man."

"You don't know?"

Luis hesitated before answering. "I don't know."

"You two are pretty close, aren't you? He's one of the few people in that office who's loyal to you, rather than Emilio, right? I can't imagine the two of you never talked about the shootout."

"He was in a bad situation a while back and I saved him from it. I think he's grateful."

"So if you needed an emissary, someone to arrange a meeting

or to make sure Emilio showed up without getting your own hands dirty, you'd send Everett."

"I never said that."

"And he'd do it, because as you said, he's grateful to you. He might even do it without being asked."

Another long pause. "I can't speak for another man. Talk to him."

"What happens now that Emilio is free, due to his convenient immunity agreement?"

"My understanding is that the agreement forbids him from returning to his old business activities. He's getting outta town."

"Leaving you in charge. The whole situation couldn't have worked out better for you...if you'd planned it." He looked up. "No more questions, your honor."

CHAPTER FORTY-SEVEN

DAN FOUND A PRIVATE CORNER IN THE COURTROOM HALLWAY to huddle with his team—avoiding the consultation room. They had fifteen minutes, which wasn't nearly long enough.

"How do you think that went?"

Maria appeared upbeat. "I think it went as well as you could possibly hope. Luis didn't confess to anything. But you established a strong motive. Maybe the strongest yet."

Jimmy piped in. "Looks to me like we've given the jury three strong alternate suspects. Maybe four. If they buy any one of those, they have to acquit."

"That's a big if. If they think we're just stirring up dirt, or trashing innocent citizens, they might resent it. It might make them want to convict Gabriella even more."

Jimmy shook his head. "No one thinks Luis is a completely innocent citizen."

"He handled himself well, given the circumstances."

"He's a former gang member. And some people will never believe he's come clean."

Garrett agreed. "I'm afraid that's true." He stopped a moment. "Are we all comfortable with this business of making the jurors suspect innocent citizens?"

"That's our job."

"Our job is to give Gabriella a reasonable defense, and you have. But I worry about standing up there and accusing other people of being murderers. You know how much media coverage this case is getting?"

"I saw the headline in the *Herald* this morning."

"It's not just the newspapers. It's all over. Social media is blanketed with it. Every fifth post in my Facebook news feed this morning was about the case. I spotted at least three different Reddit groups discussing it, and when I plugged key terms into Google Alerts, I found thirteen different Internet bulletin boards discussing the case. Most of them thought Gabriella was guilty. Called us sleazy lawyers trying to put criminals back on the street."

Jimmy frowned. "Internet trolls. Losers. I don't care what they think. Do you, Dan?"

He replied. "I didn't get into criminal defense because I thought I would win popularity contests. I can take the heat." He placed a hand on Garrett's shoulder. "I get what you're saying. I don't like it either. But I'm not letting any stone go unturned. We must get Gabriella off."

Garrett's voice dropped lower than a whisper. "What if she's guilty?"

"She's not."

Maria stepped in. "We assume she's not. We assume that about all our clients. We are required to do so."

"Plus," he added, "she told me she didn't do it."

"Oh," Garrett said. "Well, that proves it."

"Do you have a problem with the way I'm handling this case?"

Garrett shook his head. "I don't know. I've never been involved with a case that got this much heat."

"Take a few minutes," Maria said. "Go for a walk. Have a Monster energy drink. Sometimes I start to feel despondent when I've been in the courtroom too long. Clear your head, then come back. We need to be able to count on you."

Garrett nodded. "You can count on me."

Maria checked her watch. "We're almost out of time. What else do you need, Dan?"

"We haven't even talked about the main issue. We have two choices. We can rest our case, and I spend my closing reminding the jury of all the other possible suspects." He drew in his breath. "Or we put Gabriella on the stand."

"I don't want to do that," Jimmy said. "I don't think she'll hold up."

"She might be tougher than you realize."

"Does that mean you want to put her on the stand?"

"Honestly, I don't know. She's got a lot of skeletons in her closet."

"Then why would we do it?"

"Because if we don't, the jury will always wonder why we didn't."

"And no matter how many suspects we throw at them," Maria said, "we have no way to answer Ramon Alvarez, who talked about her coming home covered in blood and saying she'd taken care of everything."

He nodded. "The only witness who can address that is Gabriella. And if we leave that thread hanging..." He shook his head. "I just don't know."

Maria looked him in the eyes. "It's your call, Dan."

"It shouldn't be. You're the master strategist. What do you think?"

She swallowed. He could tell she didn't want to answer.

"Honestly. Tell me what you think."

She took a deep breath, then spoke. "I've been watching the jurors the whole time, while you've been working. I've been watching their faces."

"And?"

"I think if you don't put Gabriella on the stand, we lose. And we may lose anyway. But if they don't hear a denial from her own lips...we're sunk."

He nodded. "Kind of what I thought too. Thanks for being honest."

"That's what friends are for."

CHAPTER FORTY-EIGHT

"YOUR HONOR, WE CALL THE DEFENDANT, GABRIELLA VALDEZ, to the witness stand."

The jurors' surprise was palpable. Several eyebrows rose. And a few people smiled. This was what they wanted—to hear what the defendant had to say for herself.

He just hoped it didn't destroy her.

Gabriella had taken the news that she was going on the stand better than he expected. In fact, if he wasn't mistaken, she was pleased. Perhaps she welcomed a chance to tell her own story. He had cautioned her about everything that would likely come out, that she should expect an absolutely cutthroat, razor-sharp, no-holds-barred cross-examination. But that did not deter her.

He started slowly, asking her simple questions. He let her give a great deal of her personal backstory, starting with how she came to the United States from El Salvador, the struggles she had here, jumping from one poor job to the next, one low-rent shack to the next. Initially, she didn't know the language and she had no education. But she finally managed to establish herself, find a passable place to live, obtain US citizenship, and help others in the community. He hoped the jury would see that working for Emilio part-time was a small compromise that could have been much worse. Instead of being completely consumed by gangs and criminal activities, she ran the occasional errand to make ends meet.

"How did you meet Esperanza?"

Gabriella's demeanor changed when she started talking about the young girl. She told the whole story of how she was initially reunited with Esperanza's mother, her distant relative. Her eyes darkened and her voice halted when she recounted the death of Esperanza's parents, the traffic accident, and the effect on the girl who lost both parents in one night at such a tender age. Some children might have been devastated, might've been scarred to such a degree they would never recover. Esperanza took it hard, but in time, she displayed an amazing resilience. She was strong, smart, stable. A worthy addition to the community.

"When did you decide you wanted to adopt her?"

"Soon after her parents' death. An immigration agent suggested it to prevent her deportation after her temporary protected status was revoked. I did not know how to go about it and I could not afford lawyers. I turned to Emilio. He was the only person I knew who might be able to make it happen."

"And was he helpful?"

"No. Always excuses. Always too busy. He said the government was out to get us. In time, I realized I would have to go somewhere else. I went to Family Legal Aid. They said they couldn't help."

Mr. K must've heard about it and somehow contacted Gabriella. What about this case triggered K's interest? he wondered, not for the first time. Could K have possibly imagined where it would lead?

Gabriella continued. "You came into our lives, offered to handle the adoption without charge. For the first time, I had hope. Esperanza and I had hope. We could see a better tomorrow." Her eyes lowered. "And then all this happened."

"Gabriella, let's make one thing clear up front. Did you have anything to do with arranging the showdown between Emilio and Sanchez?"

"No. I wouldn't know how. Emilio contacted me. He asked me to bring him a weapon. That's the only reason I was there."

"You brought him your own gun."

"It was the only weapon I could find so quickly."

"Why did you have a gun?"

"In my neighborhood, you need one, for your own protection."

"Were you surprised when Emilio asked for a weapon?"

"Not after I heard who he was meeting. Only a fool would go to a meeting like that unarmed."

"Did you know how to use the gun?"

"Yes. I trained."

"Were you good?"

"I could hold my own. I always told Esperanza—if you're going to do something, do it well."

"Gabriella, one of the previous witnesses testified that she saw you holding the gun. That in fact, she saw you extend the gun as if aiming to fire."

Gabriella nodded. She was keeping cool, thank goodness. And she wasn't denying anything unnecessarily. She didn't seem defensive. "I did hold it and aim it—but only after the shooting started. In a matter of seconds, I was surrounded by gunfire."

"Did you kill Sanchez?"

"No. I fired twice into the air. He was down before I drew my gun."

"He was already dead?"

"I don't know if he was dead. But he had fallen to the ground. Emilio ran for cover. I had to defend myself. I pulled out my gun, fired, and retreated. I tripped over—" She clenched her eyes shut. "The girl. The one who was so badly wounded. I fell on her. That's why I was covered with blood." She swallowed, took a minute, then continued. "I panicked and ran. It's a miracle I made it out alive."

He nodded, giving the jury a moment to absorb what she said. "After you fled, where did you go?"

"Home. I worried about Esperanza. Fortunately, she was fine. She had the sense to hide till I got there."

"And your friend, Ramon Alvarez, was also there?"

"Yes. I didn't want him there. But he was. He had offered himself to me as a husband, but I turned him down. I did not think him...suitable, and I did not think marrying him would help me keep Esperanza in this country."

He paused. Something was nagging at him, but he couldn't quite place it. "Did you call the police?"

"No. They already knew about the shootout. Calling would only make me a suspect."

He couldn't argue with that. "Did you call anyone?"

"Yes. I called Jack Crenshaw, the immigration agent."

"Why?"

"He was the only law enforcement person who had ever reached out to me. The only one I trusted. He had spoken to me about Esperanza. He was in charge of her deportation. I wanted to see if he could do anything to prevent this from destroying us both."

"And did he?"

"He didn't answer the phone. It was late at night. I left a message. We talked the next day."

"What did he say then?"

"He suggested that I find a lawyer."

"Ramon Alvarez has testified that you changed out of blood-stained clothes. Is that true?"

"Yes. I could see that my blouse was disturbing Esperanza. I took it off. I later burned it."

"What did you do with the gun?"

"I put it in a box and hid it beneath a floorboard under the bed in my room. A safe place, or so I thought. A place Esperanza could never get to it."

"You didn't put it in your backyard?"

"No. Someone else must've done that."

"One last thing. Alvarez said that you told Esperanza not to worry, because you had taken care of everything. What did you mean?"

"I was talking about the adoption. Ramon heard what he wanted to hear, not what I said. Crenshaw told me the main obstacle that might prevent me from adopting Esperanza was my connection to gangs. So that night, when I arrived, I told Emilio I would not work for him anymore. That's all I meant. I was just trying to take care of that precious girl." Her chin trembled, and tears welled up behind her eyes.

He let that hang in the air for a few moments. "Thank you, Gabriella." He turned toward the prosecution table. "Your witness."

———

JAZLYN DIDN'T HESITATE. "MS. VALDEZ, WE'RE ALL MOVED, I'M sure, by your story. But let's focus on the facts for a minute." She led Gabriella through her prior arrest record, minor theft charges, all more than five years distant. She didn't spend much time there. She seemed to be in a hurry to move on. "Even after that, you worked for Emilio, right?"

"A little. For a time."

"That time was actually more than four years, wasn't it?"

"That sounds right. I needed the money. And I needed it more once I was caring for Esperanza."

"Come on now. You could've found a real job. An honest job."

"I had an honest job. Two of them. But they did not pay enough. We live in an expensive world. All anyone seems to care about is money. Money money money."

"You worked at a nail salon, correct?"

"Three days a week."

"And you also worked at a waffle house."

"Also three days a week. I tried to get more work. There are only so many hours in a week. And I needed to be home at night for Esperanza."

"There must've been other jobs."

"For a person in my neighborhood?"

"Your English is good."

"But I have no education, no degree. Getting work is difficult for the people in my neighborhood."

"But some have done it."

"*I've* done it. But it never pays enough. Perhaps life was different for you, with your white skin and your law degree. But I grew up in a different world and I still have to live in it."

He winced. Guilting the Caucasian community was probably not a brilliant move, since most of the jurors were white. But it had already happened. He hoped they would see her frustration and not make too much of it.

Jazlyn continued. "Ms. Valdez, your lawyer talked with the previous witnesses about motives they may have had against Sanchez, so I think it's fair to do the same with you. Because of all the people involved in this story, you had the strongest reason to want Sanchez dead. Didn't you?"

Gabriella lowered her head. "I barely knew the man."

"He's your relative, isn't he?"

"I knew of him, but I did not know him."

"You knew what he did. And you knew what he wanted, right?"

"Yes."

"You knew he was involved in sex trafficking. Often with very young girls."

Her eyes seemed stony. "Yes."

"And you knew that if Esperanza were deported, she would be delivered to El Salvador and probably ultimately sent to Sanchez."

"Agent Crenshaw told me that. He said he had no choice, that regulations required him to do this."

"And you had to be worried about what would happen to a

pretty young girl in Sanchez' hands."

"He would've forced her to become a whore. She would've had no choice about it. He would've sold her virginity to the highest bidder. She would have been destroyed, just as he destroyed my sister."

His jaw clenched. Stay cool, Gabriella. Stay cool.

Jazlyn continued. "You didn't want to see that happen, did you?"

"Of course not. No one who cared about her would want that to happen."

"And you would do anything to prevent it, wouldn't you? And it looked like you couldn't prevent it unless Sanchez was dead, right?"

"I did not kill Sanchez."

"There are many people with dubious contrived remote theoretical motives, but the person who had the strongest motive to kill Sanchez was you. You might even say, once Sanchez was dead —you'd taken care of everything."

"Sanchez was just a man. The cartel goes on. Agent Crenshaw says his younger brother will now be in charge."

"Maybe the brother will be the next one to meet a violent death."

He sprang to his feet. "Objection!"

Judge Le nodded. "Sustained. Anything more, counsel?"

Jazlyn nodded. "One last question. Ms. Valdez, were you saddened by Sanchez' death?"

He bounced back up. "Again I object. Her feelings are not relevant."

The judge tilted her head. "I can't agree with you this time. Overruled. The witness will answer."

Jazlyn repeated the question. The silence in the courtroom was palpable.

"No," Gabriella said. Her eyes were like hardened coals. "I was glad he was dead. I was very glad."

Jazlyn nodded. "No more questions."

CHAPTER FORTY-NINE

DAN CLOSED HIS EYES, ATTEMPTING TO CONCENTRATE. HE HAD no desire to re-direct Gabriella, but his brain was trying to tell him something, had been for some time. What was it?

Judge Le looked toward the defense table. "Is that all, Mr. Pike?"

Maria tugged at his arm. "We're done, aren't we?"

He didn't answer.

"I know that didn't go as well as you wanted," she whispered, "but I think we're done, right?"

He shook his head. "If we quit now, Gabriella is finished."

"We don't have any more witnesses."

He barely heard her. He was deep-diving into his brain, trying to pull something elusive to the surface. But what was it?

He scanned the gallery, trying to recall everything he knew, everything he had seen. Trying to connect the dots. Put it all together.

Tattoo. Earring. Scar behind the neck. Small shoes.

No. That wasn't it. He kept scanning.

Hat. Ink stain on left finger. Hymns.

No.

Boots on the desk. Strong arms. Bolo tie...

Getting warmer.

Luciana's head wound. The gun in the hedge. The torn photograph. The mutilated corpse. I don't know how Sanchez got in. Some months I can barely pay the mortgage.

His eyes flew open. He rose to his feet.

Judge Le leaned forward. "Mr. Pike? Are you all right?"

"Yes, your honor. I'm sorry. I was…thinking."

"Are you ready to rest your case?"

"No." He scribbled a note on his legal pad, then tossed it to Jimmy. A second later, Jimmy bolted out of the courtroom. "I have one more witness."

The judge's head turned. "You do? I thought we were finished."

"I did too. I was wrong." He turned to the gallery and pointed. "The defense calls Agent Jack Crenshaw to the witness stand."

In the third row of the gallery, Crenshaw looked stunned. "What?" he said softly. "I'm just monitoring the case. No one told me anything about this."

Jazlyn asked for a bench conference. The judge waved the lawyers forward and covered the microphone. Jazlyn protested the surprise witness. He reminded her that she had pulled much the same thing earlier with Ramon Alvarez.

"But that was based upon newly discovered evidence."

"Well, so is this. Sort of."

The judge squinted. "I'm sorry?"

"This is based upon…a newly realized revelation."

"I have no idea what that means."

"It means I've been a damned idiot. But I figured it out. I know what happened. Look, I'm not required to submit a witness list, so you can't say the prosecution has suffered any disadvantage. Let me put this witness on the stand. *Please.*"

"There's also an issue of fairness," Jazlyn said. "The witness had no knowledge he would be called."

He gave the judge a firm look. "And that might be for the better."

Judge Le frowned. He could see she was deliberating.

"Crenshaw is in the courtroom, after all," he continued. "It's not like he's being inconvenienced. Why should he object to telling the truth about what he knows?"

"All right," Judge Le said. "I always love me a good surprise. You may disappoint some jurors who are ready to get home. But let's do this." She looked up and uncovered the microphone. "Agent Crenshaw, please take the stand."

Crenshaw didn't move. "No one said anything to me about testifying. I haven't prepared. I doubt I can offer anything useful."

Judge Le shook her head. "Sure about this, Mr. Pike?"

"Yes, your honor. It's absolutely essential."

Crenshaw continued. "Someone wants to call a witness from my office, there's mounds of paperwork. Official channels. He can't just haul me up there against my will."

The judge disagreed. "You came into this courtroom of your own free will. You're subject to the jurisdiction of the court."

"It's a waste of time," Crenshaw insisted. "I don't know anything."

"Then this shouldn't take long." The judge pointed. "In the interest of justice, and for no other reason, I will allow this. But I want to see the relevance, and I want to see it fast, Mr. Pike. Do you understand me?"

"I do."

"No messing around."

"Heaven forfend." He suspected Crenshaw now wished he had not hung around the courtroom.

Of course, he'd been hanging around for a reason.

After a few more moments, Crenshaw marched his cowboy boots up to the witness stand and was sworn in. He quickly established the witness' credentials as an immigration officer, then had him explain his involvement with Gabriella and Esperanza.

"Could you give the jury some idea how many cases you're currently monitoring?"

Crenshaw shrugged. "A whole bunch."

"Would it be fair to say you oversee hundreds of cases?"

"Thousands, to some degree. Since the current administration revoked protected status to six different nations, my work has skyrocketed."

"That must be incredibly burdensome."

"I'm not the only cowpoke on the posse." He smiled a little. "But yes, it does keep me busy."

"And yet," he continued, "what has struck me from the start was how much detail you had at your fingertips about Gabriella and Esperanza."

"I try to stay hands-on with my work. Especially when a minor is involved."

"And how many of your cases involve minors?"

He tilted his head. "Lots."

"Hundreds?"

"Probably."

"But you always knew all about Gabriella. Is there, perhaps, some reason her case attracted your attention?"

Crenshaw's head tucked in a bit. "I am... not sure what you mean. It's a distinctive case. Smart little girl. Orphan. Ties to the sex trade."

He took a few steps closer to the witness stand. "Another mystery that's been plaguing me is how that whole shootout, the confrontation between Emilio and Sanchez, warring gang leaders from different nations, came about. Everyone seems to have been there, but nobody knows how it was arranged." He looked at the witness intently. "Do you know how it was arranged?"

Crenshaw frowned. "How would I know that?"

He smiled. Answering a question with a question was the first move of the evasive witness. "So you don't?"

"I have no idea why those two murderers met up that night. It had nothing to do with me."

"Are you sure?" He pulled out his phone and checked it. Nothing. Damn. It was always hard to stall for time, but worse when the judge had given you specific instructions to move things along quickly. "Let me phrase that differently. Do you know why Sanchez was in the country?"

"I assume that he had business reasons. Trying to expand his empire. Like I told you before."

"But you don't actually know?"

"I have no firsthand knowledge."

"Do you know how he got into this country?"

Crenshaw slowed a step. "Now...what?"

"You do work for Immigration, don't you?"

"Yes."

"A customs official would have to issue a visa before Sanchez could get into this country, right?"

"Unless he snuck across the border."

"Did he?"

Crenshaw hesitated. "No. He had a visa."

"Are you in the habit of issuing visas to suspected sex traffickers?"

"Of course not."

"Then how did he get one?" He checked his phone again. Still nothing. "Can you explain that?"

Crenshaw turned toward the judge. "This highlights the problem with ambushing somebody who doesn't expect to be put on the stand. Had I any notice, I might've been able to do a little research. Check the records."

The judge nodded sympathetically. "Mr. Pike, I asked you to get to the point quickly. So far, you've made no point whatsoever."

"I'm about to, your honor. Promise."

She held up a finger. "One minute."

Come on, Jimmy. *Come on.* "You knew Sanchez was involved with sex trafficking, didn't you?"

"We had strong suspicions. My office has been tracking him for a long time."

"And yet he still got into this country." Pause. "It's almost as if someone wanted him here."

"This stuff happens, unfortunately. People with the kind of money Sanchez had are able to pull strings. One connection leads to another."

"But at the end of the day, someone has to authorize the visa, right?" He felt a buzzing in his pocket. He pulled out his phone and glanced at the screen.

He tapped out a hasty response.

"Yes," Crenshaw said. "I've already told you that. I don't know why—"

He cut Crenshaw off. "And in this case, the person who signed the paperwork granting Sanchez' visa application—was you."

A hush fell across the courtroom.

"You made sure he could get into the States, didn't you? Because you wanted him here."

Crenshaw's lips parted slowly. "I—I don't know what you're talking about."

"I think you do. You didn't use your own name on the forms, of course, which is why no one noticed till now. But my colleague is a handwriting expert and he says the signature is yours. He's on his way to the courtroom now with a copy."

"You're bluffing."

"Not today. I have a crack team, including someone who knows the records system inside out and is also a trained handwriting analyst. He's got the goods on you, so you might as well come clean."

"This is completely outrageous."

"I'm asking you point blank, Agent Crenshaw. Please remember that you are under oath and subject to the penalties of perjury. So how do you want to play this?" He allowed several seconds of silence. Crenshaw's eyes burned into his. "Did you allow Sanchez into this country?"

"Damn you," Crenshaw muttered. His eyes grew steely. His jaw tightened. "I did."

He had the jury's attention now. Time for the money shot. "So when you said you had no idea how or why Sanchez was here, that wasn't entirely correct, was it? You're the whole reason he was here."

"This is part of an undercover sting operation," Crenshaw replied. "Top secret. You're trespassing into an ongoing investigation. I don't care what the courtroom rules are. I can't talk about this. If you sent my office a subpoena, as you should have done, we might have been able to work something out."

He wasn't buying it. "How can there be an ongoing investigation? Sanchez is dead."

"His cartel had many people in it. Some of his operatives and some of the men and women he turned into sex slaves are still in this country. Stop trying to thwart justice with smoke and mirrors and let us do our job."

He kept pressing. "You're saying the government let a major cartel figure into the country so they could investigate him? And to accomplish this, you put a false name on the visa paperwork? And somehow Sanchez knew his visa application would be granted by someone who wanted to investigate him? I'm not buying it. I think you let Sanchez into the country because you wanted to do business with him. You wanted a piece of the action."

"That's absurd."

Jazlyn started to rise, but he cut her off. "First time I met you, Agent Crenshaw, you complained about how little the government pays you. Couldn't pay the mortgage, right? Working with Sanchez would solve that problem. And this could also explain why you knew so much about Gabriella. And Esperanza. You knew, because Sanchez told you he was Esperanza's nearest relative. Sanchez very much wanted Esperanza, and you very much wanted to please Sanchez. That meant you needed to do something about Gabriella, to get her out of the way."

"This is a complete fantasy."

"You contacted Luis, Emilio's assistant, who wanted Emilio out of the way so he could be captain of the ship. And you got hold of someone in Sanchez' outfit. Maybe his little brother, Diego? You set up the meeting to take out both gang lords. But you still wanted to eliminate Gabriella, probably to curry favor with Diego Sanchez."

"It's a lie! A disgusting filthy lie."

"You must've been paid something up front, for getting Sanchez across the border. Maybe you used some of that to bribe Luis and Diego. Where's the rest of the money? Offshore accounts?"

"You have no proof of that."

"Not yet. But I have a crack research team, and they have experience dealing with foreign bank accounts, which aren't nearly as impenetrable as they used to be. We'll find your account."

Crenshaw turned toward the judge. "Do I have to put up with this unsubstantiated mudslinging? This is offensive not only to me but to my office and the United States government. He's meddling in an ongoing investigation."

The judge was slow to respond. "You are required to answer Mr. Pike's questions. I will remind Mr. Pike that he is supposed to be asking questions."

"Fine. Here's another one. How did you know about Gabriella's sister, Luciana?"

Crenshaw seemed startled. "Well... Gabriella...told me about her sister."

"Really? According to Gabriella, you told her Luciana was in the country. How did you know?"

"That's not accurate. Gabriella asked me to check up on the gal."

"When did Gabriella tell you about her sister?"

"I don't remember the date."

"How did it come up?"

"Her name was in the file."

"You gave me copies of those records. I saw no mention of Luciana. I knew nothing about the sister till I heard about her in court."

Crenshaw hesitated. "Well...I don't remember exactly. This is all very confusing."

"One way or the other, you're going to be called on your lies."

"I'm not lying!"

"Here's the truth. Sanchez told you about Luciana, just like he told you about Esperanza. He'd used Luciana until there was almost nothing left of her. Brought her here—with a visa you arranged, I'll wager—for leverage against Gabriella, but she kept escaping and became a threat—which you dealt with. You went to work on her, didn't you? Drugs, captivity, isolation. Who knows, maybe even a little torture. You wanted to make sure she couldn't identify you, couldn't testify against you, couldn't tell people you were involved with Sanchez. We know she and others were confined in a storage locker, apparently for days at a time. Someone took her apart, destroyed what fragile remnant of a mind was left after years of sexual degradation."

"These are all lies!"

He could see Jazlyn preparing to object, and to be fair, she had cause. He pivoted and gave her a stern look.

His meaning was clear. Don't interrupt. I'm onto something here.

Jazlyn settled back into her seat.

"You know what Luciana told me when I talked to her? She babbled about someone who wanted to hurt her. She kept talking about the eyes." He concentrated, recalling the scene. "She repeated the phrase. 'The eyes, man.' And I was so stupid, I let her true meaning get lost in her broken voice and heavily accented Spanglish. She wasn't saying eyes—she was saying ICE.

She was talking about the ICE-man. Meaning you. The Immigration and Customs Enforcement agent who had beaten and tortured her."

"I'm not putting up with this any longer." Crenshaw stood as if to leave. The judge gave him a fierce look and motioned toward the bailiff.

In the back of the courtroom, Jimmy burst through the doors, waving papers above his head.

"You see that?" he continued. "We've got the goods on you. The visa application with your signature. Soon we'll be able to prove you let Sanchez into the country, met with him, learned about Gabriella's sister, and arranged the meeting that led to the shootout. I bet you were the one who instituted deportation proceedings against Esperanza. Even by the standards of the current administration, rushing the deportation of a little girl who's lost her parents is inhumane. You pushed for it, right? Don't bother answering, I'll prove it. Once I get the FBI involved, we'll find all kinds of telecommunications between you and Sanchez. And Sanchez' brother."

"I would never work for men like that! They disgusted me!"

"So you admit that you knew them?"

Crenshaw fell back into his seat. Sweat trickled down the side of his face. "I want a lawyer. I'm taking the fifth. Man's got to protect himself against lies. I'm not saying another word."

Yes! Nailed it.

He exchanged a glance with the judge, then continued. "You told me the cartel planned to expand the sex-trafficking business to the US. Wouldn't they need a point man here to assist? Who better than you? You're so well connected in the immigration world. You could get almost anyone in or out."

Crenshaw stared back at him, his teeth clenched shut. "I'm not talking."

"Then let me explain what happened. You knew Gabriella had a gun. You searched her house while she was at work and Esperanza was at school till you found it, which probably didn't take you long. You planted a lookalike gun in its place. You set up the shootout, hid in the shadows, and killed Sanchez with Gabriella's gun. Probably tried to kill Emilio. You mutilated the body to make the murder look personal. Later you switched the guns again, taking back yours and planting Gabriella's, the murder weapon, in her backyard. Then you called the cops and gave them the anonymous tip."

"You don't know what you're talking about," Crenshaw growled.

"I think I do. I'm going to prove everything I've said and make sure you're locked up for the rest of your life. If anyone deserves to be on death row, it's you, and I will not rest until—"

Before anyone knew what had happened, Crenshaw had a gun in his hands. Pointed about a foot from Dan's forehead.

CHAPTER FIFTY

"DON'T MOVE!" CRENSHAW SHOUTED. "NO ONE MOVES!"

The bailiff took a step forward. Crenshaw cautioned him with a wave of the gun. "Anybody moves toward that door or me, they're dead. I've got nothing to lose now. Don't push me."

His hand waved the gun back and forth, erratic and trembling. "I may kill you all anyway. Starting with you, Pike. Followed by your client."

Dan's heart pounded madly against his chest. He had hoped to get Crenshaw excited—but he hadn't expected this. He should've realized the man might have a gun on him. Like all law enforcement personnel, state or federal, he was allowed to carry weapons into the courthouse. They waived him past the metal detectors.

"I'm getting out of here," Crenshaw said, "and nobody's gonna stop me. Including you, Pike."

He took a deep breath and tried to stay calm. He liked extreme sports, he told himself. Staring down the barrel of a gun had to be the most extreme one yet. "Let's say you get out of here, which I doubt. Then what?"

"I got money. I can go anywhere."

"Can you? You can't leave the country. I doubt you can even make it to your car."

"I've already made arrangements. Contingency plans."

"You're thinking Diego will take care of you. Forget it. You just made yourself untouchable."

"You'll forgive me if I try."

"Aren't you a poker player? Surely you know it's time to fold."

"I'll fold when I'm dead."

"And that's exactly what's going to happen, probably in the next ten minutes, if you don't put down that gun."

He noticed the judge slowly sliding under the bench, out of the firing line. The bench was probably steel-reinforced. He knew judges were trained for emergencies. Too often, they became targets.

Maria looked stunned, terrified. He laid his hand on her shoulder, trying to calm her. Gabriella, by contrast, seemed oddly calm. Perhaps because this scene vindicated her. But he thought it was more. Finally, she was seeing the truth revealed, the truth about what she and so many others had suffered.

Crenshaw climbed out of the witness stand and headed down the center aisle, keeping the gun trained. "Here's a word of advice for you, judge. If you're thinking about calling security, think again. No one's going to draw on an immigration officer. And if they try, they'll end up dead."

Judge Le, to her credit, was not cowed. "Sir, you are in my courtroom, and you will obey my instructions. Put down the weapon."

"Your courtroom? You're a joke. The whole justice system is a joke. Immigration is a joke. Politicians and bureaucrats give speeches and nothing ever changes. We have a real immigration problem and no one is doing anything about it. How much longer can we go on like this, paying the way for people who can't support themselves? Are we going to be dominated by the people who contribute the least? It has to stop somewhere."

"We can talk about this," he said, breathing deeply. "Just put down the gun."

"I tried to help people, but what did it get me? A crappy house, a broken marriage, a job no one respects. Just once, I tried to do something for myself, tried to make a little money on the side. But of course, you won't let that happen. Rights are only for illegal leeches."

"You're not thinking straight," he said, holding out his hands. "I think you need some help. And we can get you that. But you need to put down the gun."

"You're even worse than they are, Pike. Putting murderers back on the street for cash. You have no idea what justice is."

His face hardened. "I know my father did fourteen years for a crime he didn't commit. And then he died, when I was seventeen. I swore I'd never let the government railroad anybody else. Not if I could stop it."

Maria looked at him. "Dan…I had no idea."

"Doesn't matter." He turned back to Crenshaw. "Please put down the gun before someone gets hurt."

"I am so damn sick of this. I'm sick of everyone!" Crenshaw took several steps forward and pointed the gun directly at his face. "But most of all I'm sick of you, Pike. I tried to warn you off. The doll, the photo. But you wouldn't listen. *Damn you!*" The gun swung wildly all around him. "I may not get out of here alive. But I won't die alone!"

Everything happened at once. He leapt backward, pushing over the defense table to serve as a shield. Gunfire erupted. He grabbed Maria and Gabriella and held them tight. He heard a rush of footsteps, then screaming. A mad blur. Crenshaw's knees buckled and he fell forward. More people screamed.

The gun fired again.

And then the courtroom was filled with an eerie silence.

He and Maria exchanged looks. What happened? Was it safe?

A few seconds later, he leaned out from behind the table.

Crenshaw lay on the floor, arms twisted behind his back.

Garrett sat on top of him. The gun was on the carpet a few feet away.

"What happened?"

"Well," Garrett said, "someone had to do something."

"I had security people—"

"And they weren't moving," Garrett replied. "So I did."

Armed officers burst through the back doors of the courtroom. Garrett raised his hands. The cops took custody of Crenshaw. Jimmy slowly raised his head out of the aisle. Garrett walked back to the defense table. "You okay, Dan?"

"I'll live. I think you just saved my life."

"Well, I didn't want to go through the whole process of getting another new team member. Too damn much trouble."

CHAPTER FIFTY-ONE

MUCH TIME PASSED BEFORE DAN FELT REMOTELY NORMAL again. He wondered if he would ever feel normal again. His heart pounded like a stroke was imminent. He let Maria calm Gabriella. She seemed much calmer than he expected to be anytime soon.

The police spent the next hour taking statements. No one was allowed to leave. Eventually they hauled Crenshaw away.

He quizzed Garrett. "What the hell did you think you were doing?"

Garrett shrugged. "I expected your security guys to cut in, but they seemed paralyzed."

"So you decided to play Superman?"

"I held back when he was confessing. I thought that might help our case. But when he started babbling about immigrants, I couldn't stand it anymore. Losers like that give conservatives a bad name. While he was distracted by you, I tackled him from behind. He fired into the ceiling a couple of times, but I knocked the gun out of his hand and pinned his arms behind his back. No big."

"You saved my life, dude. And probably a lot of other people's lives too."

"I could hear the officers outside. They were probably afraid they'd draw fire if they burst through the doors."

"Just the same—thanks. That was speedy thinking."

"You were pretty speedy yourself, Dan," Maria said. "I think you leapt ten feet to get that table down to shield us."

He pointed at his feet. "Air Jordans. Not just a fashion statement."

Judge Le looked shaken, but she held herself together and spoke directly to Gabriella. "We still have much to learn, Ms. Valdez. I suspect the investigation will continue for many weeks. But it's clear that you are a victim here, not a perpetrator. I believe the charges against you should be dismissed. Any objection from the prosecution?"

"Definitely not," Jazlyn said.

"Gabriella Valdez, you are free to go."

Gabriella melted into his arms, tears streaming down her face. "I can't believe it. I never thought—" Her voice was buried beneath tears.

Maria closed in beside him. "I'm just as surprised. And just as pleased."

"You didn't think we could win this?"

"I didn't think anyone could win this. And a few minutes ago, I thought you'd solved the case and your reward would be a bullet in the head. But somehow you managed to win and survive. You really are a miracle worker."

Jimmy came up behind them. "Could we please have a normal day? One with no threats, gunplay, or racing after documents?"

"Someday soon. By the way, thanks for your help."

Jimmy frowned. "The line at the records office was a mile long. All the schmoozing in the world would not have gotten me cuts. I'm sorry."

Maria looked confused. "What? I thought—"

Jimmy held out the piece of paper he'd been waving around. It was blank.

"Jimmy! You lied?"

"Dan texted me. Told me to burst into the courtroom waving paper in the air."

"Then you didn't find the visa application? You didn't analyze the handwriting?" She glared at him. "Dan! You lied to the witness!"

He tilted his head, eyes upward. "I baited the witness. And it worked."

CHAPTER FIFTY-TWO

DAN WAS IMPRESSED BY HOW MUCH DIFFERENCE A GOOD night's sleep could make. This morning, he almost felt like a normal person. He slept well, except for the three times he woke with night terrors, convinced that Crenshaw was about to drill him. He almost left the boat and checked into a hotel, but ultimately, terra firma would not have made anything better. He still got the best night's sleep he'd had in days.

He was at the courthouse as soon as it opened. He noticed several reporters seated on the front row of the gallery. That was unusual for an adoption hearing. But he supposed Gabriella was still a subject of interest.

She sat waiting for him, looking happier than he had ever seen her. He sat beside her and smiled. "We're in the home stretch."

Judge Hawkins called the court to order.

"Thank you for hearing this on such short notice," he said.

The judge nodded. "I understand there are exigent circumstances. I've received a summary report from Judge Le. I know what occurred in her courtroom. Of course, it's all over the news. Are you all right, Mr. Pike?"

"Never better." He felt jubilant, confident. At last they were on the downhill slope. No one had filed a brief in opposition. Esperanza's guardian ad litem was present to protect her interests, but what objection could be made? This should be a snap.

He launched into a standard presentation, basically echoing the information presented in his brief. Gabriella knew Esperanza and loved her. She had demonstrated that she could take care of a young girl, even in difficult circumstances. She was pursuing new job prospects. The media coverage worked in her favor. People were lining up to help this wronged woman who put her life on the line to save a little girl. Dr. Kazan had offered her an apartment in one of his nicer buildings, rent free for the first six months. Her life was about to improve in a way she could never have imagined.

"It's a complete win-win, your honor. Gabriella has a safe place to live, a good job, and a kindly spirit. Esperanza adores her. Once the adoption is completed, I've been assured that all deportation proceedings will cease. I strongly urge the court to grant this adoption."

Judge Hawkins nodded. "Thank you, Mr. Pike. Anything from the child's guardian?"

A thin woman, Ramona Clarkson, rose. Brown dress. Flats. Upswept hair. Fidgety hands.

She spoke in a quiet voice. "I'm afraid I do object, your honor."

His head whipped around. *What?*

He felt Gabriella's hand clutch his wrist. "No," she whispered. "No."

Clarkson continued. "I'm glad to hear Gabriella's life may be improving. Perhaps in six months, or a year or two, she would be a better candidate for adoption. But I have to put the best interests of the child first. Gabriella would never pass muster with any adoption agency. She couldn't even be approved as a foster parent. She has a criminal record. Until recently, she worked for a known drug pusher. She's been connected to sex trafficking."

"Wait a minute—"

"She was accused of murder."

"She was acquitted," he practically screamed.

"No," Clarkson continued, "the charges were dismissed, after a witness had a breakdown during an intense cross-examination, followed by a dramatic courtroom confrontation. Clearly the man suffered from mental illness, but that doesn't prove anyone's guilt or innocence. The authorities are still investigating what happened."

"Gabriella didn't do it," he said firmly.

"I'm not arguing with you about that. But the fact is, she wasn't acquitted, and the reason she was accused in the first place is because she has made poor choices and surrounded herself with the criminal element. She is simply not a suitable adoptive parent."

He couldn't believe what he heard. "Have you spoken to Esperanza about this?"

"Of course Esperanza adores her. Gabriella has been the only adult protector in her life since her parents' passing. That doesn't prove Gabriella is a suitable parent."

"All Gabriella's criminal activities were in the past."

"She was working for Emilio Lòpez until quite recently."

"But not in a criminal capacity. She hasn't done anything wrong recently. She hasn't—"

Clarkson cut him off. "She was in possession of a gun."

He stopped. Took a breath. "She owned the gun legally. It was registered to her."

"It was in the home with a minor. It was apparently hidden in the bedroom where the minor could easily have laid her hands on it. The mere fact that she had it violates most adoptive or foster parenting regulations."

His voice dropped to a low rumble. "She needed a gun for protection."

"In that neighborhood, yes, she probably did, which points out again what an unsuitable parent she is."

"She's moving."

"Over and over again, Gabriella has made unwise decisions. I have to base my recommendation upon the best interests of the child, and I can only do that considering what has happened in the past. I hope Gabriella will improve in the future, and as I said, we might be able to revisit this down the line."

"Esperanza won't be here a year from now. She won't be here a week from now. Do you think she'll be better off if she's deported?"

The guardian shook her head. "I can't take that into account, and it would be inappropriate for the judge to consider predictions about the future. We can't recommend an ill-advised adoption based upon speculation. The only proper consideration for this court is whether Gabriella is a suitable adoptive parent. And by every objective standard we use to measure such things, she is not."

He jumped to his feet. "Your honor, may I respond?"

To his surprise, Judge Hawkins shook her head. "No, I don't think there's any need for that. You were responding constantly during the guardian's presentation. You've said what you have to say and I don't need to hear it a second time. I've given this matter a great deal of thought and investigation. I'm sorry to tell you this, Mr. Pike, but I almost always accept the guardian's recommendations because they are in the best position to know the truth. In this case, I completely agree with Ms. Clarkson. I realize you're only trying to help, Mr. Pike. But the fact is, Gabriella is not a suitable adoptive parent."

"She's the only person eligible. ICE will only permit adoption by a relative."

"And they have that restriction for a reason—to prevent someone from engineering an inappropriate adoption just to thwart immigration procedures, which is exactly what you're trying to do now. You may be sincere in your efforts to help, but I can't let that influence my decision. The law is the law."

"If Esperanza isn't adopted, she's dead."

The judge drew in her breath. "I will instruct the reporter to strike the last remark from the record. And I will instruct counsel to stop interrupting or I will have him removed from the courtroom."

He buttoned his lip.

"Neither you nor I can perfectly predict what might occur in the future. Fortunately, courts are not required to do so. The decision whether to grant an adoption is based upon the suitability of the parent based upon present circumstances. I don't think Ms. Valdez fails as a prospective parent on every count. I do believe she loves this girl and the girl loves her. But unfortunately, that's not enough. The eyes of the world are upon us. We have to play by the rules."

Was that the problem? he wondered. Was she speaking to him, or the reporters in the courtroom? Was she afraid she'd be criticized in the press if she allowed the former accused murderer to adopt a child?

Gabriella clutched his wrist so tightly she drew blood. A soft cry emerged from her lips. She had been through so much—and now this. The whole reason for everything, every risk she'd taken, slipping through her fingers. After so much fighting, it would come to nothing.

"I wish all the best for the child," Judge Hawkins continued. "But at this time, I cannot grant the adoption." She banged her gavel. "The petition is denied."

CHAPTER FIFTY-THREE

That evening, back at the office, Dan huddled with his partners, trying to come up with a solution. Unfortunately, no one had one. They'd experienced such elation after the charges against Gabriella were dropped. In his arrogance, he had assumed the adoption would be a piece of cake. He should've known better. Nothing in the law is ever easy, and no judge's decision is ever predictable.

He received a call from the detention center. They were processing the deportation orders. Esperanza had only a few days to remain in the United States.

"I realize I barely knew her," Garrett said. "But I'm going to miss her just the same."

Maria nodded. "We all are. She really burrowed into our souls, didn't she, Dan?"

He tried to remain stoic. "She's a smart girl. And she's endured so much. Only to be sent to—" He stopped short. He couldn't say it aloud. He couldn't even bear to think about it.

"There must be something we can do," Maria said. "We just haven't thought of it yet."

"That's what I used to think. Every problem has a solution. Every piece of evidence can be admitted. Every witness can be tricked into spilling the truth. But as it turns out, that isn't always true."

"Was I the only one," Garrett asked, "who was floored by what Crenshaw started spewing as he tried to make his way out of the courtroom? About immigration and the justice system, and how it totally doesn't work."

"At the time, I was more focused on the gun."

"Likewise," Maria agreed.

"He's not completely wrong," Garrett said "The system is a mess. If a bright girl like Esperanza gets deported, something is not working."

"I love that girl so much," Maria said. "I can't believe that after a few more days, I'll never see her again."

Jimmy pressed his fingers against his forehead. "This is so sad. It's just like when Superman fell in love with Lori Lemaris, and he asked her to marry him, and she was forced to reveal that she wasn't in a wheelchair with a blanket over her legs because she was handicapped, but because she was...a mermaid." His voice choked.

"I'm not quite sure I see the connection..."

"Don't you? Dan, he loved her, and she loved him, but they were from two separate worlds and they could never be together."

His eyes widened. "Oh my gosh. I remember that story."

Jimmy's head turned. "I thought you said you didn't read comic books."

He looked away. "I might've seen one somewhere. In a... barbershop or something." He tilted his head. Something else triggered in his brain. "Wasn't there some awful place where all of Batman's crazy archenemies went? Until they escaped, which was about every other week."

"Arkham Asylum. Denny O'Neill came up with that. Named it for a town in the Lovecraft mythos. He—"

"Wait a minute." He snapped his fingers. "Wait just one second. That's it. Arkham *Asylum*."

All three looked at him strangely.

"We've been so wrapped up with everything else. We forgot something." He rushed to the kitchen counter and opened his laptop. "We're not down yet, partners."

"What?" Maria said, rushing beside him. "What is it?"

"We've got one more arrow in our quiver. One more way to save Esperanza."

DAN HAD NEVER ARGUED ANYTHING LIKE THIS BEFORE. He had never appeared before Judge Franklin, but he knew the older man—only a year and a half from retirement— had a reputation for being a strict constructionist. He would apply the law as it was written, and would not be receptive to any emotional appeals or arguments about bending the rules.

That probably would not work to their advantage. But he would give it his best anyway.

Esperanza was scheduled for deportation tomorrow morning.

He grasped Gabriella's hand under the table. She had been through so much. Incarceration, trial, losing the adoption petition. He didn't want her to end up like her sister—but how much could anyone bear?

He turned and saw Jazlyn entering the courtroom.

She had actually come. She told him she would, but he still found it hard to believe. He was not accustomed to perceiving his adversaries as admirable human beings.

He crossed into the aisle to meet her.

"Sorry I'm late," she said. "Stopped by my boss's office. I thought you'd like to hear what's going on with Crenshaw."

"Have they charged him?"

"Just ten minutes ago. They wanted to be cautious and make sure they got it right. As it turned out, the documents he had on his laptop were more than enough to justify pressing charges. We're building a strong case."

"So he was working with Jorge Sanchez?"

"At first. Till he found it more promising to shaft Jorge and partner with the brother. Found a bank account in the Caymans we're almost certain is his. We think the taste of real money sent Crenshaw over the edge. Once he was firmly installed in the organization, he probably planned to quietly retire from ICE, and no one would be the wiser." She smiled. "Until you figured it all out."

"Until we did," he said. "Working together. Making the system work."

Jazlyn shook her head. "I can't take any credit for this. I was about to convict the wrong person. I would have, but for you." She reached out and laid her hand softly on his shoulder. "I want to thank you for that. You stopped me from making a hideous mistake." She passed him a cardboard box. "This is filled with documents. Amazing how cooperative ICE can be, once you've unearthed a traitor operating unchecked in their system."

The bailiff appeared in the doorway.

"Okay," he said, "looks like it's show time. Hey, would you mind hanging around after the hearing?"

"Sure. Why?"

"Later."

Judge Franklin entered the courtroom. He took up the papers on the bench. "We have a petition for political asylum. For a young woman named Esperanza Coto."

He rose. "That's correct, your honor."

The judge continued. "I've been sent numerous background documents, a complete dossier. I think I know everything I need to know. I gather you're representing the minor?"

"I am, your honor."

"And we also have a representative from Immigration and Customs Enforcement? Brendan Abrams?"

Abrams rose. "We do, your honor."

"And you oppose this petition?"

Abrams spoke slowly. He was young and fair, a little awkward.

"On technical grounds, your honor. We do not believe this petition meets the standard for granting political asylum. We think it's important that these applications not become a ploy for evading legal deportation."

"I understand. Mr. Pike, since this is your petition, I'll allow you to speak first."

He stood and addressed the court. "Your honor, it's very simple. If I may remind the court, Esperanza was brought to this country from El Salvador many years ago by her parents, who were tragically killed, both at the same time, in a traffic accident. Now she's on her own and she needs our help."

The judge did not appear moved. "During the entire time she and her parents were in the United States, did they apply for citizenship? Or asylum?"

"No, your honor, but to be fair, they had no need to. The government had granted protected status to immigrants from El Salvador. They came to this country legally, through legitimate border-crossing venues. They had no way to anticipate that the current administration would suddenly, without explanation, revoke protected status for people from El Salvador and several other countries. This political move may have pleased some niches of the populace, but it had a devastating effect on those who—"

The judge cut him off with a wave of his hand. "We're not going to debate politics here, counsel. The law is what it is. Protected status has been revoked. The minor will be deported unless you can explain to me why she should be granted asylum. So why don't you get to that?"

He drew in his breath. "As I said, she's alone in the world. She's been cared for, and cared for well, by the woman seated beside me, Gabriella Valdez."

"This is the woman whose adoption petition was denied?"

"Yes, your honor."

"So this asylum petition is your last-ditch effort to keep an illegal alien in the country."

"She's only an illegal alien because the government, by executive order, changed the rules."

"Be that as it may, she's an illegal alien."

"If you will recall, your honor, the current administration also issued an executive order forbidding applications for asylum by people who have not entered the country legally. It was unclear whether that would apply to people like Esperanza who lost protected status but remained in the country. A federal court struck down those restrictions, though, opening the possibility of political asylum once again, at least until the Supreme Court speaks. People like Esperanza can claim asylum and obtain legal protection in the US if they're facing or could face persecution back home based upon their race, religion, nationality, political opinion, or membership in a particular social group."

"I am familiar with the law, counsel. What's your argument?"

"Esperanza Coto is an extraordinary young woman. Strong, intelligent. Despite serious economic handicaps, she has excelled at school. She's generous, kind, hard-working. She is exactly the kind of citizen we want in the United States."

The judge looked at him sternly. "And none of that has anything to do with political asylum. You need to show a present threat. You need to show me that she is in danger in her home country."

"And she is," he insisted. "If you've read my brief, you know what awaits this young girl in El Salvador. Our customs authorities will deliver her to their Salvadoran equivalent, which will almost certainly deliver her to her nearest living relative, which in this case is Diego Sanchez, who runs a sex-trafficking cartel." He pushed forward the box Jazlyn brought him. "I have numerous documents here detailing Sanchez' connections to the largest sex cartel in that country. He also has connections here in the United States. If we deliver this young girl to him...there's little doubt about what will happen to her."

"You can't prove that. You're speculating."

"I'm using common sense," he said quietly.

"You can't say there's persecution against her in El Salvador. She's been in the United States for most of her life."

"She's a member of a protected social group that faces persecution."

"And that would be...?"

"Young women. Who are habitually treated like chattel in many corners of the world."

"That's not a protected class."

"Then it should be. When will we start protecting women from these predators? When will we stand up and say, hey— time's up. We're not going to allow this anymore."

"I believe you're showing your cultural bias. We can't force our values on other nations."

"This isn't Western cultural bias. Sex trafficking is illegal in El Salvador too—but it happens. This is an incredible young girl and we shouldn't let a total scumbag get his hands on her just because they're related."

The judge leaned back, steepling his fingers. "This is most irregular."

"Granted, this is not like most claims for political asylum. But her case meets the standard. And there is also the matter of justice. And mercy. Which may not be written into the statute, but I like to think it underlies every decision made by every court in this country."

The judge turned toward Mr. Abrams. "Anything from the United States?"

Abrams seemed hesitant to speak. "As I said before, your honor, we oppose on technical grounds. But as Mr. Pike has said, this is a special case. These facts are unlikely to be duplicated." He cleared his throat. "Before I entered the courtroom today, I had a long conversation with Jazlyn Prentice, a prosecutor I trust and respect who knows all there is to know about this case. She's as honest as the day is long. She's sitting in the gallery right now."

Jazlyn tentatively raised a hand.

He bit his lip. Maybe everyone working for government wasn't quite as villainous as he thought.

"Ms. Prentice believes everything Mr. Pike said. So I'm not denying it either." Abrams paused, his eyes darting downward. "It is simply the policy of this office to oppose asylum requests from people who do not currently have legal status in the United States."

"I've got the general idea," the judge said. "And I want to thank all parties concerned for their honesty, for putting aside politics and focusing attention where it should be. On the child. So far as the law allows, we need to do the best we can by her."

Judge Franklin gathered his thoughts. "It is clear to this court that the threat of persecution exists. I'd like to have more time to consider this and write an opinion, but clearly that time does not exist. That being the case, I will rule from the bench. This petition for political asylum is granted. Mr. Pike, please prepare the appropriate paperwork."

He felt Gabriella squeezing his hand under the table. She understood. A small cry escaped from her lips.

"What's more," the judge continued, "just to make the intention of this court clear, I'm issuing an immediate restraining order against Immigration and Customs Enforcement. There will be no deportation, no detention, no incarceration of any kind, while we complete the paperwork necessary to make this young woman a citizen of the United States."

The judge looked up. "And when you next see that young lady, Mr. Pike, please tell her that this old conservative fart will be proud to have her as a fellow citizen of my country."

CHAPTER FIFTY-FOUR

GABRIELLA MELTED INTO DAN'S ARMS. HE FELT HER WHITE-hot tears, even through his suit. Barely a second later, a much smaller person wrapped herself around his legs.

"Had her waiting outside," Maria explained. "Just in case."

"You didn't mention—"

"Thought you had enough pressure," Maria said, then she joined the group hug. And as if that weren't quite enough, barely a few moments later, Jimmy wrapped his big arms around everybody.

He looked down. "Do you understand what happened, Esperanza?"

She beamed up at him, nodding vigorously.

He feared the judge might be upset at this breach of decorum. That did not appear to be the case. It was subtle, but he thought the judge was smiling. With his eyes.

Before he knew what was happening, Maria had leaned forward and planted a kiss on his forehead. "Don't get the wrong idea," she cautioned. "That's a congratulatory kiss. Nothing more."

"Understood."

"You did good work today, champ. Very good work."

"What does this mean?" Gabriella asked. "I need to hear it from your lips."

"It means Esperanza will not be deported tomorrow. Or ever."

Gabriella's eyes clenched shut.

"Is it over?" Esperanza asked in a tiny voice.

"We still have some work to do. But it's nothing we can't handle."

"But Esperanza is so young. She can't take care of herself." Gabriella bowed her head. "And I cannot be her parent."

He nodded. "You can and should remain a part of her life. You should see her every day. But she's going to need more."

"I will do anything for this girl. Anything."

"I know you will."

He pulled out of the embrace and pivoted. Jazlyn stood behind them. "I had my doubts about this asylum business. But you pulled it off. Once again, you're the miracle worker. Could we talk for a moment?"

"Of course." He glanced down at Esperanza. "Excuse me. I'll be right back." He and Jazlyn stepped a few feet away so they could speak privately. "What's up?"

"Nothing important. I just wanted to say...oh wow. This is so awkward."

"Out with it. Jump into the deep end."

Jazlyn sighed. "I just wanted to...amend something I said earlier."

"And that would be?"

"Oh, you remember. That night. Dinner. The sailboat."

"I do remember. Not my most successful night on record."

"Well, having to work a little harder for it would probably do you good. I meant those comments I made. Earlier that day, at the courthouse. I said I admired you...but I didn't respect you." She shifted her weight, tilting awkwardly to one side. "I just wanted to say that has... changed. Somewhat." Her eyes scanned the celebration in the courtroom. "I respect what you're doing, and I respect who you are."

He checked his instinct to make a stupid joke, or to turn it into a come-on. "Thank you," he said quietly.

She threw up her hands. "Okay, enough of this. I need to get back to the office."

He reached out and grabbed her wrist. Was it his imagination, or was there a little electricity there that couldn't be attributed to the carpet? "I remember something else you said that night. At dinner."

"What would that be?"

"Something about your clock ticking."

"Oh. That."

"Since you came clean with me, let me come clean with you. I think you would be a terrific parent."

"I don't know anything about parenting."

"No one does, until they've done it. But what I've learned these past few weeks is that there's a real person hidden under your steely prosecutorial shell."

She held her finger to her lips. "Shh."

"You would make a fabulous mother. And I know a little girl who needs one, the sooner the better."

Jazlyn's mouth gaped. "Are you—Are you kidding me?"

"Totally serious."

"Oh man. That is...completely..."

"You know how bright Esperanza is. Given the right education, she could accomplish anything. And you're on the board at St. Teresa's, right? Prep school for girls. You could get her in."

"I don't know...Maybe..."

He turned and found Esperanza not far away. He knelt down to her level. "Esperanza, I'd like you to meet a good friend of mine. Her name is Jazlyn. She works in courtrooms, just like I do."

"Well," Jazlyn said, "hardly like you do." She bent down and extended her hand. "Hi, Esperanza. Glad I finally got to meet you. I've been hearing people talk about you for weeks."

Esperanza smiled. "Nice to meet you, ma'am."

"You two girls have a lot in common," he added.

Jazlyn arched an eyebrow. "Like...?"

"You're both extremely smart. You both know how to apply yourselves in tough situations and get the job done. And you're both—" He took a breath, then tried again. "You're both on my A-list."

Silence filled the air. They all looked at one another wordlessly.

"Hey, it's a beautiful day," he said. "Let's all go to that fabulous park Kazan built."

Jazlyn nodded. "I'm embarrassed to say I haven't seen it yet. Let's make it a party. My car is big enough to hold everyone." She reached into her purse and withdrew her keys.

Esperanza's eyes widened like balloons. "Hello Kitty!"

He blinked.

Esperanza reached out and grabbed Jazlyn's hand. Which was holding a Hello Kitty keychain. "You like Hello Kitty!" Her eyes were saucers, and for the first time in this whole ordeal, he saw tears gushing from them. "You like Hello Kitty!"

Jazlyn shrugged. "Doesn't everyone?"

Esperanza pointed downward. "I have Hello Kitty sneakers! Mr. Dan got them for me!"

"Did he really?" She gave him a piercing look. "Did you notice my keychain before?"

"I don't know what you're talking about."

And a moment later, Esperanza had wrapped her arms around both of them.

He cleared his throat. "I think this is the beginning of a beautiful friendship."

Esperanza pulled back and looked straight into his eyes. "I

knew you were the one, Mr. Dan. I knew you were the one who would save me."

He felt a strange itching behind his eyes. For once, he didn't know what to say.

knew you were the one, Mr. Dan. I knew you were the one who would save me.

He felt a strange itching behind his eyes. For once, he didn't know what to say.

CHAPTER FIFTY-FIVE

DAN SAT ON THE SOFA WITH HIS TEAMMATES, STARING AT THE big screen television with no picture. Mr. K was on the other end of the line.

"I want to congratulate you all on exceptionally good work," Mr. K said. "I mean, technically, all I asked you to do was handle an adoption, which you botched. But you found Esperanza a good home. And saved Gabriella from wrongful conviction. You even managed to tag the actual culprit."

"I hope he goes away forever," Maria said.

"What I can't believe," Jimmy said, "is this whole thing started as just an adoption. That was your original assignment."

He heard a chuckling emerging from the television.

Maria gave him the side-eye. "Dan, what does the chuckling mean?"

"Hey K—did you know where this was going?" he asked. "Did you know we would end up handling a complicated and controversial murder trial?"

Even though he couldn't see K's face, he could hear the smile. "I'm the boss. I don't have to answer questions."

"Then why—"

"Suffice to say, there are some seriously vile forces out there trying to undermine the justice system. And no, I'm not talking about Democrats or Republicans. I'm talking about people addicted to power. People motivated by hate. Bad enough on their own, but when they organize...well, we don't need to go into this now. I'm going to do everything possible to stop them. And I need your help."

"Anything you ask," he said. "I'm there."

"Good to know. You've all earned your paychecks this month. The last-chance lawyers can expect to see a first-rate bonus."

Maria beamed. "I like the sound of that. There's a purse at Louis Vuitton that's got my name on it."

"Enjoy yourselves. But I'll have another assignment for you soon. So party hardy while you can. That's an order."

Jimmy gave them a stern look. "Hear that, team? We have our orders."

"I THOUGHT YOU SAID HIS POWER TO STRIKE WAS FOUR."

"It was four. Now it's eight."

"How did that happen?"

"He got a power-up card."

"I have a power-up card."

"You used yours."

"I don't understand this at all."

"Yes, we get that."

The four of them sat around a table covered with a dungeon map, painted figures, and more cards than Dan had ever seen in his life. As best he understood from the opening scenario, they were on some kind of quest infiltrating some kind of castle keep. Motives were a bit murky. He had hoped he could follow their lead and do what everyone else was doing, but that wasn't working.

Jimmy cleared his throat. "Let me explain the rules to you again, Dan."

"You spent more than an hour explaining the rules."

"It's only hard the first time."

Maria flipped over some cards. "If you can handle a murder trial, Dan, you can handle Gloomhaven. Just takes a while to get the hang of it."

"Because there are roughly fifty thousand rules."

"Still simpler than courtroom procedure."

"Hey, Dan," Garrett said, "did you take that treasure beside the portal?"

"I did. I landed on it."

"I didn't see you move."

"Guess I was too fast for you. I wanted the treasure."

Jimmy nodded. "You're definitely getting the hang of it. Nice move."

He smiled. "Now I'm starting to like this game."

"I knew you would. Ready for your costume?"

He pulled back. "What? I'm not wearing a robe."

"Of course not. You're not a wizard. You're a warrior." Jimmy handed him a feathered Robin Hood hat and a quiver filled with plastic arrows.

"Swell. Is Maria going to be the beautiful princess in the cone-shaped hat?"

"Boy, are you living in the Dark Ages," Maria said. "I'm the dark enchantress. I know all the secrets. I pull everyone's strings." She slipped on a stylish leather jacket. "And of course, I wear the best clothes."

Jimmy put on his zombie mask. Garrett wore a wizard's cloak.

He put the Robin Hood hat on. It fit perfectly. "Well, now I feel like a warrior."

"Good," Jimmy replied. "but I have one more prop for you. A substitute player token." Jimmy held out a small action figure.

His eyes bulged. "The Mego Aquaman!"

"Indeed."

"You took it out of the plastic!"

"And if that doesn't prove I like you, nothing will. All right, are we going to take this dungeon?"

He counted his coins. "I don't think I can afford it."

"Individually? No. As a team, absolutely."

He looked at every one of them, then smiled. "You know, I've never actually been a member of a team before."

Maria arched an eyebrow. "And?"

He tilted his head to one side. "I might be able to adjust."

She nodded. "Thank goodness. We're stronger together."

ABOUT THE AUTHOR

William Bernhardt is the author of forty-seven books, including the bestselling Ben Kincaid series, the historical novels *Challengers of the Dust* and *Nemesis*, two books of poetry (*The White Bird* and *The Ocean's Edge*), and the Red Sneaker books on fiction writing. In addition, Bernhardt founded the Red Sneaker Writers Center to mentor aspiring authors. The Center hosts an annual writers conference, small-group writing retreats, a monthly newsletter, a phone app, and a bi-weekly podcast. He is also the President of Balkan Press, which publishes poetry and fiction as well as the literary journal *Conclave*.

Bernhardt has received the Southern Writers Guild's Gold Medal Award, the Royden B. Davis Distinguished Author Award (University of Pennsylvania) and the H. Louise Cobb Distinguished Author Award (Oklahoma State), which is given "in recognition of an outstanding body of work that has profoundly influenced the way in which we understand ourselves and American society at large." *Library Journal* called him "the undisputed master of the courtroom drama." *The Vancouver Sun* called him "the American equivalent of P.G. Wodehouse and John Mortimer." In 2019, he received the Arrell Gibson Lifetime Achievement Award from the Oklahoma Center for the Book.

In addition to his novels and poetry, he has written plays, a musical (book and score), humor, children's stories, biography, and puzzles. He has edited two anthologies (*Legal Briefs* and *Natural Suspect*) as fundraisers for The Nature Conservancy and the Children's Legal Defense Fund. In his spare time, he has enjoyed surfing, digging for dinosaurs, trekking through the Himalayas, paragliding, scuba diving, caving, zip-lining over the canopy of the Costa Rican rain forest, and jumping out of an airplane at 10,000 feet.

In 2017, when Bernhardt delivered the keynote address at the San Francisco Writers Conference, chairman Michael Larsen noted that in addition to penning novels, Bernhardt can "write a sonnet, play a sonata, plant a garden, try a lawsuit, teach a class, cook a gourmet meal, beat you at Scrabble, and work the *New York Times* crossword in under five minutes."

ALSO BY WILLIAM BERNHARDT

The Daniel Pike Novels

The Last Chance Lawyer

Court of Killers

Trial by Blood (November 2019)

The Ben Kincaid Novels

Primary Justice

Blind Justice

Deadly Justice

Perfect Justice

Cruel Justice

Naked Justice

Extreme Justice

Dark Justice

Silent Justice

Murder One

Criminal Intent

Death Row

Hate Crime

Capitol Murder

Capitol Threat

Capitol Conspiracy

Capitol Offense

Capitol Betrayal

Justice Returns

Other Novels

Challengers of the Dust

The Game Master

Nemesis: The Final Case of Eliot Ness

The Code of Buddyhood

Dark Eye

Strip Search

Double Jeopardy

The Midnight Before Christmas

Final Round

The Red Sneaker Series on Writing

Story Structure: The Key to Successful Fiction

Creating Character: Bringing Your Story to Life

Perfecting Plot: Charting the Hero's Journey

Dynamic Dialogue: Letting Your Story Speak

Sizzling Style: Every Word Matters

Powerful Premise: Writing the Irresistible

Thinking Theme: The Heart of the Matter

The Fundamentals of Fiction (video series)

Poetry

The White Bird

The Ocean's Edge

For Young Readers

Shine

Princess Alice and the Dreadful Dragon

Equal Justice: The Courage of Ada Sipuel

The Black Sentry

Edited by William Bernhardt

Legal Briefs: Short Stories by Today's Best Thriller Writers

Natural Suspect: A Collaborative Novel of Suspense

9 781087 868660